The moment the world shifted, I felt as if I was waking up from a long nap. What I had thought was life—mine and everyone else's—had been a collective dream, and like dreams I knew I had to write down as much as I could remember before it faded away. In the dream, the world had been taken over by intelligent, non-human entities that called themselves tulpas. They appeared human and claimed they were from this planet, but born of a being, called the Maker.

It seems unlikely that I would forget that, but I was already losing memories of distant parts of the dream. Was I married? No, I was divorced and I typed... Shara, ex-wife. My daughter was Kari. I wouldn't forget that because she was here with me. I sensed that most people would have no memory of how the world had been before Dominion. They would simply accept rule by tulpas as the normal way. The bastards were playing with our minds.

ISBN 978-1-948929-31-8

For information address Crossroad Press at 141 Brayden Dr., Hertford, NC 27944
A Mystique Press Production - Mystique Press is an imprint of Crossroad Press.
www.crossroadpress.com

First edition

TULPAS

By Rob MacGregor

MYSTIQUE PRESS

PART ONE

I & I

The true complexity and importance of the dream world as an independent field of existence has not yet been impressed upon you. Yet while your world and the dream world are basically independent, they still expert pressures and influences, one up the other.

—Jane Roberts, *The Unknown Reality*

Finally, I knew that dream figures were much more complex than people realized. Some appeared to possess a type of awareness, a type of conscious volition. Perhaps they were sub-personalities, conscious fragments, or archetypal energies, but their independent agency increased my uncertainty about the dream realm.

—Michael Waggoner, *Lucid Dreaming: Gateway to the Inner Self*

Prologue

ALEX

Just as I settled down for breakfast in the sunny courtyard of the old hacienda—converted to hotel—my phone vibrated. I really wanted to sit here amid the flowering bougainvillea and enjoy a leisurely breakfast, but I sensed that wasn't going to happen. Shara had called me half an hour ago and said she would text if there was any news.

Her message was brief and urgent: *Dom heading into Merida. Get out before they take the airport, Alex. Get out now!*

My empty stomach groaned as my gaze fell on my untouched breakfast of eggs, potatoes, bacon, half an avocado, toast and coffee. I texted back: *Maybe I can still make contact.*

I started speed eating, but was barely a quarter way through my meal when Shara replied. *Alex, NO! Go now. Those 6 journalists captured in Cancun found dead this a.m., decapitated on the beach.*

I gobbled down two more bites, swallowed half a cup of coffee, swiped a cloth napkin across my mouth. I set my plate down on the Mexican tile courtyard floor next to a dozing scrawny pale brown dog, and hurried to my room. I packed and checked out in five minutes.

I stepped out of the hacienda and looked for a taxi. Carlos at the front desk said there was always one nearby. Always except this morning. A tree-lined boulevard, cluttered with early morning vendors selling colorful hammocks, fruit and pastries, separated the two lanes of traffic.

Maybe if I walked out to the boulevard I could flag a taxi from either direction. I spotted a truck across the way loaded with armed men dressed in black. Instinctively, I stepped back toward the shadow of the hacienda wall. I wasn't afraid, just cautious. I'd always been lucky as a journalist in foreign lands and made friends with the locals, even when they had good reason not to be friendly to an American.

But I'd had a couple of close encounters with Dominion forces in Cancun two days ago, and had barely avoided capture when I turned a corner and nearly collided with several armed men in black. Armed kids, actually. They looked about fourteen, at best. My press badge was in full view and that was probably what set them off. I kept my head down and moved around them, hoping they would ignore me. One of them ordered me to stop, but I kept going.

"*Matalo!* Kill him."

The instant I heard the command, I bolted into an office building, raced up a staircase and down a hall. I clambered out an emergency exit and jumped the last six feet to an alleyway. I spotted more armed men at one end, their backs to me. I darted out in the other direction and merged into a crowded market. I knew I needed to flee Cancun.

I took another step back under the awning of the hotel and bumped into someone. "*Lo siento,* sorry."

A lean, grizzled old man with a scraggly white goatee nodded and smiled, revealing crooked front teeth. I expected him to hold out his palm and automatically reached into my pocket for change. To my surprise, the *viejo* addressed me in fractured English, a nasal tone. His voice was high pitched for a man and some of the words literally squeaked out of his mouth. "You want Dominion. I take you. Sí, sí, I take you to *el jefe*? Only fifty dollar."

I let the change drop back into my pocket. Since arriving in Merida yesterday afternoon, I'd made several inquiries about meeting a Dominion leader. I'd guessed that Dominion was coming here and figured an advance team was on the streets. Now I was torn between doing my job and saving my neck. Never had that phrase meant more. I hesitated, then made a bargain with myself.

"Twenty dollars, no more."

I figured the old man would walk away. But I was wrong. "Twenty-five and I take you right now."

"How do I know I can trust you?"

"Es facil. You no pay until you meet *el jefe."*

"I don't mean the money. How do I know it's safe, *seguro*?"

"Tu no sabes. Yo no se."

Great. No assurances. It sounded damn risky, especially after what Shara had texted me. Thirty-six was too young to die. Shara would get over it. After all, we were separated, heading for divorce. However, our daughter Kari, who'd just turned twelve, would be devastated. She kept saying she wanted to live with me rather than her mom and Charles, whom she despised.

A taxi eased up to the front of the hacienda. The driver leaned toward the curb and called out, *"Aeropuerto*?"

That made up my mind. *"Si, un momento."*

I turned to the old man as I pulled out a twenty-dollar bill. "Take this for your trouble, *su trabajo."*

The old man waved off the bill. "I go with you. *El* jefe *esta alla."*

"What, he's at the airport?"

"Sí, sí, vamonos."

I hesitated a moment, then shrugged. Whatever. We both climbed into the back of the taxi. Maybe I could get an interview and get out safely. That was my new plan, sketchy as it was.

As the taxi pulled away from the curb, I decided to see how much the old man knew about Dominion. *"Me nombre es Alex Brooks. Como te llamas*?"

"Hector."

I started to ask another question, but he held up a hand, nodded toward the driver, and touched a finger to his lips. *"Espérate. El jefe* will answer your questions."

As if on command, the blare of salsa filled the car and the driver kept fiddling with the volume on the radio. I settled back in my seat and stared out the window, feeling a sense of unease about all of this. We moved through the narrow cobbled streets lined by one-story shops, most of them painted a pale green, and gradually the old city fell behind and a few minutes later we arrived at our destination on the outskirts of town.

The airport seethed with bedlam. Dozens of distraught and confused people, many of them tourists, milled outside the entrance with their luggage. Soldiers in black uniforms and berets directed traffic, patrolled the crowd, and guarded the entrances.

Shit. They're here. But what did I expect, just one friendly representative of Dominion waiting for me? The taxi stopped and the driver opened the trunk and took out my luggage. *Buen suerte,* the driver hissed when I paid him.

I would need more than good luck, I thought grimly, turning toward the entrance. Hector moved directly toward a small group of Dominion soldiers. He spoke briefly to one of them, then motioned me to follow him and the soldier who cut a path through the crowd. Foreign and Mexican passengers were on their phones trying to get answers, trying to find a way out, their lives on hold. Worry, anger, and indignation rolled off of them in waves. Some were here on business no doubt, but the couples, especially the ones with children, were on vacation. The families reminded me of what was missing in my life. I'd taken this assignment partially to escape my ravaged personal life.

I'd returned from a three-day trip to Los Angeles and found that Shara and Kari were gone. She'd left a note, telling me she'd moved out. We'd grown apart and she'd gotten too close to her partner. FBI agents in love. That was three months ago and she was trying to make it up by feeding me as much information as she could about Dominion. The problem was that very little was known about the group. They'd materialized in Mexico as if out of nowhere.

The soldier leading Hector motioned toward the guards at the entrance and they immediately opened the doors. Boss man must have known we were coming and told the guards to let us in. I caught a brief glimpse of myself in the tinted window next to the door. I looked burdened and disheveled, my usually trim beard bushy, khaki-brown hair mussed. Still young, but feeling the years. The extra pounds I'd gained since the break-up didn't help my appearance, either.

I'd been told that I should be doing television news, not because of my reporting abilities, but because of my supposed rugged good looks, square jaw, straight nose, pale blue eyes. But the only appeal television news had for me was the possibility of a bigger paycheck. Print journalists were still the best, as far as I was concerned.

The chaos outside the airport was matched by the turmoil inside. A rippling black wave of armed men moved across the concourse. Here and there groups of travelers huddled together on the floor, soldiers holding them at gunpoint. Workers in the shops looked stunned and frightened.

We were guided to an unmarked door, entered into a private lounge. The chaos vanished. A hostess greeted us in Spanish and English and asked if we would like to order food and drinks. Hector waved her off and led me past the comfortable chairs and couches to a table in the far corner. I took a seat and was surprised when Hector joined me. I scanned the empty room, waiting. Hector stared at me, his arms folded over his chest.

Donde esta el jefe?

"*Aquí.* Right here," Hector said. "You're looking at him." He held out his left palm revealing a tattoo of a trident inside a circle. "What do you want to know?"

Hector's crisp English had lost its thick Spanish accent.

"Whoa, I'm confused. What are you talking about?"

"I'm telling you that I'm in charge, commander-in-chief of all Dominion forces."

It seemed unlikely. Yet, there was a distinct change not only in his speech, but the way he held himself and, oddly enough, his appearance. I definitely wouldn't mistake this man for a beggar. He'd donned wire-rimmed glasses and looked more like an intellectual. Or maybe even the leader of a rebel force.

"What's your full name?"

"This interview is about Dominion, not me. Just call me Hector, and don't ask anything about my background."

"Can I record the interview?"

"No recording, no notes. Just listen and remember. I am testing you."

What did that mean? "Okay. Why did your militia take

on the same name and uniform as the rebels in Iceland, who overran the government last week?"

"We are not a copycat movement as the international press has claimed. We are the same. We are one. We are Dominion, and the truth will soon be known."

"Why were the journalists killed in Cancun?"

"Many people died there."

"But why the journalists? They weren't combatants."

"Our followers are sometimes overly enthusiastic in their missions. They see the journalists as propagators of lies."

I nervously tapped my index finger against the table, wishing I could be writing what I was hearing. I would take notes as soon as I could. "About your followers. Why are people so attracted to Dominion?"

"They understand that we are saviors, that we are the future, that we will lead them from poverty and hopelessness. They know that those who oppose us must be eliminated. Simple as that."

He sounded dangerous and simple-minded. "So the rich are your enemy?"

"Not necessarily. The well-to-do are welcome to join our cause, but there will be no more free rides for them. No more socialism for the rich."

"What about the poor?"

"Everyone deserves a place to live, food, and health care."

"How can you guarantee any of that?"

Hector leaned closer to me, his expression intense. "We are here to bring the world into balance with appropriate population, with appropriate distribution of wealth."

"Where are you from?"

"Earth, just like you, just like all of the Dominion leadership. I am descended from the mind of man."

What the hell was he talking about? "How are you going to control the birth rate?"

"I did not say anything about the birth rate. You must listen better." He abruptly stood up. "That's all I will tell you now. You will be put on a private jet to Miami. You will write the truth. If you don't, expect to die like the others in your profession."

Shaken and baffled, I stood and picked up my luggage. I wanted to ask why I was getting the story, but decided not to push my luck. Hector guessed my thoughts.

"I selected you, because you survived Cancun and came to the right place at the right time. How did you get here?"

Oddly, the question made me uneasy. "Well, I took a bus." I remembered ducking into the bus station and looking for a bus to Merida.

Hector smiled. "Oh, did you? Think carefully about that. You might learn something very important."

What the hell did that mean? I just wanted to get away from him, and to Miami.

Hector stood erect and seemed younger and more capable than the old man I'd met. "I won't mislead you, Alex. I have no need for deception. But you and the world are not yet ready for the truth. When the time is right, all will be known."

1

Blind Date

LANG

I must be nuts to go on a blind date with a police psychologist. That's what Sal said. And my old buddy didn't know how close to the truth he'd come with that comment. Maybe I *was* nuts and just wanted to confirm it. I considered the matter from behind the wheel of my pickup parked in the lot outside the Hogfish Grill on Stock Island.

It wasn't really a blind date, more of a digital one. I'd met Risa Ferraro through an on-line service. We'd exchanged a few text messages before agreeing to meet.

There, that's her.

A slender, redhead in a sky-blue dress and block-heel sandals crossed the pavement from a sedan and passed within twenty feet of me. She paused outside the entrance, and looked back as if sensing my presence. Perceptive, I thought.

As I got out, she turned away. "Hey there!"

She let go of the door handle and slowly swiveled her head. I smiled, waved awkwardly.

"Hey there, yourself." Was she smiling or smirking? She placed a hand on her hip, a seductive pose. Or was she annoyed?

I was forty-six and felt like I was going on my first date. Since my divorce eight years ago, I'd gone out with women who, for the most part, were friends of friends and, like me, divorced. To my surprise, some of them, well, actually most of them, didn't want to waste time getting to know me. They wanted dinner, then off to the sack.

I thought it was men who wanted to skip the small talk and head to the bedroom. So I was surprised when women got impatient with me, and moved on to the next guy. It seemed like a reversal of traditional roles.

Tonight was going to be different. I was dating someone who listened to others as a profession and I had something unusual to talk about. The thing that was making me feel a little nuts.

"Hello, Risa. You are Risa, I hope."

"I am, if you're Bruce Lang," she said with a throaty laugh.

"Then let's go." I motioned with my hand. She was a decade my junior, fit and attractive, and I'd been pleasantly surprised when she'd decided to go out with me.

"Do I look like my picture?" she asked, pausing as he opened the door.

"Even better."

A beat passed. "No kidding. Then I guess I'm not very photogenic."

"I didn't mean it that way."

She touched my shoulder. "Relax, man. We're in the keys."

"Yeah, I noticed." A hostess motioned us to a table with a waterfront view of the harbor.

The restaurant was Key West casual without the tourist crowd that thronged Duval Street. A funky bar and wooden tables with benches instead of chairs. A long-time Key West resident, Risa had chosen the place. A local hangout.

Six p.m. on a Friday, every bar stool was taken, and more than half the tables were occupied. Mostly locals, a few tourists, and at the end of the bar two middle-aged men, both of them carrying, one with an ankle holster, the other with a weapon on his hip. Off-duty cops, I guessed.

Risa noticed my gaze. "That's Anderson and Waz, Monroe County deputies."

"You want to say hi to them?"

"They're not my friends."

"Clients maybe."

She smiled. "Or friends of clients."

The waitress came by and we ordered beers.

"So, Risa Ferraro, police psychologist."

"Who doesn't date cops." She met my gaze. "Bruce Lang, retired police detective, Miami Beach. Now a mystery writer living on Sugarloaf Key. Guess that novel did fairly well for you. Retiring in your mid-40s."

"Especially after it was optioned for a television series. I gave up my rights on it and a chance to be a producer, and took the money. They can do whatever they want with it. Of course I'm hoping for the best."

A couple of beats passed. "Isn't Sugarloaf a little boring for a single guy?"

"Not yet. I get plenty of visitors in the winter and lobster season. My former partner at Miami-Dade, Sal, lives on Big Pine and runs a bait shop now. We fish a couple times a month."

Risa rested her chin in her palm. "Okay, let's hear it. Why would a retired cop want to go out with a police psychologist?"

She didn't waste any time. "I wanted to talk to someone who would listen. I've got a story."

"So you figured it was cheaper on a date than an office visit. Is that it?"

"I'm not asking for professional services, just an ear."

The beers arrived and I opened the menu. "What's good here?"

Risa tapped the menu. "Hogfish sandwich with Swiss cheese, onions and mushrooms is my fave. Everything's good. Fresh fish everyday. You can bring your own catch and they'll cook it for you and Sal, or whoever."

After we ordered, Risa sat back and crossed her arms. "Is this about a cold case that you've been brooding over? You know who did it, but can't get the evidence, right?"

There was that, but not what I wanted to talk about. "Good guess, but wrong." In our exchange of text messages, I told her I'd worked the last nine years of my career on cold cases. "There were some interesting ones, but I didn't take any of them into retirement with me."

"Okay, what's on your mind, Lang? Never cared for the

name 'Bruce.' Sounds too much like booze and bruise, and reminds me of my work with cops."

"Yeah, I can see that. Lang is fine."

"So tell me your story."

I wasn't expecting to get into in this fast. I figured we'd get to know each other first, at least share some idle chatter. But here I was getting rushed into something again with another date. What the hell. I thought a moment, not wanting to make it sound either too strange or too insignificant.

"Well, I had a dream that wasn't like any dream I've ever had. I was awake, I was there, only it wasn't me. It was like I was inside someone else. I was watching this person's life through his eyes. I finally started to worry that I was becoming the person. That's how it ended. I jolted awake and for a moment was confused about where I was, and who I was. Pretty strange, uh?"

"Yeah, but I'm missing something."

"That's what happened to me. You haven't heard what happened to him."

She sipped her beer. "Tell me. Don't leave anything out."

"I'll tell you what I remember. The man's name is Alex Brooks, he's in his mid-thirties. He's an investigative reporter for an on-line news agency. I think he lives somewhere in Florida, and he's in Mexico. There's an uprising or a revolution involving a group called Dominion."

I took another swallow of my beer as I reached the point in my story where Alex was leaving his hotel in Merida with an old man, Hector, who promised to take him to meet the leader of Dominion. "That's when I woke up and drank a glass of water. I was really confused, because for several seconds I thought I was in Mexico and wondered what I was doing in bed."

Risa lifted her head and cleared her throat as the two cops from the bar approached our table. "Gentlemen, how are things this evening?"

Ankle holster spoke up. "Hey, Risa. I got something to say to you."

"Shoot, Waz."

He grinned as if he thought her reply was a joke. "You

could've gone easy on Emilio. He was a good guy."

"It wasn't my decision."

"But it was your recommendation. That's all I've got to say." He stared a moment at Lang, studying him. "You look familiar. Who do you work for?"

My stomach tensed. I felt uneasy under his gaze. "Myself."

"Good for you." They walked off as the waitress arrived with our fish sandwiches.

"What was that about, or don't you want to talk about it?"

"Drugs, booze, abuse and suicide. The dark side."

"Yeah, you don't have to go into it."

I wanted to ask her what she thought of my dream, but I could see she was upset and, as we ate, she told the story of a narcotics cop who got too deep undercover and lost his direction. She tried to help him, and recommended that he be transferred off narcotics and given a desk job until he recovered from his addiction. He reacted by pistol whipping two suspected drug dealers, and beating up his girlfriend. He was suspended, then fired when he refused to meet Risa for any more counseling sessions. A week later, he shot himself in the head outside her office.

"I had to step over his body to get out of my office, and the rumor started that I went to lunch, that I was a cold-hearted bitch."

"Did you?"

"I sat in my car and cried for half an hour. I kept it to myself. It's better for a woman to be seen as tough than weak. Or so I thought."

"I believe it."

"Problem is I'm not a cop. I'm a psychologist with a contract with the sheriff's office. So I'm seen as an outsider." She paused. "Enough about me. That dream of yours. What's it mean to you?"

"I was hoping you would tell me. But let me continue. There's more to it. I went back to bed and the dream picked up where it left off. We arrived at the airport."

"You and the old man, Hector?"

"Right."

I'd written all I remembered as soon as I had awakened. Yet, I was certain that I would've recalled this dream, even if I hadn't written a word. It was so real, so unusual. When I finished relating all the details, I pushed my empty beer bottle toward the middle of the table.

"Like I said, I felt like I was there."

Risa remained silent for a few moments, lost in thought. "It's puzzling. I'll say that. But one thing you said might be key."

"What's that?"

"Hector told you that he was descended from the mind of man. To me, that suggests your unconscious mind is telling you that the characters were spun out of your imagination and represent different aspects of your personality."

"So you think it *was* just a dream?"

"What else would it be?"

I shrugged. "I don't know. It's just odd that I wasn't the main character. That I was part of this guy, Alex, or inside his head. It wasn't like a regular dream."

"Dreams can be very creative like that. But usually the scenarios are reflections of elements of the everyday world. For example, your Dominion militia sounds like ISIS with the black uniforms."

"But they weren't fighting in the Mideast. Not that I could tell."

"I know. Mexico, a place to the south, down below us, like the unconscious. Also Iceland. Odd place for a rebellion. But dreams sometimes include puns. Think about it. Iceland. ISIS or ISIL. Sounds sort of similar. And the message of ISIS is or was world *dominion*."

I shrugged. "Yeah, you're right. I should've known you would be able to disassemble my dream."

She reached out and touched my hand. "I'm just helping you understand it. I'm not trying to belittle it." She drew her hand back, shook her head, and laughed. "Here I am counseling a cop, just what I said I didn't want to do on a date."

"Ex-cop." I sat up in my chair. "Wait. Oh, shit. I just realized something that I overlooked. Alex and I both have ex-wives who were FBI agents. Alex's ex is named Shara, mine is Sharon. We both have one daughter. But their names and ages are different. My Jennifer is in college, his Kari is a pre-teen."

Risa scrutinized me as if I were some sort of strange bug. "Promise me one thing, Lang. If you have any more of these dreams…"

"Don't call you, right?" he said, finishing her sentence.

"Actually, no. I'll have another busman's holiday with you. Most likely the dream was a one-time phenomenon. If it happens again, though, with the same dream character, I might re-think what I said."

"Why do you say that?"

"Who knows? Maybe you're unconscious mind is projecting into an alternate reality. It's possible, but not very likely."

It was no doubt a playful comment, but I had a response for her. "Interesting. Guess I should tell you then."

"What?"

"I've already had a second one. That's what made it so disturbing. It gets more complicated."

"Oh, really. Well, don't hold out on me. I want to hear it. But let's go somewhere else."

"How about my place?" I blurted.

She studied me a moment, undecided.

"I'm not a serial killer, if that's what you're wondering."

She laughed. "I didn't think so. Okay. Let's go."

2

The Interview

ALEX

I looked around my sparsely furnished condo, hunting for my keys. Not too many places for them to hide in my tiny box on the nineteenth floor of the Waverley. I didn't consider my sterile, two-bedroom abode as home, but rather a place to crash when I wasn't traveling. I loved our house in Winter Park, but I couldn't stay there after Shara and Kari left. Too many memories. Once I was certain they weren't coming back, I rented the place and moved downtown. Well, Orlando's version of downtown, a mini-downtown.

I stepped out on the porch to see if I'd left the keys on the low table next to the chair where I liked to sit and take in the view of nearby Lake Eola. I moved back inside and spotted a lump under a manila envelop at the end of the kitchen counter. I lifted the envelope and snatched my keys. I was out the door in seconds, locking it, then striding down the hall. For a moment, I thought I should go back for my laptop, but then I realized there was no need for it. Regretfully, I would be the interviewee, not the interviewer.

As I waited for the elevator, I reviewed everything that had happened over the past few days. I'd scored a journalistic coup with my interview with the man who described himself as the commander-in-chief of Dominion. The article was picked up by news outlets around the world. Hector's proclamation that Dominion was a worldwide movement was widely dismissed. However, the article, combined with rumors that Dominion forces were gathering in several countries, prompted governments around the world to go onto high alert.

I was inundated by calls from reporters who wanted to question me, almost as if I were a spokesman for the group. The alternative, getting their own interview, was a difficult and dangerous task, especially in the aftermath of the slaughter of captured journalists. Rather than answering questions over and over again, I decided to hold a press conference in the bandstand on Lake Eola, a ten-minute walk. But first I had a personal interview.

A local TV reporter, Lydia Cabrera, pestered me for the past two days with calls and e-mails and even a couple of visits to the lobby of my building. She pleaded with me to give her an interview. Grudgingly, I'd agreed to do so one hour before the press conference. Now I was regretting my decision. Sure, she was persuasive and persistent, but so were other reporters.

I'd agreed to meet her at the top of the parking garage where she said she could capture the cityscape in the background. I realized now there was another reason for that location. The concierge had called me five minutes ago and said that reporters were gathering in the lobby, waiting for me, even though the press conference would be in the bandstand shell half a mile away.

I rode the elevator to the rear exit, crossed the street to the parking garage, and took the steps two at a time to the roof. Half a dozen cars were parked under the sun. I spotted a white van with station call letters covering the side and a satellite TV dish antenna rising like an enormous invasive weed from the top of the van. Next to it was a cameraman and a dark-haired woman in black slacks and a pale blue blouse. She wore high heels and held a mike in her hand. I headed over to them, introduced myself and shook their hands. Lydia was attractive with bold features, large eyes and full lips, a long thin nose. She was someone who caught your attention and I'd definitely seen her on the local news.

"I'm not sure what I can tell you that wasn't in the article."

She had a ready answer. "Not everyone who watches the

news read your article, though they might've heard about it." She smiled and moved closer. I started feeling mesmerized, then checked myself, noting that I was just the story of the day, nothing more. "Besides, I'm assuming no one was asking you questions when you wrote the article. I've got a few."

"I bet."

"Let's go over to the corner so we can get more skyline and less concrete in the frame," she said. "We're going live with this exclusive. We'll have it at least an hour ahead of anyone else."

I couldn't help thinking the so-called exclusive was going to be a re-hash of my article published two days ago. I glanced at my watch. "Let's do it then. As I said, five minutes. That's it."

After a few minutes of preparation and cell phone chatter with a producer at the station, Lydia was on the air talking about Dominion and their rapid expansion across Mexico and into Central America. She summarized my article, then turned to me. "Alex Brooks, one of the most puzzling aspects of Dominion is their supposed connection with the group that overthrew the government in Iceland and now there are militias using the same name in Malaysia, Guatemala, and Spain. What can you tell us about that?"

"The man I interviewed, who called himself commander-in-chief of Dominion, boasted that the movement would spread worldwide. He said the Mexican and Icelandic Dominion were part of the same militia."

"But where did they originate? Where are they from?"

"I don't know. I thought the commander, who only gave his name as Hector, was Mexican when I met him. But later his speech changed and, strangely enough, he looked different to me."

"How so? How different?"

"He looked younger and more Caucasian, and I thought I heard a hint of a British accent."

"What about their philosophy? You wrote that they're not religious, that their followers are from all religions and political stripes. How could that be?"

"Well, it could be propaganda, as I pointed out in the article. But it does seem that Dominion has an appeal that's hard to quantify. Somehow they're uniting people in their cause. Even Mexican soldiers, who are supposed to be fighting them, are taking off their uniforms and joining Dominion."

"I suppose the benefits for the Mexicans is seen as economic, improved living conditions. But would that message work in Western countries?"

As she spoke, a black Suburban moved slowly in our direction and stopped a hundred feet away. The doors opened and to my amazement, Hector stepped out of the passenger side. Three others joined him, triple extra-large beefy guys, dressed in Dominion uniforms, their faces hidden by black ski masks.

"We've got trouble."

Lydia and the cameraman turned as the three goons rushed forward. Two of them shoved me and the cameraman and the third one wrapped a muscular arm around Lydia's waist and picked her up like a rag doll. She screamed, kicking her legs, and beating her fists against his back as she was dragged to the Suburban. Just before they reached the vehicle, she ripped off his ski mask, scratching his cheek as she did so.

"You crazy fucking bitch," he shouted, pulled her head back by the hair, punched her jaw, knocking her out.

The cameraman struggled to get past the intruders. He snatched up his tripod and swung his camera, but it bounced off one of the burly men's shoulder. The Dominion thug retaliated by driving the cameraman back to the edge of the roof and against a three-foot concrete barrier. He lifted him up and tossed him head-first off the roof. The cameraman's cry lasted barely two seconds before he slammed into the ground.

The other masked thug pulled my arms tightly behind me and jammed my wrists between my shoulder blades. He kicked my feet out from under me and I fell forward, my chest and chin striking the pavement. Ski Mask held onto my arms and pressed a boot into my lower back.

Hector leaned over me. "Pay attention, Alex Brooks, or you will join the cameraman. No press conference. The media is trying to stir up fear. That's no good. If you look at your history, you'll see that fear and suspicion are what has eroded your democracy and turned it into a game of power plays among corporate entities and individuals with great wealth. You're living with the results of that divisive enterprise. But we are here to unify America and the world."

"Let the woman go. She didn't do anything."

"She's collateral. You'll write what I tell you, or she dies."

"Let her go. Take me."

"Suit yourself. We'll take both of you."

The Suburban pulled up and I was shoved into the backseat. Lydia was lying on her side in the rear of the vehicle. A moment later, a hood was pulled over my head. Everything went black and I felt a noose tighten around my neck. "That's to keep you from jumping out," Hector said as the Suburban pulled away. "Try it and you will be dragged and choked."

3

Another Dream

LANG

I glanced into the rearview mirror and saw that Risa was still behind me in her Honda Civic. I'd surprised myself by asking her to my house. I hadn't expected that, but it just seemed the natural thing to do. I not only found her appealing, but she actually listened to me, and was interested.

I slowed as I approached the blinking light at mile maker 17. I'd almost suggested the tiki bar behind the Sugarloaf Lodge, which was right here at the intersection, but was glad I didn't. That would've sounded like a half-assed attempt to get her to come home with me. She would've seen it as her second try-out of the evening, and a chance for me to bail out.

I imagined her reaction to that scenario: *Oh, we're only a couple of miles from your house? That's interesting. But I better go home.* Yeah, better that I'd been direct.

I turned right and headed toward the Atlantic side of the island. While Lower Sugarloaf passed by in the blink of an eye on U.S. 1, the island actually extended several miles before reaching the open water. Halfway to the ocean, I turned onto my street. Houses shrouded in tropical splendor were setback from the road and barely visible.

My place was at the end. I'd left the old green wooden gate open and eased into my parking space. Risa pulled up next to me, got out, looked around, and walked over to the boat ramp.

"Right on the water. Nice. You've got both a canal and open water."

"It's a lagoon, a big one, that leads to a bay. It takes a good twenty minutes to get to the ocean."

"And look at this boat."

"My fishing boat, a Boston Whaler."

"Does it go fast?"

"Pretty fast. Two ninety-horsepower Mercs. Take you for a ride sometime. If you're interested."

"Sounds fun."

She walked over to the coral rock break and gazed out over the moon-lit water. "Nice view, and a nice big lot. Very private." One side of the property was a tropical paradise, the other side was beach-like, with pale sand instead of grass, and was, littered with fallen coconuts. A hammock hung between two palms. She maneuvered onto the hammock, clasping her hands behind her head and staring at the stars. "Very nice. Ah, those coconuts up there are a little scary, though."

I laughed. "So far no one has gotten beaned. The no see ums are a bigger problem. Worse than mosquitos, but only out at night. C'mon in."

The bottom floor was screened and furnished with decks chairs, a low circular glass table and a pool table hidden beneath a green plastic covering. Two pool cues rested on top of it, identifying what lay beneath.

I opened a door leading to a wrought iron spiral staircase that climbed to the main floor. Risa pointed at another door to the left. "Where does that one go?"

"Into a one-bedroom apartment. Waterfront with an open porch. I might rent it out at some point, but nobody's living there now."

We climbed the stairs and Risa paused at the top. "Wow, gorgeous!"

"The open floor plan makes the place feel larger than it is. Two bedrooms, two baths, and a loft." I pointed up to another level.

"Seems very roomy for a single guy."

"I guess. You want another beer or something else?"

"How about a cup of coffee?"

"Sure."

She settled onto a stool by the kitchen counter and I felt her watching and assessing as I brewed a pot of Cuban coffee. I hoped she liked what she saw. I poured two cups and suggested we sit out on the screened-in porch that wrapped around three sides of the house.

We relaxed on cushioned chairs and gazed out over the water. "I feel like I'm on a cruise ship up here." Risa sipped her coffee. "If I lived here, I might never go into Key West. I'd tell my clients they'd have to come here. Then again, I wouldn't want to ruin the pleasant vibe this place has with the negative energy that comes into my office some days."

"So you want to hear the second dream?"

"Of course." She slid a hand under her shoulder-length hair, lifting it off her neck. "It's so pleasant out here I almost forgot, but not really. Please, go ahead."

"Let me get my laptop. I'll read it to you."

I slipped away and returned a few moments later, computer in hand. I settled down again, opened the laptop and brought up the file.

"It was just as vivid as the first one. Again, I felt like I was inside this guy's head. I knew it wasn't me, but I became totally involved with his life. I actually knew his thoughts. It began with him leaving his apartment in Orlando a couple of days after his article on Dominion had been published."

Risa put down her cup of coffee and listened intently as I began reading. When I finished several minutes later, I sat back in my chair and stared off into the night. "That's all I remember, except I was worried that I was also a captive inside Alex's life. I woke up as the car drove away. Alex and Lydia were captives. I felt concerned about them, but also relieved that I'd gotten back to my own life."

"These Dominion folks are truly nasty bastards. So what's going to happen to Alex and Lydia?"

"I don't know. I'm not making up this stuff."

"I know."

I smiled. "But what? I hear a hesitation in your voice."

"You must read a lot of novels."

"More non-fiction, actually. Research. But I know what you're getting at. No, the dreams aren't like anything I recall reading."

She nodded, thought a moment. "But you're a novelist, you create worlds."

I turned up my palms. "I'm totally aware that these dreams are probably creations of my subconscious mind. But they're so vivid, so real, that when I wake up, I'm disoriented. It's almost like I temporarily forget who I am."

"It's good that you wrote down that one. You preserved a lot of detail. Dreams are fleeting. You might think you'll remember a very dramatic dream, but five minutes after getting up it just fades away."

"But both of these dreams still remain very clear to me, as if they were my own recent experiences, as if I was awake. I've never had dreams like that."

"Since you were awake in the dream, did you have any control over the action?"

"None whatsoever. I was a trapped observer."

She frowned. "How do you feel trapped in your life?"

I tried not to show my annoyance that she was looking at the dream as if it were symbolic of my life. "I don't. My life is great. I'm very lucky."

That didn't stop her. "What was it that Hector said about the downfall of democracy? Is that what you believe, that we're not a true democracy any longer?" When I didn't respond immediately, she added: "I'm not interrogating you. I'm just interested in how much your everyday thoughts influenced the dream."

"That part is odd, because I try to avoid politics and just live my life. My daughter tells me I'm living with my head in the sand and that I should be more informed. But it feels good to isolate myself from all of that. So Hector's politics, or any political rhetoric, isn't something that's on my mind."

"It sounds like he's a liberal raging against corporate democracy. That's not the politics of ISIS, that's for sure. They're ultra-religious, ultra-conservative."

I frowned a moment, then a smile crept over my features. "This might sound naïve, but I really don't think I've ever heard that term corporate democracy. It sounds like an oxymoron."

"Well, it is." She clasped her hands behind her head and gazed out over the water. "I could just sit here all night. This is so beautiful, and it's your private domain."

"I never get tired of sitting out here." If she wanted to stay, I had no problem with that. But I figured she was about to say it was time for her to leave.

A loud splash caught our attention and we both bolted out of our chairs and over to the screen. "Look at that! How many are there?" Risa gasped.

"Looks like a pod." Dolphins frolicked in the moonlight barely ten feet from the edge of the property.

Her hip brushed against my leg as she leaned toward the screen. "There must be a dozen of them. But why are they so close to shore?"

"It's the waterway, you know, like the highway. The first thirty feet are dredged for boat traffic. Past that the lagoon is shallow, only two to four feet deep, depending on the tide. So there's more fish for them in close."

"They're beautiful."

"My daughter, Jennifer, should be here. She loves dolphins. She even worked as an intern one summer at Dolphins Plus in Key Largo." I recalled a story Jen had told me. "Have you ever heard about the legend of the shape-shifting dolphin?"

She reached for my hand. "No, please tell me."

"This story comes from people called *Rivereños,* who live near the shores of the Amazon River. When there was a party in the village, a handsome stranger would show up and dance with the most beautiful girls. Then he would lead one of them over to the nearby river where he would convince her to go swimming with him. Once they were in the water the stranger changed into a dolphin and took the girl to his home deep below the surface. A couple of days later, she would come back and tell her story. Soon she would become pregnant and everyone would know that the dolphin did it."

Risa laughed. "Good one. Sounds like a convenient excuse

for getting pregnant out of wedlock. The dolphin did it."

"That's a sociological interpretation. But maybe the girl was telling a true story." I tried to sound serious. "Supposedly, the stranger wears a Panama hat to cover his blowhole."

She playfully shoved my shoulder, then slid her arm around my waist. I turned and embraced her. Our lips met and I knew immediately that she was right for me. I felt the chemistry that was lacking in other sexual encounters over the years since my divorce.

She pulled her head back after a few seconds. "What about the dolphins?"

"They don't care."

"You're not one, are you?"

I touched the top of my head. "No blowhole."

"That's good. So what're we going to do?"

"I could show you the master bedroom."

"That would be nice, especially if I could look at the ceiling."

"What? Oh, I get it. Sorry I'm a little slow."

"Not that slow. You got me with that dolphin story."

We barely made it to the bedroom when we embraced again and my hands sculpted her body. Our clothes fell away, and we tumbled onto my bed. "Am I blocking your view of the ceiling?" I whispered.

"I don't give a damn about the ceiling," she said between gasps.

It had been more than a year since my last interlude, and damn, it was worth the wait.

4

Captive

Lydia stirred in her sleep. Her jaw ached and spittle ran down her jaw. She felt as if she were awakening from a night's sleep, but quickly re-oriented herself. Her hands were bound behind her back and a black hood covered her head. With a sinking feeling, she realized she was in the back of the Suburban.

She heard a commanding voice, but it wasn't addressing her.

"I was hoping I could trust you to communicate my message to the world, Alex. But you focused on death, not the promise for the future. You even called Dominion a killing machine. You dismissed my message that Dominion is about creating a more just world for everyone, not just the fortunate few at the top."

So they'd kidnapped Alex, too, she thought. That was somehow reassuring, especially when he responded, defending himself.

"It sounded like propaganda. The reality is you *are* killing masses of people, including many of my colleagues in the media, depriving people of family and friends and neighbors. Where's the justice there?"

Way to go, Alex. She heard a smack and a groan, and guessed that Alex had taken a blow to the head. On second thought, rebuking the Dominion honcho wasn't going to play well with these thugs.

She wasn't sure how long they'd been moving, but the sound of traffic and the numerous stops suggested that they were still downtown. They traveled another fifteen minutes, remaining on side streets, avoiding I-4 and the 408. Finally, they turned off the pavement and onto a gravel drive. They drove about fifty yards, turned to the right, then stopped.

Doors opened and hands pulled her out of the vehicle. She was walked rapidly away from the vehicle. Alex stumbled along behind her. The men guiding him cursed, and it was clear to her they were Americans. They were taken into a house or building. Another door opened, and she was shoved down into a low chair. The plastic handcuffs were removed, the hood pulled off.

Alex lay on the floor on his side, and he was freed from his bindings. The three men in ski masks and black uniforms left the room, locking them inside. She immediately stood up and helped Alex to his feet. She ran a finger over his red and swollen cheek and cut lips. Blood speckled his beard from a cut below his left eye. "My god, are you okay?"

He ran his hands over his face. "I guess, how about you?"

"My jaw is sore where the bastard slugged me. Otherwise, I'm okay. What do you think this is about?"

"Nothing good." His split lips were swollen and his voice was thick. He moved unsteadily around the room as if looking for a way out. There was nothing they could do, but wait. The room had no windows and resembled a walk-in closet without the clothes. Two lounge chairs that looked like it should be poolside were pushed sideways against opposite walls.

She crossed her arms, hugging herself. "What are we going to do?"

Alex sat down on one of the chairs and gingerly touched his face. "Whatever they say. No arguing. That was a mistake on my part in the car. If we want to live, we go along with them. That's our only choice."

She sank into the other chair. "I'm sorry I got you into this, Alex. I had no idea they would be following you."

"It's not your fault. I should've canceled. I had a bad feeling about it. Maybe they're just trying to scare us and will let us go in awhile."

She hoped Alex was right. She wanted to go home. She wanted her freedom. And mostly she wanted to tell the world about these bastards posing as saviors. She closed her eyes, and wished away her predicament. Moments later, the door burst open and two large, muscular men barreled in. They grabbed Alex by the arms and dragged him away. Lydia pressed her fists against her mouth, stifling a cry. Fucking barbarians.

Risa sat up in bed and looked around. It took a moment to place herself. She smelled coffee and glanced at her watch. Seven-thirty, time to get up, and get moving. She swung her legs over the side of the bed. She wore a long t-shirt that Lang had given her the night before. She started to stand up, but her knees nearly buckled as the impact of the dream hit her. She sat back down.

"Hey, Lang, can you come here?"

"Hang on," he called out from the kitchen and in a few moments appeared with two cups of coffee. "Milk or sugar, both?"

"Give it to me black."

He frowned, handed her a cup, then sat down next to her. "Is something wrong?"

"Something is weird. I had the dream."

"What?"

"Your dream, except I was the girl. I was inside the TV reporter. They were both captured by Dominion. In Orlando, of all places."

A couple of beats passed in silence. "You're not joking, are you?"

"No, I'm not."

"Shit, this is getting really strange, Risa."

She tried to make sense of it, and mentally tried to put some distance between herself and the dream, allowing her to analyze it. She smiled and slipped a hand over the back of his neck. "Amazing how the mind works, isn't it? You filled my head with those stories and my subconscious went to work."

"Is that what you think?"

"What else would I think, Alex?" In spite of her attempt to explain it away, she was still baffled. "I don't remember many dreams. But this one seemed real. Even now, it's more like recalling something from my life than from a dream. I sensed her fear and shock. I was right there with her, and…" She shook her head.

"What is it? Tell me."

"It's like you said about your dreams. I felt that if I wasn't careful, I would become her or a part of her. Stuck in the dream, I guess. Which doesn't make any sense."

Lang helped her to her feet. "No, it doesn't. But that feeling, that sensation, is real and scary. Hey, I'll make us breakfast and you can tell me the whole story. I can't wait to hear it."

She reached for her purse and pulled out her iPad. "While you're cooking, I'm going to take some quick notes so I don't lose it. Then I'm going to take an even quicker shower and get ready to go."

Risa walked out of the bedroom ten minutes later, her head wrapped in a towel. "What a great view! All these sliding glass doors and glass walls looking out on the water. It's like we're on a cruise ship."

"Yeah, come and eat before it gets cold."

"Do you know you don't have a hair dryer?"

"Never knew I needed one."

She sat at the serving counter, rubbed her hair for a few seconds, then laid the towel over another chair. "I guess the wet look will have to work this morning."

"Works for me." He passed her an omelet with slices of turkey bacon on the side. "It's goat cheese, mushroom and tomato. I hope that's okay."

"It's wonderful. You're a good cook."

He laughed. "How do you know? You haven't tasted it yet."

She took a bite, nodding. "I was right. What's that seasoning?"

"Oh, the Adobo, a Cuban thing. Gives it some spice." He tipped the coffee pot over her cup.

"I have to say, Bruce Lang, that I never expected to find myself here this morning."

"Nor did I expect to be making breakfast for you," he replied between bites.

"As I drove to the restaurant, I asked myself what was I doing going out on a date with a cop."

"Retired cop."

"As you told me. I almost turned around, but then I reminded myself of your new profession. I kept going and I'm glad I did. It's been a quite remarkable encounter."

He set down his coffee cup. "And it's not over, I hope."

"I have get to my office to prepare for a 10 o'clock appointment. But this is a two-way dream fest now." Slowly, she began recounting the details, pausing here and there as she continued eating. She finished recounting the dream as she took her last bite.

"Interesting. You definitely tuned into something. Considering what happened to Alex, I'm glad it was your dream, not mine."

Risa rested her chin in her hands, her elbows on the counter and met his gaze. "There was one other thing. In spite of being held against her will and frightened, Lydia was secretly enjoying her time in captivity with Alex. She was quite taken with him from the moment he arrived on the rooftop of the parking lot. He's a handsome fellow, a few years older than her."

He put his dishes in the sink. "Well, you seem to have gotten quite nicely into her head."

"Maybe. Or into my own head."

"Oh, you mean you see some parallels between their new relationship and ours?"

"Hmm, I think they're more into bondage."

"Good one."

"Then there's the relationship between you and your ex and Alex and his."

"Yeah, both ex-wives are FBI agents who ran off with fellow asshole agents. The only difference I'm divorced, he's separated."

"You and Alex have a lot in common."

"Excellent deduction, Dr. Ferraro."

"Don't doctor me, Lang. After last night, you'll never be my client."

"Why, am I too crazy?"

"Maybe. And apparently I'm joining you."

"Do you really think your dream was just your subconscious mind making up a story based on my dreams?"

"Do you have another explanation?"

"Maybe we're both tuning into something that's dark and disturbing that has a reality of its own separate from us."

"Hmm, maybe."

"I know you've got to get going, but I want you to read something first. I got up at six-thirty and started writing. I had a dream, too. I wrote it down, and I wanted to keep writing. I actually sensed what was going to happen beyond the dream. It was a little scary. I felt as if I was being pulled back into it while I was writing. So I stopped myself."

"I can't believe you didn't say anything."

"I didn't want to interrupt you." He walked over to the dining room table and raised the top of his notebook computer.

She slid off the stool, glanced at her watch, and stepped over to the table. She settled in front of the laptop. "I thought we were finished with our dream-telling, but I guess not."

ALEX

I heard the jingle of keys at the door. It was too early for lunch. I'd been here four days now. Meals arrived three times a day, served by one of the Dominion thugs who had accompanied Hector when Lydia and I were captured.

When they dragged me from my room, I thought I was either going to get released or executed. They'd hauled me into a room in the same building that looked like it might be a bed-and-breakfast. It was neatly furnished with a sailing theme that included pictures of tall sailing ships at sea on the windowless walls and a model sailboat on the dresser. There was even a copy of *Moby Dick* on the back of the toilet in the adjacent private bathroom. The shower curtain featured a bearded sailor in rain slicker and rain hat clinging to a tiller in a storm.

Hector walked in, unaccompanied, and closed the door. I was amazed by what I saw. The man had transformed again and now stood fully upright. His shoulders seemed broader, his chest larger. The gray-haired man who had appeared seventy when I first encountered him now looked fifty, his dark hair streaked with silver.

In spite of the transformation, I had no doubt I was in the

presence of the same man and truly believed for the first time that Hector was not just one of the leaders of Dominion. He was *the* leader, just as he'd said. I couldn't help feeling a sense of awe and wonder. Who exactly was this man, where had he come from, what was his background? I knew virtually nothing about him.

Hector looked around, smiled. "Nice room. A bit larger than your friend's."

"Is Lydia okay? Your helpers don't say shit to me."

"She's frustrated, angry, fearful. What you would expect? She lacks your patience."

"What do you want with us?"

"Please, sit down." Hector pointed at the bed.

I sat on the edge of the mattress, like an obedient boy about to be lectured by his father. Hector remained standing. I remembered my pledge to play along, but my natural tendency was to rebel against authority. And the Dominion leader was clearly the authority figure in my life. My momentary admiration for Hector had vanished. I was in the presence of a mass murderer.

"Congratulations, Alex."

"For what?"

"You are world famous now. The video from the rooftop has gone viral. It's everywhere."

"You're in it, too."

"Only for a couple of seconds, a blur of black uniforms."

"Aren't you concerned about being caught? Orlando is not exactly your stronghold."

He smiled. "You don't think so? Things are moving very rapidly. That's why it has taken me a few days to get back to you. Now that you are famous I have a request. Think carefully before you reject it."

"What is it?"

"I want you to pledge that you are with us. You are part of Dominion."

"Why would I do that?"

"Maybe you want to live." He moved closed and touched my shoulder. "Don't be a fool, Alex. You're getting the offer of your life, a chance to be close to the inner circle, if not part of it."

"How long do you think your rebellion, or whatever you call it, is going to last?"

"The world is changing rapidly, Alex. The old ways are falling away. So is the opposition. You'll see when I take you and Lydia out of here."

"Where are we going?"

Hector's answer was the last thing I expected to hear. "Disney World. It's our headquarters, at least for the time being."

"You're taking us to Disney World?"

"That's right. Lydia has already agreed to work with us. You two will do very well in the new world."

"Disney seems kind of conspicuous. An easy target for bombs."

"Not so easy any more. Patrick Air Force Base has flipped. They're with us. They're guarding Disney. The military considers them captives, and won't attack."

"How could that happen?"

"Many strange things are happening. You will understand better when you become part of us."

LANG

I could tell from Risa's body language that she was perplexed. She leaned back in her chair as she finished reading and gazed up toward the loft. "What do you think?"

"Strangely enough, it seems to fit with my dream. They were separated."

"But what do you think it means?"

She stood up. "I've got to run." She stepped closer, poked me in the chest. "You're messing me up, Lang. That's what I think."

"Sorry. Guess it comes with the territory."

She leaned forward, lifted up on her toes, and kissed me lightly on the mouth. "But it's nice territory. I've got to think about all of this. I'll call you from the car."

She stopped at the top of the spiral stairs and turned. "Disney World...really?"

I laughed. "Definitely a dream, right?"

"Yes, but our so-called counterparts don't act like dream characters. They seem too real. And then there's Hector. Whoever he is, whatever he is, doesn't feel good to me." She waved and disappeared down the stairs.

I cleaned up the kitchen and started my laundry, all the while puzzling over the two new dreams—Risa's and mine. They were clearly interconnected with each other and my earlier two. I didn't know what to think about the story line, but I felt damned good about how Risa and I and our dreams had melded together. It was like I'd found a missing part of myself, and if it took a few weird dreams to explore our relationship further, I was all for it.

A few minutes later my phone rang. It was Risa, probably calling from the road. "How's traffic?"

"Light, fortunately. But I won't have much time to prepare for my client."

"How do you prepare?"

"Look at their file and see where we should go. But actually, this morning, it's not really a client. It's my lawyer. The wife of that cop I told you about, the one who killed himself, is suing me. She says I aggravated his condition and should be held responsible."

"Sorry to hear that."

"Yeah, me too. Especially since I'm not getting any help from my employer, the county government."

"What about the union?"

"Lang, I told you, I'm a contract employee of the sheriff's department. Not a cop, not in the union."

"That's right."

"Let's talk about something else. Your new novel. Is it about aliens?"

Now it was time for me to set *her* straight. "I'm a mystery writer, not science fiction."

"I know. But if you were writing about aliens, your dreams might make more sense."

"Why, Hector isn't an alien?"

"So he said."

After a few moments of silence, I laughed. We both did.

"This conversation is getting weird, Risa. You realize that?"

"Yeah, no shit. Our relationship is based on strange conversations."

And great sex, I thought, but didn't go there. "Strange dreams, too."

"And I hope it continues," she said, her voice husky, then abruptly changed her tone. "Okay, Gotta go. Talk to you later."

5

Lang's World

LANG

After pouring myself another cup of coffee, I sat down at the dining room table where I did most of my writing. I needed to stop thinking about Risa and this dream stuff and get to work. I was two-thirds through my third novel in the mystery series, and intent on finishing it. My second novel would be published in three weeks, and the publisher had arranged a publicity tour that would take me away from writing. Meanwhile, I was also a script advisor on the TV series based on my first novel, and shooting for the first season was underway in Miami.

I was thrilled with my good fortune, but only to a point. My old friends and former colleagues treated me differently now. I wasn't one of the guys any longer. The novel didn't change things, but the television series did. Everyday someone said, *Why are you still working here?* It was almost as if I didn't fit any more. It was time to go. Besides, I had a deadline for my second novel.

I struggled to focus on my story. Whenever I couldn't move ahead, I went back and read the last couple of chapters. But I'd already done that yesterday and nothing had come of it. The dreams, it seemed, had infected my muse, who my daughter called the dude in the basement, a reference to Stephen King's muse. I didn't have any idea where my mused lived. Outside, probably, by the water. One thing I wasn't going to do was let Dominion sneak into my book. It didn't belong there, even as a dream.

My cell rang. Jen. "Hey, let me guess. You need money for something."

"Dad, I don't always call you about money." I'd bought her a new car after the TV series came through, even though Sharon had admonished me for it. *Jennifer should earn the car by improving her grade-point average,* she'd written in an email.

"How's your Prius?"

"Wonderful, of course. I'm saving a shit ton of money on gas."

"But…?"

"I want to do on-line courses for the new semester."

"Why? I thought you already registered."

"I can still change. It's just the first week. I want to come down there and live with you. Remember you told me I could always stay in the apartment downstairs."

"Yeah, but what about your apartment there in Miami?"

"I can sub-lease it. I know someone looking for a place and my roommates already know her. It should work out."

Probably a boyfriend issue, I thought. "Are you trying to get away from someone? You know it's usually best to confront your problems with other people, rather than running away from them."

"It's not about that. I'm over Dan. That's done. It's something else. I don't want to talk about it on the phone. Can I come down today?"

"Sure, but what about your mother?"

"I've already told her. She's pissed at me right now. But she'll get over it."

"Well, you spent the holidays with her in California. Now it's my turn. But did you tell her your reason for leaving?"

"I just said that I wasn't happy here and wanted a change. I'll see you later this afternoon. We'll talk."

She disconnected before I could say another word and I stared at my computer screen, wondering what that was about. Then it hit me. *Oh, shit. She's pregnant.* She probably intended to get an abortion and didn't want to tell her mother. Or maybe she wanted to have the baby down here. The thing with kids was that even when they'd left home, they were still your kids, you were still connected to them, worried about them, wanted the best for them.

But I couldn't worry about it now. I would find out soon enough.

Try as I did to focus, the words on the screen kept blurring as my thoughts turned back to Jen and the possible scenario that would unfold. Finally, a light blinked in my head. Jen's scenario gave me an idea, a new twist, and I wrote for the next hour and a half until I was interrupted by a call from my old partner at Miami-Dade.

"Sorry, Sal, no fishing for me. I've got to get this novel done."

"All right, man. I thought you might be getting bored with your success. You know we can always meet for lunch, even if you don't have time for bone fishing."

"Lunch at that place in Big Pine, as soon as my novel is finished."

"I'm holding you to it," Sal said.

I stared at the screen, trying to focus again. But now my mind slipped back to the day shortly after I'd resigned when I'd driven down to the keys to see Sal. He'd retired three years earlier after winning a sizable settlement from an insurance company, and had opened a bait shop on Big Pine Key. We'd made an odd pair. I was six-two with an average build, while Sal was five-six, barrel-chested with biceps that strained against his uniform sleeves. I had a full head of salt and pepper hair and Sal's top was thin and receding. Now his head was shaved and he wore a graying goatee.

We'd gone out trolling for bonefish in the mangrove channels, and afterwards over a beer at a marina bar on Cudjoe Key Sal had talked me into looking at a house that was for sale on Sugarloaf. He knew the owner and was certain that I could get a good deal on the place.

"It's his second home and he needs the cash now. His business took a dive and he's trying to get out from under his debt," Sal said in his New Jersey accent. "He owns a chain of camera stores in the Northeast, but the Internet's killing him. People come in and look at his stuff, then go home and buy what they want on-line."

"They probably get a better deal."

"Right, but then the brick-and-mortar guy gets stuck with leases and insurance and all that goes with operating a business the old way." Sal downed a shot of whiskey, then went back to his beer. "Fortunately, fishermen don't go fishing for gear on-line. Not so much. Fishing rods, you know, are like shoes. No one wants to buy them on-line."

Sharon bought shoes on-line, I recalled, but didn't want to bring up her name or Sal would carry on about what an asshole she was for leaving me for an FBI agent. Like a lot of cops, Sal didn't care for G-Men and their haughty attitudes.

"Besides, once they get down here on vacation," Sal continued, "there's no time to order shit. It's spur-of-the-moment shopping, for sure. And I got what they want."

"You picked the right business, I guess. You want another beer?"

Sal slapped his hand on the bar. "I'm good. Let's go see that house."

"I don't know, Sal. I don't want to intrude on the guy."

"You're not intruding. He's not even there. But I know where the key is. C'mon, take a look, at least. I know you'll like it, and I know you can afford it now. Don't lose your fucking money in the stock market. Put it in real estate in the keys. If you decide you don't like living down here and want to go back to the traffic and crime in Dade, you can sell for a profit."

"Christ, Sal. I haven't even seen the place and you got me buying and selling it already."

"Hey, what are friends for?" He patted my back as we walked out to the parking lot.

Snap out of it, I told myself. *Keep writing.*

Again the phone rang. I saw it was Risa. "What's up? How did your meeting go with the lawyer?"

"He thinks the wife is going to drop the suit. There's no way a counselor can be blamed for a suicide. Not unless I was encouraging him to take his life and it was recorded."

"That's good."

"That's not why I called though. I have a client coming

in this afternoon. She's an Iraq war veteran with PTSD. She wants to talk to me about her latest dream. She wrote it out and e-mailed it to me."

"Yeah, and…?"

"You've got to read it."

"Really? Can you forward it?"

"Normally, I wouldn't. But this isn't normal, not by a long shot. I'm removing her name and e-mail address. But promise me that you won't say a word to anyone about this woman's dream."

"Who the hell am I going to tell, Risa? The dolphins?"

"Okay, Talk later."

Lang clicked onto Risa's email. The subject was simply: Dream.

Hi Risa. You told me to label my dreams so I'm calling this one, Disney. It's so weird. I was in Disney World walking around, but it wasn't really me. Well, it was me. But I was different, a few years younger and I had a little girl. I always wanted a girl. Never happened.

But that's not the only thing. Disney World was really strange. It was full of these soldiers in black uniforms and berets. They'd just come in and taken over. There was a battle with security people. I didn't see it, but I heard gunshots. At first, I thought it was an invasion by foreign terrorists. But these people spoke English and were Americans. I never thought of dream characters as having nationalities, but these did, and that seemed to be important for some reason.

I wanted to get out, but the soldiers rounded everyone up and moved us to Tomorrowland near Space Mountain. We were all frightened, but they said they weren't going to hurt us. Some of the younger soldiers passed out water bottles and when one of them handed me a bottle, I said, "Who are you guys?" And he said one word: Dominion.

That's all I remember, except the person who was me seemed really frightened when she heard that word, Dominion. She knew who they were, or something about them.

I leaned back in my chair, astonished. The woman sounded convinced that the dream character was herself, even though she appeared different. I couldn't help wondering if the same was true about Alex. Considering the similarities between us, it seemed that he was a version of me. But did he actually exist separate from my dreams? Hard to believe. Yet, even stranger, Risa's client had somehow tuned into the Dominion-Disney scenario.

I punched her number, left a message. "I'm baffled. Talk later."

I turned back to the computer. But now I wasn't in the proper frame of mind to write. Besides, I needed to get the apartment ready for Jen.

I was mopping the tile floor when she arrived, carrying a large backpack that she'd bought for a trip to Ecuador she and a friend had taken last summer. They'd volunteered at an animal rescue center in the Amazon for three weeks, then traveled the country.

Jen dropped her pack and gave me a hug. "Daddy, great to see you. But you didn't have to clean the place up. I could've done that." She was lean and fit, a long-distance runner. Her dark blond hair was mussed. Her sparkling green eyes, which always caught everyone's attention, seemed dull, almost as if she were wearing contacts with a faint yellow tinge on them. She looked tired and worried.

"It was mainly dusty and needed airing out. I fixed the thermostat on the air conditioner, too. I'd been planning that for a few weeks."

"Thanks." She walked out the front door to the porch, thirty feet from the coral rock break at the edge of the property. She gazed out over the lagoon and took a deep breath. "This is so nice. I already feel at home."

"Well, you might get bored here. It's not Miami."

"Fuck Miami. I needed to get out of there."

Jen had the same salty mouth as her mother, and he and Sharon had agreed that it would be hypocritical to tell her to watch her language. She was bright enough to know there were social situations when curse words were not appropriate. As a result, Jen always felt as if she could express herself and not hide anything from her parents.

However, I figured it wasn't the best time to question her about her seemingly abrupt change in plans for the new semester. "I'll let you get settled in. How about if we go out to dinner at Mangrove Mamas?" When she hesitated, I added: "Or would you prefer going to Key West tonight?"

"Oh, hell no. Not tonight. Mangrove Mamas is fine. It's just that I had a sub on the way down. I'm not really hungry now."

If you're eating for two, you'll be hungry soon enough, I thought. "We can wait awhile. I need to work on my book."

"How's it coming?"

"Good. But I've had some disruptions lately."

I left it at that and headed back to my domain. As soon as I sat down, I knew how to move ahead. My protagonist awakened from a dream that gave him a lead on the case he was pursuing. The block gone, I wrote several pages over the next couple of hours.

My phone chimed and I saw it was Risa. "So did your client show up, the one with the dream?"

"She certainly did. You sound a bit groggy. I hope I didn't wake you from a nap."

"Nope. But that's not a bad idea. As long as I don't end up in Disney World."

She laughed. "I barely know you, but I feel like we're old friend."

"Well, so far it hasn't been boring. What do you make of your client's dream?"

"I'm starting to wonder if these dreams might be hints of a possible future. But I don't think it's a foregone conclusion by any means. Dreams are often symbolic and not accurate in terms of every day world events."

"So what're you saying?"

"Maybe some sort of catastrophic event happens at Disney World. Maybe it even involves a terrorist group that wants to rule the world. I hope I'm wrong."

"I wonder if I should make some calls regarding security at Disney."

"Do you think they're going to beef up security on the basis of a couple of dreams?" Risa asked.

"Might be worth a try." But even as I said it, I knew she was right. The bottom line was that the FBI would take an interest in me. In my twenty-plus years of law enforcement, I never had any luck with psychics. Others had, but a couple of times the person providing the lead became a suspect.

"I think we need to talk about this more before we consider going public," Risa said. "How about dinner tonight at my place. I'm thinking shrimp scampi."

"Sounds great, except I can't make it tonight. My daughter just arrived a couple of hours ago, and I need to spend some time with her."

"Oh, of course."

I looked up to see Jen standing at the top of the stairs. "Talk soon," I said to Risa, and ended the call. "C'mon in."

"Dad, you don't have to cancel your plans on account of me. I'm fine."

"I didn't cancel any plans. Just turned down an invitation. Remember we're going out to dinner."

She smiled. "I'm ready if you are."

The hostess at the funky roadside restaurant greeted me by name and led us to a table in the courtyard. A couple minutes later, a waitress appeared. "Your usual, a cab?"

"You got it, Renie."

"I'll take a Gray Goose martini straight up with two olives, extra dirty," Jen said and proudly flashed her ID. She'd turned twenty-one two months earlier.

I smiled. "I guess you've got your drink order down."

"Yeah, and the waitress has yours," she said with a laugh. "Is this your hangout?"

"One of them. They know me pretty well at the Tiki Bar behind the Sugarloaf Lodge."

"Yeah, you could walk home from there."

"I usually ride my bike."

When our drinks arrived, we ordered dinner, mahi tacos for Jen, seafood quesadilla for me. I held up my glass. "For a good stay and for as long as you like."

"I'll toast to that." Our glasses touched.

"So tell me, why did you want to leave campus?"

"It's a combination of things. I wasn't looking forward to bumping into Dan. I mean, I'm over him, like I said, but seeing him is a reminder, and the asshole acts like he doesn't even know me, and that hurts."

"Sounds like a song."

"No doubt. But that's not the whole reason."

"No, it's something else."

Get it over with, I thought. "Okay, let me guess, you're pregnant."

She laughed. "No, I'm *not*. But I see how you might think that. It's something deep and emotional, but not part of my ordinary world. I mean…what I'm trying to say, Daddy, is that I'm having really strange nightmares, and I'm afraid."

I didn't like the sound of that. "Why are you afraid?"

"I know this sounds weird, but I keep thinking I'm not going to get out of the dream. It's very real when I'm there and I feel like I'm being pulled into it."

My throat tightened, my temples pounded. My head felt as if it were spinning. And it wasn't the wine. I'd barely sipped at it. I needed to know more. "How many of these dream have you had?"

"Six or seven. At first they were short, but they're getting longer and scarier."

"Tell me about them."

She sipped her martini. "When I'm in this dream, I'm young, eleven. It's me, but it's not me. It's hard to explain. She's a redhead with a round face. Her name is Kari, but she's me and I'm her. What's wrong? You're frowning."

"Sorry. Go ahead. I want to hear more."

"Her parents are divorced, and her father is a journalist. He wasn't really in the dreams until recently. That's when it got scary. He was captured by this bad army that is taking over everywhere. It's like mind control or something. People and even regular armies are joining this bad army."

"You mean, Dominion?"

Her eyes widened. "Yes! How do you know?"

"I've had the dream, too. I was inside the journalist, who was captured. I think he was going to be taken to Disney World, which is Dominion controlled."

"Yes, that's it. I think he became one of them. That really frightened me. He and some woman reporter were sending out stories about how Dominion was changing the world for the better."

"Go on. What else?"

"You kept using the same phrase over and over: Resistance is futile."

"Wait. I know that line." I couldn't help laughing. "It's from a *Star Trek* episode. An alien force was taking over and this robot-like character just says that over and over. My guess is that Alex, your dream character's dad, is sending out a cryptic message."

"And maybe he knows the line because you know it."

"It's a dream, right?"

Her eyes narrowed. "Yeah, but why are we both dreaming the same thing? How could that happen, Dad?"

"I don't know."

She shook her head. "I don't know whether I should feel better or worse that you're involved in these dreams."

Worse, I thought, but didn't say it. Our meal arrived and as we ate, I considered telling her about Risa and her client, and their dreams. But I thought better of it.

My phone buzzed in my pocket and I pulled it out, thinking it would be Risa.

"Go ahead, take it," Jen said.

"It's just Sal, my fishing buddy. I'll talk to him later."

After a few moments, I heard a chirp, indicating that Sal had left a message. I listened to it and groaned softly to myself.

"What is it, Dad?"

I hesitated, then put on the speaker. "Listen."

"Lang, sorry to bother again. Got a question. Is there something going on with Disney World I should know about? I don't see anything on the news, but I've had three people today ask me if I know how secure Disney World is against a terror attack. Any idea what that's about?"

Jen let her fork fall out of her fingers. It clattered off the edge of the table and dropped to the floor. "It's spreading. Dad. This freaks me the fuck out."

I squeezed her hand and tried to reassure her, but my words fell flat. "You're safe. It's just a dream. Try not to think too much about it."

She looked at me, incredulous. "It's more than just a dream and you know it." She sounded irRisable, angry, and who could blame her? She knew I didn't believe what I'd just said. "I'm afraid to go to sleep, Dad. I'm afraid I'll get stuck inside that eleven-year-old girl. That's really why I left school."

"Tell you what. Let's see if we can get together with Risa, a psychologist friend of mine in Key West. We'll talk about it then."

Jen held my gaze for several seconds. "She knows, doesn't she?"

"Yeah, she knows."

6

Propaganda

ALEX

The moment Hector strode into the room, I knew Lydia and I were about to go to work. His arrival meant fresh news, and we would be busy working the rest of the day. That would make the time go faster and we wouldn't have to think about how fucked up our lives had become as house slaves for the leadership of a militarized movement that seemed to be swallowing the world.

I hated being a Dominion mouthpiece, and every day had thought about refusing to do anything and just face the consequences. But Lydia's presence kept me going. I didn't want to take her down with me. To justify what I was doing, I added a coded message in my press releases, hoping those in power would understand that I wasn't a convert, that I was working on the inside.

Hector didn't greet us. Didn't say anything. He paced while Lydia and I took our places at a long wooden table equipped with computers. Kahil, one of Hector's lieutenants, a slender man in his late twenties with distinctive white hair, had bolted to his feet the instant the door opened. He often acted as the cameraman for Lydia's reports and put them up on the Internet. He'd been lounging on a leather couch for an hour before the Dominion commander appeared. Now, like us, he waited for orders.

Hector paused behind us, arms crossed. He'd been absent

for three days and we'd been stuck with Kahil or one of the other lieutenants, who simply reviewed events in the world news with us, feeding us only what they considered important. But now, with Hector back, I would soon be working on an article presenting the Dominion point of view, and Lydia would record two or three short reports for YouTube. All of it would be distributed through the Dominion website, picked up and digested by other media sources.

Considering that we were captives, our accommodations were spectacular. We were housed in a junior suite on the third floor in the Holiday Inn Resort Hotel at Buena Vista, a short hop from Disney World. Dominion had assumed control of the hotel a short time after the takeover of the theme park. High-ranking American soldiers, who had joined Dominion, also resided here, while thousands of soldiers and volunteers had set up a camp in the parking lots outside the entertainment complex. Other than the fact that Hector moved around, staying in different locations each night, they didn't seem to fear infiltration of the ranks, or an all-out attack from the U.S. military.

Our suite included two bedrooms with queen-sized beds, a third spacious room with the couch, tables and computers, and a kitchenette with a microwave, refrigerator, and dishwasher, as well as a balcony overlooking the pool. Meals, provided by the hotel restaurant, were initially delivered to our room. After a few days, we were given more freedom to roam the hotel and surrounding grounds. But Kahil or another guard followed us and we knew we were watched by cameras and listening devices inside the room.

While our communication skills were highly prized, we were still considered risks. After all, we were captives, not volunteers. We publicized ourselves online as the only reporters embedded in Dominion. We insisted our reports weren't edited and we were free to write or broadcast what we saw and heard. In truth, everything we wrote was closely monitored and a critical story not only would get killed, but probably would get us killed.

Editors usually added that authorities suspected we were captives and our stories no doubt contained propaganda and disinformation. And they noted the death of a cameraman at the time of our disappearance. Some Internet news sites weren't so kind, and just assumed we were traitors. But as the days passed, we noted fewer scathing attacks against us or Dominion as military units—companies, regiments and brigades—astonishingly switched sides.

The only serious setback for Dominion came a couple of days after we were ensconced in the Disney hotel. Hector decided to make a personal appeal to the governments of all nations, telling them to surrender now while they could do so with minimal loss of life. The broadcast was initially greeted with derision from all parts of the world. Within days, Hector's appeal was used as a platform for new alliances between nations that had previously been at odds. But governments continued to fall when military commanders and their troops switched sides.

I felt as if I were lost in a hallucination. Here I was at the heart of it, supposedly the inner sanctum of Dominion, an outsider with an insider perspective. Yet, in spite of my position, I still didn't understand the nature of the beast. I was like an ant crawling on the back of an elephant. I only saw a small part of the tough exterior. I couldn't see the creature in its entirety, and I didn't know where it came from.

Members of Dominion's inner circle varied in race, age and physical stature, defying any sense that they were from a particular culture, race or religion. Kahil, had Nordic features, pale skin, eyes like ice chips, and that ghostly hair. He was lean and muscular, submissive in Hector's presence and always vigilant. In all my conversations with Kahil and the others, they'd been tight-lipped about their origins. Were they aliens, alien-human hybrids, bio-engineered robotic being? Whatever they were the populace was mesmerized by Dominion and increasingly identified it as the planet's savior.

As I waited for Hector to begin, the Dominion logo—a trident within a circle—glared at me, emblazoned on the screen of my computer. It was the first thing that appeared when I turned it on. The Dominion leadership was tagged with the logo on the palms of their left hands. I recalled Hector showing me his trident in Mexico. At the time, I was confused and uncertain who he was and what the tattoo meant.

Hector opened the session by describing his plan for the United States, which would require total capitulation by federal, state and local governments. It sounded like a fantasy. But then, so did so much else related to Dominion. I mean, *Disney World* as headquarters? In fact, all five Disney parks were now in Dominion control—Disney World, Disneyland, Tokyo Disney, Disneyland-Paris, Hong Kong-Disneyland and Shanghi Disneyland.

But why the keen interest in taking over these parks? Did the fantasy element of these places somehow play a role?

I focused on his comments, typing away. The U.S. would be divided into five semi-autonomous states—the Southeast, the Northeast, Texas, the Midwest and the West. The federal government essentially would be dismantled.

"But how can you have control if there's no central government?" Lydia asked.

Hector turned to her and smiled. "Lydia, the new central government is international. There's no need for a federal government in this country. The current one is falling apart fast."

He was right about that, I thought. The government and military was immobilized because so many Americans, including soldiers, were pledging support to Dominion.

"Washington realizes that if they bomb Disney World, they will be attacking not only an American institution, but American soldiers, and they will have no guarantee that they eliminated the heart of Dominion," Hector continued. "Their plan is to infiltrate us and take out the leadership."

It seemed like a good plan to me. "Aren't you concerned about that?"

"Not in the least. Even though we can't turn individuals as easily as groups, we can easily detect intruders and eliminate them."

I didn't like that. Did he know that I was faking my allegiance? That I would rebel against him in any way I could?

"I think Americans will welcome this new direction of

the country if they see it as a way of uniting people in their particular regions," Lydia said, interrupting my thoughts. "But I don't know if Americans will support a world union."

"They don't have to support it," Hector answered. "It's just the way things will be. What do you think, Alex? I see you're mulling things over."

The Dominion symbol faded from my monitor as the screen went black. I touched the escape key and it reappeared. "Right now Dominion is the new thing on the block." I carefully edited myself, avoiding saying *you're* the new thing. "People everywhere are unsatisfied with the way things are going in the world and see Dominion as a powerful force standing up to whatever they don't like. That can be a lot of different things, but they all see Dominion as providing a viable answer. However, I suspect the sheen will wear off and they'll start questioning Dominion's authority."

Hector walked over to the couch and sat down at one end. He motioned Kahil to sit, and turned to his colleague. "What do you think about what Alex just said?"

Kahil blinked his eyes and the ice chip pupils seemed to glow for a moment. Or did I just imagine that? "What he said is impossible. We have their hearts, we have their dreams. They are attached to us. There is no turning back."

Resistance is futile, I thought. My inside joke for Trekkies. A point of rebellion for me.

In the days that we'd been here, Dominion had gained power in the Baltic nations and battles raged in the streets of Russia and Europe. Governments in the Mideast were falling into Dominion's hands, and no one doubted any longer that it was a single international force with many arms.

I was seeing events from the control tower, so to speak. I was a part of it. Sometimes I actually felt proud of my role as a propagandist. It seemed as if a wave of energy rolled over me on occasion and each instance left me feeling more powerful and more aligned with Dominion. But I knew what was happening to me. I was succumbing to the Stockholm syndrome. I tried to fight it by repeatedly impressing on myself that I was a captive, that my actions were taken under duress, that these positive feelings were like injections of a behavior-control drug.

Since our words and actions were being recorded, Lydia and I didn't talk about our true feelings. At first, we exchanged meaningful glances from time to time when listening to Hector or one of his colleagues. But Lydia no longer responded to those looks, and I was starting to wonder if she'd lost her sense of independence.

It was time to write and tell Americans and the world what the future of America would look like. Hector was sly and never said this is what we must write, but whatever topic he discussed was what he wanted publicized.

Hector and Kahil stood up, the meeting complete, or so I thought. Kahil, who had been quietly reading the *New York Times* before Hector arrived, approached me and pointed to an editorial. "Look, you two are famous. Or is it infamous?"

I saw my name and the word *traitor.* I didn't want to read it and looked away. They were all watching me, waiting to see my reaction. "I guess we're making an impact," I remarked, trying not to sound disturbed. "Or at least the *Times* thinks so."

"You don't look too pleased by the way you're being singled out," Hector said.

I shrugged. "Nothing I can do about it."

Hector stepped closer. "I guess they aren't *Star Trek* fans on that editorial page."

I caught my breath, tensed, but gave Hector a blank look. "I don't know what you mean."

"I think you do, Alex. *Resistance is futile.* You keep putting that phrase in your articles. The Internet is very handy. All I had to do was enter the phrase on Google and there it was, linked to Borg, a fictional alien cybernetic race that appeared over and over again on *Star Trek* as antagonists. That was their favorite line.

"I guess it was a subconscious thing. I wasn't aware of that connection."

"I disagree. I think you're sending out a signal, letting the people in Washington know that you're still on their side, that you're on the inside working for them."

Hector pulled out a small hand-held device from his pocket and pressed a red button. Instantly, the door opened and two more of his lieutenants rushed in. I recognized Rom, who was tall and thin with dark skin, combined with European features, and long, straight black hair tied in a ponytail. The other one was Chen, stout and muscular with Asiatic features and a ruddy complexion. Like Hector, they spoke English as if it were a second language.

Hector gave a hand signal and they quickly moved in around me, pulled my chair away from the long table, then clasped my arms and lifted me to my feet.

This is it, I thought. They were about to kill me.

"Don't hurt him," Lydia shouted. "He didn't mean anything by it."

Hector turned to Kahil. "Take her to the other room and close the door. Now!"

Lydia glanced at me, and I mouthed the word, "Go!"

She turned, head hanging, sobbing, as Kahil led her to her room, shut the door, and remained in front of it, arms folded over his chest.

"I have something to show you, Alex," Hector said and motioned to Kahil. The pale, white-hair man crossed the room and returned seconds later holding an iPad.

"Play it for him."

Kahil pushed the screen in front of my face and I heard a scream and saw someone struggling against two men. I realized it was a child, a girl. *My girl! Kari!*

The men spun her around to face the camera. "Say hello to your daddy, Kari."

It was Hector, standing behind her, grinning into the camera just as he was doing now a couple of feet in front of me.

I lunged toward him, attempting to butt my head against his jaw and knock that grin off his face. But Rom and Chen tightened their grips and jerked me back.

"What did you do to her?" I shouted. "Where is she? I want to see her."

"In time, Alex. In time. As long as you're a good boy."

7

Connections

LANG

I bolted out of bed and clambered down the stairs in my t-shirt and drawstring shorts, hurried over to the apartment, and rapped on the door. No answer. Seven-thirty. She was probably still sleeping. I pounded harder, called out to Jen. I tried the door handle. Locked. I bounded back up the stairs for the key. Maybe I was over-reacting, still under the influence of the dream. But I had to make sure she was here, that she was okay.

I hurried back downstairs, my heart pounding from exertion and worry. I unlocked the door, called out her name. Still no answer. The bedroom door was partially open. I stepped over to it and pushed. I could see an impression on the covers and the pillow where she'd laid. But the bed looked as if she hadn't slept in it.

What did that mean? Where was she? I needed to call her phone and started to turn away when I heard a slider open. I stepped out of the bedroom. Jen stood in the doorway to the porch, outlined against the pale blue lagoon.

"Dad, what's wrong?"

"I was about to ask you the same thing. Where have you been?"

"Right here. I was sitting on the rocks, watching the sunrise. Before that I was reading out on the hammock." She held up a book and a slender flashlight.

He stepped closer to her. "You didn't sleep in your bed."

"I didn't sleep at all."

I could see the dark circles around her eyes and knew she was telling the truth. "You must be really tired."

"I didn't want to go to sleep. I was afraid what might happen."

"Don't be silly, Jen. You've got to sleep."

"I know. But will you wake me up every hour? I'll feel better if you do. Promise me you will."

I forced a chuckle. "Sure, but you'll probably tell me to leave you alone."

She didn't laugh. "I won't." When I didn't say anything, she continued. "Daddy, please don't let this dream world swallow me."

"Get some sleep. I'll be back."

I went upstairs and made myself breakfast, a bowl of homemade granola and blueberries. Afterwards, I took a second cup of coffee over to my computer and stared at the screen. My story felt distant, as if I was reading someone else's book. My thoughts kept returning to Jen and alternate realities. To me, it seemed the dream world was getting closer and closer to our reality by the hour.

I tapped Risa's number and reached her voice mail. "It's Lang. Call me." I went back to my book and read over the last couple of pages that I'd written. But again the dream scenario filtered into my awareness and I knew I needed to do something. I opened a blank document and tapped out a phrase: *Resistance is futile.*

I knew that phrase just as Alex knew it. But I realized there was more, a second phrase that followed. *Assimilation is inevitable.*

That was what was happening to people in Alex's world. They were being *assimilated* into a reality dominated by Dominion. But I couldn't help thinking I felt the same way, that Jen and I and Risa and maybe others—possibly lots of others—were also being assimilated.

Who is Dominion? What is it?

I stared at the words I'd typed and felt like I was in a chat room waiting for an answer. Sometimes when I was stuck in my novel, I would type questions addressed to the characters and often I'd find a way forward. But now nothing came to mind.

Okay, if you won't answer that, tell me this: Why am I being pulled into Alex's life?

I closed his eyes, suddenly feeling drowsy. My fingers were still on the keyboard and suddenly I typed an answer. I was aware of what I was writing, but it felt as if the thought was coming from elsewhere.

Dominion is weakening the veil.

Play with it, I told myself. *Why?*

The words poured out as if I'd hit a vein of good material for a scene. *They want to absorb all the dreamers from your world to make this world physical."*

Who are you?

You are me; I am you.

Alex?

My daughter, your daughter. Where is she?

I blinked, stared at the last sentence. I sat upright, glanced at my watch. Shit. Two hours had passed already. I hurried down the spiral stairs and over to the apartment. I stepped inside and peeked into the bedroom. She was sleeping soundly. If she were dreaming, there was no sign of any anguish. Her body was perfectly still. Maybe I shouldn't disturb her.

I went over to the foot of the bed, reached down tugged on her big toe, like I had when she was a baby in her crib. No response. "Jen?" I shook her shoulder. "Jen, you wanted me to wake you up."

She continued breathing softly and didn't react. "Oh, well. I'll let you sleep. I'll come back a little later and wake you."

I paused at the bedroom door and looked back. *Make sure you wake me up, Daddy.* Suddenly, a feeling of dread passed over me. I rushed forward, grabbed her shoulders, and pulled her upright into a sitting position. Her head lolled forward. "Wake up, Jen. Wake up!"

I shook her harder now. No response. "Damn it, Jen. Wake up!" I slapped her face. No response. I set her back down. "Shit!"

I rushed into the bathroom, filled a cup of water, hurried

back, and splashed it on her face. She didn't wake up.

ALEX

I jerked awake, looked around. I knew where I was, and a terrible heaviness pressed against the center of my chest. The bedroom door was half-open and a gray murkiness that hinted of dawn seeped into the room. Someday I would like to wake up and not find myself in this Disney hotel. If only I could find Kari and escape far from anything related to Dominion.

As I pushed up on my forearms, memory of a dream flickered through my awareness. I was in a house near water, writing on a laptop. It was me, but not me. It was like I was talking to myself, holding a conversation on the computer. I couldn't remember exactly what was said, but I knew it was about Dominion.

Then I remembered Kari was in the dream. She was downstairs in an apartment. I rushed down. It was Kari, but it wasn't. This girl was older and she wouldn't wake up. I kept shaking her, and that's when I woke up.

It was all about Kari, and my concern for her. If I hadn't gone to Mexico and sought out the Dominion leadership, she would be with her mother, not trapped in some Dominion stronghold. It was my fault for not seeing the true ruthlessness of Dominion. These bastards didn't play fair. It was one thing to face my own extinction. I took that chance. But I wasn't bargaining with my daughter's life.

I heard Lydia moving around in the kitchen, clattering dishes, and I could smell coffee brewing. She'd come out of her room yesterday as soon as Hector and the others left. "I can't believe they got your daughter," she hissed.

Then she saw my bruised and swollen cheek and started to curse the Dominion leader. I'd quickly stopped her, quietly reminding her that we were being recorded and observed.

"Let's just do our job. I don't want anything to happen to Kari. Or to you."

She stepped back and her attitude suddenly shifted. "You don't have to worry about me. I can take care of myself. You need to be more cautious. You're only endangering yourself and your daughter by playing games like that." She'd spoken loudly and sounded annoyed. I couldn't tell if she was covering up for her momentary lapse or if she really felt what she'd said. I kept to myself the rest of the day and she worked in her room. When Kahil came to take us to dinner, I told him I wasn't hungry. They left without me. Lydia didn't even glance back, and I felt very much alone.

She stepped aside from the coffee machine as I entered the kitchenette. "Your cheek still looks swollen, and it's red."

"Thanks for telling me."

"Let me look." Her face was close to mine as she examined my cheek. Her long ebony hair brushed against my arm and her dark, appealing eyes met my gaze. Her full lips beckoned. I basked in the surprising attention and imagined pulling her close, kissing her deeply. "They got me on the other cheek this time. But I'm okay, at least physically."

She touched my jaw and turned my head, as if examining the injury. She moved even closer and I was tempted to slide my hands over her rib cage and around to her lower back. "Look over my shoulder," she whispered. "Do you see it, Alex?"

At first, I didn't know what she was talking about. Then I spotted a note stuck to the mini-refrigerator. I leaned closer. *Go to the porch when you hear the music from our neighbor.*

The music. I glanced at my watch. It was due to start any minute. Loud classic rock blasted from the neighboring suite for half an hour and made it impossible to sleep past 6:30. What were we supposed to do, get up and dance at dawn every morning? More than once I'd muttered under my breath that the former U.S. Army officer who resided there was a fucking traitor with bad taste in music. When we complained to Kahil one morning when he arrived for a briefing, he cheerfully responded that we should use the music as our wake-up call.

But now Lydia had hatched an idea on how to take advantage of the sonic intrusion. What would be the leadoff song today? I wondered. Would it be Chicago's *25 or 6 to 4* again? Hopefully not *In My Room,* by the Beach Boys, which kicked off yesterday or *I Started a Joke,* by the Bee Gees from the day before. Maybe it was time again for *Islands in the Stream*, by Kenny Rogers and Dolly Parton, another of his favorites. Please not Rod Stewart's *Do You Think I'm Sexy*, not at this hour. All were songs played at full volume and seemingly selected to make me want to puke.

I didn't have to wait long to find out. I shook my head as I recognized the song within two or three beats, another repeat from our neighborly daybreak disco jock. *In the Navy*, by the Village People. And the colonel wasn't even in the navy. Even *YMCA* would be preferable.

I walked out to the porch with a cup of coffee. Lydia was standing at the railing holding a glass of what looked like diluted orange juice. We'd never come out at this hour because of the music. But now it was the music that brought us here.

"Do you think it's some kind of mind control thing?"

"What, the music?" she asked. "It's just plain obnoxious. Harassment. They don't want us to sleep late, I guess."

"Or maybe the colonel really likes this music."

"Anything's possible."

I'd never seen the colonel, only heard that he'd brought an entire regiment to Dominion. I would like to ask him what he was thinking about when he did that. How could an officer turn on his country, his way of life, his vision of what was good? Of course, I couldn't express these ideas, but I could look him in the eye and I'm sure I would see something there. Maybe fear. Maybe insanity.

I still held hope that the American government and military weren't unraveling, that turning regiments and divisions over was a tactic to defeat the enemy from the inside. But Hector was confident that he knew what motivations were at play, and that weakened my certainty that the military was holding strong. I'd heard that less than ten percent of troops rebelled when the shift was made. Those who refused to change their allegiance were immediately incarcerated to await court martial hearings, and a firing squad if they continued to hold out. At least, that was what we reported.

Now that we found a place to talk without being overheard, I didn't know what to say, where to begin. So I just lamely asked how she was doing.

"I thought you had bought the goods," she replied. "You were playing the role of convert."

"Me? I thought the same about you."

I was about to say something about the dangers of the Stockholm syndrome when *In the Navy* ended. I held my breath, hoping for the first time that wasn't our only wake up tune. Then along came the Bee Gees with *I've Got to Get a Message to You.* This time I didn't groan or want to cover my ears. I knew this song from long ago. My mother had liked the Bee Gees, and this was one of their older songs from the late Sixties. She'd played a CD, or maybe it was an old album with this song. It was about a wife trying to get a message to her husband who was awaiting execution.

Why that song? Why now?

These bastards were inside my head. There was no way of hiding from them. I felt like leaping over the railing head-first to the concrete bed along the side of the pool. I squeezed my hands on the railing, looked at my bare feet.

No, they weren't inside my head, I told myself. It was just more harassment. In spite of their powers to manipulate, they couldn't control everything. They couldn't know everything that was going on all the time. They wanted us to believe they were all knowing, as ubiquitous as gods, but they weren't. They could sway the masses somehow to act against their own best interests, but they couldn't know what everyone was thinking.

Lydia moved a few inches closer. "We've got to get out of here. But we need a plan."

"I can't abandon my daughter. They'll kill her if I run."

"I know that."

"What do you want to do?"

She held up the glass as if to toast my coffee cup. "I'm going to make myself sick with a little concoction I mixed. They'll take me to sick bay and I'll see what I can find out about people coming and going from the base."

"Shit, don't poison yourself."

"I won't. It's six ounces of warm water, two teaspoons of mustard, one of hot sauce and a tablespoon of salt. It'll make me vomit and look really sick. I used to do it when I didn't want to go to school."

She tipped the glass and gulped it down. The Bee Gees went quiet.

"You're looking a little pale."

She gasped for breath. "I don't feel very well, either."

Instead of another big hit from the musical past, a voice boomed from the adjacent porch. "Well, what do we have here?"

From the first word, I knew it wasn't any American turncoat colonel. Hector stood on the porch, his hand clutching the back of my daughter's neck, her blond hair falling over her face as she cried out. "Daddy, help me! They kidnapped me!"

Hector pushed Kari toward the edge of the porch as if he were about to toss her over. I was ready to leap across the railings separating the two porches when Kahil appeared behind Hector aiming a pistol at my heart.

Suddenly, Lydia retched and hot vomit spewed over the railing through a beam of morning light, fell two stories, and splattering next to the pool. She tottered and collapsed, her head striking the railing.

8

Coma

LANG

A beeping sound from a machine brought me awake and out of a pop-rock nightmare that had ended with a glimpse of a frightened red-headed girl a decade younger than Jen. I was slumped in a chair in a large, dimly lit room with curtains separating beds, the ICU at the Key West Medical Center. Jen was in a coma and they'd allowed me to stay with her overnight.

The beeping continued, lights blinked. A nurse rushed into the room. "What is it? What happened?" I asked, bolting to my feet.

The nurse didn't answer. Dr. Valencia, who I'd talked to earlier, moved into the room, followed by another nurse. "What's going on?" I asked again.

The second nurse turned to me. "Please go to the waiting room. We'll let you know as soon as we can."

I didn't want to go, but I knew I couldn't help Jen by getting in the way. I'd told the EMTs, nurses and doctors that Jen had stayed up all night, that she had been afraid to go to sleep, that it related to a series of frightening dreams. I didn't go into my own dreams, because I was sure they would find them irrelevant and might even question the validity of what I was saying about Jen's dreams.

I sank into a cushioned beige chair in the antiseptic waiting room, checked my watch. It was 4:15 a.m. and the waiting room was deserted. *C'mon, Jen. Pull out of it. You can do it. Come back to me.*

In spite of efforts to make the place appear friendly with bucolic paintings on maroon walls, the room felt cold and vaguely depressing, probably a reflection of the mental states and emotions of past visitors who had spent hours in these chairs.

My phone buzzed. I guessed it was Sharon, who was flying in from San Diego. I wasn't looking forward to talking to her, especially right now when I couldn't tell her how Jen was doing. To my surprise, it was Risa. "You're awake. How are you feeling?" I asked her.

She paused. "I should be asking you that question. Are you with her now?"

"No, something happened. The machines started beeping and they made me leave."

"Maybe she's waking up."

"I hope so. I dreamed again. Hector had Alex's daughter and threatened to throw her over the porch railing. That's when I woke up to the beeping sound."

"What happened to Lydia?"

Details of the dream exploded in my mind, a hand grenade of emotion. Alex and Lydia on the porch, the blasting music, then Hector and Kari appearing, Lydia collapsing.

"She threw up, on purpose, so she could get out of there."

"That's weird. I felt really nauseous when I got up a few minutes ago. I had the feeling I should call you, that you would be awake."

"Did you dream?"

"No, not that I remember. I'm going back to sleep. I just wanted to call."

I stood up as Dr. Valencia entered the room. His dark hair was streaked with silver threads even though he looked barely thirty. "How is she?"

"Her heartbeat shot up to 195. That's what it might be if she were running a couple of miles. So when it happens in a coma, it's definitely something out of the ordinary. Her brain activity increased as well and her eyelids fluttered. I thought she might be waking up, but that wasn't the case. Now she's stable, but still in a coma."

"What caused the changes? That sounds pretty dramatic."

"That's really hard to say. We don't know what people are experiencing, if anything, while they're in a coma. It could be that she briefly came out of the coma and became aware she was in the hospital, and that frightened her."

Or it could be that Jen experienced Kari's fear out on the porch, I thought. I could still see that scene, hear that music. I realized the doctor was asking me something. "Sorry, what was that?"

"You said your daughter wasn't on any medications, but do you know if she had a drug problem? Sometimes these things are kept secret from parents."

"Jen has always been very open with me and my ex-wife. And if I didn't know something, Sharon definitely would know about it and she would've told me."

"About forty percent of comas are related to drug overdoses. Another twenty-five percent are the result of hypoxia, a lack of oxygen to the brain. That condition is usually related to cardiac arrest. Strokes account for another twenty percent and the remaining fifteen percent are related to trauma to the brain, malnutrition or hypothermia. There's no clear sign that Jen had any of these symptoms."

"Well, I know she definitely didn't have hypothermia in the keys."

"Interestingly, hypothermia is also a treatment for coma symptoms. When we lower the body temperature slightly, it helps reduce swelling in the brain."

I noticed that Dr. Valencia had a nervous habit of tugging his right earlobe. It reminded me of a sign to steal second base that the third base coach used when I played college baseball. "If it's not dangerous, I'm all for trying it."

"Let's see if we can find the cause first. You said she stayed up all night reading and you saw her about 7 a.m. just before she went to bed. Did she seem as if she was under the influence of any drugs?"

"Not at all."

Valencia looked at his notes on his iPad. "But she said that she was afraid to go to sleep. That sounds like someone who might be coming down from being high on amphetamines."

"She told me that she'd been having nightmares."

"Did she describe these nightmares?"

"They were very vivid and seemed like real life, she said, not a dream. She would find herself inside the head of another girl, and was afraid that she wouldn't be able to get back."

Valencia looked perplexed. Whether or not he thought her concerns were valid or logical didn't matter. The fact was she didn't wake up and he saw the link between her fear and what happened. He tugged on his earlobe, then shook his head. "This is very unusual. There are two other patients in ICU that are also in comas. Both went comatose within the past three days, and both were having frightening dreams and afraid to go to sleep."

"Do you think the three cases are related?"

"The symptoms are definitely similar. There might be a connection. I can't release their names right now, but one is a 38-year-old black female, the other a 54-year-old white male. Both live in Key West. Any chance your daughter would know either of them?"

"Not unless they've spent time in Miami recently. My daughter has been attending classes at the University of Miami and living near the campus."

Valencia's fingers went to his ear again. "I would appreciate it if you could wait here for awhile, Mr. Lang. I want to get in touch with relatives or friends of the other two and find out if either of them have visited Miami recently."

"You think it's something that's contagious?"

"It could be a new type of virus. At this point, I don't know. But I understand there are other hospitals getting similar cases."

"Jen doesn't have a fever."

"There are viruses with no fever associated them. It's usually body aches and soreness, but this one, if it is a virus, seems to be associated with mental distress and confusion."

I considered telling Valencia that I was dreaming too, and felt the same sensation, that I might not get back. But if I did, I might end up under observation in the psyche ward.

"I'll do all I can to help your daughter, Mr. Lang." With that, Valencia turned away.

9

The Getaway

The drink was worse than she remembered. It felt as if her entire stomach and everything in it was rising into her throat and exploding out of her mouth. As soon as she vomited, Lydia stumbled, banged her head against the railing and lost consciousness. A few seconds later, she groaned. Alex hovered over her.

It was a good show for Hector, more real than she wished. Alex started to help her up, but Hector ordered him to leave her where she was. "If you stand her up, she might fall down and hit her head again." *Hector the caregiver, what irony*, she thought. *Que cabron.*

She lifted her head and felt a sharp pain above her left eye. She lowered her head back down, rested it on her forearms. Alex knelt next to her, a comforting hand on her lower back. In spite of her injury, or maybe because of it, her plan was working. Hector was on his phone, calling for help. Karl was no longer with him on the porch.

She would get out of the hotel and look for an escape route, maybe by finding a sympathetic soldier or orderly. Would she escape if she had the chance and leave Alex behind? She could hear her mother telling her not to worry about anyone else. *Think of yourself, Lydia,* mi hija, *and think of your poor mama worrying constantly about you.*

Yeah, Mom. I get it.

But she would try to help Alex, if she could. She liked him, liked him a lot. In spite of being held against their wills, being constantly spied upon, and required to work for an enemy, she felt comfortable around him. Sometimes when they were working together, sexual tension filled the air and she would have an urge not only to reach out and hug him, but to lead him into her bedroom.

In different circumstances, she might've followed through, or allowed him to do so. But not here. Not with these creepy voyeurs lurking around. Instead, she tried to remain aloof from Alex and sympathetic toward their captors. She could never truthfully identify with them or defend them, but she went through the motions every day.

Kahil showed up in less than five minutes with the hotel physician in tow. The overweight doc was flushed from hurrying after the Dominion officer and his thinning hair was mussed. He introduced himself as Dr. Alan Harwood and asked her what happened.

Lydia let Alex explain.

"Did she purge first, then hit her head?" Harwood asked. "That was the order?"

"Yeah. Is that good or bad?" Alex asked.

Lydia didn't like Harwood's use of the word purge. It sounded as if he suspected that she'd instigated the incident. If that was the case, they'd keep a close eye on her, nullifying any hope of escape.

"It depends. If vomiting follows a head injury, it's usually a sign of a concussion. When it precedes a head injury, it means something other than the fall caused the vomiting."

Get me out of here. Now.

As Harwood helped her sit up, the porch spun around her and she felt a sharp pain above her eye. She winced as he examined her pupils with a small light, asked her several questions that indicated he thought that she might've suffered a concussion. Then, as if Harwood had heard her silent request, he said he would like to do some tests at a hospital. Harwood told her to lie back down and wait until EMT assistance arrived.

Within minutes, she was strapped onto a gurney and on her way out of the hotel, her first time off the property in three weeks. An emergency medical technician, a young Latino who introduced himself as Enrique, guided the gurney into the rear of the ambulance and joined her for the ride. "I'm supposed to make sure that you don't go to sleep?"

"This isn't exactly a comfortable bed for sleeping," she replied.

"No te preocupes. Don't worry. I'll unstrap you when we arrive. But right now I don't want you taking a tumble on a sharp turn."

"Where're we going?"

"Celebration Health Hospital. It's not far, just outside of Disney."

"How long have you been with Dominion?"

"Chica, we're the people who are saving your ass. You are in the hands of the U.S. Army now. I'm Sgt. Enrique Cabrera."

"What do you mean? Do you know who I am?"

"Of course. This is a rescue mission."

She wanted to cheer, but her head hurt too much. *Thank God!* She started to say how much she appreciated his help when she noticed a camera lens pointed at her. She bit her lower lip. Did emergency medical vehicles videotape everything? Maybe. But she was so used to Dominion cameras that she couldn't shake the idea that they were setting her up to see if she really was with Dominion or trying to escape. Maybe she was just being paranoid, but she wasn't taking chances.

She focused on a patch on the upper sleeve of his jacket that read: *133rd Medical Detachment.* Now she remembered Kahil saying something the other day about an army medical detachment flipping to Dominion. Besides, how would the U.S. Army know that she was trying to escape this morning.

"I don't need to be rescued, Enrique. I'm fine where I am. I'm performing an important service."

"For Dominion or for us?"

She hesitated, but only a moment. "Dominion, of course."

Enrique didn't look either disappointed or pleased by her answer. He was just doing his job, and she was pretty sure he had flipped. Her head throbbed and she didn't know if she could continue with this game for long.

"We'll take care of you." He put his fingers to an earpiece, concentrated, as if he were listening to instructions. "Yes, sir," he said.

"What was that about?" she asked.

"I'm not supposed to talk to you if you are not interested in escaping."

Now she was more confused and confliced. She badly wanted to flee, but decided it was best not to respond. A few minutes later, they turned onto a winding road and slowed as they rolled over a couple of speed bumps, then stopped. She was lowered to the pavement on the gurney and wheeled into the emergency room. Someone she couldn't see directed Enrique to move her into a nearby hallway.

Enrique loosened the straps holding her down. "I'll make sure you're taken care of." With that, he turned and headed back to the waiting room. Was the hospital free of Dominion? She hadn't seen any soldiers in black uniforms. But if Enrique was in the army, where were *his* fellow soldiers? Were they simply out of sight?

She slowly sat up and winced as she touched the swelling above her brow. No wonder it felt as if someone was drilling into her skull. She wasn't in an examination room yet, but she'd bypassed everyone in the waiting room. Was that because she'd come in an emergency vehicle or because patients linked to Dominion received special treatment? Maybe Enrique had been telling the truth and she was being freed. But this hospital was so close to the Dominion headquarters that she could've walked here. She needed to look around and see what she could find out.

No one was paying her any heed. So she carefully swung her legs over the gurney and dropped her feet to the floor. If this was her only chance to escape, maybe she should take it. Alex would understand and surely they wouldn't kill him for what she did.

She made her way along the hallway and back to the double doors leading into the waiting area. She touched the swinging door and was about to push it open when she peered through the small window and spotted Enrique about ten feet away. He was talking to a slender young man with white hair and pale skin. *Damn it, Kahil.* He and Enrique were about the same age and could've been buddies in the army. Except Kahil was at the heart of Dominion. So much for Enrique's heroic effort to rescue her. No doubt he'd been flipped with the rest of the medics in his detachment.

She backed away, wondering how to find another way out of the hospital. But even if she did, what would she do? Where would she go? Without a vehicle there was little she could do, short of hijacking someone's car. Besides, maybe this was a test. Maybe they were watching her.

She walked back to the gurney and sat down, her head pounding, her heart aching. There had to be something she could do. A nurse greeted her and asked her to explain what happened. As Lydia told her story, she wondered if the nurse would help her escape. She was close to Lydia's age and had an open, kind face framed by blond hair pulled back in a ponytail. Her name tag read Andrea Hardy, R.N.

She took Lydia's blood pressure and temperature, examined her pupils and asked most of the same questions she'd heard from Harwood. Lydia told her that she hadn't felt ill until they'd walked out on the porch. "Maybe it was the music coming from the next suite that wakes us up every morning. Can you give me a Tylenol for this headache?"

"Ibuprofen can cause swelling and bleeding. If you have a concussion, which I think you do, you don't want that. I'll get you something else, but let's finish here first."

Unlike Harwood, nurse Hardy kept pursuing the matter. When had she eaten, what had she eaten? Was she allergic to any foods? Finally, Lydia took a chance and blurted the truth about what she drank. "Andrea, I'm a captive and I wanted out of that place. Are you going to turn me over to Dominion now so they'll shoot me?"

The nurse studied her in silence for several seconds. She took a quick look about, leaned closer. "The hospital is officially neutral. We are not reporting any gun-inflicted wounds or deaths or any other suspicious injuries to local authorities or Dominion."

If nothing else, that showed the power Dominion held on the hospital's administration, which gave them equal status with local authorities. But maybe they would make an exception in her case. "I'd like you to report my case to the sheriff's department so they'll get me out of here."

Andrea considered the request. "I know who you are. I've seen you on television. Like a lot of people I've become sympathetic to the Dominion cause. They're fighting to change the world for the better. Governments everywhere are corrupt and out of control. The American government no longer represents the will of the people. It's time for a revolution. You, of all people, know that."

Lydia's head throbbed worse than ever. She was appalled that Andrea was saying nearly word-for-word what she had been broadcasting day after day. "Andrea, nobody really knows what Dominion is or what it will do. The leaders..."

"They're heroes," Andrea interrupted. "I heard you say it yesterday."

"They force me to say what I do. The leaders aren't human. They're something else."

"How are they different? Are they from another planet? That's a lie. You've said it yourself."

It was as if Andrea didn't hear her saying she was a captive and spouting Dominion propaganda in order to stay alive. "I don't know what they are."

Andrea's amiable features hardened. "I'll be back in a few minutes. Please don't wander off like you did before."

Great. Dominion was brainwashing the world, and her voice and image were what people were hearing. What now? She heard her mother again, as if she were here talking to her. *Use your God-given talents, the ones that you've buried. You can see behind closed doors.*

Yeah, right, Mom.

She closed her eyes and pushed away the thought. By the time she was in elementary school, her mother had recognized her ability to know things that she shouldn't know, to see things that were going to happen. Lydia thought these abilities were natural, that everyone had them, that future events were as accessible as memories from the past. Her mother warned her not to talk to others about such things. But Lydia had to find out for herself. When she told a neighbor kid, he was going to fall from his bike and break his arm, her young friends became frightened of her when it happened a couple of days later. They whispered that she was some kind of freak, that she'd caused the accident. They moved to a new neighborhood in Miami—as Lydia knew they would—and she made new friends, and vowed never to look forward again. That was how she had thought of it as a kid.

Yes, wake up your talent, Lydia. But don't abandon Alex.

Her eyes blinked open. *What the hell.* She'd mistaken that voice in her head. It wasn't her mother at all. But who was it? What was it? *Who are you?*

I'm you….but not you.

Leave me alone!

Silence. Whatever it was receded. Yet, she sensed an etheric presence that seemed to hover just outside of her awareness. She needed to use those hidden talents to seek answers.

Closing her eyes again, she took a couple of deep breaths, turned her focus inward, searching. The voice didn't seem evil. It was part of her, yet separate. A woman. Suddenly, she felt a tingling sensation along the back of her neck and she knew someone was watching her. But now it was different. It was outside of her, not the inner presence.

She opened her eyes, and slowly turned her head. Enrique and Kahil stood just inside the double doors at the end of the hallway near the waiting room. They watched her as if she were some sort of strange creature. She forced a smile, then laid back down on the gurney. Her abilities were back. Maybe they'd always been there, latent, waiting for her to rediscover them. The voice had awakened them.

And she would escape. Soon. She felt it. She was confident of it. However, she didn't have a clue how she would do it, or where she would go.

"Okay, Lydia. I'm going to move you now," Nurse Hardy said as she returned.

"Where're you taking me?"

"Just lay still. We'll get you out of the hallway and into a bed."

Andrea wheeled her into a curtained bay in the ER and helped her off the gurney. She handed Lydia two pills and plastic cup of water. "Dr. Harwood will be here shortly."

"Please don't tell him what I told you. They'll kill me."

Andrea picked up the chart at the end of the bed. "I've written that your vomiting was self-induced by the mix you described. I didn't provide any explanation. You can tell him whatever you want."

She didn't like what she heard, but it could've been worse. "Okay. Thank you."

"I'm sorry, but it's my job."

More than an hour passed before Harwood arrived. He greeted her, then studied her chart. Lydia couldn't help wondering what the hell had taken him so long. He'd given her the impression that he was heading right to the hospital. Did he have another emergency patient to see in the hotel? He probably had breakfast in one of the hotel restaurants, taking his time, knowing the nurses would be tending to her. Then he'd arrived and no doubt chatted with the staff before making his way here.

He lowered the chart. "Okay, we've solved the source of the emesis, I see."

"The what?"

"Medical term for vomiting. Can you tell me why you did it?"

"Of course. I wanted a day off. I've worked twelve days in a row. So I did what I used to do in high school if I wanted to stay home." It wasn't true, but it sounded good.

"And here you are."

"Well, I wasn't expecting to get a concussion."

He examined her head again, asked her about the pain, and noted the swelling had started to turn a faint purple. "I want you to have an MRI."

"Who's paying?"

"Your medical expenses are covered."

By my captives, she wanted to say. Did Harwood even know she was a captive? Did he care? If he was the hotel's doctor, he was working behind enemy lines. More likely, he was like Enrique, a flip-flopper, working for the enemy.

Harwood said he would make his rounds, then check on her before he left. Twenty minutes later, a muscular black guy with dreadlocks tied back in a ponytail came in the room. His biceps bulged under his hospital scrubs and his nametag said Reginald Jordan. He smiled and told her that he was the MRI technician. He helped her into a wheelchair.

"Reginald, you should know that I get claustrophobic in small spaces."

He laughed. "Don't we all. No worry, Ms. Lydia, my machine gives you a sense of openness. You can choose your music and even watch an outdoor video of open spaces. You'll be out in twenty minutes." As they moved down the hallway, he added: "By the way, Reginald is my name tag. But I'm Reggie."

"Okay, Reggie. Some relaxing music would be nice. Escapist music." *Hint, hint.* Did he get it? If so, he didn't respond. Her hopes of finding an ally were fading, especially since it was too dangerous to speak her mind.

When they reached the MRI room, she asked to use the restroom. She stood in front of the mirror, leaned closer and examined the purple swelling above her eye. Her features were disturbingly distorted, but she laughed at the thought of standing in front of the camera for her next report looking as if someone had knocked her silly. Even makeup wouldn't cover the swelling. *Too bad, Hector. No on-camera work for me for a day, maybe two or three.*

By the time she left the bathroom, however, she was feeling vaguely depressed at the thought that there seemed no way out. She moved to the center of the room and onto a padded slab that reminded her of an autopsy table. The MRI machine looked like an oversized front-loading washing machine or dryer.

Reggie gave her instructions not to move once the red light came on, then retreated to an adjacent room with a glass window. She heard a hum and the slab started to move into the mouth of the machine and quickly swallowed her.

She took a deep breath, exhaled, trying to relax. Environmental music filled the tube—sounds of nature, chirping birds, running water, wind chimes, backed by the hollow echo of flute notes. It was accompanied by bucolic scenery on the monitor overhead. Mountains and streams, woodlands and fields, lakes and ocean vistas flowed past. Maybe this was the escape she'd sensed, a fabricated one. The soft lighting that illuminated the interior of the machine gave her a sense of openness. She could almost go to sleep.

She lost track of the time until the red light started blinking. Done, she thought. The music was abruptly interrupted by three beeps, like a wake-up call. The screen on the monitor went blank. She was ready to get out, to sit up and stretch her arms. But the slab didn't move and she remained trapped.

Words, sentences, a message appeared on the monitor: *We will get you and Alex out. Be on your porch at two-thirty. Trust no one.*

What? She read it again. The scene went black again. Music and soothing scenery returned for a couple more minutes before she heard the technician telling her that the MRI was complete. The slab slowly pulled out of the machine and she sat up. Her headache had eased. Maybe it was the pills combined with the relaxing music and video. But now her mind was racing.

The door to the adjacent room opened and to her surprise Harwood stepped out and moved over to her. Careful, she thought. *Trust no one.*

"That wasn't too bad, was it?"

She smiled. "No, better than I expected, actually. How does it look?"

He shrugged. "Actually, MRIs or Cat scans rarely show anything when the symptoms are a mild concussion. Like yours."

"Then why bother?"

Harwood smiled. "I'll let you figure that out. My friend, Reggie, will wheel you back to the waiting room where your ride is waiting for you."

With that, he walked away. It was Harwood's message, she thought. She felt like cheering. He was the link to the world outside of Dominion that she'd hoped to find. Harwood wanted to save them. He disguised himself well. She'd totally misjudged him.

But what about the tech? *Trust no one.* Yet, Harwood

had called Reggie his friend, not his assistant. But did he call everyone he worked with his friend? She walked over to the wheelchair and settled into it. Reggie moved toward her and let her know he was in. "You got the message, right? On the monitor," he added when she hesitated.

"Yeah, thanks."

"Thank the doc. He set it up."

"Where's the U.S. military, anyhow? Why don't they do something?"

He laughed. "I don't know how much they're telling you back in that hotel, but it's total chaos. Most of Congress has flipped. Nobody's heard from the president for days. As for the military, half of the soldiers are with Dominion. Hundreds, maybe thousands are dead or they deserted their posts, both here and overseas."

"It's worse than I thought." She looked around for cameras. "Aren't you worried that they're listening? We're so close to their headquarters."

"This room is shielded for the MRI. It's a safe room, but even so the doc didn't want to talk to you directly. I'm sure he doesn't like me talking, either. Even in here."

"I guess you better get me back to my keepers, if that's the plan."

"Yeah. We'll get you two out."

"Two? No, three. Alex's daughter is captive, too. She was in the next hotel room this morning."

"I don't know anything about that. But I'll pass it on."

"It's good that everyone's not buying the Dominion bullshit Alex and I putting out."

"You know, as Doc Harwood says, it's like an epidemic. There are always a certain number of people who are immune, or get better, and that's why everyone doesn't get wiped out. Dominion is a new form of virus."

"Well put."

As he started pushing her toward the door, Lydia heard a distant chiming, repetitive and insistent. She couldn't tell where it was coming from. She was about to ask Reggie if he heard it, when she realized it was inside her head.

Risa rolled over at the sound of her cell phone and looked at the clock. Eight-thirty. She'd called Lang four hours ago before going back to sleep. She reached for the cell.

"Lang, thanks for waking me. I've overslept. I've got to get to the office."

"It's Saturday."

"Oh, yeah. That's good."

"I guess you haven't heard the news."

"About what?"

"The CDC has issued a warning that an unknown virus has left dozens of people in comas. The numbers are growing by the hour. I think we know what this is about."

She was stunned into silence. When she didn't immediately respond, he added: "After we talked earlier, Jen's doctor asked a lot of questions. He was very interested in the dream scenario. Interested and disturbed. He said he had two other patients in comas and they both had been afraid of their dreams."

"This is not good," she said, finding her voice.

"Risa, the dream world is literally swallowing people."

"Harwood, was that his name?"

"Who, the doctor? No, it was Valencia. Why? Who's Harwood?"

She shook her head. "Harwood is someone from the dream world. Lang, if you hadn't called me, I don't think I would've gotten back. I was totally part of Lydia. I was starting to lose touch with my life here. I tried breaking away, but couldn't do it. Not until your phone call jerked me awake. Five, ten minutes longer and I don't think it would've mattered."

"I'm glad I called. I would hate to lose two people."

"I appreciate the thought. But don't compare me to your daughter, you hardly know me."

"Right now, Risa, with Jen in a coma, I'm feeling closer to you than anyone else. Did you see her, did you see Jen, or rather Kari? You know what I mean. You're the only one who knows."

"No, the dream started after I fell. I was taken…no, I mean after Lydia fell…she was taken to the emergency room of a nearby hospital. I want to tell you about it. I think they're going to try to escape. Can we meet for an early lunch, say about 11?"

"I don't know. I should stay here at the hospital with Jen."

"Lang, Jen isn't there. You know that. You need to hear my dream."

"I guess you're right. How about meeting at Pepe's on Carolyn?"

"You don't have to give me the address," she said with a laugh. "See you there."

She walked into the bathroom and stared in the mirror just as Lydia had done. Seeing her image helped ground herself in the real world. But she touched her forehead, half expecting to feel tenderness and a swelling. "It is like a virus," she whispered, "a dream virus."

10

Making Contact

LANG

I claimed a table in the courtyard of Pepe's and ordered a cup of coffee from a waitress who had worked here forever. With my life and my sense of reality shifting like a series of tremors, this old establishment represented stability, something I seriously needed now. More than a hundred years old, the restaurant had existed longer than any establishment in the Florida keys, and was open every day of the year.

For me, it encompassed the old town atmosphere of Key West, a place that seemingly never changed. The rusted historic sign outside that advertised a full breakfast for 75 cents looked as if it might fall down at any moment. But Pepe's existed in a timeless reality—part of the daily world, yet outside of it.

Risa joined me a few minutes later and ordered an ice tea. She flipped open the menu, then immediately closed it. "What are we going to do, Lang? That's the question. Or maybe, is there anything we can do?"

She seemed more intense and disturbed than she'd sounded on the phone. "We have to take it day by day and see what we can figure out." Even as I spoke, I knew it was the wrong thing to say. I knew damn well it wasn't true.

Risa leaned across the table toward him. "Are you kidding? There is no day after days left. It's hour by hour, no, minute by minute. Next time I fall asleep I'm gone and there probably won't be any room in that ICU for my comatose body."

"I just might beat you there. I didn't get much sleep last night. I woke up every time a nurse entered the room. That's probably what kept me here. But if I go home and take a nap after lunch..." I shook my head. "News on the radio on my way said there are hundreds in comas, not dozens, and it's probably a huge underestimate. Think about all the people who might be sleeping in their homes with no one around.

The courtyard was slowly filling up with new arrivals. A half dozen locals sat at the bar in the rear. Everything looked normal, Key West relaxed. I sipped my coffee. "Who could've guessed that the world actually *will* end with a whimper instead of a bang. No violent catastrophes. No floods or earthquakes or hurricanes, no nuclear bombs. Everyone just goes to sleep and they don't wake up."

"It probably won't be everyone. Some people, the unlucky ones, will be left with the remains."

"Yeah, maybe this will become the dream world, and the Dominion-controlled world will be reality."

"Damn. That's a scary thought. But this will be more like a nightmare world."

I motioned toward the bar. "Look how happy people seem. Laughing, drinking, eating. Maybe they haven't heard the news. Or maybe they don't think it will affect them." Like every other time he'd been here, the television above the bar was tuned to The Weather Channel.

He reached out for her hand. "Maybe Alex and Lydia will become better friends. But it won't be the same, you know, being the watcher. Hell, we might even lose our awareness completely. Our lives here will be a dream that faded away."

"That's real comforting, Lang. Let me tell you my dream. I think there's some hope. I was able to communicate with Lydia, to push her to think in a way that she knew wasn't her own thoughts. She was aware of me."

The server came by and I told her we weren't ready to order. But I would take more coffee.

"Start from the beginning, after you, or rather Lydia, fell."

I listened carefully and the everyday comforting reality of Pepe's vanished as I lost myself in her story. When she finished,

I sat quietly as the waitress finally returned with the coffee pot. Risa ordered ceviche. I wasn't hungry, but maybe it was my last meal. "I'll take an order of conch fritters."

When she walked away, I turned my attention back to Risa. "Maybe the reason you were able to communicate with Lydia is because you've got some psychic talents yourself just like her."

"Maybe. But I think you can connect with Alex. With Lydia's help. I'll have to work with her more. We've got to try something or we're fucked."

That, I thought, aptly summarized our situation. I noticed the bartender, a big guy named Larry, was aiming the remote control at the television, changing channels. "Yeah, and who knows how much time Alex and Lydia have left before they're eliminated. I mean if that escape plan fails…"

"I know."

"Alex isn't going to leave his daughter—my daughter—behind, is he?"

Risa tapped her fingers nervously on the table. "Good question. I'm not sure he'll leave without her."

"I hope not."

If I was going to be dragged into that world, then I had one goal. Find Jen, even if she was lost inside Alex's kid. I'd failed to wake her up. I'd allowed her to drift away, and more than anything I needed to let her know that I hadn't abandoned her. If I could push Alex, as Risa had done with Lydia, maybe I could somehow reach Jen. But then what?

Jen in a coma in Key West. Jen lost inside of Kari, and Kari a captive of Dominion.

By the time our lunch arrived, a cluster of people had gathered near the bar and were staring at the TV, now tuned to cable news. A man in a coat and tie was talking in an official manner. I guessed it was a CDC press conference and things had gotten even worse, much worse from the looks on the people staring up at the screen.

"Let's enjoy our lunch, then I'm going back to the hospital to sit with Jen for awhile."

"After that, why don't you come to my place?"

As if in response, a trill of notes erupted from my pants

pocket. I smiled, and reached for my cell. "A text message."

"Oh, I thought it might be something else waking up at my suggestion."

"Hey, good one. Oh…my ex. She must be at the hospital." I read in silence, panic building in the center of my chest. "It doesn't look good. Sharon says the halls of the hospital are overflowing with comatose patients. She said it's total chaos, that I shouldn't even try to approach the hospital. That she would stay with Jen."

"Pretty bad."

I nodded and leaned toward her and when I spoke, I heard the urgency in my voice, the pulsing fear. "We've got to do something. If we're looking at our last day, then we need to act *fast*. If we can nudge Alex and Lydia, maybe they can broadcast a warning and somehow short-circuit Dominion."

"It's a slim chance, Lang. But we can try. Let's get our lunch to go, and head to my place."

"I'll drive."

"We'll both drive, I don't want to get a parking ticket, just in case the world doesn't end today."

I laughed. "Good point. And I like your optimism.

Risa knew what she had to do by the time she turned off Elizabeth Street and pulled into her narrow driveway between the side of her house and a row of palm trees. The trick would be getting Lang into Alex's head without allowing him to fall asleep and drift away, never to return.

Lang edged his car in behind her. She led him to the front door, unlocked it, and they hurried into her modest-sized living room.

"Hey, nice place."

"It's tiny, barely a thousand square feet, but it's enough for me." The two-bedroom house, she explained, was more than a hundred years old, and had been totally renovated. The house had tile floors and bright yellow walls with thick swirling paint strokes that reminded her of a Van Gogh painting of sunflowers. The bathroom had stone tile walls in the shower and all the fixtures looked new and upscale. She led Lang to the kitchen that recently had been renovated with granite counter tops and high-end appliances.

She opened the back door that led out to a small enclosed yard with a spa, benches and a brick walkway, all surrounded by lush tropical plants. "Nice. Very nice. But, ah, where's your bedroom?"

"Oh, aren't you in a hurry."

"No, just looking," he said with a laugh as she showed him her bedroom and office on the other side of the bathroom.

"Just remember that going to bed might be our last act."

"Yeah, we're not there yet. But what do you have in mind?"

"Glad you asked." She told him her plan, and Lang thought about it a few moments. He nodded. "Hypnosis, huh. Okay, I'm game. But can I have a glass of wine first?"

Risa laughed. "Actually, one glass might be a good idea. But only if I can join you."

"Suits me," Lang said as they moved into the kitchen.

"In fact, I've got a bottle of Cabernet here that looks like it's ready to be opened." She handed him the bottle and a corkscrew.

She removed two wine glasses from the cupboard and wondered aloud about what happened to Lydia in the aftermath of her experience at the hospital. "I'm sure she couldn't rush into their suite and tell Alex the good news that someone wanted to rescue them. They seem very aware of all the monitoring devices."

"Yeah, I don't think they can take a crap without someone at least listening. But, since we're both awake and here, do you really think anything is happening?"

She frowned. "I don't understand what you're saying."

"I'm trying to figure out what's going on so I'm looking at it like a crime scene. We've got people who were kidnapped. It's just that we're investigating another fucking reality where things are not the same."

"You're funny, Lang. And you're right. You can't play detective very well when you're not dealing with the ordinary world."

"Right. But hear me out. When Jen was a kid, she would get lost in television shows and get mad when there was a commercial break. She always wanted to know what she was missing during the commercial, and I would have to tell her there was nothing going on. I would say that the actors were also watching the commercial."

"Oh, you're bad," she said with a laugh.

"My point is that I don't think there's anything going on in the dream world when we're not dreaming. Everything there seems like it is here in the physical world while we're dreaming it. But when we're not linked in, so to speak, their world doesn't exist." The cork popped out of the bottle and he unwound it from the corkscrew.

"I get it. It's like commercial time. You could've been a psychoanalyst. But I don't completely agree with you. We tune in where we left off because we're intricately involved. It's our dream, but it's also a collective dream, like the Middle World in shamanism—a non-physical world that's a reflection of our world.

Lang filled the two glasses. "I'm not very familiar with that philosophy."

"Look, we're connected to these characters through our dreams, but they're also independent. They don't think of their lives as a dream any more than we think we're dreaming our lives."

They moved into the living room and settled on a comfortable black sectional couch, the only furniture in the living room besides a coffee table and lamp. "Do you see my point, Lang? We wouldn't stop existing when these other versions of us woke up from their dream."

He shrugged. "That all depends. Maybe things would look seamless to us. Maybe our minds would fill in the gaps, and maybe that's what happens with Alex and Lydia."

She nodded. "Maybe you're right. Maybe they're not such independent beings. However, a consensus reality has developed in that world, a dream reality that reflects our world to some extent."

"Right, but why do I only dream about Alex now? What happened to my regular dreams?"

Risa sipped her wine. "The virus. Or whatever it is. We're fighting it, but we've got it."

"Let's face it, it's all guess work." Lang set down his wine glass, then excused himself and headed to the bathroom. Risa took advantage of the break to think about how she was going to proceed.

When he returned, she was ready. "Why don't you stretch out on the couch with your head down on this end." She moved to an adjacent upholstered chair.

"All right. I hope this works. I've never been hypnotized before."

"All we can do is try. I've had plenty of experience working with people who think they can't be hypnotized. You'll be surprised how easy it is. I'm going to take you into a relaxed state, then lead you to Alex. When you're with him, raise an index finger. I want you to contact him. Say something. See if he responds."

Lydia began by directing Lang to focus on his breath and take slow deep breaths, in and out. After a couple of minutes, she guided him through progressive body relaxation. Starting with the crown of his head, she told him to imagine invisible fingers massaging his scalp, then his forehead and temples, around his eye sockets, along his cheekbones and down his jaw. She continued with his neck, shoulders, arms, wrists, hands and fingers. Then she directed his awareness down his torso, relaxing all the muscles, tendons and ligaments, then over his lower body all the way to his feet and toes.

Risa could tell before she was even halfway through the relaxation process that Lang was drifting into a deeply calm state and she realized he was an excellent subject. There was a fine line between guided hypnosis and meditation, mainly that the hypnotist directs the subject toward a particular goal. But Lang didn't need the guidance. He lifted an index finger before she even had a chance to tell him to look for Alex.

"I'm with him now," he said in a slow, soft voice. "I'm inside his head, but I can see him from the outside, too, a strange sensation."

"Tell me what you see. Keep talking to me."

ALEX

When Lydia walked in the door, I knew by her expression that something happened at the hospital. Kahil followed her in and watched us closely.

"How'd it go?"

Her eyes locked on mine, another hint that something important had developed. "Hi Alex. Good to be back. I got an MRI, but it didn't show anything."

Yeah, right. Good to be back.

"It was interesting, though."

How was an MRI interesting? I wondered. "Do you have a concussion?"

"A small one, nothing serious. The throbbing is almost gone." She touched a finger to her forehead. "It's just tender where I hit the railing."

I moved closer and examined the purple swelling above her left eye. "I don't think you'll be going in front of the camera for a couple of days."

She glanced over at Kahil, who sat comfortably in a full-lotus position onto the couch, something I'd never seen him do. "I'm sure there are other things I can do."

"Are you hungry?" I asked. "How about getting some lunch at our favorite restaurant?"

Kahil brightened. "The Bonjour French Café, correct?"

"Yeah, man. That's the place."

Lydia nodded and glanced at her watch. "I haven't eaten anything since my accident."

Kahil was already on his feet. There was never any privacy when we left the room. Always one or more of Hector's lieutenants accompanied us. Kahil, who was the most relaxed of the three regulars, actually seemed to enjoy our company.

"Crepes, croissants, and salads. Excellent choice," the pale skinned, white-haired young man said with a laugh.

"You would make a good maître d, Kahil," Lydia said. "You are very enthusiastic about restaurants. But you never eat with us."

"I am working, so I do not eat."

"What do you like to eat?" I'd never seen any of them,

including Hector, eat or drink anything.

"I like everything. Wait until you see. I will be a big eater."

What the hell did that mean? We left the room and headed to the elevator. Kahil was more talkative than usual and seemed almost excited. "Now you will get served by your favorite waitress, Go-Go Girl," he said as we descended to the first floor.

Lydia and I exchanged glances as the elevator door opened. That was the name we privately called Gogola, who usually waited on us at the restaurant. I was sure we'd never mentioned that name in Kahil's presence. But our room had ears and he must've heard us talking about her.

Gogola greeted us by name and led us to our usual table in the corner. She was an attractive, ageless blond, somewhere between her mid-thirties and early fifties, very attentive, always smiling. I'd never seen her without her hair in a ponytail or single braid and she always wore a white apron over a casual dress or jeans. She was the perfect server. Yet, something about her suggested that she didn't belong here, or wasn't staying here for long. I assumed her heRisage matched the restaurant's cuisine, though her accent and peculiar name didn't exactly resonate as French. But then Disney World attracted transitory employees from around the world.

Kahil sat with his back to the wall so he could see what was going on in the restaurant and the foyer of the hotel. As we settled in, I was surprised when he opened a menu, something he'd never done before.

"Are you going to order?"

Kahil's pale blue eyes gazed over the top of the menu. "No, not yet. But soon."

We exchanged looks again as Kahil turned back to the menu. In spite of more than three weeks among the Dominion inner circle, I knew very little about the core members. I didn't know where they came from, how many there were, even what they were. Especially that. The lack of any alien spaceships hovering over cities suggested Hector was telling the truth that they weren't extraterrestrials. But maybe that scenario only took place in the movies and on TV. Whatever they were, they were changing the world, manipulating masses of people into their mold. If they were human, they were extra-human. That was my conclusion.

The fact that Kahil had actually spoken at the table was a first. Whenever they'd addressed one of the guards during a meal, there was no response, not even a shake of the head. The rule was no talking to them at the table. Of course, Lydia and I could never talk openly about what was on our minds, so we tended to talk about our lives before Dominion. That way we'd gotten to know each other through our personal histories.

I decided to test Kahil, to see if he would say anything further. "See anything you like?"

He folded the menu and laid it on the table. "I told you. I like everything."

"I'm glad you're talking to us," Lydia said. "It's awkward when you just sit and watch us eat."

"I suppose I should remain quiet, but things will be changing very soon. Even now I feel the change taking place."

"What kind of change?"

Kahil didn't reply as Gogola returned with two glasses of water and asked for our orders. If it surprised her that their companions never ate anything, she never showed it. I guessed that she knew who we were, but she seemed neither impressed nor particularly sympathetic. When we ordered salads and ice tea, Kahil said: "Good choice." It was a line that Go-Go Girl often used. She looked at him and smiled. "Nothing for you. Not yet. Right?"

With that, she walked away. Gogola had never taken any notice of their guards, but now she'd said virtually the same thing he did about ordering a meal. *Not yet.*

I was even more baffled. "What's going on, Kahil?"

"Don't you know? The conquest is almost over. The victory is coming very soon."

I gave him a doubtful look. "Really. No one told us. What exactly is happening?"

"Governments everywhere are preparing to concede victory to Dominion."

"How could that be?" I pressed. "Why would they give up? Two weeks ago, they were still calling Dominion a start-up terrorist group."

"Not any more. They are surrendering because many, if not most, of the powerful leaders have already switched sides. Most governments now are controlled by people who support Dominion. Besides, they found out something important about us."

"Oh, what was that?" Lydia asked.

"That we cannot be killed."

"What do you mean?" I said with a frown. "A lot of Dominion soldiers have been killed."

"Only people who joined us. The heart of Dominion is unscathed."

That was really scary, if it were true. But maybe Hector had directed Kahil to expound at lunch on their invincibility and supposed victory to see how we would react. My natural inclination as a reporter was to ask a hundred questions: Why couldn't they be killed, who were they, what were they? Would there be reprisals against the defeated enemy? What changes would they implement, and how fast would they do so?

But I didn't ask any of those questions. Instead, I felt an inner nudge, a voice deep inside—a voice called Lang that seemed part of me, but separate as well. It urged me to ask something else. I didn't quite grasp the meaning of the question, but sensed it was important. "But what's the bigger picture, beyond the victory? What else is happening?"

Kahil pointed at me. "You surprise me, Alex. You are quite perceptive. The bigger picture, as you say, the new picture, actually, goes hand in hand with our victory. We call it the merger."

"What is it?"

"You will find out very soon. That is all I will say."

That didn't tell me much, except to expect something more dreadful than we'd already experienced. But Lydia reached for something positive. "Does that mean we can go home?"

Good question. "Yeah, and can I get my daughter released?"

"Hector will decide your fates. But I think he will recognize your valuable contributions. Your daughter is safe and won't be harmed."

"Thanks," I said, uneasily.

Don't believe him. Ask to see her.

It was that same voice, like a presence inside me, a part of me that I'd never recognized. "Can I see her now?"

"Talk to Hector."

"Where is his daughter?" Lydia asked.

"She is someplace safe and not far away."

Send her a message through Kahil. Tell her you love her.

The inner voice was upset, in turmoil, then I felt its absence.

LANG

I blinked my eyes and felt the couch beneath me. I'd been aware that I was here with Risa. Yet, my attention had been with Alex, and I'd prodded him. Vaguely, I recalled Risa telling me to do so. I sat up and turned to her, anxious to tell her what I'd learned. The merger Kahil spoke of had set off an alarm.

"I got through to him. How much did I tell you? I think I stopped talking."

"She sat quietly in the chair, eyes closed, not moving, not responding.

"Risa?"

I leaned toward her and spoke in a softer voice. "Hey, are you okay? What's going on?"

She lifted an index finger from the arm of the chair. She'd hypnotized herself, I thought, feeling relieved. She was still here, but there, with Lydia.

Lydia watched Kahil closely as he told Alex that he would take the message to Kari. He seemed sincere. Of the three guards, Kahil seemed the most understanding. Maybe they could get closer to him. She glanced at her watch. Already one-thirty.

Go-Go Girl arrived with their drinks. How could she be so gracious and good-natured all the time? She always acted as if she didn't have a care in the world. Or maybe she just didn't care, or pay attention, to what was going on in the world. Ignorance is bliss.

"Can you tell us more about yourself?" Lydia asked when the server walked away. "Where are you from, Kahil?"

He didn't answer immediately and it seemed to Lydia that he was listening to something. After a few seconds, he nodded. "I am from Earth, just like you. But not like you."

"Where did you grow up?" she asked.

He smiled somewhat sheepishly. "I never grew up, so I can't say where."

Was he trying to make a joke? *Keep pushing him.* That voice. She'd heard it before. Now it seemed stronger. *Ask about his mother.*

"Okay, where does your mother live?"

"I have no mother, only the Maker."

Maybe they were finally getting some answers. She stole another peek at her watch.

"Who is the Maker?" Alex asked.

Again Kahil didn't hesitate. "The Maker is the first of our kind. From the Maker, we are all descended."

Lydia still didn't understand, but they were actually getting answers. If they weren't aliens or bio-robots, what the hell were they? "What is your kind called?"

"You called us angels."

She regrettably remembered the comment from one of her video reports. "I said 'like angels.' I don't believe you are angels, even if I seemed to imply it."

He paused again, tilting his head as if he were listening. "We are *tulpas.* We came from the Himalayas."

In that brief response, Lydia had just found out more about their captors than she'd learned in all of her meetings with Hector and the others. "How many tulpas are there?"

Kahil tensed, tilted his head slightly again. "I've been allowed to talk to you, because the merger is so near. What was secret is coming to light. Our Maker decided the number would be 23,000 to achieve victory, and she was right. We are in every country. We control more than half of them and within hours, Dominion and our great masses of sympathizers will dominate the world."

Lydia placed her hands in her lap because they were shaking. She knew that Kahil was telling them the truth.

Alex spoke up. "How did the tulpas move around the

world, crossing borders?" She knew Alex was concerned about his daughter, but he couldn't help playing the role of journalist.

Kahil smiled. "How does anyone move about in this world, Alex?"

It sounded like a simple answer, but something about it disturbed her. He'd touched on something important, but she didn't know what it was. She quickly changed the subject and asked if there would be elections. She'd asked that same question to Hector, who had dismissed it as unimportant for the time being.

"The world will be Dominion and Dominion has no parties," Kahil explained. "There will be no need for petty arguments. We will act in the best interest of the world."

"Explain what *tulpas* are," Alex said. "I don't understand."

"We are manifestations of the Maker, who was the first."

Right, and Eve was made from a rib of Adam. Again, the voice resonated in Lydia's mind. It triggered a question, something Lydia had wondered about concerning the Dominion power structure. "Are *tulpas* only men, are there no women? I haven't met any."

Kahil laughed, but fell silent as Go-Go Girl arrived with lunch. *Finally,* Lydia thought, knowing they had to eat and run, so to speak. The server smiled as she set the plates down and asked if they would like anything else. Lydia thanked her, and told her she was fine.

Kahil nodded toward Go-Go Girl as she walked away. "There's one, a *tulpa.* There are many other women."

"A waitress? Really?" Lydia said. "Are there women in more elevated positions?"

"Gogola is not just a waitress. She can play many roles. You will see."

11

Call to Action

LANG

Risa's breath was shallow and she hadn't moved for twenty minutes. I had to do something. I couldn't lose her. I couldn't make the same mistake I'd made with Jen and let her fall into a coma.

I crouched in front of her, gently touched her knee. "Risa, come back now. Can you hear me?" I raised my voice. "Risa!" I moved her legs back and forth. "Snap out of it. Oh, fuck. No! C'mon, please, wake up."

I was about to grab her shoulders when her eyes blinked open. "I'm okay. Give me a few moments." She glanced around the room, orienting herself, then nodded. "I'm back."

She rubbed her face with her hands and I sank back onto the couch, relieved. "I was getting worried."

"Sorry to drift off like that. I slipped into a trance when you stopped talking and I was pulled right into Lydia."

"I couldn't talk. I needed to concentrate."

"The last thing I remember you saying was that Dominion was about to claim victory. How did that happen?"

"Apparently, Hector and his horde have converted masses of people to their cause. But they've also worked their way into the halls of power. Governments are collapsing. It all gathered momentum quickly."

"They didn't convert Alex and Lydia, and they were right under their noses."

"I think I know why. It's simple. It's because they were taken captive. That's what saved their asses. It blocked Dominion's ability to sway them."

Risa considered the idea. "Maybe. How did you get back?"

"I got upset because Kahil wasn't going to help Alex get his daughter. I was angry and just popped back."

"I'm glad you didn't pull me back right away," Risa said. "I learned something that might be important, or it might be a trick, more misdirection by Hector."

"What is it?"

"Lydia was prodding Kahil to talk about himself, and he actually provided a name and a place of origin. They're called *tulpas,* and they're from the Himalayas."

"What the hell are *tulpas*?"

"I vaguely recall reading something about that term. *Tulpas* are some sort of mythical beings in Tibet. But it was a long time ago and that's all I remember."

I took out my smart phone and typed the name in Google. Within seconds, I was immersed in a document.

"Well, tell me," Risa said impatiently.

"In the early 1900s, an adventurous young French woman, named Alexandra David-Néel, traveled in disguise to Tibet, and became the first Western woman ever to visit the Tibetan capital of Llasa. She mentioned *tulpas* in her writing. She called them thought forms created in deep meditation. She said experienced meditators could give these thought forms enough energy so that they could take on a life of their own, and could actually free themselves from their maker."

"Yeah, okay, now I remember. I read about her and got interested in Tibetan mysticism. In fact, as I recall, thought forms are mentioned in *The Tibetan Book of the Dead.*"

"She said she created one herself in her time in a monastery in Tibet. And the being became so independent that she and her monk guide destroyed it."

"Does the article say how the monk destroyed Alexandra's *tulpa*?"

I shook my head. "I don't see anything about that.

Unfortunately. But I want to go back. I think I can get a message to Alex. He needs to be pushed. He knows now that Dominion is a non-human force and he's got to get the message out."

Risa looked confused. "How does any of this relate to us, to what's going on here?"

"That's the question, isn't it."

She straightened. "Wait. Kahil mentioned a merger that's coming with the victory."

"That's right. It changes everything, he said."

"It's got to be about us…about the virus. We're getting merged. Everyone is."

I was excited and frightened at the same time. "But if the tulpas are exposed, maybe it's not too late."

"Hold on, Lang. If we go in there with guns blazing, so to speak, it's only going to get Alex and Lydia killed, and who know what that means for us."

I crossed my arms. I didn't want to think about that. "Maybe you're right. But we can't sit here and do nothing. At least, we know something about what's going on."

Risa shrugged and moved from the chair and sank next to me on the couch. "I should've known that getting involved with a *retired* cop is like getting involved with a cop. Let's see if we can both reach them through meditation. Maybe we can get them to take some action before they make their escape attempt."

"Good. I still find all of this hard to believe. I mean part of me says it's just a dream. But then I think of Jen and I know it's real. I want to know if there's any way I can save her. Even if it endangers Alex's life, and my life, fuck it, I want to try."

"To protect and serve. You're a good cop, Lang."

"I don't think we have a choice. Look at the alternative. I don't want to be absorbed into Alex and live in that *tulpa* world. If there's any chance we can stop it…"

Risa leaned over and hugged me. "I'll lead us into self-hypnosis. Sit back, relax and quiet your mind."

There was just forty minutes before their supposed rescue and Lydia hadn't even told Alex about it. She'd rushed him to finish his lunch, saying she wasn't feeling good and wanted to lie down. But now Khalil was accompanying them back to the room. As they entered, she turned to him.

"Would you please find out if Alex can see his daughter? It will make our work much easier if he has a chance to talk to her."

Kahil hesitated, then nodded. "I think you want some privacy. I will talk to Hector about the girl. But I am locking you in."

Lydia didn't like hearing that. But as soon as he'd left the room, the lock clicking behind him, she suggested they go out onto the balcony. "For some fresh air."

Alex opened the slider. "Something's definitely up," he hissed. "What kind of merger was he talking about?"

Lydia shook her head. "Whatever it means, it can't be good." She noticed that the porch's concrete floor had been cleaned in her absence, leaving no sign of the vomit she'd spewed. That incident felt like it happened days ago now, not hours.

Alex glancedout at the neighboring porch where Hector had held his duaghter.. "We're not seeing the big picture."

She swept a hand through her long, dark hair, lifting it off her shoulders. "I'm more concerned about the little picture right now. Us and our immediate future." She made a pouty expression that highlighted her full lips and drove guys crazy. On impulse, she turned, pulled him close, and kissed him. He tensed, but quickly overcame his surprise and responded, pulling her even closer and deepening the kiss.

After a few seconds, she drew back, then pressed her cheek against his. "Listen, Alex, there's an escape plan. Dr. Harwood is behind it."

"When?"

"Two-thirty. Right here on the porch."

"So that's why you keep looking at your watch. And why you kissed me."

"Well, that kiss was a long-time coming. We better not wait out here. It'll look suspicious."

Lydia turned and froze. Hector stood five feet away, smiling, arms crossed. "I see you two are finally becoming better friends.

How sweet and just in time for you both to become *really* physical." He laughed. "You don't know what I mean, do you?"

Neither of them replied.

"Well, you will find out soon enough. Now I have more work for you. A brief article from Alex, and a short broadcast from Lydia. Possibly the last ones. After these messages to the world, everything will change."

"Are you going to let us go?" Alex asked.

"Oh, I thought you were worried about your daughter. Now you are concerned about yourself, I see."

"I want my daughter sent back to her mother."

"Don't worry about her. As long as you do as I say, she will be fine."

"Can you bring her here?" Lydia asked. "I think that's only fair. He wants to see her."

"No, I don't think so. Not quite yet. But soon. Oh, she did give me a message to pass on to you, Alex. She said, 'Tell my dad I'm okay. I have an invisible friend, an older girl, who's helping me.' What do you think of that?"

"What do *you* think about it?" Alex responded.

"I think lots of people are starting to hear the voices from invisible friends. However, I don't think they will last long. You see, we are approaching a major transformation, my friends." He paused. "But I'm getting ahead of myself. Please sit down at your computers and take notes."

They did as they were told. Lydia opened the top of her computer and the Dominion trident—a curse upon her life—flowed and throbbed like the beat of a heart. Hector had told them that the symbol was from Greek mythology, that Poseidon, god of the sea, used his trident to cause earthquakes, tidal waves and tsunamis, and that Dominion, like Poseidon, was shaking up the earth.

"My message is simple, but momentous." Hector moved behind Lydia. "You should say that. It's a startling way to open. Then tell the world the good news: All nations have conceded power to Dominion. We control every government, and you, the people, are saved from the tyranny of small minds."

When he didn't say anything more, Alex asked: "That's it?"

"Not quite." He stepped back and looked toward the door as if expecting someone to open it.

Lydia sensed a presence again, a feeling of being inhabited. It's how she felt when the voice spoke in her head. She didn't want her thoughts interrupted or invaded, so she typed: *Don't bother me. I'm working.*

To her surprise, her fingers tapped across the keyboard and a message appeared on the screen. *We need to talk.*

Who are you? How do you know me? She typed in reply.

I'm part of you; you are part of me. We are part of the same soul. I am Risa.

Why are you here? What do you want?

My world is crashing into yours. Both worlds are being destroyed, as we know them, by Dominion.

Dominion is powerful.

Only because people are entranced. Break the trance.

How?

Broadcast a warning to governments and citizens not to concede defeat, that Dominion is not human. Tell them about tulpas.

Hector moved closer and Lydia quickly closed the file.

"Let me see that. Bring it back."

She tapped a few keys and brought up her list of Dominion files. She needed to do something to put him off. If he read that inner conversation, it was all over.

The door opened and Hector, distracted, turned away. Lydia opened the file, quickly erased the exchange, and scrolled up to the notes from Hector.

"Look who's here," Alex whispered, nodding toward the entrance.

Lydia gaped as Go-Go Girl walked into the room. Did Hector order a meal? Was he actually going to eat in front of them, rather than the other way around?

But Gogola didn't have any food with her and, instead of her uniform, she wore a long black dress as if she were working as a server at a formal affair. Her hair was loose and flowed over her shoulders. Hector moved next to her and for a moment Lydia thought he was going to introduce her as one of their kind.

"Now Gogola will provide you with more information for your final report before the shift."

"The *waitress*?" Alex sounded as amazed as Lydia.

"Yes, your waitress, but she's much more. Gogola is the Maker."

Lydia was stunned. How could they have overlooked Gogola and simply played with her name? Incredibly, they'd never even asked where she was from. It was career bias. Lydia had overlooked her because of the server role she'd played.

Gogola smiled and nodded. Her eyes seemed to gleam. "Sorry to mislead you both, but I wanted a chance to observe you without either of you being aware I was doing so."

"Why?" Lydia asked.

"You two have played a valuable role, more than you realize, more than an entire army regiment of converts. You reach hundreds of millions of people in a way that we could never do. While we are very persuasive behind the scenes, so to speak, when we appear before cameras, we tend to generate suspicion."

That made Lydia feel worse about their propaganda reports. She and Alex acted to save their lives, not to destroy the world. But if they were so influential, as Gogola apparently thought, then maybe there was still a chance they could turn things around.

"I want to start by saying that we are all living in a dream. But the dream world is about to end. Everyone will soon feel changes, both in body and mind. That's because we are moving into full physical reality."

Alex stopped typing and turned in his chair. "Isn't that a Buddhist thing, that we're living in a world of illusions?"

"It happens to be true. This world lacks physical reality. You and everyone else are reflections of a physical reality and so you think you are physical."

"How will this new reality be different?" Lydia asked.

"For us, Hector and me and the rest of our kind, it will be very different. We constantly recognize and experience the instability of this world. You're blinded to it, and you only get glimpses when you consider your past and all the gaps in your life. For example, Alex, you found yourself in Merida where you met Hector. But how did you get there from Cancun? You knew it was the right place to be, and you were there. Things like that happen to you and everyone else all the time, and you are all mostly unaware. That's the nature of the dream world."

Alex looked as if he were about to argue with her, but Hector motioned for him to turn back to his computer. "Write. Get to work."

Gogola walked over to Lydia and peered down at her screen and gave her a quizzical look. Lydia couldn't help thinking of her as Go-Go-Girl, but that image was fading. "You each have a counterpart in the physical world. Everyone does. But I sense that your counterparts are recognizing what is happening. They might even understand they and everyone else in their world are about to be absorbed as we become physical. You two will feel more human, more physical very soon."

The door opened again and Kahil entered. Next to him, a girl rushed ahead to Alex, her long blond hair flying behind her. "Daddy!" Alex hugged Kari tightly and nodded to Kahil, thanking him.

"Did I tell you that you could bring her here?" Hector glared.

"No, but I thought she shouldn't be left alone if the merger is about to happen."

"It's not a problem," Gogola said in a firm voice, glancing at Hector. "Come to me, honey. Your daddy's working."

"No, I want her next to me."

Hector moved forward, but Gogola raised a hand, stopping him. "That's fine. She can stay. I understand that humans are very emotionally tied to their offsprings. For better or worse."

Lydia stole a glance at her watch, then bolted to her feet as she realized their rescue was imminent. "Okay, I'm ready for my report." She didn't know if she would be able to send out an uncensored message. It might be suicidal, but if Gogola was right about the importance of their role, she wasn't sure she wanted to live in a new Dominion-dominated world that they'd help create.

Kahil conferred quietly with Gogola and Hector. "Let's do that," Gogola said.

Hector gripped Alex's shoulder. "There's no time to write. Both of you will speak to the world together and we'll do it live. No time to edit. I can feel the change coming and the world must be immediately prepared."

"Why don't we do it on the balcony?" Kahil suggested.

"I like that," Gogola said. "Go. Now."

ALEX

Maybe they knew something was about to happen. Why else would Hector, Kahil and Gogola—the Maker—all arrive here just when we were about to escape? Now we were being told that no one would edit our report. We literally could say what we wanted in our live broadcast from the balcony. I knew it might be the last thing we would say. We probably would be tossed right over the railing to the concrete floor below. I couldn't let that happen, especially with Kari here.

I stood by, nervous and restless, while Kahil set up the camera on the balcony. I could only imagine what Lydia was thinking. We both stole glances into the courtyard.

The door of the suite opened and the slovenly doctor walked in. How the hell was Harwood going to rescue us? I was confused, feeling trapped. The voice inside my head nudged me. *Just say they're not human and not here to help.*

They'll kill us. They'll kill Kari. I can't do it. It's too late. They won.

The red light on the camera blinked on, but before Lydia said a word, Alex reached for her arm and spun her halfway around. "Don't do it!"

She pulled away from him. "What are you *doing?*" She turned to Kahil and the camera, which was still running, catching it all. "They're not human. They're called tulpas. They're not angels, they're monsters and they want our world. Don't trust them," she blurted.

Before she could say another word, Hector charged into the scene and shoved both of us toward the railing. I tripped and pulled Lydia down with me.

I looked up as Hector faced the camera. "It is true that

we are not fully human, but neither are you, and that is why our video presence leaves you feeling uneasy. Like you, we are inspired by humanity and we are here to make you truly humans, not fragmentary personalities. We are fierce angels fighting for your future. Prepare now for the changes that will unfold within you."

I noticed Harwood reach into his medical bag. Abruptly, he raised his arm, aimed a gun at Hector. Just as quickly, Kahil pulled out a weapon. "Shoot him," Hector hissed.

Both guns fired. Kari screamed. Hector and Gogola collapsed.

"Kahil's with us!" Harwood shouted. "Let's get out of here!"

PART TWO

The New World

One way of thinking...is to suppose that the waking world and the world of the dream have begun to merge so that...the laws that operate in the dream, the laws that operate in hyperspace, can at times operate in three-dimensional space when the barrier between the two modes becomes weak.

- Terence McKenna from New Maps of Hyperspace in *Archaic Revival*

12

The Merger

Hector rolled over onto his side and listened to the silence. Slowly, he sat up and looked around. He was alone on the concrete floor of the porch. He noticed a tear in his bloodied white shirt, and poked a finger into it, touching the tender skin on his chest near his heart. He undid several buttons, exposing a small hole that was shrinking even as he stared at it.

Tulpas couldn't be killed in this world, but he never considered the question of what happened to the bullets. His thought was answered instantly by Gogola.

Dream bullets fade away. We know they can't harm us. But the collective mental structure of this reality was enough to empower those bullets to temporarily disable us.

She could tune into any of them. All the *tulpas* could send out messages on the open channel that connected them, but Gogola controlled the invisible reply button. Hector was expected to keep tabs on those who worked closely with him, but he'd failed and that was going to be a problem. Kahil not only took orders directly from him, but he was Hector's creation, his only one. They were in daily contact, so how could he have overlooked a traitor in their midst?

Come here.

She'd no sooner spoken when Hector realized he was no longer on the porch of the hotel suite, but somewhere in Disney World. He looked up to see a sign that read Adventureland. He stared at it for a moment, then took in his surroundings.

There were a few troops and employees milling about, but he didn't see Gogola.

He wasn't surprised that he was here. He was used to such sudden jumps. *Tulpas* were fully conscious of the nature of the dream world. Humans, on the other hand, overlooked the anomalies. Their minds weren't capable of comprehending the true nature of their existence and they clung to the idea that they lived in a physical world and their counterparts, who actually did, were mere dream images.

The planes, trains, cars and busses were imaginary, and so was the rest of the world. Some people did travel by these vehicles of the mind, but mostly they only thought they did. When Alex had fled Cancun, he made it on foot to the bus station. Then he simply appeared in Merida. His intention to escape was all it took. Of course others didn't escape and died. Their belief that they were trapped was too strong.

For Hector, the world could appear stable for a couple of hours, but then would quickly fold into mental quicksand when the laws of the physical world vanished, and reality shimmered like a desert mirage. The fact that it was still happening meant one thing: the merger had failed.

No, just delayed. I'm here, the Enchanted Tiki Room.

He was standing right in front of it. How convenient. He noticed that he was wearing a fresh blue shirt with a Dominion insignia near where the bullet struck. The world definitely hadn't shifted. Gogola was manipulating events, pulling Hector's strings. She had that power, but would she lose it after the merger...and would the dream bullets then be real? She was the Maker and master *tulpa,* the only one who had ever experienced physical life and she was committed to doing everything possible to return to it. She would take them all, and they would understand.

He entered the Tiki Room and scanned the tropical pavilion with its lush flowing vegetation, mysterious carved wooden tikis and equally strange audio-animatronic birds. There was no sign of her, though Hector knew she was here. She might appear in disguise. Gogola could shift her image at will. The pavilion room appeared empty, except for a table in the corner occupied by three figures—Mickey Mouse, Goofy and Donald Duck. Mickey motioned for him to join them.

Hector hesitated, then slowly walked over to the table. He didn't know what to say or do. Was Gogola posing as one of them, maybe all three of them? While Hector had kept on a maintenance crew and other necessary employees, most of the service workers and entertainers, including the costumed ones, had been relieved of their positions since the early days of the occupation.

A door to a restroom opened and an attractive, youthful brown-skinned woman wearing a flower-patterned mu-mu stepped out and smiled. She had shoulder-length ebony hair, prominent cheekbones, a Polynesian beauty.

"Hector, sit down."

He recognized Gogola's voice, if not her appearance. Gogola joined him and motioned toward the characters. "You see these guys, Hector? They are the heart of the Magic Kingdom. You don't go firing them. As caretakers, we're maintaining the magic here. I want our troops to enjoy these theme parks on their down time. Soon you will understand human emotions, and not think of the attribute as a genetic flaw." Gogola and the costumed characters gazed silently at Hector, then she added, "I want everything operating after the merger. People will need this place more than ever. Do you understand?"

"Of course."

Gogola turned to Mickey, Goofy and Donald. "Do you know what merger I'm talking about?"

They shook their heads.

"It's not like LucasFilm merging with Disney, my friends. It's bigger, much bigger. It's a merger of two worlds. You will feel a shift in awareness, and you will feel awake and complete."

She paused, giving them a few moments to comprehend what she was saying. "Any questions?"

"Will we still have jobs here?" Goofy asked.

Gogola looked up at a palm frond a few feet away where an audio-animatronic toucan continually bobbed its head and made sharp, raspy croaks that sounded like a cross between a frog and a pig. "You weren't listening very well, dog. Of course you will."

"What will become of this world?" Mickey asked in the voice of a young woman.

Gogola rapped her knuckles on the table. "Not to worry. This will be the real, physical existence. You can go now. Or as Hector would say, 'You're dismissed.'"

With that, the Disney characters quickly vacated the Tiki Room. They were no doubt relieved to get away from these new bosses of the Magic Kingdom, Hector thought. If he were perplexed by the merger, he could only imagine how they felt.

Abruptly, Hector was no longer in the Tiki Room or Adventureland, or Disney World. They were driving on a wide beach with hard-packed sand, Gogola behind the wheel. She was back in her familiar blond image, wearing a thong bikini.

"Daytona Beach," she said. "And stop staring. I know it's more surprise and curiosity than lust. But watch what happens after the shift." She laughed.

He wasn't sure what was so funny. He knew all about sex and the physical world, and no doubt he would sample the process to find out what all the kerfuffle was about. "Why are we driving on the beach?"

Instantly, the car vanished and they were walking barefoot at the edge of the water. "You're right. Why drive, when we can walk?"

Gogola looked out to sea in anticipation. She felt the breeze and the faint penetration of salt air against her skin. This was the place to experience the shift, to fully embrace the power. Meanwhile, Hector couldn't stop wondering if they would be safe here and if the physical world would be as wonderful as she described it.

"I know you and the others are more or less content with your existence, but you never experienced the physical as I did with my creator, Norbu. I moved between the physical and the dream worlds at will. I was the monk's secret companion. I learned about the physical world from him, even though he was far removed from it. Through deep meditation, we explored the world, and even manifested physically in many different places on Earth. That was how I came to love physical existence."

"I'm sure I will enjoy the pleasures of the physical. But will we remain safe from common deaths?"

"We will experience the physical, Hector, but we will remain *tulpas,* the best of both worlds."

Hector, like all *tulpas,* was aware of their heRisage. But Gogola had never spoken directly with him about her history, and she knew he wouldn't let the opportunity pass.

"Was it difficult to move about the world as you and Norbu did in the physical?"

"Hardly any humans can do it. Norbu was a master and he taught me well. It takes strong desire and endless practice to teleport from place to place. It's *not* like here where it's merely a twitch of your nose or it happens when you don't even think about it."

"Or want it," he added. "How did you learn to create *tulpas?*"

"Norbu showed me. He never thought I would be able to do it. And I almost gave up trying. Manifesting *tulpas,* as you know, is not easy, especially the first time. Eventually I succeeded. As did you."

Gogola had been impressed with how Hector had manifested Kahil on his one and only attempt to serve as a sub-maker. It almost seemed as if he had invisible outside help, like someone who is suddenly able to lift a car to free someone trapped beneath it. However, he'd found the effort so overwhelming that he never wanted to do it again. But now he was concerned that his creation had become mentally defective, and he didn't want to talk about it. He furtively tried to hide his thoughts from her, but failed as always.

"Did Norbu like your first *tulpa?*"

She considered the question. "It was not well received. The creature was distorted. It looked like an egg with short arms and legs. It squatted in the corner of Norbu's cell and wouldn't leave."

Hector laughed. "I would've liked to have seen that."

"It wasn't funny to Norbu. Creating *tulpas* was forbidden and he feared he would be exposed and forced out. He said my *tulpa* needed to be eliminated. That's how I learned the technique for the dispersal. After that, I never created another one while Norbu was alive. He wouldn't allow it."

The dispersal, or dispersing the essence, was the term Gogola used for the elimination of *tulpas*. She had never taught the technique to any *tulpas*, and rarely invoked it, other than eliminating defective 'newborns.' But it was a skill that Hector longed to know. Because of their nature, *tulpas* were difficult to kill through normal means. Destroying their bodies was a useless endeavor. Unless she applied the dispersal technique, *tulpas* typically re-manifested within an hour. That was a major reason they had conquered their enemies. Nothing stopped *tulpas* and their willingness to lead their human allies into battle had reinforced loyalty among the human troops.

She enjoyed listening in on Hector's thoughts and fears. He was certain that Kahil needed to be eliminated and he hoped she would finally teach him the technique. But he was worried that she might've already eliminated Kahil, and had summoned him so she could apply the same technique.

"How were you able to stay in the monastery if *tulpas* were forbidden?"

"I wore a monk's habit with the cowl up. If anyone saw me, they thought I was one of Norbu's students and no one was allowed to talk…" She stopped in mid-sentence, peered toward the sea. "It's here. Now! It's happening."

An enormous tsunami wave, hundreds of feet high, rushed toward the beach. Hector whirled to flee, but Gogola grabbed his arm. "Look!" she commanded.

Rather than a wall of water, it was an enormous, shimmering mirage, a dragon with wings spanning the ocean, and a moment later the glistening appendages enfolded them. Gogola felt as if she were under water, but still breathing. The collision of forces pinned her to the earth and sucked away at her life force. Her mind drained of thoughts, but something new and formidable—deep emotions—punctured her heart, pummeled her gut, and spread throughout her being. *Back in the physical!*

She crawled on hands and knees, then dropped to her belly, and hugged the warm sand, feeling a tremor, not of the earth, but from within her body. She thrust her hips repeatedly into the earth and was overtaken by an orgasm that sent her spiraling into the cosmos. She knew she was being 'acclimatized' to the new world. But there was more.

Music, from cosmic and ethereal to dark and dissonant, welcomed a massive migration of beings as their essence entwined with their counterparts. Even with eyes shut, she could 'see' the merger of worlds as the dream world gave birth to a new physical reality.

13

The Escape

ALEX

We fled the Disney hotel in a white van, the kind an electrician or plumber might use for his equipment. No seats or side windows in the rear compartment, just a scruffy rug covering the metal floor. Kari and I were huddled together on one side, Lydia and Kahil on the other. Reggie Jordan drove the van and Harwood sat in the passenger seat. The doctor was busy tapping on a cell phone, and I wondered if Dominion might zero in on our location through it. We were moving fast, at least 80 miles an hour, and I guessed we were on I-4.

I had no idea where we were headed. I just hoped it was safe from Dominion. I wanted to get Kari back to her mother as soon as possible. It was too dangerous for her to stay with me. I considered calling Shara, but Dominion might already be monitoring her calls.

Hector and Gogola were hit multiple times and should be dead. But if the rumors were true, they would quickly recover from their wounds. I wanted to ask Kahil about that, and why he had turned on his own kind, but the steady roar of the road made conversation too difficult.

Meanwhile, I comforted Kari. She clung to one of my arms and I was afraid she was in shock. After a few minutes, she fell asleep, her head lolling against my side. I'd managed to grab the notebook computer I used for my Dominion articles before we fled and now I noticed Kahil staring at it. He crawled on hands and knees over to me and asked to see it. As soon I handed it to him, he slid his fingers along the bottom and detached something. He held up a small silver-colored object about the size and shape of three dimes stocked together. A monitoring device. He passed it upfront to Jordon, who tossed it out the window.

"What about the cell phone?" I called out, pointing to Harwood, who was tapping on it again. Kahil waved a hand, indicating it was safe.

Now we were followed a winding road, and I felt the vehicle climbing and descending, an unusual experience in Florida, where there were few hills. I couldn't see out the windshield from where I sat, and the back window was caked with dirt and dust, obscuring the outside world.

When did we leave the interstate? For that matter, how did we get out of the hotel alive? The room was fully monitored and the hotel was heavily guarded.

I was about to dismiss the questions, but instead hung onto them. These kinds of thing happened all the time. Not just to me, but to everyone. We were so used to it that it wasn't even jarring when we shifted from one scene to another, sometimes seamlessly from one conversation to another. People took it for granted, like falling asleep or waking up. It was something that just happened, and everyone dismissed such happenings as "mere twinks." If there was one taboo subject among scientists, it was this one. There was no quicker way to ruin your career, to become a pariah in your field, to be mercilessly ridiculed, than to propose a research project on twinks.

So why was I thinking about the matter? Only people confined to institutions talked about twinks and played with them as if they were mental candy rather than poison. But now I was coming to realize they were not only important, but key to unraveling a mystery about the nature of our existence. Sure I was thinking like the crazies, but I didn't care.

The thought vanished as Kari tugged on my arm. "What kind of town is this, Daddy? Where are we?"

We were standing outside the van near the front of an old two-story Mediterranean-style hotel with a long porch. I had the creepy feeling that the hotel had eyes and was watching the new arrivals. The street that ran alongside the hotel was narrow and dipped downhill. Several people walked leisurely down the middle of the road that was lined by old wood-framed houses.

"I don't know, honey." Then I noticed the sign on the building across the street, a white wood-frame structure with a porch facing the hotel. *Cassadaga Bookstore.* Cassadaga. I'd heard that name. Someone had told me I should go to Cassadaga and write a story about the place. Something odd about it.

Lydia smiled at Kari and stooped over to speak to her. "Don't worry, Kari, your Dad will take good care of you. He's a good man." She stood up. "Have you ever been to Cassadaga before, Alex?"

"I was about to ask you the same. I'm not even sure how we got here." I was about to mention to Lydia that I was becoming more aware of twinks when Harwood motioned us to follow him. We moved along the sidewalk to the entrance of the hotel, and entered a quaint lobby with wood floors, antique furniture, an old piano. I felt as if we'd entered another time. The front desk was more like a closet compared to the typical expansive check-in counters at most hotels. I wandered over to a shop that sold crystals, stones books and herbs.

Now I remembered. Cassadaga was a spiritualist community somewhere north of Orlando...and now apparently our hideout from Dominion. But how long would we be safe here?

If anything, it seemed the events of the world were affecting this tiny town in a positive way. The parking lot outside was crowded. A dozen people milled about and the adjacent restaurant was surprisingly busy, considering it was still late afternoon.

Now I was standing on the porch outside my room. Kari had stretched out on the bed and had immediately fallen asleep. I didn't remember coming out here, but here I was.

"Are you looking for anything in particular, sir?"

I realized I was inside the bookstore across the street from the hotel and was staring intently at a bookshelf. How did I get over here? How long have I been here? It was another *twink,* of course. Gaps in awareness? Leaps in awareness? Whatever they were, they seemed to be happening all the time now. Maybe they always had and I'd just overlooked them. Why was I even thinking about it?

I smiled at the round-faced, middle-aged woman who wore a patterned loose-fitting dress that reached to her ankles. "Maybe something about Cassadaga."

She laughed. "You're in the right spot."

I'd been staring at the titles of several books on the history of Cassadaga and spiritualism. I thanked her and picked one off the shelf.

"Are you interested in the ghost tour this evening? It's only once a week and tonight's the night."

"Maybe. I'll ask my daughter about it."

I opened the book to several pages of old black-and-white photos at the center. One showed a man wearing a floppy hat standing next to a horse. The caption read: *George Colby was told during a séance that he would someday be instrumental in founding a Spiritualist community in the South, far from New York, where he grew up. The prophecy came true in 1875, when Colby was guided through the wilderness of Central Florida by a spirit named Seneca to an area of uncommon hills. Colby homesteaded land and in 1895 deeded over 35 acres to the Cassadaga Spiritualist Camp Meeting Association.*

"Hello, Alex."

Lydia stood next to me. "Hey, you sneaked up on me."

"What do you mean?"

"Well, a moment ago you weren't there."

She gave me an odd look. "Now I am." Before I had a chance to think about it, she continued: "There's a ghost tour leaving here tonight."

"I heard." She wore shorts and t-shirt and seemed surprisingly relaxed, maybe because we were no longer stuck in the hotel room under the stress of constant scrutiny. She also looked incredibly appealing, and I had to force myself not to stare.

"Do you think it's safe to go?"

I was about to jokingly ask if she was afraid of ghosts, when

I realized we were standing on the hotel porch, embracing outside her room, and I no longer had the book in my hand. I was pleased by this development in our relationship, but startled and astonished by pace of the twinks. Our lips met and her small, firm breasts pressed into my chest.

We were in her room, naked and making love. What happened to foreplay? How did we even get here? Did it matter? *Enjoy the moment.*

"Alex, are you okay?" She gazed into my eyes as our bodies continued slow undulations.

"I'm fine, real fine! I just want this to go on. I don't want to find myself somewhere else."

"You don't have to go anywhere. Let's just take our time."

Lydia's back arched in ecstasy, she gasped beneath me, we melded closer and closer with each thrust. *What happened to taking our time?* I blinked and for a moment the dark-haired beauty was a redhead and I was another man—Lang, then I was me with Lydia again.

The atmosphere suddenly seemed to condense around us, thickened, the walls rippled, the air shimmered. Lydia gasped, "What's going on?"

"I don't know. I don't know. Wait…this must be it. The merger…the merger." My eyes rolled back, I shuddered in a prolonged climax. I finally collapsed on top of her, rolled to the side. Our hearts pounded, our eyes were still locked in those final moments of utter joy. The bed rolled and rippled beneath us and the room spun so fast I felt dizzy, nauseated. The joy of the moment vanished.

Lydia clutched her head as if it was about to explode. "Jesus, it hurts, I hate this, I…"

Her voice pulsed into silence, I could no longer hear her, hear anything. I'd experienced earthquakes in my travels, but this felt different. It infected all my senses, all my thoughts. My entire sense of reality seemed to be cracking open, coming apart.

I heard a voice inside my head, a familiar voice that echoed as if I were in a canyon. *This is it, it's happening.* Lang, it was Lang, shouting as he was swept along and hurtled into a new world. I rolled off the bed and lost contact with him. I crawled over to where I'd dropped my clothes, started jerking them on.

Lydia lifted up on her elbows. "What are you doing?"

"I've got to get to my room. To Kari."

I headed down the hall, keeling like I was trying to negotiate the deck of a ship tossed about in high seas. I lunged for the doorknob to my room, steadied myself. It felt like a big wave was washing over us. I opened the door and was relieved to see Kari sitting up on her bed, her arms wrapped around her shins.

"Daddy? I feel weird, and the bed was moving. What's going on?"

I made my way over to her bed, lowered myself to the foot of it. "Something… is changing."

"Jennifer told me I should stay here and wait for you. She said I could talk to her anytime."

"Jennifer?"

"You know, the teenage girl who's with me. She's nice." Kari raised her head. "But she's kind of sad now."

What the hell was she talking about? "Why is she sad?"

"She thought her father would be here with you, like she's with me. But he's not. She wonders what happened to him."

A wave crashed and the sea flowed up the beach, over Hector's shoes, then retreated. He realized he was sitting in a puddle of water. Gogola sat next to him. "Help me up, Hector."

He stood, unsteady on his feet, feeling disoriented. Gogola extended a hand and he pulled her up. He thought himself fresh, dry clothes. But nothing happened.

"Why are we still here?" he asked.

"What's wrong?"

"My clothes are still wet."

She laughed, an appealing trill, and he felt oddly attracted to her as never before. She pointed down the beach. In the distance, a black SUV sped toward them through the haze, tires kicking up sand. "Our ride is coming."

"Are we human now?"

"We are *tulpas* in a physical world."

When the SUV stopped, Hector opened the back door and

stuck his head inside. He didn't recognize the driver or the man in the passenger seat. They both held up hands, as if in greeting, but they were actually showing him the Dominion logo on their palms—the trident in a circle. To humans, the logo looked like a tattoo. But to *tulpas,* it appeared to glow. That way no one could fake their way into the Dominion circle with an ordinary tattoo. Anyone doing so would be instantly revealed and eliminated.

He moved aside to allow Gogola to enter. She paused in the doorway and smiled. "Thanks for the protective gesture, but it was totally unnecessary. I know our kind from farther away than you can imagine."

She always managed to amaze him. He nodded and slid in after her. Hector was always nervous around her. He never knew how he should act. He wanted to show her his command and leadership prowess, but he didn't want to overstep his authority. "Where should I tell them to take us?"

Gogola laughed again, this time a low and husky sound, and he felt the attraction again. "You're already acting very human, Hector. You're going to do well in this world, once you're fully adjusted. They know where we're going."

He heard her clearly in his mind. *Back to Disney World, of course.*

He felt embarrassed, a new sensation, and wondered why he couldn't keep in mind that Gogola had superior abilities through the thought network. As they cruised along the empty beach, he tried to relax. He stared out the window, mulling over his situation, and all that had happened. He was starting to feel cravings, a sensation that he'd never experienced. He knew of the desires for food and sex, but had never felt the urge to indulge in the way that he did now. But he also noticed that he was much more wary and uncertain. Was that part of the nature of being physical?

"So Hector, ask your questions. I can feel them mounting in you."

He wanted to know where Kahil and the others had fled and what she would do about them, but he thought better of it. No sense reminding Gogola that Kahil was his right-hand man, his creation. Did she know what was on his mind, or only that he had questions? He decided to play it coy. "It's a personal question."

"Go ahead."

"Was Norbu in love with you?" Hector had never asked her or anyone such a question. Emotional matters were almost non-existent in *tulpas*. But now in the physical world, they easily bubbled to the surface, and he felt confused about the tug of war between thoughts and emotions.

Gogola peered curiously at him. "He was a monk, Hector. But, yes, he had feelings for me, more like a strict parent than a lover. Since I was in his world, I had feelings as well. I was upset when he threatened to disperse my essence if I made another *tulpa*. He was terrified that I was getting out of his control."

"So were you happy when he died?" Hector really wanted to ask if she'd killed him.

"His death meant that I was condemned to the dream world. That's when I began creating our kind. At the same time, I studied the dream world with new interest in the hopes of finding a way back into the physical realm."

Her willingness to confide in him impressed him. Was he falling in love with her? Was that what the tightness in his chest meant? Talking to Gogola about her history was fascinating, but he realized he faced new challenges that he hadn't ever considered. "Now that the worlds have merged and there's no longer any active resistance, what should be done about the massive armies we've built?"

Gogola tapped her fingers impatiently on the armrest. "We will talk about that and more tomorrow. First, I want you to experience a day as a physical being."

Hector nodded, but he felt an unexpected uneasiness. He had the feeling he wasn't going to like what Gogola had in mind.

14

What's Outside

LANG

Making love might seem like an inappropriate response to a global meltdown, but that's exactly what we did. Maybe it was the only thing we could do. *When in doubt, make love. When seeking peace, make love.* The litany of the Sixties.

Risa tugged my arm, drawing me into her bedroom, and we tumbled onto the bed, pulling off our clothes, and embracing, fondling, our mouths melding. Not that we needed justification, but we'd agreed that the more sensually aware we were, the more chances we had to maintain our physical awareness and save our asses from being absorbed into Alex and Lydia. And that was what was happening, *absorption.* If it didn't work, it was a fucking great way to go.

We moved in a wave-like motion, taking our time. I felt Risa rising to a climax, but I held back as best I could. Pausing tensing, slowly thrusting, rising toward orgasm only to back off again. I realized that our love-making might be our last act, at least in this body, and I wanted to enjoy every moment of it. Drenched in sweat, gasping for breath, we climaxed together, our bodies heaving in exaltation. And in the heat of the moment, I was Alex with Lydia, then myself with Risa, and we were being swept along, pulled toward a new world.

"The shift! I feel it. I'm with him. I'm there, I'm here. I'm dead, I'm alive." Was I talking or thinking? I'd lost my bearings,

I was split in two. Here and there…folding in toward Alex.

"No!"

I forced myself to break the connection before I was swallowed into him. I focused on Risa, her eyes rolled back, her body limp, and thought immediately of Jen. Where the fuck was my daughter? What was happening to her? I tried to ground myself, shook Risa's shoulders. "No, no, come back, come back! Don't leave me! I can't lose you!"

First Jen, now Risa. Fuck that. I slapped her face, she groaned, sucked at the air. "I felt it too. I was with Lydia." She blinked rapidly, focused on me, rubbed her cheek. After a few moments, she lifted up on her forearms, her round, compact breasts heaving. She touched her cheek again. "Damn, you nearly broke my jaw."

"Sorry, but I had to."

"I know. I know. I feel like I was spat out of the spin cycle."

I sat at the edge of Risa's queen-sized bed. "Either the shift happened or we had the simultaneous orgasm of a lifetime."

"Or both."

I slid a hand along the side of her body, feeling her ribs, her slender waist, and the flare of her hip. "But we're still here. We weren't absorbed."

But why was Jen absorbed? And what exactly did that mean?

"Where is *here*?" Risa threw her legs over the side of the bed, stood and grabbed a pale blue silky robe off the chair in the corner. She shrugged it on and hurried over to the bedroom window that looked out onto her tiny backyard. "Everything looks the same, as far as I can see."

"Yeah, which isn't far." I joined her at the window. "We've got to go out and see what's going on."

"CNN first. Let's see what they're saying about the comas. It should be the top story."

I grabbed my clothes and followed her out into her living room. She turned on the TV, I pulled on my khaki shorts, and stared intently at the screen. A reporter stood in front of the White House, but the sound was too low to hear. When Risa ratcheted up the volume, I expected to hear a dire report about the spreading epidemic that had left thousands of people, including my daughter, in a comatose state. Instead, I gaped at several armed men in black uniforms with berets posed behind the reporter, who was talking about the Dominion security force that guarded the White House. She sounded as if they were folk heroes guarding our legacy.

Stunned, I couldn't speak.

"Now I want to play a clip from Lydia Cabrera, spokesperson for Dominion. You might've heard this before, but it's worth having Lydia repeat it."

Risa dropped the remote, gripped the sides of her head. Her jaw dropped open, her shoulders shook. Her mouth moved, but no words came out. On the screen, an attractive dark-haired journalist talked about how life will be so much better under Dominion rule. "The world as we have known it has vanished," Lydia said.

"Holy shit. You can say that again." Even though our immediate environment seemed unchanged, CNN was telling us we were in another world. But why hadn't we vanished inside our dreaming selves? Wasn't that what was supposed to happen? "We've got to go out and see for ourselves," I whispered. I collected myself and worked the buttons on my shirt.

"I don't want to go out there." Risa swept up the remote, hit the mute. "I want to hold onto what we had as long as we can."

"Look, sooner or later, we have to."

"I want to go back to bed and hide under the covers. I want to dream our world back into existence. Maybe we can do that."

She sounded manic, but I considered what she'd said. "My guess is that falling asleep is still dangerous. We're awake and we haven't been swallowed whole. That's something."

"How did that happen?"

I shrugged. "Sex at the right moment?"

"Maybe that combined with the fact that we knew what was coming. We were tuned in through Alex and Lydia."

A couple of talking heads were conversing with a CNN commentator. At the bottom of the screen, a quote from President Burns rolled past. I *don't care where they're from. They're here to help us and bring justice and fairness to the world.* "Who the hell is President Burns. Never heard of him."

"Christ, let me get dressed. You're right," she conceded. "We should go out." She switched off the TV and retreated to the bedroom.

I sat down on the couch, knuckling my eyes, struggling not to think about Jen, about what might have happened to her. I tried to tune in on Alex to find where he was hiding, but didn't sense anything. Had the connection between us been severed? Maybe the image of Dominion forces guarding the White House had shocked me into some hyper state of awareness that no longer needed Alex. After all, unless Risa and I were hallucinating what we had seen on TV, we were in the same world as Alex and Lydia.

A dream world turned physical.

Risa came back, dressed in Key West casual, shorts, a t-shirt, and sandals. "I'm ready."

I suddenly felt weary, heavy, burdened, like a shit load of wet cement had been poured down my throat. Risa hurried over to me, hooked her arm through mine. "Don't weird out on me, Lang. You went all pale just then. We're each other's reality gauge."

For all I knew, we might be in separate padded cells in some nuthouse and all of this was a hallucination, vivid and colorful and frightening, but madness nonetheless. "Gauge," I finally managed to say, my voice sort of choked, way too soft. "That's a good word. If we really are elsewhere, then we need to know the lay of the land. The rules. The parameters."

"Yes. Exactly." We started toward the door. "And we should share our observations, okay? You may notice stuff I don't. And vice versa."

I reached for the door handle, but stopped. "Wait. We should take a weapon. Just in case. Do you have a gun?"

"Yeah, don't you?"

"Sure, at home."

"It's not going to do you any good there. Fortunately, I've got two guns." She let go of my arm and hurried over to a desk. She opened a desk drawer, brought out a pair of weapons, held them between her index fingers and thumbs.

"You're kidding. *Pink guns?*"

Both were sub-compacts, a Ruger, a Springfield, both the color of bubble gum. "I don't suppose you have any other color choices?"

"Sorry, that's what you get for leaving yours at home. I bought the Ruger after I began working with police, then inherited the Springfield from my mother."

"Nice." I took the Ruger. "I'll take my chances with this one." I checked to make sure it was loaded. "At least it fits nicely in my pocket."

"Let's go out the back."

I followed Risa to a door at the rear of her compact home and we walked out into a fenced-in backyard, no larger than a postage stamp. She opened a gate at the backside that led into an alleyway shrouded by flowering trees and shrubs. We were just a few blocks from the tourist mecca on Duval Street, but this back street was empty.

As we moved along, I had an eerie feeling that the entire island was deserted, that we were the only ones alive. I walked over to a wood fence, reached up and closed my palm over one of the vines of a flowering bougainvillea.

Thorns jabbed my palm.

"And why did you do that?"

"I wanted to make sure I wasn't dreaming."

Risa stopped and turned my hand up as speckles of blood bloomed on my palm. "You don't think you can bleed in a dream?"

"I don't know anymore. But I feel whole and physical."

"Yeah, you were acting pretty physical back there in my bed."

I laughed, but it sounded nervous, chopped up, uncertain. "I'm just confused."

She brushed away the blood and planted a kiss on my palm. Then she pointed at our shadows on the ground. "Do figures in dreams cast shadows?"

Was that one of the parameters? The rules? The heat felt more intense than it had earlier and sweat now beaded on my forehead. We crossed a street, our shadows keeping pace with us, and still we saw no one.

Key West felt different, the air heavier, the shadows darker.

Risa alternately hooked her arm through mine or grasped my hand, her palm cool and moist. The sound of our sandals flip-flopping along the pavement punctuated the tense silence. I glanced about, imagining people watching us from behind shaded windows, through slats in fences, from treetops, behind shrubbery.

"Maybe we're still in our world, but the people have been absorbed into the other world." It seemed that the only thing I had to offer right now was speculation.

Risa considered it. "Then how do you explain what we saw on the news?"

"A bleed-through. Like how we drifted into that dream world and out."

"Where are all the bodies?" she asked.

"They're gone, everyone's gone. Our world is now the dream world." *And Jen? Where the hell is Jen?*

"Oh, okay. We're the only ones left? Sounds like a good set up for a horror story, Lang."

"Not if there's no one here to read it."

She punched me lightly on the shoulder. "Good point."

"Unfortunately, it might not be a joke."

"I don't buy it."

At the next corner, laughter rang out. We paused. "See, we're not alone," she whispered. Three young men and a woman tottered along the opposite side of the cross street.

"This is great. I feel drunk and I haven't even had a beer yet," one of them called out.

"We're all drunk on life," the woman shouted. "I feel much more alive than I've ever felt."

"I know. It's incredible," one of the others joined in. "This is real life. Everything from before feels like a dream. Hey, let's go to Pepe's. I heard they're giving out free beer."

Risa squeezed my hand. "Hey, now we know Pepe's is still standing."

"Meaning what? Things are the same—but different?"

"I don't know what it means, Lang." She sounded irRisable. "It's just an observation. You learn the rules of a place through observation and analysis."

The chatter and laughter continued as we moved down the street. I suddenly pulled Risa back toward a shrouded fence at the corner. "What're you doing?"

I jabbed my thumb toward the dusky green army truck moving down the street. It passed the intersection and stopped by the four revelers of life, blocking our view of them.

A moment later, we heard gunshots, screams, then silence. We pushed back deeper into the shadows, the shrubbery, hearts hammering, branches poking us in the faces, the arms. Fear overpowered discomfort. We weren't in Kansas anymore, Toto.

Several soldiers dressed in Dominion garb dragged the blood-soaked bodies to the rear of the truck and hurled them in like bags of garbage.

The truck pulled away, continuing its sweep of the streets, cleansing Key West of tourists. Crouched low in the shrubs, I whispered, "We need to get outta here. Let's head back to the house."

We moved out of the shrubbery bumped into a tall, gaunt black man. I wrenched back, but he pointed at the disappearing truck. "I knew those fuckers were no good. Golems, that's what I call them. Golems and all the blind idiots who joined them."

15

Lost Identities

Everything seemed so damned normal, Risa thought.

She and Lang sipped coffee at the patio table behind the house. Birds chirped and fluttered past, the sun had risen an hour ago and now burned white against the blue sky. The air was still, hot, like high summer. It seemed like their world, but it wasn't.

Two days had passed since they'd ventured out, and they'd remained here, locked within the walls and fences of what was familiar, known. When it got dark, they didn't turn on any lights. That first night they played Scrabble in a windowless bedroom closet and had finally fallen asleep on a bed of thick quilts she'd arranged on the floor. The second night, they had sat in the yard, in the shadow of the house, and talked intermittently about the rules and parameters of this new place. They waited. And the wait seemed interminable.

Even if they hadn't arrived at any firm conclusions about this new place, they had some practical facts. If they ate meagerly, she and Lang had enough food to last a week. Hopefully, by the time they ran out of supplies, they'd be able to safely forage the streets to replenish their coffers.

But she didn't want that. She wanted to leave, and soon. If Dominion turned Key West into one of its bases, there might be no escaping. She had a gnawing urge to find Lydia, her counterpart. If anyone could understand their predicament, it would be Lydia and Alex. But what would happen when they met?

"No gunfire since last night."

Lang set down with his coffee cup. "Not yet."

She suspected Key West wasn't the only city under assault. Every couple of hours, while it was light, she tried to get online—nothing—and then turned on the television and toggled through the channels. But the network and cable news shows were blacked out, replaced with monotonous background music, the screen displaying a series of pastoral settings. It only confirmed her growing belief that a worldwide onslaught was underway as Dominion 'cleansed' the world of overpopulation, or whatever other excuse they were telling their zombied human troops.

Their situation sucked, they both knew that. With only one road out of the keys, there was no way they could chance driving to Miami. She figured Dominion had set up roadblocks along that route and who knows what they would find if they reached Miami.

She studied her phone out of habit. No one had called her or Lang since the merger. Their contacts, e-mail, and all their apps had vanished, and the few numbers that she'd memorized didn't work. Same for Lang.

Their best shot for escaping the island was by boat and she knew Shelly, an artist who lived next door, owned a catamaran. But was Shelly there? Someone was. They'd seen lights. She stood up. "I'm tired of sitting around Lang. I'm going next door to see for myself."

"I don't think that's a good idea."

"Yeah, well, I've got to do something."

"I'll go with you."

"No, she doesn't know you. I don't want to freak her out."

"You don't know who's in that house, Risa."

"Well, I'm going to find out. I mean, maybe we're wrong. Maybe this *is* our world and Dominion somehow has invaded it." If that was the case, then Shelly would be living next door and she would probably be happy to see a friendly face, Risa thought.

"I'm not sure that would be any better." Lang unlocked the front door, eased it open, and scanned the neighborhood. He nodded, and she hurried outside, covering the short distance to

Shelly's door in record time.

She knocked, waited, knocked again. A muffled voice called out from behind the closed door.

"It's me, Risa."

"Who?"

"Risa, from next door."

A click, then another. The handle turned and the door opened. A tall blond peered out. She wore her hair in a ponytail and was dressed as if she were going to the gym. Shelly had dark hair and was twenty years older than this woman. "Oh, is Shelly here?"

"There's no Shelly here. How did you get in that house?"

"I don't know who you are, but that is my house. I own it, and I've lived there for seven years."

"And I've lived here five years, and I've never seen you before. The owners of that house live in Montreal half the year, and half the year here."

"I've got papers that show I own it. C'mon over and I'll show you."

"I'm not feeling well and you're not helping me." With that, she slammed the door and the locks clicked in place.

Lang was waiting for her as she stepped inside, concern written across his features. "What happened?"

Risa didn't answer. She looked around in amazement. Her living room furniture had vanished, replaced with tasteful, expensive mahogany tables and China cabinet and dark leather sofa and chair. Nice, but not her style, not hers at all.

"What's wrong?"

"Are you kidding? What happened while I was gone? Everything's different, where's my furniture?" She rushed passed him and into the bedroom. The walls were burnt orange, a mahogany king-sized bed with a huge carved headboard had replaced her queen. She opened the door to her walk-in closet. Not her clothes, a man's on one side, a woman's on the other.

"Oh, shit. You're right. It's all different. Why didn't I see it?"

Risa sat down on the edge of the bed, stunned. "It's all perception, Lang. We were living here in a cocoon, a memory of our world. As soon as I talked to that strange woman next door and she told me I didn't live here, I moved fully into this world. You did the same, as soon as I told you what I was seeing."

"Why didn't it happen when we went out and saw the Dominion troops?"

She shrugged. "Maybe because no one challenged our beliefs."

He walked over to the window facing the patio. "That is totally crazy, but I think you're right. Our coffee cups are still there, but…"

She moved next him, feeling dizzy and disoriented. Her faux wicker table and chairs had been replaced by black metal. The cups were a different design and shape. "I don't feel comfortable here anymore. It's not my house. I feel like an intruder. And what happened to all my stuff, my clothes, everything?"

"Shit. Our cars." Lang loped to the front door, Risa behind him. They ducked over to the alleyway at the side of the house. Their cars were gone, replaced with one encased in a plastic cover. Lang lifted a corner of the cover, revealing the trunk of a Prius.

Back inside, Risa looked around the altered kitchen. A wooden countertop had replaced her pale green granite. The cabinets were mahogany. Whoever lived here really liked that wood, she thought, and had the money to afford it. Utensils hung from a circular carousal and among the kitchen tools was a key ring with a keyless entry device for a Prius.

She snatched it off the carousal and tossed it to Lang. "You want to go for a ride?"

"A joy ride in a stolen car with Dominion troops patrolling the roads? I don't think so."

She opened the refrigerator, the freezer, then inspected the pantry. "We've got to do something. We've got oatmeal, coffee, a selection of salad dressings, half a jar of blueberry jelly, and a box of crackers. No doubt stale. Not much else."

"Yeah, it's a problem. The proverbial rug has been pulled out from under our feet."

"The rug and all the furniture on top of it."

"Who was next door?"

Risa leaned against the kitchen counter, still marveling how everything had changed from the tile floor to the upgraded appliances. "Nobody I know. Yet, when she said that there was no one named Shelly living there, she blinked her eyes really fast. I think that was Shelly's dream character, and Shelly got sucked into her."

"Could be. This is a nightmare."

"But it's real. We're not dreaming. I'm still puzzled by how we avoided getting swallowed up by Lydia and Alex."

Lang rubbed the back of his neck. "Like you said, we were aware and in communication with our dreaming selves. But I'm still going with the sex connection, too."

She laughed. "Somehow, I'm not surprised. Here's a question. What do you think would happen if we found them, wherever they're hiding?"

"That it might be another way of getting ourselves killed."

They moved out into the living room and she noticed her TV was gone, replaced by a larger screen on the same wall. "You mean besides stepping out the door and taking a walk?"

"Yeah, right. Seriously, though, I was thinking the same thing. What else can we do? We need to find them, and we need to do it as quickly as possible," he responded.

"Hold on. We don't know where we're going."

"We've got to get out of here. You know that. Your house isn't yours anymore. I'm sure my house isn't mine, either. No doubt our professional lives don't exist. I'm not a mystery writer or a former cop. You're not a shrink. We're squatters in your house, squatters in this world. Alex and Lydia are the only ones who can help us. Or at least hide us."

"You're scaring me, Lang."

"I'm scaring myself. *We're* the aliens. We're from another world!"

She sank down on the unfamiliar black leather sofa. "Where was Alex when you saw him last?"

Lang settled next to her. "In bed, the two of them. Just like us."

She laughed, and reached for his hand. "That doesn't help."

"I did get a sense of where they were. I was seeing it through his recent memory. It had the feeling of a small town. Kind of hilly with pine trees. There was something different about the place. Not sure what."

"I saw Lydia sitting at a table on a long porch overlooking a narrow street. She'd just spotted Alex walking out of a wood-frame building across the street. Then they were in bed."

"Huh, wonder where it is."

"I had the feeling that the rebel group already had a plan and it didn't involve staying on the road for very long where they would be vulnerable."

"Let's try contacting them again before we leave."

Lang made a face. "Yeah, I suppose. You're better at this hypno-contact than I am. I wish I could just ring him up and ask for directions."

"That might be dangerous."

"No kidding."

"Okay, let's relax and let go of everything, except the idea of contacting our counterparts." Risa took a deep breath, and slowly exhaled as she closed her eyes. She directed Lang to take several deep breaths. She did the same, doing her best to shed her fears about remaining any longer in this house that was no longer home. She extended the relaxation, telling Lang, telling herself, to let go of all concerns, everything outside of them, and to go deeper. Finally, she said in her most soothing voice. "Now, let's reach out to our dream selves. Dream selves who have become physical beings, like us. Who live in this same world."

At first she sensed nothing. She focused on her breath and tried to relax even deeper. She called out to Lydia. Again and again. 'Lydia' became her mantra. Nothing. It was simply a meditation. No contact, no immersion in someone else's life. She drifted in a dark void and lost track of time.

She thought she heard a voice. A warning cry. Was it from Lydia, from a deeper part of herself? Her heart leaped in response to something unknown and dangerous. It was coming, it was right here...right now.

A pounding erupted at the door.

16

Cinderella's Castle

As Hector walked toward the majestic castle with its spires and turrets, he felt nervous, an unfamiliar sensation. Cinderella's Castle represented both a fairy tale and a time when castles were a symbol of strength, power and rank. He got that. But here in Disney World the castle represented fantasy, and he had difficulty understanding Gogola's attraction to the theme park. After all, escaping fantasy, becoming 'real,' was what she was all about.

Adjusting to the physical world meant changing perspective in so many unexpected ways. One of them was moving into a greater sense of time. In the dream world, his awareness was focused on the present moment. Now he was conscious of history. Information arrived in packets when needed, and he'd just unwrapped an enormous one filled of knowledge about the past.

As he approached the castle, he marveled at how solid and physical he felt.

The fabric of life seemed denser and time felt incredibly linear, one moment following another. The dream world had fluctuated, existing like a movie that he both watched and participated in, ideas manifesting as a collective dream.

Now the movie had merged into reality with an explosion of sensation, extraordinary colors and textures and shapes that could be touched and sensed. Even the fantasy world of theme parks assumed a mechanical reality, rather than a Magic Kingdom without foundation. Best of all was the new sensation of consuming food and experiencing taste, hunger and satisfaction.

But there was something more, something less definable than sensual desires. Never born of a woman, never existing as a baby or child, he had arrived fully developed, a flower blossoming from a mental bud, with the collective knowledge of his kind. Now his sense of self had migrated from the collective vision of *tulpas* to his individual notion of self, what the humans referred to as ego. To that end, his individual will needed nurturing and protecting.

A pair of Dominion guards stood at the door, both of them dark-skinned, tall, muscular. He didn't recognize either of them, probably because they were freshly minted. The plan was to continue creating *tulpas*. "I'm here to see Gogola."

Neither questioned him. "The Maker awaits you, Commander." They spoke in unison and Hector realized they were twins. He entered a massive entryway that looked new, but with style and character embedded in the past.

He was handed off from the entry sentinels to a stout man with Asiatic features. He wore a black tunic and beret. "Hello, Chen. I see you've moved up in the new world." Gogola had praised Chen for his work with military and civilian authorities.

His ruddy features remained unchanged, masking his reaction. "I've been called to assist the Maker. Follow me."

Chen led the way down a majestic hallway with a domed ceiling and crisscrossing beams. Enormous fairytale murals framed the hallway and Hector, with his new knowledge, felt as if he'd moved into the era of knights and chivalry in a royal court. They entered the great hall with its massive fireplace, signets and tapestries, and full suits of armor seemingly guarding the entrances.

They passed through the hall into Cinderella's Table, a circular banquet hall with a high cathedral ceiling and a long oval table in the center. He'd met with Gogola here on several occasions, but never comprehended what he was seeing. He stopped by the table, ready to sit and wait. But Chen motioned for him to continue. They exited the banquet hall, moved down a narrow corridor, then climbed a shadowy, curving staircase inside one of the castle's towers. The red-carpeted stairs were illuminated by light streaming through a lone stain glass window.

They reached a landing at the top of the stairs where Chen knocked on the heavy door. He paused a moment, then opened it. Hector knew that his guide had received a signal through Gogola's net. Chen nodded, stepped aside, and Hector cautiously moved into the castle's opulent master suite, the only bedroom in the massive structure.

He entered the sitting room with its ornate brocade couch and loveseat. He peeked into the adjoining bedroom. Like the rest of the castle, the suite was furnished in seventeenth and eighteenth century antiques. A king-sized bed with a majestic hand-carved frame dominated the room. The covers had been turned down and an impression was left where Gogola had slept.

"In here, Hector."

He walked over to a door that was partially open, paused, then slipped inside. She was sprawled in a luxurious spa with Corinthian-style columns at the corners, antique stained glass windows, and a deep purple glass ceiling speckled with stars.

"Are you hungry, Hector? Order some food, if you like."

"I just ate. I'm full, as they say." *But I have other cravings and you're looking good.* The water was sudsy, but he could see the outline of her full breasts.

"This is where I go into my meditation to create more of us. I never know what will materialize now that we're physical. I've created half a dozen since the merger. They're coming out as twins. But I dispersed all but two. We don't need deficient twin *tulpas*."

"I see that Chen is your chief aide now."

"He's very efficient and persuasive when he needs to be." After a moment, "Why do you ask about him? Are you jealous?"

"Not at all. I just wanted to confirm his role."

She adjusted her position and her pointed nipples briefly surfaced. "The water feels so sensual." She slid her hands down her body, tempting him further. "I could stay here all day. But there are things to do. Hand me my towel, Hector."

She stood up as he spread out the towel, blocking his view.

But what he'd seen had aroused him. She wrapped the towel around her, held it with one hand, and pressed the other one to his crotch. "Oh, I see you are attracted to your maker. You know, that is taboo among humans." She took his hand and led him into the bedroom. "But of course we are not human. And we don't make babies."

He couldn't hold back any longer. As they stopped by the bed, he pulled away her towel and pushed her onto the bed. She spread her legs willingly as he quickly pulled off his clothes and mounted her. "But we can enjoy the fruits of the physical," he whispered in her ear.

Her coy expression showed a mix of lust with something else, something deceptive, possibly something cruel. A warning. But he couldn't stop now, not with the passion rising as he fondled her and worked his way into her. The Maker was his. Her eyes rolled back in her head, her back arched. Her body stiffened beneath him, then relaxed. He plunged on, but she was gone. Gogola simply stared ahead, taking long slow breaths, her eyes half-closed, mouth slightly open.

He uttered a cry as he finished, but she remained impassive. Confused, he rolled off her, gasping for breath, his heart pounding. He'd never experienced anything like it. He wanted to do it again. Even though Gogola hadn't acted quite as he'd expected, he now understood the human fascination with sex. He closed his eyes and seconds later started to drift off. He didn't know how long he'd slept when he felt the bed shake. He blinked his eyes open. Gogola remained entranced, unmoved.

He propped himself up on his elbows, and discovered they weren't alone. A naked man lay on the other side of her. Hector looked on in disgust as he saw the man's penis was erect and rising off his belly.

A new tulpa.

Hector threw his legs over the side of the bed, reached for his clothes, and hurried to the bathroom. When he came out, he found another *tulpa,* a female, curled in a fetal position in the exact same spot he'd just occupied. Both new *tulpas* were blond with similar features—long noses, pointed chins and thin lips. Twins.

When he'd created Kahil, the process had been torturous. Under Gogola's guidance, he was directed to enter a dream without losing consciousness, controlling the action within the dream, and manifesting a *tulpa*. He'd found it impossible to hold his conscious awareness more than a few seconds before drifting into sleep. As soon as he did so, Gogola would wake him up, and tell him to do it again, repeating over and over…*a dream within a dream* until he could hold his conscious awareness long enough to change his mantra to…*a tulpa within a dream.*

She pushed him over and over, and finally he begged her to stop. That was when he found the pale-skinned, white-haired man lying on the bed next to him. After that, she dismissed him as a sub-maker. She'd found more success with female *tulpas.*

Now that they were in the physical world he wondered if sexual stimulation played a role in the creation of *tulpas.*

"Of course it does, Hector." Gogola was sitting up, her breasts modestly covered by the sheet that threaded under her arms. She read him perfectly. "So we are finally physical beings, the manifestation of my dream, so to speak. But we are still *tulpas,* and our babies come full grown, a creation of the mind, abetted by sexual arousal."

"I thought it would take longer." Hector pulled on his clothes.

"At first it did." She looked over her shoulder at the stirring *tulpa.* "But now I can instantly enter the dream yoga state that Norbu taught me." She examined the twins as they slowly stood up and moved to the end of the bed and faced her. "They appear acceptable, but will be tested, of course."

Gogola was assisted by a team of *tulpa* 'mid-wives,' women, sub-makers themselves who took over the immediate care and testing of all new tulpas. It's something he knew very little about, and found somewhat repulsive. "Do the men all arrive in that condition?"

She laughed. "You mean with erections? No, that's a first. And it must relate to your presence as my source of stimulation. Very interesting." She raised her head. "My assistants are almost here. You should leave."

Hector quickly finished dressing. He had no desire to

remain a minute longer. He realized Gogola hadn't given him any directives. He was amused by the thought that he might've come on a sex mission. "Is there anything else, Gogola?"

"Yes, of course." She was garbed in a pale silky robe that clung to her body. "I'll be direct, Hector. You're not longer supreme commander of Dominion. There will be eighteen command centers around the world. Each general will command autonomous zones and report directly to me. You will be commander of the Southeast U.S. zone."

His shoulders and his gut tightened in a defensive posture, felt anger and outrage, then wariness and self-pity. *So this is what ego is about, a protective self-awareness. I want power and she is taking it away.*

Before he could reply, she continued. "Of course you know that I always monitored your actions as commander and changed your orders when I saw fit."

He knew that, but it had never offended him. Not like now. Before the shift, he had considered himself her loyal servant, nothing more. Now status and power were foremost in his mind.

He knew what this was about. "I'm sorry about Kahil. I should've known that he was getting too close to the humans."

"We'll take care of Kahil and the others with him. But right now there's a more important matter. As you know, the troops are out of control. They're ransacking cities and randomly killing whoever they encounter."

Not my fault. "It's the humans, not *tulpas*."

"I'm aware of that," she snapped. "Their new physical awareness is channeled into combat and their enemy is everyone who stands in their way. But you've done nothing to stop them."

Hector didn't follow her logic. "You've said the population had to be reduced. Why not let them do it?"

She looked disappointed. "We have the people in our control. They believe we are their saviors, that we will create a better world."

"We tricked them."

She moved into the next room and motioned for him to sit down on the couch. She remained standing. The light passing through the stained glass window highlighted her body and he felt his desire for her growing again. He imagined pulling her down to the couch and taking her once more. But that wasn't feasible with the new tulpa in the next room and the midwives on their way.

"You don't understand, Hector. The merger of worlds was only accomplished because of the willingness of the vast majority to believe in us, in our cause. Which became their cause. When they accepted us, they empowered our cause to become physical. We conquered them, but they are the ones who created the merger."

"But it's over. It's done."

"If we don't stop the chaos and killings quickly, the people will turn on us."

"You said they can't kill us."

"That's true, but if they lose their belief in us, we lose our control. We are still far too few. The army could turn on us. They can't kill us, but they can incarcerate us. There's no more walking through walls."

"What can we do?"

"Order all of *your* troops back to Disney World. Reorganize them. Reward the soldiers who didn't rampage. Punish any ringleaders who led the murderous attacks on civilians."

He stood up, ready to leave. "What if they rebel?"

"They won't. Not if you act now. The same order has already been issued to the other commanders. Their troops are complying. I'm calling a press conference and revealing myself as the supreme commander. Then I will apologize for the behavior of our troops."

He nodded, waiting for her to dismiss him. She moved closer. "After you've given your orders and made certain they are being followed, I want you to take a truck load of troops and go to a small town north of here. It's called Cassadaga. You'll find Kahil and all the betrayers hiding there. Capture them, and bring them to me."

"What about Kahil?"

"Bring him here and I will show you the technique for dispersing the essence of a *tulpa*."

He saluted. “Yes, my commander.” He started to leave, then paused. “If I may ask, how did you find them?”

She smiled. “I have my ways.”

17

Captured

LANG

We both snapped out of our reverie. Who would be knocking at the door? My fleeting glimpse of Alex, real or imagined, vanished. My shoulders stiffened. I glanced at Risa and we both bolted to our feet. I pulled the pink Ruger out of my pocket and Risa darted across the room for her purse and snatched out the Springfield. She approached the door as the pounding re-ignited.

"Who is it?"

"It's me, your neighbor. I'm sorry I was so abrupt. I've got to talk to you."

Risa looked my way and I shrugged. She unlocked the door, opened it a few inches, then immediately tried to shut it. I rushed forward to help her, but was too late. A booted foot wedged in the doorway, and a moment later a tall, muscular man with an eye-patch pushed his way inside. A blond woman followed, both clad in Dominion uniforms, complete with berets. I ended up partially behind the door, pressed against the wall. Neither of our visitors had noticed me. They were armed with pistols, aimed at Risa's head. If I shot one, the other might kill Risa before I could fire a second shot.

"What do you want?" Risa asked, holding her gun behind her back.

"Let me see your hands," Eye-patch snarled.

She dropped her gun and raised her hands. "I'm leaving."

"Damn right you are," the blond said. "You aren't my neighbor. You don't live here."

"Okay, I said I'm going." Risa moved toward the door, but the woman pushed her back.

"You picked a bad time to break into someone's house, lady," Eye-Patch said. "We got orders to eliminate any troublemakers."

I couldn't wait any longer. I slipped out from behind the door. Eye-Patch spun around. I aimed and squeezed the trigger, but the gun jammed. The sight of the pink gun seemed to amuse him. In that moment of hesitation, I kicked him in the groin. He bent forward in surprise and I hammered the back of his head with the butt of the gun.

The woman whirled and fired. She would've hit me from five feet away, but Risa struck her arm and the bullet whizzed past my head. I slammed the gun against her temple, she collapsed, but Eye-Patch staggered, raised his gun, and fired into the ceiling as he fell to his knees. I chopped him in the back of his neck with another blow from the pink Ruger, and he fell onto his face.

My heart pounded, Risa rushed over and hugged me.

"Thank you, thank you. I thought I was dead. I should never have opened that door."

"We're lucky we survived. The Ruger came in handy, but not as a gun. We've got to get out of here. They'd probably been in contact with other soldiers." My training kicked in and I quickly scooped up the automatic pistols and passed one to Risa. I slid the defunct Ruger across the floor toward the kitchen.

Both intruders were moaning now, coming awake. Eye-Patch spewed a string of curses as he tried to sit up. I slapped him hard across the face, bouncing his head against the mahogany floor. "Take off your uniform or I'll do it myself after I put a bullet in your head."

Risa caught on fast and backhanded the blond as she sat up. "You heard the man. The same for you. Take it off."

Eye-Patch sat up, palms raised in surrender. "Okay, okay." He started unbuttoning his shirt and I noticed his gaze stray. He spotted the Springfield on the floor where Risa had dropped it. In spite of his size, he rolled over like an agile gymnast, grabbed the gun, spun around and aimed. I squeezed the trigger, but the safety was on. I grunted. Not my day. A gun fired and Eye-Patch fell back, a bullet in his forehead. The blonde screamed and Risa slugged her with the butt of the gun.

"Nice work."

"Yeah, after I nearly got you killed." Her eyes fell on Eye-Patch. She looked stunned at what she'd done. She hurried over to the kitchen and I heard her retch into the sink. She returned a minute later as I finished removing the dead man's boots and pants.

"Sorry about that. I can't believe I killed someone."

"It was him or me. You did the right thing."

She stared at the woman. "Did I kill her, too?"

"No, she's breathing. She's going to have a major headache."

Risa went to work removing her uniform. Ten minutes later, after struggling with the bodies, we were dressed. Risa's uniform fit fairly well after she turned up the sleeves. My uniform was another matter, too big in the shoulders, too long in the pants. "This will have to do. I just hope I don't trip over these pants."

She laughed. "You look fine, Private Kern." The uniforms had nametags above the shirt pockets.

"You, too, Schwartz. Let's get out of here." I found the key for the Prius and Risa grabbed her purse. She paused at the door, fumbling with the purse. "What are you doing?"

"Oh, yeah. No need to lock it. My keys probably wouldn't work, anyhow."

I heard the rumbling of a diesel engine. "Oh, shit." An army truck had just turned onto the street. We ducked back inside, shut the door, and turned the deadbolt. Risa peered through the front blinds, which were now mahogany slats. I waited, hoping to hear the low thunder of the engine slowly fade way. It didn't.

"They stopped!"

We darted out the rear door, opened the side gate, and moved out into the alleyway. The Prius was parked ten feet away, out of sight from the front of the house. We ran to it and pulled off the tarp. I could hear voices, then pounding on the door.

I clicked open the lock with the remote key and started the

engine. Nice. A remote starter and no engine sound. We climbed in and I drove forward along the alleyway. We turned onto the first cross street, and I glimpsed soldiers in the rearview mirror as they hustled around the side of the house. "Did they see us?"

Risa remained tense and upset. "I don't think so."

I touched her knee. "How're you doing?"

"I feel terrible about what happened back there. You don't think they were just trying to scare me, do you?"

"They had me convinced. No, I don't think they were pretending."

"How many people have you killed?"

"In eighteen years on the force, I never fired my gun, except in practice at the range. I'm only trigger-happy in my novel. That was my literary agent's doing. She said, if you show a gun, you better use it."

Risa laughed and shook her head. "I don't know if that makes me feel better or worse."

I kept to the narrow back streets, working my way toward A1A, the route off the island. The town seemed empty and quiet, a hollow shell void of life. No gunfire. No sign of rampaging troops. "Well, we've gotten away from the house and the soldiers. But we're going to need some incredible luck to avoid getting stopped and questioned."

She squeezed my thigh. "Let's just make it happen. Maybe they'll see our uniforms and won't question us."

"Somehow, I think it's not going to be that easy." I pulled over by a dumpster at a construction site a couple of block before A1A. "Let's get rid of IDs, driver's licenses, credit cards, anything with our names."

"Why?"

"They don't match the names on our uniforms. Besides, my guess is that the credit cards don't work anymore, our addresses aren't where we live, and the driver's licenses won't be registered."

"You're right. I'm confused. My address also ties us to the dead guy."

"You've got a right to be confused. We both do." I pulled out two credit cards and my license. Risa took out her cards, handed them to me. I hurried over to the dumpster, tossed the plastic, and climbed back behind the wheel.

"I had eight thousand dollars in my checking account," Risa moaned. "Guess I'll never see it." She laughed. "Then again I had twelve grand in credit card debt."

"There you go. You're in the black. We've got to stay positive. The way I figure it, we're wild cards, anomalies, real outliers. We came from another world and that's got to count for something." With that, I put the car in gear. "Onward." We turned onto an empty A1A near Smathers Beach and headed toward the turn off to U.S. Route 1. In spite of my attempt at optimism, my thoughts were more on surviving the next few minutes, the next hour, the rest of the day.

I held my breath as we reached the top of the island, and waited at the red light. I was tempted to run it, but decided against it. Even though there were no cars in sight, trouble could be hiding on the side of a building or behind shrubbery. My thoughts turned to Jen and I wondered if I would ever see her again.

Finally, the light changed and I turned onto U.S. 1 in the direction of Miami and crossed over to Stock Island. I'd barely gone half a mile when I made a sharp turn onto a narrow roadway.

"What the hell you doing?" Risa asked.

"The hospital. I've got to look for Jen."

"Lang, she won't be there."

"You don't know that. Maybe she is there."

"Oh, god. You're going to get us killed." She slumped into her seat and we continued on, and passed by a tropical park. We rounded a curve and I expected to see the Lower Keys Medical Center straight ahead. I hit the brakes. Instead of a hospital, a townhouse complex appeared at the end of the road. A sign read on the side of the road read confirmed it: *Key West Naval Station Housing.* A hundred yards ahead, a gate crossed the road next to a guard house.

"Did I take the wrong road?"

Risa leaned forward. "No, this is right. Except it's not. I've been here enough, mostly visiting patients in the psych ward. But..."

I considered driving ahead and asking for the location of the hospital. But Risa was right. Jen wouldn't be there. A figure in black wearing a beret stepped out of the guardhouse and peered at us. I quickly backed away and turned around. "Let's get out of here."

We caught the green light this time and I turned onto U.S. 1 and away from Key West. We passed by the turnoff to the Hogfish Grill where I'd met Risa a lifetime ago in another world. I was about to mention that when I spotted a man in uniform waving his arms. No sign of a roadblock, just a single soldier signaling us to stop.

"What're you doing now?" Risa asked as I pulled over.

"Just being cautious." I closed my hand over my new weapon, a semi-automatic Sig-Pro. As the man ran up to the driver's side, I lowered my window Wiry guy, late twenties, angular features. He wore the Dominion uniform, but no beret. His thick dark hair fell over his collar and a three-day stubble covered his jaw. His eyes looked red from lack of sleep.

I kept the car in gear, ready to pull away if he lunged at me. In spite of my concerns, I wanted to hear what the soldier had to say. Maybe he knew something important.

"Hey, can you give me a lift? Oh, shit. I wasn't expecting uniforms. Sorry."

Surprised, wary, he started to back away. "Wait. Where are you going?"

He took a second look, his concern turning to suspicion. "Where'd you get this car?"

Risa leaned toward the driver's side. "I live here. It's my car. Answer his question. Why did you wave us down?"

"I'm trying to get to Big Pine Key. My dad lives there. I want to check on him."

"We're going as far as Sugarloaf. For now."

"That works. I can walk from there, if I have to, another ten or twelve miles. It's just another march, but without the heavy pack."

I clicked on the safety and slid the gun behind my back. "Where're your pack and your weapon, soldier?"

"My name's Phillip. I'm unarmed. I ditched everything

when I saw what was going on. I grew up down here. These are my people."

I turned to Risa and spoke in a low voice. "What do you think?"

"I think he's okay, but I'll sit in the back and keep an eye on him."

She got out and motioned for Phillip to come around to the passenger side. She climbed into the back seat and he took her place. He put on his seat belt and thanked me for the ride.

"So what was going on when you lost your weapon?"

"Stuff I don't want to think about. You must've seen it. Didn't you get into it?" He craned his neck to see my name tag.

"I thought the orders were not to kill anyone." That was a bluff, but it paid off.

"Shit, I didn't hear about any such orders, not until this morning when they told everyone we were heading back to Disney for re-training or something." I could feel him staring at me. "So why didn't you get into a troop carrier? What's in Sugarloaf?"

"We're heading up to Disney, but I wanted to check on my house and make sure my renters are okay after the rampage."

"That's cool." He laughed and looked back at Risa, studied her a moment. "I got the feeling we're not the only ones who are missing in action."

"You think we'll hit roadblocks, Phillip?"

"Yesterday if you tried to leave, yes. Not today. We're all heading out. I'm just glad I found you before a troop carrier came by."

And we were lucky to find him, someone who seemed a bit separate from the mass mind of the troops.

"Why do you think the troops started slaughtering people?" Risa asked. "Who gave the order?"

Phillip shifted in his seat again. "No one gave the order. When everything changed and we got real, we just went wild. Killing everyone without uniforms. I heard it happened all over. Not just here."

I was fascinated by his description of the transformation. "Do you think we weren't real before the shift?"

He gave me an odd look, like *Where are you from, dude?* "Of course we were real, but the world was only half real. At least, that's the way my commander explained it, and he got that straight from the tuppies. You know, *they* were the ones who made the world real."

"Tuppies, you mean *tulpas*?" Risa asked.

"Yeah, whatever. They're like super beings. You can't even kill them. They're here to help us. That's why they made us real." He paused, frowned. "I'm surprised you don't know this stuff. I thought we all got the intel upgrade."

"We're just sort of confused about it," Risa said. "We heard that two worlds merged and now we're fully physical, but everyone has a dreamer caught inside them."

"If that's true, then you've got intel above my rank. Shit, that might account for the voice I've been hearing."

"What's it say?"

"I don't know." He slapped the side of his head as if he was trying to shut it up or knock it out. "It's like someone yelling at me inside my head. Like really annoying. Driving me fucking nuts."

"Do you hear it now?"

"No, only when I'm alone."

"Best to keep that stuff to yourself. We're with intelligence," I said and glanced over my shoulder at Risa.

"Yeah, that's right," she agreed then added: "People don't need to know what they don't need to know."

Phillip nodded. "Mmmm." He settled into his seat and didn't say anything more. We'd gained a substantial amount of insight from him and had become intelligence officers for our own cause.

The highway, which usually had a steady flow of cars in both directions, was eerily quiet. A few cars were heading out of Key West, but we didn't pass any coming into town. I paced a troop carrier that was about half a mile ahead, making sure I didn't get too close to it.

A few minutes later, as we approached Mile Marker 17, I eased to the side of the road. "This is where we're turning."

"You're not going to report me, are you?" Phillip asked.

"Not to worry."

He got out and walked off at a quick pace. "Well, that was enlightening," I said as Risa returned to the front passenger seat.

"Yeah, he seemed okay, I think. I didn't like the way he stared at my nametag, though." She adjusted her beret. "I hate this uniform and everything it represents."

"Me too. But it's keeping us safe right now." I turned onto Sugarloaf Boulevard. "If my place is abandoned and we can get in, we can take the uniforms off and hide out for awhile."

"Yeah, we might be safer there than in Key West, and we can wait until all the troops have left. But I don't want to stay too long. We've got to find…"

"Yeah, I know. Finding Alex and Lydia is the only thing that makes sense."

It actually felt like an instinct, I thought, like birds with their inner drive to migrate north or south, depending on the season. After a couple of beats, I added: "And finding out what happened to Jen."

"I think we know the answer, Lang. She's inside Alex's daughter."

"Well that's fucked. I want her back."

After a couple of miles, I turned onto Flying Fish Drive and slowly drove to the end of the road. The neighborhood was quiet, just the way it always was. My place was on the left. Except it wasn't. "Holy shit."

We stared in astonishment. It was an empty lot behind a high wire fence. I got out of the car for a closer look. Cinder blocks were stacked to one side of the lot and weeds had grown around them. It looked as if someone had planned to build a house, and hadn't gotten very far. A faint outline was visible where my house had stood as if the foundation was still buried beneath the weeds.

"So much for hanging out here," Risa said as she joined me.

"Yeah, too bad. It was a nice house. Wonder why they tore it down."

"Oh, they probably planned to build a bigger one, but something happened."

As we walked back to the car, the reality of our situation

settled around me, weighing heavily. "So neither of us has a home."

She shook her head. "Yeah, it sucks. All we've got is a stolen car."

I heard a pop just as a bullet slammed into the rear window of the Prius. We ducked behind the car as a second bullet ricocheted off a steel fence post. I peered out, but couldn't see anyone. I figured someone with a rifle was firing from more than a hundred yards away.

I opened the back door. "Get in and lay down." Risa dived in headfirst and I closed the door. The driver door was still open and I slid behind the wheel. I made a quick semi-circle and laid on the gas pedal. We passed a wooded lot and I heard another pop and a bullet pinged off the hood.

I turned onto Sugarloaf Boulevard. "So much for these uniforms protecting us," Risa said as she sat up.

"Yeah, I was thinking the same. But it's good to know that not everyone is falling for the Dominion message."

Just before we reached U.S. 1, I pulled over. "C'mon up here, Risa. I'm not your taxi driver."

She climbed out and quickly joined me. We turned toward Miami and had covered about a mile when Phillip appeared in the distance, walking along the side of road. "Why don't we give him a ride," she suggested.

I slowed down. "Yeah, we'll take him to Big Pine. He could easily be picked up as a deserter or get shot."

The kid seemed to hesitate when I stopped a hundred feet in front of him, then he hurried toward the car. He paused outside the rear door, stared at the bullet hole in the back window, then climbed in. "That's new. I guess it was a short stay at your house."

"We decided it was best to keep going after someone took a couple of pot shots at us."

"Smart thinking."

"Guess some people still aren't on board with Dominion yet," Risa said.

"Not surprising, especially after all the random shootings. Crazy stuff."

"We'll get you to Big Pine, if that's where you still want to go."

"Yes, sir. I've gotta check on my dad. He's got a bait shop there."

"Really. What's his name?"

"Arnie Keller."

I couldn't help wondering if it was Sal's bait shop. I didn't recall him ever talking about any competition on the island. I glanced into the rear-view mirror and saw Phillip take out his phone and start texting. "I'm letting him know we're on the way."

When he finished, he slipped the phone back in his pocket and slumped deeper into the seat and closed his eyes. I didn't disturb him until we approached Big Pine. I turned at mile marker 33 and headed toward my old partner's place.

Phillip stirred as I asked for directions. He glanced around and said I was headed in the right direction. He pointed toward a dirt road leading through dense wooded landscape, but I'd already slowed for the turn. I knew where I was and that the road led to Sal's shop…or where it had been. "You seem to know the way."

"I've done some fishing up here. I only know of one bait shop in Big Pine."

"Cool. I hope he's okay."

Fortunately, Phillip didn't quiz me about his father or the bait shop. From what I'd seen of my own place, it was clear that the shop could look completely different from Sal's. I knew nothing about the owner, other than the fact that his son sat in the back seat.

A minute later, the Prius crunched over the gravel parking lot near a canal that led to open water. The two-story wood-framed building looked exactly like Sal's bait shop. Sal had lived in an apartment on the second floor. I had an urge to rush inside and call for him, even though I knew better.

But I caught myself when I saw the wood decking leading to the canal. The back of Sal's place was dirt with sparse clumps of grass. A couple of boats were docked, and I couldn't help wondering if some hardcore keys fishermen were still at it in the aftermath of the merger and the chaos that followed. It was probably a good way to escape it all.

Phillip slid out of the passenger seat. "Thanks a lot for the ride…or rides, both of them! Hey, you two want to come in? I'll get you a beer or something for the road."

"Sure, go ahead. We'll be right in."

I turned to Risa. "What do you think, Schwartz, should we take a look?"

"Your call. This is your friend's place, right?"

"Wrong tense. It *was* his place in our old world. But he's not here. Sal didn't have a son."

I started to open the door when Risa touched my shoulder. "But it's strange, though, that we ended up here. Maybe there's some significance. It could be a synchronicity, you know, a meaningful coincidence."

"Does that mean we're on the right path?"

"Hopefully, but sometimes synchronicities can be a warning, too. So let's be cautious."

We got out and walked to the shop. The beer cooler was right by the door, same as Sal's. Two men were standing at the counter in the center of the store checking out, containers of bait in hand. Sal's counter had been in the corner. The middle-aged man at the cash register was tall and slim with a receding hairline. Phillip stood beside him and it was apparent they were father and son.

When the fishermen paid up and left, Phillip introduced us as Privates Kern and Schwartz. "Nice to meet you, Arnie. You've got a good son. He didn't like what was going on in Key West, and he was right. That's why we're all being recalled."

"Yeah, we're headed up Disney," Phillip said. "Everything's getting re-organized after all the…all the bullshit."

"I heard about them killings. Maybe some deserved it. Key West has always been a hangout for rebels, and it's good that they didn't get established there."

"What we saw was mostly attacks on tourists," Risa said.

Arnie looked between us as if he was trying to figure something out. I hoped he didn't look too closely at our ill-fitting uniforms. "You're kind of old to be in this army as a foot soldier, aren't you?"

"Yeah, pretty old. I believe in the cause," I lied. "I want to do my part."

"Dad, lots of older men and women have joined. Not that you're old, Private Schwartz. The cutoff age is fifty."

Arnie nodded. "I guess you're never too old to offer your service to your country. Especially in times like this."

"Dad, would you get them a beer or something to drink and maybe a snack or two. I'll be right back. I've got to run upstairs and get my keys. I'm taking my car up to Disney."

"You two go pick out what you want," Arnie said.

I found a ginger beer and Risa grabbed a bottle of Perrier. We added bags of chips and peanuts. "This should hold us over until we get to a restaurant. How much do I owe you?"

Arnie waved a hand. "It's on me. You helped my son."

"Thanks. So where were you when the shift happened?"

He frowned. "When the shit happened? Which shit was that?"

"You know, the merger, when we became more real, more physical."

He rubbed his chin and looked at Risa for help.

"Out of the dream, into the real world."

Arnie shook his head. "I can't say I know what you're talking about. Let me see what's taking Phillip so long." With that, he headed for the door that led to the stairs.

"What do you make of that?" I asked.

"Interesting. He seemed clueless. I've got the feeling he's not the only one."

"What do you mean?"

She crossed her arms and leaned against a freezer case. "You know how when you have a vivid dream and think that you'll definitely remember it as you're laying there, but then a few minutes after you get up it starts to fade, and pretty soon you can't remember it at all. It's like that, except in this case, the entire memory of the dream world vanishes."

"Phillip remembered it," I pointed out. "He knew about the merger."

"Here he comes. Let's ask him."

But there was no need to ask. "Hey, what were you saying to my dad about a shift?"

"You know, what we we're talking about on the first ride, how the merger changed everything." I could tell by his expression that he didn't remember.

Phillip stared out the window toward the canal. I couldn't see what he was looking at. "I vaguely recall something about dreams." He shook his head. "That's about it. What's the big deal?"

"It was something the Dominion leaders talked about," Risa said. "Now I can't remember what it was, either. Can you, Kern?"

She lightly kicked the back of my ankle. "No, I can't remember what it was." As I spoke, a boat pulled up to the dock. A half dozen soldiers, all wearing berets, disembarked. "We've got company. I wonder what they want?"

I figured it out, but too late. A cloud of black uniforms flooded into the bait shop, weapons drawn. All three of us were knocked to the ground. I glimpsed Arnie in the center of the shop, hands raised. "I'm the owner."

The bastard had reported us, but when did he do it, and why would he turn in his own son? A moment later, I realized I had it wrong.

"That's my son," Arnie said, pointing at Phillip. "He's the one who called you."

No, he'd texted them in the car.

Two of the soldiers pulled Phillip to his feet. "They're the ones. They're wearing uniforms of two soldiers from my unit, Schwartz and Kern. I bet they killed them."

An officer stopped in front of us. "Show us your picture IDs."

That was going to be a problem. Fuck. So much for picking up hitchhikers.

18

Cassadaga

Lydia left the Cassadaga Hotel and walked outside just to feel the sun on her face, to stretch her legs, to smell the air. A scent of gardenias, of fertile earth, of green. Everything here was a deep, rich green. She crossed the street, intending to walk over to one of the bookstores or cafes, but suddenly felt so exhausted she turned back.

She spotted Alex and Kari sitting on the side porch outside of their room. He waved and she blew him a kiss. She made it as far as the front porch of the hotel and simply had to rest. Lydia settled in the hanging loveseat, bewildered at her fatigue.

They'd been here two days, and she was having a difficult time, physically and mentally. She felt as if she were underwater and confined by a sharper sense of time, one thing precisely following another. She'd always thought of time as merely now, an expansive sense of the present that loosely followed 'before' and generally preceded 'after.'

At the same time, she felt a greater sense of physicality and sensuality, and razor-sharp self-awareness. In the old world, things happened that made no sense and were best ignored. Twinks. Apparently, the acuteness of time in the physical world had eliminated such distractions. Limitations and constrictions abounded. But she was real now, whatever that meant. She had always felt real, but reality itself had been unstable, a dream world where events sometimes flickered in and out. That was something she'd never really been aware of until after the merger. Yet, she lacked something. She felt an emptiness, a void, a gaping hole inside her.

She wanted to go home to her apartment, her old life. She wanted to talk to her mother. But it was too dangerous. She would no doubt be killed if she were captured again by Dominion. Besides, what remained of her old life?

Her nose twitched at the smell of cigarette smoke and she realized she wasn't alone. A heavyset, round-faced woman with hair tied up on top of her head stood near the door from the lobby, cigarette poised in her right hand. She wore a billowy patterned dress that reached her ankles. Lydia guessed she was one of the local mediums.

"I hope I didn't disturb you," she said. "Are you okay?"

Lydia smiled. "I'm fine. I'm just getting used to all the changes."

The woman sat down at a table between her and Lydia. She took out a small copper bowl from her large multi-colored purse, set it on the table, and tapped her cigarette against the edge. "Harley Diamond. I'm one of the readers here at the hotel."

"Oh, really."

"You're with the group of people who showed up just before the shift."

Lydia touched a foot to the floor and stopped swaying on the hanging seat. "And who are still here. I'm Lydia."

"I know who you are." She paused, waiting to see Lydia's reaction." I've seen you on TV. My guess is that you and your friends aren't just hanging out here. You're hiding out, right?"

"You getting that psychically?

Harley smiled. "Just observation."

"So are we in trouble?"

"Not with me. In fact, not with anyone from the spiritualist community. We have a better understanding of these beings than most people."

"Then you have better insight than I do. I spent weeks with them and I don't understand them. They act so human, but they're not."

Harley stubbed out her cigarette in the copper bowl. "Actually, they consider themselves superior to humans, and deserving to inherit the planet from us."

"But they need us."

"For the time being. They'll probably thin out the population in a pandemic. Of course they won't be affected by the disease."

"I don't care for the picture you're painting."

"They can be stopped."

"How?"

Harley dragged on her cigarette. "I wish I knew." She gazed off again, as if an invisible being was talking to her. "You've lost something important, more important than you understand."

Lydia didn't reply and waited for her to continue. "You've lost a part of your being that you should've absorbed. So did your friend and accomplice, Alex. That's why you're feeling weak and uncomfortable."

"What can we do?"

"You know what you must do. You have no choice in the matter. You can't survive without re-connecting."

"You're talking about our counterparts from the other world. Why didn't they join with us?"

This time Harley dropped her head back and gazed up as if she were reading a message off the ceiling. She lowered her eyes and studied Lydia for a few moments. "That's interesting. You're quite talented psychically. Both of you are. You were both able to communicate with your counterparts while awake, and that's unusual."

"Actually, I think they reached out to us."

"Most people don't listen. They block the channels. But you heard them and acknowledged them. They knew what was happening and because of that they didn't get absorbed."

Confused, Lydia said, "I wished they could've stopped it from happening."

Harley shook her head. "They couldn't, no one could. It was meant to happen."

"But why?"

"It's like many other terrible disasters. They were meant to happen as part of the evolution of humanity, the evolution of the self."

Lydia shook her head in disbelief. "It sounds more like

destruction of the self to me. I'm just feeling so empty."

"Ha. You think *you* feel isolated? Imagine what your counterparts are feeling here in this world with no friends, no family, no lives. Their homes aren't their homes. Their careers have vanished. They're at a loss."

"They're here?"

"And looking for you two."

Risa. Where are you? She realized now that Risa had always been a part of her, even though she'd been unaware of it. "Where is she now?"

Harley's eyes turned glassy again and she stared off into the distance. "I see water around her. Lots of water. She's confined, surrounded by water. That's all I'm getting. She's trapped. She can't do anything."

"How can I help her?"

"You can't. You need to help yourself. The longer you stay here, the more dangerous it becomes." Harley's cell phone chimed. She dug it out of her bag, glanced at the screen, but didn't take the call. Instead, she started tapping the screen.

Hector had allowed her and Alex to keep their iPhones in order to monitor news stories. They could call each other—which was hardly necessary—or Hector and Kahil. But all other calls were blocked. Since the escape, she'd turned off her cell and had kept it off.

"What are people saying about the merger?" Lydia asked.

"Initially, there was a surge of confusing comments. But within hours they tailed off. I don't see anything about it now."

"That's weird. You'd think it would be all over the social media and the news sites."

"No, people have adapted quickly by forgetting that they existed in a dream world. The merger was just a dream that has faded away."

"I don't understand how they could forget that experience. It's like forgetting you just went through a category 5 hurricane or an 8.0 earthquake."

"The physical world is overpowering, Lydia. People are unaware that the source of their former dream lives have been absorbed into them."

"Will you forget, too?"

"I think I already had forgotten. I'm only remembering because I've tuned into you. But you will remember. So will Alex. You two are the keepers of the memory."

"Why will we remember?"

"Because you two are different, as I told you."

Her phone played several notes over and over. Harley focused on the screen again. "Oh, you better take a look. One of the other mediums sent this to me." She passed her phone to Lydia.

Lydia's eyes widened. "Oh my God." The first thing she saw was an image of herself and Alex below a large headline that read: TRAITORS! She quickly scanned the article. "Wonderful. We're wanted for attempted murder, but no mention of escape because they don't want anyone to think we were held against our will."

She looked up to see Kahil joining them on the porch. He'd overheard her comment and responded: "I was the one who shot Hector and Gogola. But I knew they would quickly recover. We bleed, but we don't die."

Harley peered suspiciously at him. "How does that work?"

"We have a built-in recovery system."

Harley stood up. "How convenient. I have a reading coming up. Nice talking to you, Lydia."

"I want to get a reading from a medium," Kahil called out. "Do you think the spirits will talk to me?"

Harley stopped. "I don't know. You'll have to find out. You can make an appointment at the desk." Harley caught Lydia's eye, a quick look, like a warning. Then she was gone.

Kahil shrugged. "Damn, I don't think she likes me."

"She probably doesn't trust you."

"Do you?"

"We wouldn't have escaped without your help. We're all grateful." *But what was that look from Harley?*

She was about to go back to her room to stay out of sight when she noticed a shiny black Suburban had pulled into the parking lot and stopped at the base of the steps leading up to the porch. The windows were darkly tinted and she sensed that whoever was inside wasn't here to talk to spirits. Without another word, she darted into the lobby.

She had to warn Alex and Kari. They had to get away.

ALEX

"I'm tired of this weird town, Daddy. Can't we go somewhere else?"

I looked up from the computer where I'd been taking notes on everything I remembered from before the shift to where Kari stood at the edge of the porch. She reminded me of a colt, coming into her own. From a distance, she looked like a young woman. Up close, she was a child, still his little girl, only twelve.

I walked over and rested my forearms on the railing. "We're probably going to be leaving soon. We can't stay here much longer."

"I'm bored."

"Do you remember what we were talking about yesterday?"

"About what?"

"The merger."

She shrugged. "You said something that I wasn't supposed to forget, but I don't remember."

She was forgetting the dream world like everyone else, except Lydia and me. "C'mon, Kari. Think." She tilted her head to the side and smiled. "Jenny says the merger sucks."

"What else does she say?"

Kari frowned. "She's very sad and now I'm feeling sad."

He placed a hand on her shoulder. "I've got an idea, Kari-Girl. Let's go hiking. I understand there's a cool trail through the woods very nearby."

"I guess. What about Lydia?"

"What about her?"

"Don't you want to be with her?"

"Right now I want to be with you. I'll get us a couple of bottles of water." I opened the door to the room Kari and I were sharing and walked over to the mini-frig in the corner. "You like her, don't you?"

"I like her all right, but I miss Mom."

"I know you do."

"I kept telling Mom I wanted to live with you after you two broke up, but she wouldn't let me."

"I know and it was probably for the best that you stayed with her. Especially after what you've gone through the past few days."

"Yeah, living with you is an adventure. But I knew you would save me from those Dominion creeps. I never gave up on you."

"I know you didn't, but we were lucky to get away, and I get it that you want to go home. I'm sure your mother is going crazy with worry."

"Can't we call her? I mean she's with the FBI."

"I told you that it's complicated, because the FBI is part of Dominion now."

"But Mom would never be with them. She hates them."

He couldn't imagine that Shara was happy about the FBI falling under the auspices of Dominion. "Kari, we'll find a way soon to get you back to her. But right now we've got to sit tight for a while. We can't make any cell phone calls. You understand that?"

Kari looked down at her feet. "I guess."

"Don't just guess, Kari. We've got to be clear on this."

Suddenly, she was crying. "I'm sorry. I called her. But I hung up real fast. I just said I'm with you and I'm okay."

Shit. That wasn't good. I closed my eyes a moment, calming myself. No sense scolding her, the damage was done. I should've known better, and taken her phone from her. "Wait a minute." Now I was confused. "How did you get your phone? Didn't they take it away from you?"

"Yeah, they did. But Kahil gave it back to me. He's the only nice one."

Nice…or was he a fucking plant, still working for Gogola? He shot them, but he knew they would recover. No wonder we got away so easily. Gogola must've suspect Harwood was a rebel. It was all about tracking down the resistance.

"I'm sorry, Dad."

"I think we better find the others. They need to know."

Just as I turned toward the door, a pounding erupted from the inside door that led to the hallway. Insistent. Like an alarm. "Alex, are you in there?"

Lydia. Something was wrong. Was Dominion already here? I opened the door and she looked terrified. "I think they found us. We've got to run."

I grasped Kari's arm, opened the porch door, and was met by two black-clad figures. I slammed the door, locked it, but more intruders barged into the room from the hallway. I barreled into them like a running back charging the line. Hands latched onto my neck and arms. Two other hands patted down my body, searching for a weapon.

I was surprised and confused to see that the men who surrounded us wore coats and ties, not uniforms. Then I saw Shara, dressed in an expensive dark pant suit.

"Mommy!" Kari shouted and hugged her.

I was so stunned to see my ex-wife that I blurted: "Sneakers? No high heels?"

"No time for small talk, Alex. We've got to get out. Your buddy Hector and a truckful of his troops are on the way."

"How do you know that? Who are these guys?"

Harwood and Jordon hurried into the room. "They're with us. They're FBI. Or now *former* FBI. Dominion hasn't turned everyone."

"That's right," Shara said, her voice riddled with urgency. "We've got contacts with others still within the agency who are helping us from the inside. Let's go."

"Where're we going?"

"A safe house a few miles away. It's a bed and breakfast and the owners are with us, an ex-Navy Seal and his wife, a retired Army captain. You'll be in good hands."

"What about Kari?"

"She'll be safer with me, a whole lot safer. Any problems with that?"

"Not as long as you can protect her."

"She'll be fine." Shara turned to Kari. "Give your dad a big hug. We're going in separate cars."

Kari reached out to me. "I'll miss you, Daddy. I love you."

"Love you too." I leaned over and hugged her. "Do what your mom says."

We hurried out in the parking lot. Shara and Kari slid into the back seat of the Suburban and the suits piled into the roomy vehicle. A moment later, they pulled away. Reggie opened the back door of the van for Lydia and me, then climbed in behind the wheel. Harwood opened the passenger door, but paused. "Where is he? Where's Kahil?"

"He was on the porch with me when the Suburban pulled up," Lydia said.

"He's not there now." Harwood ran a hand through his thinning gray hair.

"Maybe it's for the better that he doesn't go with us," I said. "I'm not so sure he's on our side."

"Look, they're coming back!" Lydia said as the Suburban pulled back into the parking lot.

The back window lowered and Shara shouted. "Don't wait for him. He's in here with us. Get out of here now!"

As the window closed, I glimpsed Kari next to Shara, and a smiling Kahil on the other side of Kari. I didn't know what to say as we got into the van. I didn't feel good about Kahil, but maybe I was just reflecting on my weeks in confinement when he was one of my captors. Yet, I remembered how he'd taken the tracking device off the bottom of the computer after we'd escaped from the hotel. If he were still part of Dominion, wouldn't he have left it alone?

"Aren't you going to follow them?" I asked.

"They're not going to the safe house," Harwood responded. "I've got the directions. It's just over in Lake Helen, not far at all."

My thoughts about the notebook computer made me realize that I'd forgotten it in the hotel. "Wait, the computer, I've got to go back to my room," I said. "I'll be right back."

"Leave it, Alex," Lydia said.

"Go ahead, but hurry!" Harwood said.

I raced to the hotel, crossed the lobby and loped down the hall. The door to my room hung open. I snagged the computer off the bed and turned to leave, but made a quick detour to the bathroom. I could literally feel Lydia starting to panic. Did I know her that well? I zipped up and dashed out. I nearly bumped into a couple coming out of the gift shop. I maneuvered around them and rushed through the hotel and out into the parking lot. The backdoor was open.

I ducked into the van, slammed the door. No one said anything. "What's wrong?"

"Turn around," Lydia said.

I looked out the back window of the van. "Oh shit." A troop carrier had stopped on the side of the road and soldiers were in the street.

"They're stopping traffic."

"Let's go the other way," I said.

"Yeah, problem is a second carrier kept going around the bend," Reggie said. "My guess is that they're doing same, setting up another roadblock. We'll be first in line."

We were screwed and it was my fault. We probably would've gotten past the troop carriers if I'd just left the laptop. "I've got an idea. Go straight out the parking lot and down that side road. It dead-ends in a park and there's a hiking trail. Maybe we can walk out of here and get to the safe house."

"I don't see any other alternatives," Harwood said. "Let's do it."

Reggie pulled ahead and just before the van descended the steep curving road to the park where I'd planned to take Kari, I glimpsed the second roadblock. "Let's hope they didn't notice us."

Dense forest bracketed the road. We arrived at a grassy clearing with a new-looking playground and a pond beyond it. We followed the perimeter road and I directed Reggie to pull into a parking spot near a restroom. A paved walkway led into the woods.

"How's this going to help us?" Lydia asked.

"I was down here yesterday. I think we can find Lake Helen," I answered.

"If we can get there, we'll find a way to the safe house," Harwood said.

We quickly abandoned the van and followed the meandering

trail. The first quarter mile featured small placards describing the history of Cassadaga. The paved walkway ended at a sign that showed a spider web of paths crossing the forest. There was no indication which trail led to Lake Helen, but we had no choice except to plunge ahead.

"I hope there're no wood ticks in here," Reggie groused.

"I'll take wood ticks over incarceration," I remarked.

Lydia took my hand and squeezed it. "Me, too."

"If they track us down here, a bullet in the head or the back is the more likely option," Harwood said.

19

At Sea

LANG

Once we admitted that we couldn't prove we were Privates Kern and Schwartz, the Dominion Coast Guard crew, or whatever they were, treated us with about as much respect as they would a couple of cockroaches. They pulled us to our feet and literally ripped the stolen uniforms from our backs. We were pushed down to our knees in front of the freezer case where bait was stored. At least, that's what my buddy Sal kept in a freezer in the identical space.

If someone walked in now, it would look like we were about to pray to the shrimp in our skivvies. But then the captain of the patrol boat took a seat on the freezer case and tossed Risa a large T-shirt to put on. Soldiers with rifles aimed at our heads framed the setting.

"My name is Captain Adolpho Mendez. You are accused of stealing uniforms. If you can prove to me that Privates Kern and Schwartz are alive and well, your sentence will be minimal. If they are dead, you will be charged with murder. Do you understand?"

I nodded, puzzled that the soldiers who had arrived at the house hadn't reported the discovery of the real Kerns and Schwartz. But there was so much chaos in Key West over the past two days that a report of a dead man and an unconscious woman, both in their underwear, might've been buried in the chaos.

Mendez ran a finger over his thin mustache. "What are your names and where do you live?"

I should've known that was coming. I didn't know what to say. Risa spoke up. "Sir, we are Privates Schwartz and Kern, stationed in Orlando. Our IDs are in our gear in Key West. We left in a hurry because of the chaos." She nodded toward Phillip. "That man is mistaken. We've never seen him until we picked him up hitchhiking. He's a deserter."

Risa's bluff failed miserably. Phillip not only had the truth on his side, but also evidence. "That's bullshit, sir. I got proof right here that says otherwise." He moved forward and held up his iPhone. "I just found a picture of the real Schwartz and Kern with a couple other soldiers. If you zoom in, you can see their IDs plain as day."

Mendez held out his hand for the phone and before studying the image gave me a stern look. That was when I spotted the tattoo on his palm. A trident inside a circle. It must mean something, I thought. *Who gets tattoos on their palm*? Yet, there was something familiar about the tat. I'd seen it in a dream. Yes, Alex knew what it was. I could almost hear him telling me a single word: *Tulpas.*

The captain stared at the image on the phone for a few seconds, then slid off the freezer, and turned to the men guarding us. "Cuff them, take them aboard and put them below deck."

I was spun around, and a moment later handcuffs strangled my wrists. "They were going to kill us. Soldiers were killing civilians all over Key West." The word rushed out of my mouth. "They pushed their way into the house. It was us or them." The captain raised a hand, halting his men. "Is this a confession?"

"I killed the man before he killed us. But the woman was just knocked out. We took their uniforms so we could get away without being killed."

"It was self-defense," Risa said. "Actually, I was the one who pulled the trigger. They forced their way into my house." She gave them her address that was no longer her address—a potential flaw in our story.

Mendez moved away and made a call. Risa and I stood

awkwardly, surrounded by armed soldiers. They were young, all in their early twenties, tense and ready for whatever the captain ordered.

After a couple of minutes, Mendez lowered his phone and stepped closer. "They're both dead, bullets to the head. Do you want to change your story again?"

"We didn't kill the woman. I swear it," Risa said.

"You will get your chance to tell your story to a judge," Mendez replied and signaled the soldiers to take us away. As we were marched out of the bait shop, a couple of fishermen were about to enter. Startled, they moved out of the way of the departing Dominion crew with their captives.

We were in trouble, deep trouble, and I couldn't think of any way we were going to get out of it. We were hustled aboard, shoved down into a tiny cabin, and told to sit on the floor. The hatch closed and darkness closed around us. The strong smell of diesel fuel made me gag.

"I'm sorry, Lang. That was stupid of me. I hate it when people lie to try to get out of trouble, but then I go and do the same thing."

"The truth sounded suspicious to the captain, and it'll get worse if he discovers you don't own that house."

"I know," Risa responded. "The problem is we don't exist in this world, and that's not going to go over well."

I desperately wanted this entire experience to be a vivid dream. Make that a nightmare. I wanted to wake up in my own bed, in my own world. I wanted to go back to writing my novel and fishing with Sal. And, yeah, spending time with Risa, but without all of the weird baggage. "Now I know how Alex and Lydia felt when they were captured by Dominion."

"That's an interesting parallel, Lang. But I've got a feeling we're not headed to a luxury resort suite."

The engine started and it was loud down here, even while it was idling. I squinted against the light as the hatch opened and a uniform with a rifle climbed down the three steps. As my eyes adjusted, I appraised our company. He was in his mid-twenties, broad shoulders, crewcut, muscular with a surly, tough-guy look about him. If he said he was a kick boxer named Bruiser, I would've believed him. He sat on a bench facing us as the boat pulled away from the dock.

"What's your name?" I called out.

"No talking," he replied.

The engine revved and we pulled away from the dock. Sunshine filtered through the hatch providing shadowy illumination that flickered as we picked up speed. I rocked from side to side and bumped against Risa as the boat pounded over waves. We hooked index fingers behind our backs, the closest thing we could come to holding hands. I leaned over to kiss her, but our foreheads collided. At least we were still together. It was about the only thing we had going for us.

There was nothing we could do but wait to see where they were taking us. After twenty minutes, the craft slowed and I guessed we were coming to another dock. I was wrong. We continued on for several minutes at a no-wake speed, which meant we were moving through a canal.

"Where are you taking us?" I called out to the guard.

"Keep your mouth shut before I shut it for you."

Nice guy. I leaned toward Risa. "This is my fault. I never should've picked up Phillip."

Risa shook her head and tried to shush me, but it was too late. The guard bounded forward. "What did I just say?"

With that, he slammed the side of his rifle butt against my face. I dropped over on my side, my cheek and jaw screaming in pain, my head spinning. I distantly heard the guard say he had no respect for anyone who killed soldiers.

Unfortunately, Risa couldn't let that go. "What about war, that's what soldiers do? They kill other soldiers."

I managed to lift my head just in time to see the guard jam the rifle butt into Risa's gut, and she collapsed onto her side, writhing in pain.

I faded in and out of consciousness, and at some point became aware that were moving rapidly again.

I lost track of time as the boat dashed out to sea. My face was hot and throbbing from the blow, and now I felt seasick as well. I struggled not to throw up. Finally, the engine decelerated. Another uniform descended into the cabin. "What did you do to those two? They don't look so good." I recognized the captain's voice. They both laughed.

I was pulled to my feet and pushed up the steps where more hands grabbed my arms. I raised my head to see where we were, but only saw water until I was turned around and saw that the patrol boat had pulled up next to a massive ship. I was guided across the deck and strapped into a steel-framed chair that was attached to a winch from the ship. Risa was bound into another one.

"I hope you two get your sea legs, because you are going to remain at sea for awhile," Mendez said. "In fact, if you're found guilty, you might never touch land again. You two might serve as examples of what happens to those who attack Dominion soldiers."

I didn't bother pleading self-defense again. My head ached so terribly I felt like I might pass out.

Mendez gestured to someone on the ship's deck. I felt a jolt and we were hauled up to the ship, where more Dominion uniforms surrounded us and pulled us out of the chairs. No one said a word to me as the handcuffs were removed. Two soldiers walked me across the deck and down a dark passageway where I was deposited into a six-by-ten berth with a cot and portable toilet. A small porthole high in the wall provided faint light. The soldiers left, the door slammed shut. A minute later, another door slammed nearby. Risa had her own isolation cell.

At least we weren't handcuffed anymore, and I was going to make use of that advantage right away. I rapped on the wall hoping to contact Risa. When I didn't get a response, I knocked harder. This time I heard the jingle of keys and my door opened. A tall black soldier shook his head. "Don't waste your time, pal. She can't hear you. She's across the walkway."

He tossed me a rectangular package. "Here, this is your new outfit, a nice clean jumpsuit. I usually tell new prisoners to put their old clothes by the door, but I see you don't have any. So you save me a trip."

When I didn't say anything, he laughed. "Just relax, man. You're on a cruise. And be glad you don't have to scrub the deck, like the grunts."

Yeah, right. Relax. Sure thing.

Unlike the soldier who guarded us on the cutter, this one seemed more amiable and willing to talk. But I was in no mood for it. My jaw ached and my cheek was swollen.

"Any chance you could get me a bag of ice? My head is exploding."

The guard swept a hand over his bald pate. "I'll see what I can do about that. You don't look so good. But our room service is a little slow, if you know what I mean." He shook the keys. "By the way, you can call me Mr. Jingles." He laughed and jingled his keys again as he departed.

I opened the package and climbed into the orange jumpsuit. The legs were several inches short and tight in the crotch. I sat down on the hard cot and carefully rested my head in my hands. Risa and I were in deep shit.

Somehow, we'd made it into this world without being absorbed into our dream counterpart. But we'd barely lasted two days on our own. Now we were prisoners at sea, prisoners in a world where we didn't belong, our future uncertain.

In spite of our predicament and the possibility of a trial at sea, my overriding concern was my inability to find Alex. I felt an ache in my heart over the loss of a part of my being. My energy was seeping away, like a slow leak in a tire. If I didn't find him soon, and Risa didn't find Lydia, we might not survive long enough to go on trial.

20

In the Woods

Hector stood on the side porch of the Cassadaga Hotel. Across the street, a dozen tourists had gathered, watching the troops as they boarded the carrier. Until he'd arrived, he had no idea that such a town, a spiritualist community, existed less than an hour away from Disney.

"Any time you're ready, sir."

He nodded, but didn't look at the young soldier. He wasn't quite ready to return to the base. He remained hopeful that someone would come forward with a new lead. Even though he suspected there was some opposition among the oddballs here, he was confident most people here, and elsewhere, believed Dominion would improve their lives and create a secure environment. That was exactly what Gogola and all the *tulpas* wanted the world to believe.

They'd been here an hour and so far all they'd managed to do was scare the hell out of the tourists and locals in this weird little town as soldiers went door-to-door with photos of Alex, Lydia and Kahil, and searched every house. No warrants needed.

The best information they'd received came from a clerk at the gift shop in the hotel who told him that several men in dark suits and a well-dressed woman had charged into the hotel from a black Suburban. After that, they'd left with several others, including a young girl, and had driven away in two vehicles. That would be Alex's daughter, the one who had made the phone call to her mother, the FBI agent. His suspicions were growing about the possible extent of the resistance.

A waitress, whose son was a Dominion army officer, confirmed the story and told him not to trust the word of any of the mediums. Many of them had predicted the take over of the planet by an alien force that was already here. So it wasn't surprising that they were wary of Dominion's intentions.

He wasn't worried about the mediums and their alien talk. But he was concerned about the appearance of the dark suits. He'd heard that one out of ten FBI agents had resigned after the agency's director publically vowed loyalty to Dominion. The dissenters needed to be tracked down and wiped out before their cause spread.

The sooner the better. The merger and the troop riots had put people on edge. But all indications were that the populace was forgetting the shift and hopefully memories of the riots would fade as well. Hector walked back to the carrier and climbed into the front passenger seat. He held up a hand, signaling the driver to wait.

He hated leaving here empty-handed. Damn that Kahil. Whenever he turned his attention to his first lieutenant, reaching out for a connection through their mental link, he heard a wall of white sound, nothing more. He'd told Gogola that Kahil had probably removed the implant from his arm in order to prove his loyalty to their cause. But now he was carrying it too far. He'd let them get away.

Gogola had promised to show him how to disperse Kahil's essence, and he would gladly do so. Yet, he wasn't willing to completely give up on him. Maybe it only appeared that he'd joined the rebels, and was actually working his way deeper inside the resistance. He wouldn't be surprised if Gogola was aware of it, even though he was not.

He motioned for the driver to move out. The carrier jerked forward, and slowly moved past the hotel.

"Hold it, stop!" A bearded man ran toward the carrier from the hotel, waving his arms. "Let's see what he wants."

By the time he reached the truck, two soldiers had leaped out, raced over, and grabbed his arms. Hector looked over the man, who was middle-aged with salt-and-pepper hair that flowed over the collar of his shirt. His beard was neatly trimmed and Hector figured the man was one of the spiritualists.

"I have some information for you. Those people you're looking for, I know where they went."

Hector told the soldier to release him. "Where?"

"Into the trail system by the park." He pointed toward the side road.

"How do you know that?"

"I picked up on it. I saw the people you were looking for. I recognized the woman from television. I knew there was something strange going on."

"What do you mean when you say you picked up on it?"

"Oh, sorry. I'm a psychic."

Hector remembered the waitress had told him not to trust the mediums. They were against Dominion. "How long have you lived here?"

"I don't live here. I'm from Cassadaga, New York, the sister community, just visiting my sister who lives here. We disagree about Dominion. Frankly, I think the other mediums here have brainwashed her. I'm glad to see what you folks are doing. The world was a mess. Are you one of them?"

"What do you mean?"

"One of the *tulpas*."

Hector pinned him with his gaze. It was odd and disconcerting to hear a human refer to him as a tulpa. But Lydia had identified them to the world just before their escape. He thought people were forgetting the dream world, that it was becoming a confusing blur, but apparently that fact—their identity as *tulpas*—had bled through. "I'll ask the questions. What's your name?"

"David Diamond."

"If you can't tell who I am, then I'm not so certain about your abilities. But we'll follow up on your hunch, or whatever you call it."

"I knew it. You are one of them. We welcome you to our world."

"It's our world, too." *Actually, it's our world, period.*

"I think I've seen this tree already twice before. I remember that broken branch," Lydia said as she paused at one of many stretches where the trail was several feet wide. "Damn, we're going in circles. How do we get out of here?"

They'd been walking for more than an hour and hadn't found their way to Lake Helen yet. Alex had admitted the wooded area was much more extensive than he'd thought. There were so many crisscrossing trails, and no directions. But they should've found at least one path that led out to a road.

"Yes, you're right, Lydia. But I'm sure we're close to a road." Harwood wiped his sweaty brow. In spite of being overweight and out of shape, he somehow maintained his poise and determination. "I thought I heard a car, and I don't remember that particular path."

Harwood pointed to an opening in the palmetto fronds, tall slash pines, and live oaks draped with Spanish moss. It looked like a dozen others they'd explored. Harwood and Reggie Jordon moved quickly forward, their shoes crunching against fallen leaves, and disappeared from sight.

Alex paused at the entrance and looked back at Lydia, now facing the opposite direction. "Hey, you coming?"

The hanging broken branch formed a triangle with the ground and the tree trunk, and she was staring through the opening to a narrow sandy trail barely wide enough for one person. They'd tried a couple paths like this one, but both had ended in a tangle of underbrush after twenty or thirty feet. There was something different about this one, though. Paw prints and a footprint were visible in the sand. Someone had walked a dog down that trail.

"Alex, look over here." She hurried toward the trail and abruptly tripped over a hidden log and tumbled to the ground. She felt a sharp pain in her ankle. "Damn it, fuck!" She pounded her fist into the ground.

He rushed over, felt her left ankle. "What happened? Are you okay?"

She could feel her ankle swelling. "Shit, I think I sprained it. Help me up."

She took his arm and pulled herself up, balancing on her good foot. She lowered her left foot gingerly to the ground, applied pressure, and winced. She hobbled a couple of steps, then hopped on her right foot until Alex moved closer. She clasped his shoulder. "It hurts, but I don't think it's broken."

"Put your arm around me and I'll help you."

"What happened?" Harwood asked as he and Jordon returned. "I heard you shouting."

"It's my ankle. Was I that loud?"

Harwood crouched in front of her, dropped his daypack on the ground. "Take your shoe off."

Lydia sat down again. "Almost forgot. We have a doctor in the house, or rather on the trail."

Harwood lifted her foot, manipulated it, and felt her ankle. "It's going to be black and blue. It's going to hurt to put weight on it, but there's no fracture, as far as I can tell." He pulled out an Ace bandage from his pack and wrapped her foot and ankle.

Alex turned to Jordon. "Reggie, did you find a way out?"

He shook his head. "We found a familiar empty plastic bottle, the same one I stepped on fifteen minutes ago. This is getting old. We need to get out of here."

At least you can walk, Lydia thought. *Count your blessings.*

The troop carrier stopped by the playground in the park. Hector got out and told the lieutenant, who was behind the wheel, to keep the troops in place. He still wasn't convinced that the psychic was telling the truth. Diamond might've approached him with his so-called vision to create distraction. If that was true, then the rebels might still be nearby.

He headed over to the restroom and stopped short as he spotted the white van that had pulled off the road and driven a few yards into the woods. He took out his cell phone and found the photo of a white van that he'd taken from the hotel video security. He zoomed in and could just barely read the first three digits on the license. *DC9.* Or maybe *BE9.*

He hurried over to the vehicle and squinted at the license plate. *DE9.* Close enough. That's it. He signaled the driver, who was standing outside the carrier. "Everyone out. Now!"

Fifty-nine armed soldiers leaped off the carrier, and assembled in front of him. "They're in there," he shouted. "Capture, no kill! I'm doubling the bonus."

The soldiers let out a hoot and rushed into the woods. He shook his head, wishing he'd told them to keep quiet. He wanted Alex and Lydia alive. He wanted them back in the Dominion media, assuring everyone that all was well.

Harwood helped Lydia put her sneaker back on over the Ace bandage. "This will stabilize it and maybe we can make a crutch out of this broken branch."

"I knew there must be a reason I stopped here," Lydia said as Jordon snapped the branch and ripped off the twigs. Hiking in the woods had never been her idea of a good time. She got plenty of exercise in her job at the television station. But that life seemed so distant now that it felt like it belonged to someone else.

The thicker end of the branch was curved at the top and fit nicely under her arm. But it was a few inches too short. "I'll use it as a walking stick. But I don't want to continue walking in circles. You guys find the way out and come back for me."

"I'm not going to abandon you in the woods with a sprained ankle," Alex said with a laugh. "No way."

"We'll find the way out," Harwood said, handing Lydia a bottle of water, then slinging his pack over his shoulder. "We'll come back for you both." The doc seemed surprisingly agile, and acted the role of the ever-optimistic hiker.

"Hey, why don't you try that path?" Lydia stood on her good foot and pointed her stick. "See the paw prints? I thought I saw a footprint, too."

Harwood shook his head. "That's probably an animal trail. It won't go anywhere."

Lydia shrugged as Jordon and Harwood headed off on another branch. "It's better than walking in circles," she muttered.

"Let's find a comfortable place to sit down so you can take the weight off you ankle."

"I suppose, but I don't want to get too comfortable. I just want out of here." They looked up as a dozen or so cawing crows flew overhead. "If we could only fly."

"Yeah, where would you fly to?"

Oddly enough, she thought she would soar directly to Risa, wherever she was. But she responded: "Out of here, and far away."

"Listen to them. I wonder if something scared them."

"They always make a racket."

She'd no sooner spoken when she heard a shout in the distance, then another. "Shit! I think we've got company."

Lydia leaned on the stick as she stood up. More voices. They sounded like they were playing some kind of game. That thought ignited the reality of their situation. They were the target of this game and gangs of young soldiers were hunting them.

Alex must've hit upon the same conclusion. He clasped her arm. "In here. Quick!" She wrapped her arm around his shoulder and hobbled down the narrow path that she had pointed out. After ten yards, they noticed a small cul-de-sac in the trail and crouched down inside it. Palmetto fronds provided a hiding place. If soldiers charged down the path, chances were they would pass by without noticing them just five feet away.

Lydia sat on the ground, knees pulled to her chest, and tried to catch her breath. Her ankle throbbed, perspiration dripped into her eyes. She lifted the hair off her neck, trying to cool down, and wiped her arm across her sweaty forehead. More shouts rang out, and now they sounded close.

"Six hundred bucks to whoever finds them," someone called out. "But you gotta take them alive."

"Christ, was that all we're worth?" Lydia whispered.

Alex touched his index finger to his lips.

She heard a rustling of underbrush. Someone was coming along the path, but from the opposite direction where they'd entered.

"Hey, I see footprints on this side trail. I'm going to check it out." The voice came from the other direction. They were closing in from either side.

Lydia held her breath as the soldier plowed into the underbrush in his rush down the path. She saw him fly past, rifle in hand. He continued on, disappeared from sight.

A few seconds later, another soldier called after the first one. "Hey, did you see anything?"

She didn't hear any response. He'd probably walked beyond her hearing range. She squeezed Alex's hand. Something about the danger and the precarious nature of their dual existence made her feel closer to him. She didn't want to admit it and it was a crazy time to even think about it, but she was falling in love with Alex. Even if everything went well and they were able to live normal lives again, she could no longer imagine life without him. But she wasn't about to tell him that.

Alex slapped the side of his neck, and Lydia swiped her hand in front of her face. The mosquitos had found them. "How long do you think they'll keep up the search?" she whispered.

"Until they figure we've gotten away. Or it gets dark."

She didn't like that idea. There was at least three more hours of daylight left. They'd be eaten alive by then.

She glanced up to see two soldiers, who looked like they were barely out of their teens, staring at them from the path, rifles aimed at their heads. One was tall and thin, the other chunky with black-framed glasses and sideburns that reached his jaw. "I think we've just made $600," Tall Guy said with a grin.

"Stay right there. Don't move," Sideburns said. He lowered his rifle and pulled out his cell phone. Instead of making a call, he snapped a photo of them.

"What are you doing?" Lydia asked as casually as she could.

"Documenting our win. Of course."

"I saw them first," Tall Guy said.

"Bullshit. We were together. We split it."

"You think this is some kind of a game? Alex asked.

"It is for us," Sideburns replied.

"Do you understand all the terrible things that are taking place in the world because of Dominion?" Lydia said.

"Fuck you, lady. I've seen you on TV talking about how wonderful Dominion is. What happened? You get fired?"

A third soldier appeared. Blond hair flowed out from under his beret. His blue eyes widened when he saw them. "Hey, what's going on?"

"We got them," Sideburns said.

"No way. You lucky bastards. Hey, where're the other two? There're supposed to be four."

"They got away," Alex said. "You're only getting $300 and splitting it in half."

Blond Boy laughed. "You told them about the reward. You fuck-ups. That's not how you take people into custody."

"I suppose you would've shot them," Sideburns said.

"No reward if they're dead," Tall Guy said.

They turned as another soldier approached from the opposite direction on the path.

"Drop your weapons, fuckers, or you're dead meat. Do it now."

"Reggie!" Lydia said under her breath. He was armed, wearing a Dominion uniform. The others looked diminutive in his presence.

When no one responded, Jordan swung the butt of his rifle into the side Blond Boy's head. As he fell, the other two dropped their rifles.

"Hey, we found them," Tall Guy said. "You can't steal them from us."

"You wanna bet? Get your asses down that trail now."

Without another word, they fled.

Jordan grasped Lydia's arm, pulled her upright, and she hopped on one foot. He handed the rifle to Alex. "I'm going to carry you over my shoulder. Ready?"

Stunned, she nodded. He crouched down, wrapped his arms around her legs and picked her up. "Let's move." He lumbered down the trail moving in the direction he'd come.

They'd barely gone a hundred feet when they heard shouts from behind them.

21

Confined

Risa rested on the thin mattress that covered her berth and, to pass the time, she imagined that she was on a cruise. She'd taken a couple of cruises with sleeping quarters that weren't much larger than this cell, and she'd paid for the privilege. But of course on those trips she wasn't confined and awaiting trial. Big difference.

She could just as easily imagine she was confined to sick bay. The blow she'd taken from the guard had knocked the wind out of her and possibly cracked a couple of ribs. Motion sickness was complicating things. Her cell was located near the front of the ship on a lower deck and she could feel and hear thunderous waves crashing into the side of the vessel. She wondered how Lang was doing on the other side of the walkway, or whatever they called aisles on ships.

Her eyelids grew heavy and she started drifting into a half-sleep. Instead of the sterile cabin, she saw herself surrounded by a warm verdant forest. She sensed fear, as if she were lost in the wilderness or under attack, and saw a web of trails and ants running along them. Army ants. What did that mean?

She heard a jingle of keys and the door opened. A deep, resonant voice greeted her. "How are you doing in here, Ms. Risa?"

She lifted up on her forearm, feeling groggy, and saw that Jingles—that was what the guard wanted her to call him—was carrying a tray with a plate of food covered with a metal top. "How do you know my name?"

"You're on the manifest." He set the tray in front of her cot. "You look better in orange than your friend. He doesn't like his jumpsuit."

"I don't blame him. How is he doing?"

"Bruce Lang is not happy about his situation, but he's feeling better after I got him an ice pack for his head."

"Are there more prisoners on the ship, besides my friend and me?"

"I'm not allowed to say." After a moment, he added: "Though some here are calling the *SS Avenger* a prison ship. That should give you an idea.'"

"How long are we going to be on this boat?"

"Don't know. That's not my department. But I'm sure there will be a trial in your future."

"At sea or on land?"

"Don't know that, either."

The idea of a trial at sea, orchestrated by Dominion, generated another image in Risa's mind: *The captain of the ship declares the accused guilty and the penalty is that you will walk the plank at sunrise.*

ALEX

I kept looking back, expecting to see Hector's troops—a gang of young thugs who had leaped off the pages of *Lord of the Flies.* I could hear them charging through the underbrush like mythical specters of the Wild Hunt, which didn't bode well. And they sounded close, but the trail weaved through S-turns and I hadn't caught a glimpse of them.

"Are you behind me, Alex?" Reggie called as he plowed ahead, Lydia dangling over his shoulder.

"Yeah, still here. How much farther?"

"Almost there."

Almost where?

Abruptly, the trail opened, turned grassy, and a road appeared. Yet we were hardly out of the woods, so to speak. We were more exposed on the road than in the woods.

Jordan apparently had other thoughts. He lowered Lydia, who hopped until I moved in and she reached for my shoulder. "Reggie, what're we doing?"

A battered Honda Accord sped toward us, stopped. Harwood motioned from the front passenger seat. Jordan quickly opened the back door and I helped Lydia climb in. She crawled on hands and knees across the seat. I was about to follow her when I heard a shout.

"Stop right there! Don't move!" Three soldiers at the trailhead aimed their rifles at us. I recognized the blond kid that Jordan had smacked with the butt of his rifle. Quick recovery. Jordan raised his hands, as if ready to surrender. But I remembered the 'game.' "Hey, no bonus if you shoot us," I shouted. "C'mon, Reggie. They won't shoot."

My comment was greeted by the crack of a gunshot and a bullet that struck the side panel above the wheel. I quickly turned and ducked into the backseat. Reggie started to follow, but the car jerked forward partially closing the door. As he opened the door, two more shots rang out and Jordan's body jerked as he collapsed on top of me. I pulled him in as best I could and the Honda's tires screeched in the sugar sand at the side of the road. Jordan's lower legs still hung out the door, and blood soaked his shirt and spread across his back like a map of Texas.

"Reggie's hurt!" I gasped.

I couldn't see who was driving. But I smelled the scent of patchouli oil, a pungent fragrance I'd noticed in the Cassadaga Hotel.

Harwood turned in his seat, his eyes wide. "Where's he hit?"

"Shoulder. Lots of blood."

LANG

After Jingles left my cell, I lifted the cover from the plate. Greasy rice and beans, a slimy-looking sausage with what looked like a couple of slices of canned beets. Wonderful. The nightmare continues, I thought grimly. Add bad food to the explosive sound of waves battering the ship and that was life locked in a tiny cell at sea.

I'd been sitting on my cot, holding the remains of the ice pack to my head when Jingles arrived with the meal. "How do you like our room service, Mr. Bruce?" he asked with a smile.

Jailers were supposed to be grim and mean, but this guy acted like an old-fashion bellhop at a five-star hotel. Well, maybe that was an exaggeration, but he seemed excessively happy for someone dealing with prisoners. "The service is fine, the food, not so much."

"Yeah, no fresh fish. We don't do no fishin' on this boat."

It had occurred to me that Jingles might be a plant, making nice in order to loosen us up with the intent of finding out who we really were and what our intentions were when we were arrested. If that was the case, we should make up a good story to account for our lack of identification or history. In that way, we were like *tulpas* who seemingly didn't exist before the emergence of Dominion. But unless things changed, I couldn't talk to Risa about anything.

My thoughts drifted to Alex, my counterpart. I wondered if he and Lydia even knew we were in their world. If so, was there any way they could help us out of this mess? Would they even want to? As soon as I asked that question, I instantly knew the answer was a resounding yes. But I also had the discouraging feeling that they were hoping that *we* could help *them.* If that was the case, we were all fucked. Our situation on this prison boat was far worse than what Alex and Lydia had experienced while in captivity in the luxury Disney hotel. But they'd fled and were being hunted. Hopefully, they'd found their way into a rebel camp of some sort, and were safe.

"I'll be back to get your plate and bring you more water," he said, and moved to the door.

"How long have you been at sea?" I asked.

"Long enough to get my sea legs, Mr. Bruce. Long enough."

Jingles was tight-lipped concerning details about where the ship was heading and what the plans were for me and Risa, or even if there were other captives aboard. But he did let me know that Risa had asked about me and that she hadn't complained about any injuries.

I was halfway through the meal when I heard a click from

inside my head. Was it related to my head injury? I looked up and the cell vanished. I was standing in a road by a car and three soldiers were crouched down, their rifles aimed at me. I shouted something about a bonus…and heard the sound of gunfire.

The scene vanished and I was back in my cell with the remains of my dinner. I had no idea what had just happened, except I sensed it was about Alex and his predicament.

Hector bounded out into the road as the car disappeared around a curve. "How did they get away?" he shouted.

"Sir, you said not to shoot. We waited too long."

Hector's head snapped around and he focused on a young soldier with sideburns and glasses. "Yes, I want them alive. But that's not the reason they escaped. Do you know why they got away?"

Sideburns looked nervous. "Because we didn't catch them?"

"And why didn't you catch them?"

"I guess because…maybe because we were arguing about the reward."

Hector shook his head, exasperated. "The reason they got away was because someone picked them up. They had help. And I bet it was someone who lives nearby, someone who drives a silver Honda Accord. Everyone back to the troop carrier. Move!"

Lydia had been so intent on the injury to Jordan that they'd gone half a mile before she realized who was driving. Then she heard the driver's voice. "Hang on, Reggie. We're going to stop and get Doc back there with you."

"Oh my god, it's you…Harley, right?

"You got it, girlfriend. How's that ankle?"

"Better now."

Harley pulled into a convenience store and parked discreetly on one side. Lydia got out, followed by Alex. She leaned on him and he helped her get around to the passenger side. "Sit on my lap, Lydia, so Doc and Reggie can have the entire back seat."

Lydia squeezed into the front seat and settled on top of Alex, who wrapped his arms around her waist. "I'll be your seat belt," he told her.

"We're just five minutes from the safe house," Harley said, then added with a laugh. "And no lap dancing, girl."

"I'll try to remember that," she said. "By the way, how did you find us?"

Harley pulled back onto the road. "I saw you all drive down to the park and knew that you were in trouble, that they'd blocked off the road. So I got in my car and told the soldiers at the roadblock that I was going for gas."

"I waited at the little store awhile to see if you would show up. Then I drove back real slow, because I sensed you all were close by. That's when I saw Doc and Reggie pop out of the woods. I guess you know the rest."

"Harley's with us, one of several allies in Cassadaga." Harwood said. "They're the reason we came to Cassadaga."

"How's Reggie doing, Doc?"

"I've slowed the bleeding. It looks like he got lucky. The bullet ripped through some shoulder muscle, but went right through and out."

"I'll be fine," Jordan said. It was just a scratch. Alex, I thought you said they weren't going to shoot."

"Sorry about that. Those guys weren't playing by their own rules."

Lake Helen wasn't much bigger than Cassadaga. It hardly qualified as a town. They passed through quickly and followed the rim of a lake on their right and an orange grove on the left. They climbed a hill, turned into a driveway, and stopped at an iron gate. Harley tapped the code box and the gate slowly opened. They passed through a tunnel of tall tropical vegetation and into a gravel parking area near a two-story wood-frame house.

"Home safe," Harley said.

"Let's hope so," Lydia answered. "Reggie and I are in no shape to run and hide."

"Why didn't we come here right away?" Alex asked.

"That was actually the plan," Harley explained. "But there were other people staying here, relatives of the owner. They just left a few hours ago."

"Let's get you in, Reggie, so I can treat that wound," Doc

said. Reggie was already on his feet, bloodied but walking.

Lydia leaned on Alex's shoulder, staggered along to the front of the house, and carefully climbed two steps to the porch. She sat down on a porch swing and gazed out over the expansive front yard that led to the lake. It felt safe here. High fence, trees and shrubbery bracketing the property all the way to the lakefront. Yet, she felt uneasy. How long would they remain safe here?

Alex sat down next to her. "It's beautiful and private. I could hang out here for awhile."

"Yeah, it's nice. But we're not on vacation. What's our future, Alex? Are we going to be on the run the rest of our lives?"

"Well, that puts things in perspective, I guess. I was only thinking about the present moment, which is a lot better than where we were an hour ago."

"True. I guess we've got to be grateful for what we've got. But how are we going to find them?" she asked in a hushed voice. "You know who I mean."

"I know. The adrenaline is wearing off. If we don't connect with them soon, I don't know if we have a future."

Harley walked over carrying a large glass bowl filled with ice and set it down in front of Lydia. "Did I hear someone wanting to talk about the future? That's my department. Maybe later on after dinner we'll get into it. I'll give you both readings."

Lydia removed the Ace bandage from her ankle. "Thanks, Harley. We could use some guidance, that's for sure."

"Stick your foot in the ice water and relax, girl."

Harwood came out onto the porch. "Reggie's resting. I cleaned his wound and bandaged it. He's going to be sore for awhile, but he should fully recover."

"That's good news," Lydia said. "What are the sleeping arrangements?"

"You're going to stay down here, the bedroom off the porch. Alex, there's two rooms upstairs, one has two beds. Reggie and I will stay in that one, you take the other."

"That's fine." He nudged her with his knee, maybe a signal that he wished they were sharing a room. She thought the same, but she wasn't about to say so.

Alex stood up. "Great. I'm going to take a shower and then grab a nap."

"Good plan," Harley said. "We'll wake you when dinner is ready. I'll see about getting some take-out from the hotel restaurant."

"Hold on," Harwood said. "Your car is compromised just like Reggie's van. They've seen it. You can't drive it."

"Oh, shit. You're right."

"You've got to stay here with us. You'll have to share the room with Lydia. It's got a king bed. It's the biggest room."

"That's fine with me," Lydia said.

"Don't worry, honey. I don't snore," Harley said.

"No problem. What I am worried about is not having a car that's safe. I don't like feeling trapped. What if we need to get out of here?"

"The owner of the house has an old SUV we can use," Harwood said. "He lives next door. His wife is making us a big tray of lasagna and salad for dinner. We've got other friends who can help out."

Harley took out a cigarette and her portable ashtray. "I hope you're not getting too many friends involved. I'm not feeling good about that."

"What do you mean?" Harwood asked.

"It's a small town, you know. Both Cassadaga and Lake Helen. Everyone's into everyone else's business. I'm sensing someone turning on us. Best to keep the friends' list small."

ALEX

I blinked, wondering what had awakened me. Then I heard a loud rap on my door, and Reggie's booming voice. "Hey, Alex, wake up in there. You're going to miss dinner."

Dinner? What about breakfast? I wondered. Then I remembered I'd taken a nap.

"Okay, I'm coming." I cleared my throat, amazed that I'd fallen into such a deep sleep that I thought I'd slept right into tomorrow.

I got up and remembered I'd taken a shower and fallen

asleep with a towel wrapped around my waist. My room was just large enough for a twin bed and a dresser. The dark blue walls made it seem even smaller. A single window overlooked the lake. I got dressed, and peered out into the dusky evening.

In spite of the pleasant pastoral surroundings, we were barely three miles from the Cassadaga Hotel and I knew Hector wasn't going to give up easily. He would find out who owned Honda Accords in the area and when he pinpointed a silver one in Cassadaga, he would know Harley had helped us. But he wouldn't find her or her car unless someone gave him a tip. That's what worried me.

I shifted my gaze and noticed a man nearly lost in the fading light and shadows. He stood near Harley's car, wore a jumpsuit, and was looking up in my direction. Probably a service person, I thought. I had the feeling that he could see me. I glanced away, oddly self-conscious, then looked back. He was gone. He probably just walked out of view, but there was something about the momentary connection that disturbed me.

I clattered down the stairs and into the dining room adjacent to the porch. The others, including Reggie, were seated and sipping glasses of wine. "We were too thirsty, Alex. We couldn't wait for you," Reggie said. His arm was in a sling and his bloodied shirt had been replaced by a t-shirt that was borrowed from someone and was tight against his chest and biceps.

"Are you kidding? What are you doing down here?"

"I couldn't keep him in the room," Harwood said. "He's not a good patient, but he's a tough guy."

"I can see that."

"You missed our toast," Harley said.

"Oh, we can do another one," Lydia said. "Fill the sleepy guy's glass, Harley."

I smiled, rubbed my beard, feeling embarrassed, and sat down next to Lydia. "How's your ankle?"

"The ice really helped. Doc thinks it's going to be okay in a day or two." She carefully poured from the bottle, stopping when my glass was half full.

"Glad to hear that."

"It's as painful as a fracture, but not as serious, and this one should heal quickly, if she can stay put and relaxes," Harwood said.

"And there's not much else we can do here," Jordan added, "other than get in trouble if we try to go anywhere."

I lifted my glass, studied it. "Didn't Harley say to fill my glass?"

"Now, there we go," Harley said. "I've got the toast. Let's all remember, in spite of our predicament, that the glass is half full, not half empty."

"Mine is both, but I'll drink to that."

"Yeah, because you can't drink the half empty part," Jordan said and let out one of his booming laughs and everyone joined him as we tapped glasses. Harwood and Harley moved off into the kitchen and returned with bowls of salad. "I could smell the lasagna warming up and suddenly I realized how hungry I was."

"We drank to remaining safe and secure here before you arrived," Lydia said.

"By the way, I saw a man from my window standing in the parking area. Does anyone know who that was?"

"No idea," Harwood said. "What was he doing?"

"Just standing there. I thought he was a service guy. Maybe he dropped off the food."

"No, the Mitchells, the couple who own the place, brought the food over an hour ago. They were leaving for Orlando after that."

"I was outside for a few minutes. Did the guy have dreadlocks and a sling?"

I laughed. "No, it wasn't you, Reg."

Harwood stood up. "I'll take a quick look, just to be safe."

LANG

Too bad I didn't have my computer. I could get a lot done on my novel while locked in my cell. Except I would be starting from ground zero. None of what I've written existed any longer. My agent and editor were probably trapped inside their counterparts, who might be car mechanics or software developers, or any number of possibilities outside the publishing industry.

I tried to forget it all. I just let it go and saw myself as an empty shell, which wasn't far from the truth. And that's when I moved into a meditative state, deeper than anything I'd experienced. I felt as if I was soaring high above the planet, through the atmosphere and out into space. Even though I was still vaguely aware that I was in my cell, I sensed that I could travel to the moon or Mars or anywhere in the cosmos. I was finally getting the hang of meditation. All it took was spending hour after hour in isolation.

I pulled my awareness back to my cell and decided I would see if I could visit Risa in hers. To my surprise, I found myself standing outside a two-story house with a front porch. It felt as if I were really there. I looked up and saw the silhouette of a man looking out a window on the second floor and knew it was Alex. I was elated and wanted to project myself right to him, but suddenly warning bells rang in my head. I knew if I moved any closer, I would be in danger of being absorbed. If that had happened, my dead body probably would've been found in my cell. With that thought, I found myself back in my cell on the ship.

I sucked in my breath and looked around. For a few seconds, I was confused about where I was. Then it all came back. For a moment, I was disappointed that I was locked away. Yet, I also felt elated. I'd escaped the cell and glimpsed Alex.

But now a feeling of dread started to overwhelm that momentary sensation of joy. Seeing Alex while out of body magnified my need to meet him face to face, and soon. If I didn't get out of here and find him, my very survival—and Alex's—was at risk. I knew the same was true for Risa and Lydia.

My only viable option for contacting Alex was projecting out of my physical body—as I'd just done—but that was way too dangerous. I needed to warn Risa, because she might inadvertently hop right into Lydia, and I didn't want to think about what that might mean.

22

Readings

After dinner Lydia offered to help with the dishes, but Harwood told her to sit down and elevate her foot. Harley, meanwhile, poured her another glass of wine, then helped Alex finish loading the dishwasher and cleaning up the kitchen. Harwood accompanied Jordan upstairs so he could check his wound.

She was hoping the wine would help her sleep, and maybe even ease the pain. She definitely wasn't looking forward to waking up in the middle of the night and hobbling around in an unfamiliar room just to get to the bathroom. Harwood had a small supply of pain pills, but she'd told him to save them for Jordan.

A few minutes later, Harwood returned and suggested the four of them finish off the bottle of wine, a magnum, that Harley had opened for Lydia. They settled back into their chairs and discussed their plans. The consensus was that they needed to lay low until the search for them let up. There was no going back to their old lives. They were rebels as long as Dominion was in power.

Harley was concerned that her disappearance might trigger additional efforts to locate them, especially since her brother from New York was staying with her and would be concerned. "He's been brainwashed like so many others by Dominion and is convinced the *tulpas* are good guys. So I have to be careful about contacting him. I just don't trust him."

"We'll work with our other allies in Cassadaga and they can

deal with him," Harwood said.

Lydia wanted to know how they could get professional video equipment so she and Alex could take up the fight against Dominion through any friendly media and the Internet. "We need to wake people up. The *tulpas* have managed somehow to convince people that they're saving us from ourselves, that under their control the world will finally be at peace."

"I've got to say, Lydia, that you and Alex did a good job at sending out that message to the world," Harley remarked.

"It was that or be killed." She sounded defensive, but didn't care. "We decided to be their public images. But all along we were trying to figure out how to rebel and escape."

"We got the message out in the end, too," Alex added. "But it didn't seem to stick."

"I'm not trying to be critical, but it was too little, too late," Harley said. "Everybody know they're *tulpas* now, but no one cares. They think they're some kind of fighting angels—fighting for humanity's future. I think that was one of your lines, in fact."

"I get that," Lydia snapped. "But we're here and we're ready to expose them for what they are about."

"I'll work on getting the equipment," Harwood said. "There are plenty of people out there who want to see you broadcasting the truth."

Jordan walked back in the room. "Emphasize how different they are from us. As any black person can tell you, people are wary of anyone who isn't a regular person. In other words, not like them. That's where you start."

"Hey, I thought you were sleeping," Alex said.

"I not going to sleep when you're down here with that oversized bottle of wine."

"So you want us to be racists, Reggie?" Lydia asked.

"I want you to tell it like it is. Those fuckers, excuse my language, but they don't have no mamas. They are *not* like us. We are all humans no matter what race. Them *tulpa* assholes, they're not."

"I think Reggie's got a point," Harley said. "They come from nothing fully developed and absorb all the knowledge they need on whatever subject they focus on. They trick us into thinking they're like us. In truth, we're just an annoyance to them. Not just us rebels, but all humans."

Harwood set down his glass of wine. "What about Kahil? Have you used your intuitive abilities on him?" he asked Harley.

"I actually tried to avoid it, Doc, but when I was near him on the porch this morning, I couldn't help picking up something about him. I can tell you one thing, he's not who you think he is."

"Let's get to the heart of it. Whose side is he on, Harley?"

"He's an unusual one, more independent than the rest. He's playing both sides because of some bigger plan. I can't see what it is, though. I'm blocked."

"But he's a *tulpa,*" Jordan said. "He must've given away our location through some kind of psychic communication system."

"Or his cell phone," Harwood said. "But let's remember that if it wasn't for Kahil, the escape plan would never have worked."

"I think I know how they found us," Alex said. "My daughter called her mother. That brought all of them to the hotel—Dominion and the rebel FBI."

Lydia processed all she was hearing and came to her own conclusion. "If Kahil hadn't given Kari her phone, she couldn't have made the call. He's clever."

"It's complicated," Harwood said. "Kahil has been helping us for weeks. He had a chance to hide in Cassadaga and wait to be picked up by Dominion. But he went with the ex-FBI group."

Lydia wasn't convinced. Kahil was like an animal, partly domesticated, yet still wild. She didn't trust him, even though he not only had engineered their escape, but apparently was a key player in the resistance. "Maybe that's right where he wants to be."

By the time the bottle was emptied, the discussion slowed and slurred. Harwood finally stood up and stretched his arms. "Now, if you would excuse me, I'm exhausted from our day of extreme adventure. I'm going to retire."

Lydia was considering doing the same, but decided to wait. Alex had mentioned during dinner that he had something he wanted to tell her later.

"I'm going to follow you, Doc," Jordan said.

Harley pushed away from the table. She'd had less to drink than the others and still seemed sober. "Lydia, would you join me on the porch?"

"Sure." Lydia caught Alex's eye, smiled, and followed Harley. Whatever Alex wanted to say to her could wait, she guessed.

Harley lit a cigarette and stared out toward the lake. Moonlight glimmered off the surface. "This would be a nice vacation home, if it wasn't a safe house for rebels."

Lydia sat down and raised her leg again on the corner of a table. "I feel much better here than I did in that Disney hotel surrounded by those creatures mimicking humans."

"Mm. I understand that. I was going to suggest that tomorrow would be a better day for a reading for you. But it turns out that we've had some activity here that leads me to believe that I shouldn't wait."

"Really, what do you mean? What kind of activity?"

"I sensed a presence right here on the porch before dinner."

"A presence, you mean what Alex saw?"

"No, not a man, not a ghost, either. A traveler. A woman. Someone who was out of body. She had a message for you."

"Message, for me? What message?"

"She said something about a merger and that she was here now. She needs your help. Does any of this make sense?"

Lydia's eyes widened. "Yes, yes it does. It was her. My…my counterpart. She survived the shift. She's here in our world and is trying to reach me."

"Slow down. What shift?"

Lydia frowned. "You really don't remember about the merger of worlds now?"

"Sorry. I don't have a clue."

"We talked about it this morning. You gave me a short reading."

Harley stubbed out her cigarette. "I remember talking to you on the porch of the hotel. But sometimes when I get plugged in, I don't remember much of anything when it's over."

She told her about the dream world and how everyone was linked to the physical through counterparts, who had dreamed them into existence. She told her how the dream world had merged into the physical world and the counterparts had been absorbed into the dreamers who were now physical.

"That sounds vaguely familiar, like a dream, or something I heard about and forgot. But it doesn't make much sense. Nobody dreamed me. I was born by my mother. I've seen the photos from my first minutes of life."

"Yeah, it happened, but in the dream world. You remember Dominion taking over all the governments, right?" When she nodded, Lydia continued. "That happened in the dream world. Once the *tulpas* achieved domination, they were able to merge worlds, to move us into the physical realm."

"Why do you know this and I don't?"

"Because Alex and I are different. You told me as much this morning. Our counterparts were aware of our existence, aware of our world, and they managed to avoid being absorbed."

"So the one who contacted me is your counterpart. Any idea where she is?"

Lydia shook her head. "No idea."

"Why did she appear to me and not you?"

"She was probably still concerned about being absorbed, especially since she was out of body."

"I'm not going to forget this time and, if this is true, as you say, the others need to know, as well. We all need to know this, and we're fortunate someone remembers. But right now let's go to our room. Let's see what I can pick up about on your counterpart and her whereabouts." She paused a moment, as if listening. "And you know what. I think I'll be getting some extra help. My counterpart is also a medium from your world." Harley laughed. "She's wondering what took me so long to wake up to her presence."

Alex was still occupied so Lydia followed Harley into their room, and pulled up a chair from the small table. Harley settled onto a cushioned armchair, closed her eyes, and adjusted her breathing so that it slowed, deepened. She remained quiet for nearly two minutes, then shook her head. "I'm not getting anything. I'm just seeing open water, blue water, sky. Tranquil, but empty. Isolation."

"What's that mean?"

"I don't know." After another long pause, she nodded her head and cleared her throat. "Okay, it's coming to me now. I see a ship. Not a cruise ship. A military vessel. I'm being told she's inside. Locked up."

"Who's telling you?"

"My spirit guides," she answered without hesitating.

"There's more than one?"

"It's a group. They work together to help us. They're giving me a name, Rita, Riva… something like that."

"Close. It's Risa."

"She's alone. But not alone. She was captured with someone else."

"Alex's counterpart. Risa called him Lang. I don't know if that's his first or last name."

"They're in trouble. Big trouble. They have no identifications. No, it's more than that—no identities. They're untraceable. They're considered rebels, and murderers, and they can't prove they're not. Under Dominion rule, you're guilty until proven innocent. They'll be tried at sea and found guilty."

"Then what?"

"Death sentence for both."

And would that also mean a death sentence for her and Alex? She heard a tapping at the door.

"It's Alex," Harley said. "I'll let him in."

"Am I interrupting something?" he asked as she opened the door.

"Harley was giving me a reading. It's about our counterparts. And it's not good."

"What do you mean?"

She told him about the reading and how Risa had appeared to Harley on the porch. "She was trying to reach me through her."

Alex looked stunned. "I think that was Lang I saw before dinner. He was standing out by the gate. Then he was gone. That's what I wanted to tell you. Do you think they're dead and now they're like ghosts?"

Harley shook her head. "No, they were out of body." She gestured for Alex to sit down on the bed and relax. "Let me see what else I can get." Harley took a deep breath, closed her eyes as she exhaled. "Okay. I'm told they did this independently. They both had experience contacting you two. So now they're each in isolation and it was natural for them to see if they could reach you again."

Harley paused as if she were listening to a voice inside her head. "They both were surprised that this time when they projected their minds to you, it was different than before. In the past, it was like clairvoyance or remote viewing, seeing at a distance. This time they were projected out of their bodies. They nearly lost contact with their physical beings and very easily could have merged with both of you. They would've lost not only their bodies, but their sense of self. That's what happening to all the counterparts. Their individual awareness comes and goes."

Lydia swept a hand through her dark hair. Her large brown eyes darted between Alex and Harley. She was impressed with Harley's abilities. "They would be like everyone else who merged into our world and were lost in their counterparts."

"Yes, I'm seeing that now. That is the lost knowledge that you two retain."

"How can we help them?" Lydia asked.

When Harley didn't say anything, Alex filled in the silence. "If they're imprisoned on a ship at sea, there's no way we can do anything about it. We can't even leave this place to take a walk without possibly attracting attention that could lead to our capture."

His comment seemed to snap Harley out of whatever mediumistic connection she'd made. Did she really have invisible guides that whispered this stuff to her? Lydia wondered.

Harley stood up and straightened out her long billowy dress. "I know, Alex. I don't like it, either. We're all stuck here." She covered her face with her hands and made circular motions as if to break a spell. "I've got to get some sleep. I'm exhausted."

Alex stood up. "Me too."

"But they left me an idea," Harley said.

"Who did?" Alex asked.

Harley shook her head. "My guides. They said that you two can do it in reverse."

Alex laughed. "*What* are you talking about?"

"Oh, you're being a smart ass now, are you? What they meant, Alex, is that you two can project out of body to your counterparts. I'm not sure what will come of it, but it's worth a try."

"I don't know how to do that," Alex protested.

"I'll teach you. You'll be surprised how easy it is once you've gotten the technique down. It's one way you can get out of this place safely. We'll work on it tomorrow and maybe we'll start by taking that walk that we can't do right now."

"But how will that help Risa and Lang?" Lydia asked.

"I don't know, but..." Harley paused as if listening again to her guides. "They emphasize that the important thing is that you two need to meet them in person."

Alex stopped by the door, his hand on the knob. "We know that. We feel it. It's like something is missing that we can't live without for very long."

"That's exactly it," Lydia said. "But it just seems impossible, especially if they're prisoners on a ship."

"Wow!" Harley said as she stared past them at something unseen.

Lydia glanced over her shoulder. "What is it?"

Harley blinked, then met their gazes. "This may sound hard to believe, but they're telling me that the four of you together have the ability to overcome Dominion."

Alex laughed. "That's another impossible thing."

Harley nodded. "I know. But that's what they said. Good luck."

PART THREE

Revelations

That a whole world of intelligent beings could be destroyed was not an unfamiliar idea to me; but there is a great difference between an abstract possibility and a concrete and inescapable danger.

- Olaf Stapledon, *Star Maker*

23

The Lawyer

She wore traveling apparel this morning, a sleeveless black silk satin jumpsuit and heels. She thought she looked particularly chic in her current appearance—deeply tan skin, short jet black hair, green eyes behind large dark-framed glasses, full lips and high cheekbones. A distinct change from her pale blond northern Euro image when she played waitress for Alex and Lydia.

However, Gogola wasn't quite ready to set off on her journey. First, she needed to attend to her maker duties—producing another *tulpa,* a single this time.

She settled on the brocade couch in the sitting room adjacent to her bedroom. Anyone entering the room from the winding staircase in Cinderella's Castle would consider it an intimate meeting place when the boss of bosses wanted a private conversation. For Gogola, though, it was her birthing room. The only exception had been when she called in Hector as an unwitting partner in the manifestation. Since moving into the castle, she had manifested ninety-nine *tulpas* and she was ready to make it an even one hundred.

She slipped out of her heels, took a deep breath, let it go along with her thoughts and concerns about the day ahead, and focused on the work at hand. Human allies in Dominion forces vastly outnumbered *tulpas.* Clearly more of her kind were needed. She took several more deep breaths and quickly settled into a relaxed, meditative state. She followed the familiar steps that she'd learned from Norbu, her creator. She chanted for several minutes to reach an even deeper state. In Norbu's method, he would then call on the power of higher beings to bring a new entity into existence.

But Gogola had her own way. She called upon *Kamadeva*, a potent god-man—her Dionysus—a sexual beast who willingly impaled her with his massive prong. It took several minutes of concentration and imagery before she sensed his presence, and succumbed to his penetration. Her head dropped back and she gasped over and over until she climaxed. She caught her breath and heard a soft click in her head and knew she was ready.

She focused her inner eye on the image of a healthy, strong male in his mid-twenties, someone who could be trained for security duties. Another five minutes passed, then gray smoke began emanating from her solar plexus and forming an oval cloud in front of her. The energy congealed and the *tulpa* took form, its features coming into focus.

Gogola raised her head. A tall, muscular young man with shoulder-length hair, tan skin, and a curious expression on his face stood naked in front of her. "So you have arrived. We have work for you."

"Thank you. I'm here to serve."

They all said that, just what she wanted them to say. She stood up, gave him an appraising look, then opened an antique wooden chest with an intricately carved top and pulled out white drawstring pants and a white t-shirt. "Put this on."

He examined the pants, nodded, and awkwardly thrust one leg, then the other into the pants, and pulled them up. He held up the t-shirt, examined it a moment, then slid his arms and head through the openings and tugged it into place. That was good. *Tulpas* who couldn't figure out how to dress without assistance usually didn't last more than a day.

She shook his hand. "Welcome to Disney World. You were manifested here, you will live here, at least temporarily, and work here with others like you."

"Who am I?"

They always asked that, too. "Let's call you Pedro Romero." She'd given Latino names to many of the *tulpas* she'd created here. "You're a *tulpa,* like many here. You'll find out more soon enough. My assistants will be here momentarily to orient you."

"What is your name?"

That was new. No new *tulpa,* within a minute of arriving, had ever asked her who she was. "You'll call me Gogola. Or you can address me as the Maker." She preferred the term Maker over Mother. That was because there was nothing genetic about the process. *Tulpas* were essentially non-organic beings, manifested from her mind. Blood and other organic matter was an illusion that vanished within minutes. The only comparison to human behavior that she could detect was the proven ability of some humans to heal themselves through meditation or create great wealth or achieve other seemingly impossible desires.

She walked Pedro to the door, opened it, and nodded to a *tulpa* named Sean, who was posted there. No point in hiding their true identities and creating false histories, she thought. *Tulpas* were *tulpas* and they needed to know that. They arrived with basic knowledge of the world and a fragmented sense of self. Standard *tulpa* programming. Most of them quickly caught on and absorbed an enormous amount of knowledge in a short time. Like humans, some were brighter than others. Some were astonishingly intelligent, or at least possessed an enormous ability to absorb and process information. Those elite, including Hector, were moved into powerful positions of responsibility. She quickly dispersed those who remained clueless to the world around them. No sense wasting energy.

With experience, Gogola had learned how to select sex, race and general appearance. Females made up only one quarter of the *tulpa* population, because that was what she wanted. But intelligence was a random factor that remained out of her control.

"You can take Pedro to meet the mid-wives, Sean. They'll be waiting for him. If he passes, he'll start immediately. Put him on my security detail, and remember to stamp him." She closed the door as the pair walked away. With that, another *tulpa* had joined the ranks. The trident tattoo on the left palm signified that the *tulpa* was mentally and physically capable.

Now she had other business that involved travel. She

preferred remaining in the Disney castle, but something significant had caught her attention and she needed to deal with it right away. She texted her pilot and told him she was on her way. Upon arriving in her armored Humvee at the new helicopter terminal on the outskirt of the Disney property, she left instructions with her driver to be ready to pick her up at 5 p.m. She wanted to be back in the castle for dinner.

She walked over to the chopper and a few minutes later, the pilot lifted off and circled about the park. She noticed that the public parking lot was half full. Just a week ago, Disney World had re-opened three days a week. It remained a combination of military base and theme park. Gogola liked it that way. If a mouse could win the hearts and imaginations of millions, then *tulpas* could do the same. Of course, Mickey Mouse never had plans to eliminate two-thirds of the population.

The chopper turned east and headed for the coast. Some of her generals were concerned about rebel movements taking root, and wanted to quickly snuff them out. Gogola knew the rise of the resistance was a natural response to major change. A small minority of the population was always willing to fight for the past, to re-establish the way things were.

The rebels didn't stand a chance, of course. In fact, it was Gogola's wish to enhance the rebellion, to give it some legs. She wanted a challenge. She wanted to show how Dominion could overcome the opposition and, in doing so, began to reduce the population. Her goal was to eliminate four billion people, and that would be a major task. It would not only require rebels battling Dominion loyalists, but multiple civil wars, genocide, and pestilence on a grand scale, a pandemic. The latter was her catastrophe of choice, since *tulpas* were immune to human infections. Her scientists were already working on a new disease that would spawn a pandemic and threaten the very existence of humanity.

Hector's lack of success in immediately catching Alex and Lydia was a blessing in disguise. Given a chance, those two would foment rebellion far and wide. They were already picking up where they had left off in the propaganda war, but now for the cause of the puny opposition.

Hector had apologized and blamed his failure on her insistence that they be captured alive. She ordered him to continue the search and to abide by the same limitation. They could kill at will, except for Lydia and Alex. Three days had passed and she wondered how he was doing.

That inquiry set in motion a rainbow-colored mental disk in her head that spun rapidly for a few seconds, stopped, then zoomed into a purple frame that connected her to Hector. He instantly recognized the contact and understood her query. *Getting closer. I'm sure they never left the area.*

Stay on it today. Tomorrow morning be available in Orlando. More later.

When they were caught, she planned public executions, knowing well that the pair would become symbols for the rebellion. Either way, captured or free, support for the rebellion would be bolstered. That just moved her plans ahead more rapidly. Joining the resistance, to Gogola's way of thinking, was the same as volunteering to be among the first to die.

She was also enjoying the notoriety Lydia and Alex were providing her. Their first broadcast revealed her as the maker of all *tulpas*, the great manipulator, the secret power behind what Dominion called *decentralized rule* in the sectors. They called her a master of disguises, capable of changing her appearance at will. In the first four hours, there were eight million views, and by twelve hours the number has risen ten-fold. Now in the second day it was expanding by a million views every ten minutes. She was quickly becoming the most famous person on the planet. And the most powerful.

As far as Gogola was concerned, everything was coming together as planned. The merger of worlds had brought about the intended reality shift. The blend initially had resulted in murderous rampages, especially by the troops. But within two days the chaos had dissipated, the transition had been complete and the dream world had faded away, as dreams do. To her surprise, the mass killings were only a short-lived topic of concern in the media. Once the streets were at peace, no one spoke about what had happened. The incidents had disappeared from mass consciousness, the same way the shift had. The focus now was on her, and that too was something she'd been preparing for.

Meanwhile, the counterparts had been absorbed, their physical lives snuffed out, their world a cosmic nightmare. Their assimilation was so complete that people didn't seem to notice that a separate consciousness was buried within each of them.

But now she'd heard a report from fifty miles off the coast, something worthy of investigation. Could it be that two counterparts crashed through the merger and survived as physical beings? If so, how did that happen, and what were the consequences? Were these the only two cases or were there more?

LANG

I'd just gotten back from my one-hour walk on the deck and was puzzling over the behavior of the two soldiers who accompanied me when I heard the jingling of keys. Now what?

Previously, the soldiers had joked that I could always escape by jumping overboard because they weren't going after me. But today they'd said very little and seemed nervous. They'd also kept to the outside as if they were actually worried that I might jump. Something had changed their behavior. As I always did, I'd asked if Risa could join me on the walk. Instead of their usual ribald remarks about how we should be in the same cell so we could make little prisoners all day, one of them had simply said, "No, it's against the rules."

Now, just fifteen minutes after returning to my cell, here was Jingles again.

Surprisingly, I was a bit annoyed. This was out of the pattern. I'd already gotten used to the routine. Breakfast and a shower. Lunch followed by an hour of walking on the deck. Dinner and lights out at 10. I'd just gotten back from my walk twenty minutes ago and I was ready for my second extended meditation of the day. With no books and no computer, I'd turned to meditation, accelerating from my earlier experiences with Risa.

After seeing Alex standing at his window while I was out-of-body, I avoided such excursions. The danger was too apparent.

I could only encounter him in person. Instead I spied on Risa. I had glimpsed her in her cell on three occasions, but she'd been unaware of me. I wondered if she'd tried to visit me.

"What's up, man?" I asked as Jingles opened the door.

"Come with me, Mr. Bruce. You are moving up in the world."

I stood up from my cot. "What's that mean?"

"You're going to a stateroom where someone wants to talk to you. That's all I can say. So don't even ask."

Maybe the 'grand inquisitor' had finally arrived to interrogate us. Up to now no one on the ship seemed in charge of gathering statements or questioning us. I'd thought Jingles might be posing as a guard in order to slyly gather information, but he hadn't asked a single question about why I was a prisoner. He'd said that the captain would take statements from us, but he was busy with other duties. I figured that meant he was conducting trials for other prisoners.

"Put out your hands. I'm going to cuff you in front. No need for ankle bracelets. You've got nowhere to run."

The cuffs snapped on and he led me down the walkway toward the rear of the ship. "Maybe I'll finally meet the captain and find out what the charges are. Is he done with the other trials?"

When Jingles didn't immediately respond, I figured I'd guessed right. Finally, he answered. "He is indeed. And between you and me, he's got a perfect record going. No one has ever been found innocent."

That was disturbing, but probably a fair assessment of the scenario in which I found myself. Jingles stopped in front of a door labeled: 137. He opened it and guided me into the stateroom. There was a couch with a coffee table in the center of the room, and two cushioned chairs on the opposite side. The room included a bed, TV and a small fridge. What impressed me most about the stateroom was the picture window and the natural light.

Before I could comment about the impressive setting, Jingles left. I heard the click of the lock in the door. I walked over to the window, gazed out, and saw a helicopter in the distance. The thumping of its rotor grew louder. I followed its movement until it passed overhead and out of sight. But the pounding sound continued, suggesting that it was landing on the deck.

I forgot about the chopper when the door opened and Jingles ushered Risa into the room. She wore the same orange jumpsuit I did, but she looked a helluva lot better in hers than I felt in mine. It even went well with her red hair. She was also handcuffed. We touched cheeks on one side, then the other, then bumped noses and laughed. Over her shoulder, Jingles grinned, then departed.

Risa pulled back, looked around. "Lang, what's going on?"

"No idea. Maybe the captain is going to take our statements. How are you feeling?"

"Better, and you?"

"Yeah, recovering. Lots of time to rest. Sorry to get you into this mess."

She shrugged. "Which mess are you talking about?"

"The current one, I guess."

"I'm not exactly enjoying our cruise, but it's tolerable. What I'm concerned about is our future."

I laughed. "I like the way you call it a cruise. That's staying positive. Sometimes I lie on my cot and try to think of the whole thing as a dream and I'm going to wake up and realize I've got a deadline on my novel. And what was I dreaming about, anyhow?"

"So you would just sit down and start typing?"

"Hell no. I would go look for you. Immediately."

She smiled. "Glad to hear that."

"Only thing is, this isn't a dream."

"Yeah. I've pinched my arm over and over and I don't wake up."

I'd almost forgotten about my out-of-body experience. I told her about it and how I'd nearly gotten sucked into Alex.

"Wow. Me too. I did the same thing when I was trying to contact Lydia. What a mistake. I couldn't get away. Luckily, another woman was there and she could see me. It was enough interference to allow me to escape."

I wanted to hug her, but the handcuffs made it too awkward. "We've got to be careful. I've continued meditating, because it helps me keep it together. But I've avoided Alex. I've seen you though."

"Oh, I've sensed you, but I thought it was my imagination. I've also sensed Lydia trying to reach me, but again I'm not sure about it."

"Didn't you try to visit me?"

"No, I didn't want to intrude."

"What?"

"Okay, I did, but not in your cell. I timed it when you were on the deck and walked with you. You and those two guards."

"Really. I'll have to keep an eye out for you."

"Yeah. Assuming we don't walk the plank today."

The door suddenly opened. Jingles must not have jingled. An attractive dark-haired woman, who looked like she was here to model a new chic jumpsuit, walked in. I immediately sensed an aura of power about her.

She smiled and started to extend a hand, but saw that we were both cuffed. Instead, she brought her palms together in front of her upper chest and nodded. "Sit down, please." She pointed at the cushioned chairs. She sat on the couch across from us. "Guard, please bring us beverages. Sparkling water for me. What would you two like, coffee, tea, soft drinks?"

I exchanged a glance with Risa. She ordered an iced tea. "Any chance I can get a beer? I haven't had one for awhile."

"Not for prisoners." Jingles sounded formal and stern.

"Get him a beer, please."

Whoever the woman was, she was clearly in charge. Jingles nodded and left. "Thank you for that."

"No problem. My name is Heather Williams. I've been appointed to serve as your defense counsel. If you prefer to hire a private attorney, you can do so and I'll turn over whatever information you provide. Now can you tell me what happened?"

I told her our story, leaving out the matter of our identities. But that was what she wanted. "Who are you?"

"We told them our names. You should have that much. I'm Bruce Lang, this is Risa Ferraro."

Williams crossed her arms and seemed to stare right

through me. "Those were the second names you provided. First, you were wearing Dominion uniforms with the names of two soldiers who were murdered in Key West."

"Like I said, I killed one of them. In self-defense. Several soldiers entered the house just after we left. They probably killed the woman. The troops were on a rampage."

"Do you know the charges against you?"

"No, because nobody says anything to us." I glanced at Risa. "At least not to me. The guard took my fingerprints the first day. That was it."

Risa nodded. "Same here."

"You are charged with first-degree murder and theft of government property. It doesn't look good."

I barely heard what she said. I was staring at the picture window where I saw a man staring at me. The light was behind him and it was difficult to make out his features. But there was no place to stand outside the window. No ledge, no porch. The man stabbed his index finger at Heather Williams, whose back was to him. He shook his head and I heard a voice inside my head. *Don't trust her.*

"So what can you do for us?" Risa asked. "It was self-defense. We were attacked."

"It will help if we can verify your identities. You didn't have any IDs with you. Your fingerprints didn't show up on any data base and your names don't match any records. Neither of you own that house in Key West. The owners were not renting it to anyone."

The man in the window shook his head, then touched his index finger to his lips as if telling him to say nothing. His features came into focus. Full beard, ruggedly handsome with strong features, and I realized I was staring at Alex. "Yeah, that's a problem. You're not going to find anything." As I spoke, it occurred to me that we hadn't seen any identification from her, either.

"Why not?"

The man in the window faded, but I could hear his voice. *Tulpa…tulpa. Danger, danger.* "Uh, do you mind, could I see your palms, please?"

She smiled, turned up her hands. No tattoos. "I'm not hiding anything from you."

I pressed on. "Can we see your ID?"

Her eyes narrowed, anger flashing through them. "You're in no position to ask me to prove who I am. I'm providing you free counsel. You should be grateful. Without my help, you probably wouldn't get off this ship alive."

"I thought we were going to get a trial," Risa said, looking alarmed.

"Oh, you will. The captain will be the judge. The evidence will be presented. You'll be found guilty and get the death penalty. It's very easily applied at sea. You become shark bait."

"What's the alternative?" Risa asked.

"I know the captain. I can get you off this ship. You'll be in Dominion custody in the Disney World military base."

"Is that any better?" I asked.

"Much better. I can't stay here and your trial could be at any time. So you'll be on your own. But I'll be readily available as your counsel if you're at Disney."

I looked over at Risa. She nodded. "I think it's a good idea, Lang."

"Me too." In spite of Alex's warning about our lawyer, I couldn't help thinking that back in Florida we'd be closer to him and Lydia, closer to finding them. Ultimately, that was all that mattered.

I met Heather Williams' gaze and for a moment it appeared as if her dark eyes had flashed pale blue. Maybe it was an optical illusion. "Why are you doing this for us?"

"Because a defense lawyer tries to do what is best for the client. You are better off on land in a military base than out here. Have you seen any other prisoners?"

"Not a one."

"That's because there are no other prisoners. They've all been found guilty and tossed overboard."

I didn't trust this lawyer, if that's what she was. I sensed a hidden agenda. But she made a good point. Staying here was not an option. One way or another, it was a death sentence.

24

Off the Ship

Risa wanted to brainstorm with Lang to see if they could come up with a story about their identities. But that wasn't likely to happen as long they were in the air. She was seated on the floor in the luggage area of the chopper, handcuffed to a railing. Lang was cuffed on the opposite side.

A Dominion soldier sat on a fold-down bench a few feet away. He wore headphones to block out the prop noise and communicate with the pilot, and seemed content to leave them alone. They weren't going anywhere and couldn't talk to each other without yelling and attracting his attention.

She played with different ideas, even considered amnesia, but couldn't figure out how both of them would lose their memories. The lawyer was going to insist on an answer. The truth definitely wasn't an option. Not only were their counterparts on the run, but she and Lang weren't even supposed to exist separate from them. Besides, Heather Williams probably wouldn't know what they were talking about. But the *tulpas* might, and if that information got out, she had no doubt they would be killed instantly. Besides, it was all too complicated. They needed something simple.

Finally, after a three-hour flight, the chopper landed. The guard released her from the railing and handcuffed her wrists in front of her. He did the same for Lang, then slid the side door open and guided them down three steps to the pavement. A police car and two uniforms waited for them. They were quickly escorted into the backseat and strapped into place.

"I've got a plan," he hissed. But before he could explain, one of the cops slid into the front passenger seat. The driver quickly joined him. She leaned toward him. "Whisper it to me."

Before Lang could respond, Risa heard a sharp tapping on the front passenger window. The cop lowered the window and Heather Williams leaned in. "I need to speak to my clients privately for a moment, officers."

Several seconds passed. The cops exchanged glances with one another and finally grudgingly got out. In the few moments of confusion, Lang whispered: "We tell her we were drugged by the soldiers who captured us on Big Pine. We can't remember anything about ourselves."

Amnesia, she thought. They were on the same page, and at least he had an explanation.

Heather slid into the front seat. "I've got good news. A soldier has confessed to killing that woman in that house where you were staying in Key West. She came awake screaming next to a dead man when soldiers entered the house. One of them shot her in the mouth to shut her up."

For the first time in several days, Risa felt a ray of hope. "Where does that leave us?"

"I'm going to talk to the judge tomorrow in a pretrial hearing and see if I can get the charges dismissed, considering mitigating circumstances."

"That's great," Lang said. "Will we be in court with you?"

"Yes, but for this to work, I need your identities. That's especially true since you are being accused of stealing someone else's."

"That's a problem. We can't remember who we are," Risa said. "I know that sounds strange, but..."

"We were drugged by a soldier in Big Pine Key. It was after we were thrown into the hold of the cutter that took us out to the ship," Lang said.

The lawyer gave them an exasperated look. "Unbelievable," she muttered. "Okay, so we have a Jane and John Doe. What's your profession, Jane?"

"I don't remember anything about my past."

"Same with me," Lang said.

Without another word, Heather Williams exited the car and signaled the cops that she was done. She poked her head through the window once more. "So you can remember what happened at the house, but you don't remember who you are. I'll give you a night to think about it. The prosecutor will want to take your statements before court in the morning. Maybe you'll remember by then. If not, there are some less than pleasant methods of extracting personal data from prisoners that the authorities might decide to try. You should be aware of that." With that, she walked to a white SUV with darkly tinted windows. The driver's side of the vehicle showed a smiling Mickey Mouse head and the words: "Welcome to the Magic Kingdom."

The cops re-joined them and pulled away from the helipad. A couple of minutes later, they cruised onto the entrance lane of the interstate. "Where are you taking us?" Lang asked. "I thought we were staying around Disney World."

The cop behind the wheel laughed. "You thought wrong. You two are spending the night downtown in your respective drunk tanks. It should be an interesting night for both of you."

Why didn't he think of this yesterday? Hector wondered as his driver eased the Jeep into the parking lot in front of the Cassadaga Hotel. He'd been so intent on finding the vehicle that he'd overlooked an important clue.

He'd retreated to Cassadaga after the escape and within minutes found out that a medium named Harley Diamond owned an old silver Honda. He was sure it was the one. He immediately contacted local authorities, who put out a BOLO on the vehicle. Photos of the wanted five were distributed to the media, and their pictures were shown on news alerts every hour. A reward of $10,000 was offered for any information leading to an arrest. So far there hadn't been a single worthwhile lead and he assumed his prey had fled the area to another hideout.

During the night, Hector had awakened with the word *Diamond* ringing in his head. The man who had told him that the escapees were hiding in the woods had been right, and he'd mentioned a sister he was visiting who was a medium. His last name was Diamond. Hector knew it was his last chance to track down his prey. Gogola had a new assignment for him.

He walked up the steps of the front entrance to the old Mediterranean hotel, moved into the porch and spotted Fran, the friendly waitress, on a cigarette break. He smiled at the middle-aged woman whose dyed blonde hair was tied in a short ponytail. "Do you remember me?"

"Of course. I see on the news that they're still missing. They're not hiding here, or I'd know about it."

"Maybe somewhere nearby. Do you think the mediums know where they are?"

"The mediums? Like they all know the same stuff? I don't think that's the way it works. This place ain't no bee hive. It's more like the bees fighting the wasps. Lot of in-fighting, if you know what I mean. But to answer your question, if any of them know, they're not telling me."

"How about David Diamond, Harley's brother?"

"He's an outsider. Some of the ones here question whether he's a real medium."

"He told me they were in the woods. He was right."

"How do you know he didn't see them drive down there?" She pointed toward the end of the porch. "Look, you can see the road that goes down there from here."

"Have you seen him today?"

"He had breakfast in the restaurant. Look in the gift shop. He likes the woman who works there."

"Thanks."

She dropped her cigarette, ground it out with her foot, then picked up the remains, and tossed it into a coffee can by the door. "If you ask me, they're long gone."

Fran was right about where to find David Diamond. The burly, bearded man stood by the counter talking to a dark-haired woman who was a decade or younger than he was. Hector glanced around at the glass shelving with displays of crystals and a variety of polished stones, jewelry, a few books, angel figurines, and bottles of herbs, candles and incense. When Diamond spotted him standing by the door, Hector stabbed his thumb toward the lobby. Diamond quickly excused himself and joined Hector in the lobby.

"Your sister is in big trouble, David."

"I was expecting you. Harley is probably being held against her will. I know she drove that getaway car, but she didn't know what she was getting into. She wasn't involved with those people. No way."

Hector wasn't so sure about that, but he needed help from Diamond. He nodded. "I'm sure we'll take that into consideration, but right now we need to capture the rebels before they cause more trouble."

"I think they're close by. I can feel Harley's presence, but she's blocking me. She's good at that. Always has been since we were kids."

When Hector didn't say anything, Diamond continued: "Let me show you how I work. Then you'll see for yourself. Let's go to my room."

Hector followed him down the hall. Diamond chatted away, unaware of what was about to happen to him if he didn't find the hideout in the next few minutes. "I get the monthly rate here, not the daily. I couldn't afford that. And they let me do some readings. So it works out well for me."

"Why don't you stay with your sister?"

"I did for a couple of weeks. But I'm sensitive to smoke and she's like a smoke stack. The house always has a haze." He opened the door of a room at the end of the hall. "It doesn't affect her, but my lungs can't take it."

The room was small and quaint, a vision of the past. But Diamond had a window that looked out to the side porch and the spiritualist camp beyond it. Besides the bed, there were a couple of straight-backed wooden chairs, a bedside table, and a tacky metal closet. The place was apparently constructed before built-in closets.

The closet door clanged as Diamond opened it and removed two L-shaped rods with handgrips. They were about eighteen inches long, ending with a small ball at the tip. "Dowsing rods, of course," Diamond said. "It's one of my psychic talents. I've found archeological artifacts, mineral deposits, lost objects, lost people. Here, I mostly use them for ghost hunting. I've been taking groups out on Friday evenings."

Hector crossed his arms. "Is that how you've been looking for your sister?"

"It's the best way for me. I'll try it again. Maybe I can finally break through." He set the rods down at the end of the bed and unfolded a map, one of several on the bedside table. He spread it out on the bed and Hector saw it was a map of the entire state. "First, we'll find out if she's still in Florida." He made a circular gesture above the map with his index finger.

"Yes, they're still nearby somewhere."

Hector picked up one of the rods and noticed how it moved from side to side with the slightest movement of his hand. "If you can use your finger, what are these for?"

"That's for getting specific, down to the street." He turned over the map to reveal another one that only showed Volusia County, where they were now. Diamond took the rods, held them up, and they swayed from side to side. "They've got ball-bearings in the handles. That's why they're so sensitive."

"How do you know that you're not making the rods move?"

Diamond laughed. "You'll see. The side-to-side movement is only one of the attributes. Just watch." He held the rods over it, closed his eyes, and took a couple of deep breaths. Nothing happened.

After a minute he opened his eyes and nodded. "Okay, I'm ready to find Harley."

Immediately, the rods, which had been remarkably still, started slowly opening out to the sides, then closing in again, over and over. Finally, the two balls at the tips touched and the movement stopped. Hector wasn't impressed. "What's that mean?"

"It indicates that I was right. They are here on this map."

"But where specifically?"

"That's what we'll look for now." He took another couple of deep breaths. Hector noticed that his shoulders were relaxed and his eyes fixed on the tips of the rods. Thirty seconds passed when the tips of the rods came together, then bent upward, away from the map. Abruptly, they sprang apart, then back together. Diamond seemed to be fighting with the rods, pushing down as they bent upward.

"See this? She's pushing back on me, blocking me. He dropped the rods on the bed and they crackled against the map. His head dropped toward his chest, as if the effort had exhausted him.

When he looked up, he gasped, wrenched back, and raised his hands. Hector aimed his Glock at Diamond's forehead. "I'm taking you into custody."

"For what?"

"Suspicion of hiding the location of wanted terrorists."

"No, that's not true. I don't know where they are."

Diamond stepped toward Hector and eyed the gun. He stood six inches taller and fifty pounds heavier than Hector. He looked like he was about to lunge. "Back off or I'll blow your brains against the wall." Diamond hesitated, then moved back, hands still raised.

"We'll talk about it in Orlando. And take your dowsing rods and the map. You may get another chance to prove yourself. Now move!"

Risa didn't know what was worse, the isolation cell on the ship or the downtown Orlando drunk tank. At first, she was the lone prisoner. But a couple of hours later, she was joined by two women, both drunk and belligerent. She assumed that Lang was in a similar cell in the men's section, and probably with more company. She claimed a cot in one of the tiny cells that bordered the bullpen, and stayed there, ignoring the other two, who were arguing and cursing.

But after awhile, one of the women came over to her corner. She raised a thick arm and motioned toward the other woman and, slurring her words, started explaining how the other woman had called 911. Blah, blah, blah. Risa tried to ignore her, but the woman persisted until another drunk arrived. This one was younger, barely twenty-one, and crying. Risa felt sorry for her, but when the puffy-eyed blond saw Risa staring, she shouted: "Don't even get any ideas, you bitch. I'm not looking for a girlfriend. So fuck off!"

It was going to be a long night. She gradually dozed, but woke up as another drunk, then another, joined them. It was shortly after one o'clock when Risa realized someone was standing next to her inside her cell. She sat up and pulled the thin blanket close to her.

"What do you want?"

The woman didn't reply. She looks familiar, mid-thirties, dark hair, attractive, bold Latin features. "Lydia? Is that you? What are you doing..." Risa realized she could see the bars of the cell behind her. She wasn't really here. *Am I dreaming?*

I'm here with you. Don't worry. We'll get you out. With that, she vanished. Risa collapsed back down on the cot. Was it a dream, wishful thinking? She didn't know.

Jane Mackey had been Orange County chief of corrections for just six months when Dominion stormed the world. She'd assumed the post on her fifty-second birthday and became the highest-ranking black female in county government. She thought it was all over when Dominion took control. But not much changed. She still reported to the county administrator and the county commissioners. They in turn dealt with Dominion.

But now, for the first time, a Dominion officer was in her office waiting for her when she arrived at 8:15. The slender, deeply tanned man with a ruddy complexion and a wispy goatee was watching CNN on her television. She had no idea who he was and her first impulse was to lift him out of her chair and toss him out. She didn't care if he was wearing a Dominion uniform. She had her own uniform. At six-feet tall and one-eighty-five, the former sheriff's deputy had no doubt she was could handle the scrawny-looking soldier. But when she noticed the five stars on his shoulder, she hesitated. Then he held up his palm, showing her his *tulpa* insignia, and she immediately backed off.

Be nice, be courteous, and give him whatever he wanted. Hopefully, he would leave soon. He pointed at the television screen on her wall. "Have you seen this yet?"

She focused on the bearded white guy who looked like a hostage. He was giving a statement. The *tulpa* held up her remote and froze the frame. He handed the device to her. "Rewind it and watch it from the beginning. The man in the video, David

Diamond, will be escorted here in about ten minutes. I want you to take him to a quiet room where he can attempt to locate his sister using these dowsing rods and the map. He pointed to the items on her desk.

She had no idea what he was talking about. She'd heard of dowsing for water, but not sisters. "Anything else?"

"Yes. I need an interrogation room so I can interview two of your current guests in the drunk tanks. They were booked as Jane Doe and John Doe. I'm going to find out who they really are."

"I'll get them right up here for you. They'll be in room 213 down the hall to the right. Then I'll watch the video."

Hector abandoned her chair. "I'll let you get to work."

LANG

After one of the more miserable nights of my life, I was escorted out of the drunk tank at 8:30. I tried to remember what we'd told the lawyer besides the lie about amnesia. I was groggy and so damn tired it would be way to easy to spout the wrong thing. About all I had going for me at this point was that I didn't have a hangover like my roommates.

"Where are you taking me?" The guard, a surly guy with a potbelly, didn't reply. Apparently, in his mind, prisoners didn't deserve responses to their questions. "I guess you hate your job."

"I guess you should shut up."

"When I was a detective in Monroe, I liked going to work. Everyday was interesting. I also tried to be friendly and even tempered, even when people were acting like assholes."

"You don't know your name, but you know you were a cop."

Oh, shit. There I did it. Lack of sleep and I start flapping my mouth. "You think I'm bullshitting you?"

He didn't reply. We walked down a concrete corridor with jail cells on the right and a wall on the left with tiny square windows ten feet up that no one could see through. At the end of the corridor, the guard unlocked a steel gate and we passed through a screening room where the jailhouse guests were photographed and fingerprinted. The second gate required hitting a buzzer and someone on the other side to unlock it electronically.

We stood there waiting silently for more than a minute before the guard spoke up. "What's your fucking name? And don't tell me John Doe."

"I don't know."

"Some detective you would make."

The gate groaned and slid open, and the guard silently guided me down an industrial-grade carpeted hall to a locked door. He opened it and I stepped into a room that was barren except for a table and three chairs. He followed me in, told me to sit, and started to cuff me to the table.

A voice came over a loud speaker. "No need for bracelets, Sam."

The guard shrugged, put away the cuffs, and left the room. I look up and spotted a camera in one of the corners. An interrogation room. I was facing another effort to extract my real name. Fun. I folded my arms and used them as a pillow on the table. Within seconds, I started drifting off. I never took morning naps. At least, not until now. All it took was a night in the drunk tank.

I could still hear the voices calling out, muttering, cursing, screaming, crying, pleading. One guy slurred the same thing over and over. *Easy for you to say…easy for you to say.* Endlessly. He didn't even seem aware he was in the drunk tank. At least on the ship, I was able to sleep, except when large waves crashed against the port side.

As my mind drifted, I glimpsed an image of Risa. I wondered if she had already been interrogated and what she'd said. I mulled over what I'd blurted to the guard, and suddenly I made up my mind. I knew what we needed to say.

A couple of minutes later, the door opened and I raised my head. I expected to see the lawyer, Heather Williams. It was Risa. Even with mussed red hair and bloodshot eyes, she looked as attractive as ever. A female guard who fit easily into a triple extra-large uniform stood behind her. When Risa saw me, she brightened, came over and sat down across from me. The guard retreated and closed the door.

"What a night, Lang." Her voice sounded husky.

"I know. It was rough, but worthwhile. My memory came back. I know who we are." I spoke loud enough so anyone listening in could hear me clearly.

"What?"

I looked up at the camera. "If anyone's watching, we're here and ready to talk to our defense attorney."

Risa's eyes widened. She leaned forward and whispered: "Who are we?"

"I'm Bruce Lang. You're Risa Ferraro. Do you remember now?"

"Oh, yeah." She lowered her voice again. "We already tried that."

"This time we need to tell the truth. We're not from around here."

"Are you serious?" she muttered. "They'll stick us in a mental hospital."

I leaned closer. "Our lawyer seems to have a lot of power. She got us off the ship. That was good."

"Yeah, and into the drunk tank."

I whispered, leaning on my elbows, my hands at the side of my mouth. "The important thing is that she said she can get the murder charges dropped if we have names. Let's cooperate and see what happens. Maybe she can get us out long enough so we can disappear."

Risa didn't seem convinced, and I didn't blame her. We were taking a risk.

The door opened and I looked up to see a wiry man with salt and pepper hair and a goatee walk into the room. I instantly recognized him as Hector, the Dominion general. I'd last seen him during meditation before the shift just as Alex and Lydia were escaping. He'd been shot in the chest and had looked dead. But not anymore.

25

Crunch Time

Hector eyed the pair as he claimed the chair at the end of the table. Murder suspects with no IDs. They looked harmless. They'd probably been defending themselves, like they said, against the rampaging troops. He was annoyed by this assignment and was ready to believe their story about why they'd stolen the uniforms. What was so damned important about finding out who they were? He brushed off the lapels on his uniform, and wondered if they even knew what the stars meant and that they were being questioned by Dominion's top-ranking general. Recently demoted to regional commander, he thought. He couldn't shake the feeling of betrayal.

This was Gogola's idea. Probably punishment for not catching the rebels. But why had she gotten involved? Maybe because she loved to change her image and play different roles, and this one was her latest—the defense attorney for John and Jane Doe. He wondered if creating *tulpas* was driving her insane. Not only did Hector think Gogola was wasting her time, but now she was wasting his. She was getting out of control and something needed to be done. The sub-makers could continue with manifesting tulpas, if she wasn't doing it any longer. He quickly quieted those thoughts.

He'd been close to nabbing the rebel broadcasters, who were putting out Internet videos faster than Dominion was taking them down. Except for the one on Gogola. She actually liked it and crowed about it when it went viral. The attacks wouldn't be so bad if they weren't produced by the former pro-Dominion mouthpieces. That pair needed to be silenced and soon.

Right now he needed to finish this charade and get back to catching the rebels and stomping out the resistance—at least in his new domain. "I have some questions for you before you go to court."

"Who are you?" Risa asked.

"I'm with the court."

Lang looked skeptical. "What does that mean?"

"I'm representing the prosecution. It would be worthwhile for you to cooperate if you want the murder charges dropped. You told your guard that you used to be a detective in Monroe County. Very interesting, but not true. I just checked."

"How did you do that without a name?"

"We've got fingerprints, and they didn't match anyone who ever worked for Monroe. They don't match anything. You've never been fingerprinted, neither one of you. That's very odd. What are you, aliens?" Hector glanced up at the camera and laughed. "But I'm told that your memory is coming back just in time for court. How convenient."

Risa leaned forward. "We're not answering any questions until our lawyer gets here."

"That won't be possible. She's not available."

"We'll wait," Lang said.

Hector touched the Glock on his hip. A bullet in each of their heads would take care of them, but Gogola wanted answers. "She will be in court to represent you. This is very simple. All I need is your names and addresses. Nothing incriminating about that." Their sour expressions said otherwise.

Lang pointed up at the camera. "We already said our names. I'm sure they're recorded."

Hector jerked out his pistol and jammed it against Lang's head. "What is your fucking name?"

"Bruce Lang."

"Thank you." He aimed the barrel at Risa. "And yours?

"Risa Ferraro."

"That was easy. Where do you live?"

They gave him their addresses. Hector holstered his gun and typed the names and addresses on his cell phone. He stood up. "I'm going to check these names and addresses and they better be valid."

"You won't find our names on any records associated with the houses," Lang said.

"So you're renters. Doesn't matter. There should be plenty of information available about you both. If you're not telling the truth, I will end this investigation with a bullet in each of your brains. We don't have civil rights like the old days. Not with the rebels aiming to destroy the government."

Lang and Risa exchanged a look and Risa spoke up. "Don't waste your time. You're right. We are aliens. Our names and addresses come from another version of this world."

"What does that mean?"

"I think you know about the merger of worlds during the shift," Lang said. "Everyone seems to have forgotten. But I bet you didn't. I know from your stars that you are a high-ranking officer, but I'm more impressed by the tattoo on your palm."

Hector clasped his hands on the table. "You're saying that you're from another world."

"That's right. The world that was real until the shift. But we didn't merge with our dream selves. We came here as we are."

Hector took a few moments to digest what he'd just heard. Now he understood Gogola's interest. He tried to hide his anger, knowing that she might tune into his thoughts. But his emotions had their way. *Why didn't the Maker bitch say so?*

"How did you do that?"

"We don't know," Risa said.

An even more interesting question came to mind. "Who are your counterparts?"

"We don't know that, either," Lang said.

He could tell they were lying. He had ways of extracting information and he would have fun with this attractive redhead. A tap on the door interrupted his thoughts. "Yes. What is it?"

Jane Mackey filled the doorway. "Mr. Diamond insists on talking to you right away. He says he knows where they are."

Hector nodded. "Thank you, chief. I'll be right there."

He stood up. No more time to waste here. He would deal with them later, but first he would see what Diamond had to say.

"When do we go to court?" Lang asked.

Hector stopped at the door. "I don't know. Ask your lawyer." He laughed and left.

LANG

The red light on the camera faded away moments after Hector left the room. I wanted to tell Risa who our interrogator was, but held off. Revealing that I knew his identity would be saying too much. It could easily tie us to Alex and Lydia. "They still could be recording everything," I said under my breath.

Risa nodded, but didn't seem too concerned. "I hope that wasn't a mistake. But I guess we had to say something." She leaned forward and whispered: "You know who that was, don't you?"

I shook my head and lifted a hand, hoping she would read it as a stop sign. "No, I don't know," I said in a louder voice. "A general, I think."

She grimaced and leaned back. She'd caught on. We couldn't talk, not about what mattered.

She shrugged. "I wonder what happened to our lawyer. She doesn't really act like a lawyer."

"How so? I thought she was pretty good. At least until she didn't show up today."

"Yeah. Almost too good." She looked like she wanted to say more, but held off.

The door opened. The black woman who had interrupted Hector was back. The guard who had walked me here stood behind her. "Okay, you two are coming with me."

"Are we going to court?" I asked. "We haven't seen our lawyer yet."

"You're being placed in a holding cell for the time being. We'll see what happens next." She seemed like the boss lady here, but she also seemed clueless about why we were in her building.

Lydia was still half-asleep when she got up at seven-thirty. Harley, an early riser, had already vacated their room. Her ankle was still tender and she hobbled to the bathroom. But she could put weight on it now without feeling any sharp pain. She showered and put on clean clothes that Harley had left on the bed for her. Clothes that Harwood apparently had gotten from somewhere. Jeans, a pale lavender cotton t-shirt with *I've got spirit,* written across it. The clean clothes felt wonderful against her skin, even if they didn't fit quite right. She wrapped Harwood's Ace Bandage around her ankle and put on her running shoes. She ran a brush through her wet hair, and limped out onto the porch.

Everything looked the same. Quiet and peaceful, the yard sloping down to the lake, the sun rising, birds singing. She brushed off an underlying feeling of tension that crept into her reverie.

She could smell coffee and figured that Harley or one of the others was getting breakfast ready. She would like to sit out here with a cup of coffee, but she should make an offer to help with the breakfast. She turned toward the door to the dining room just as it swung open.

"Oh, Kahil!" Wearing a baseball cap, jeans, a short-sleeved shirt. "What a surprise. How did you get in here?"

"I honked and Dr. Harwood opened the gate."

When she was at the Disney hotel, he would greet her with a smile, eyes gleaming, and chirp: *Hola chica.* This morning he looked serious, his casual demeanor gone. "I was just going to wake you. Harley is too upset right now."

"What's going on?"

"You better come inside."

He held the screen door open for her and she saw the others were seated at two tables, coffee cups in front of them. The television on the wall played a morning news program, but the sound was low.

"They've got my brother," Harley said. "They're threatening to kill him if I don't turn myself in."

"Oh Christ, that's terrible." It meant their hideout was no longer safe. She knew Harley wouldn't sit here and let her brother die.

"Turn up the sound," Alex said. "They're playing it again."

Harwood raised the remote control. A bearded middle-aged man with swollen eyes was talking into a camera and he looked terrified, just like every other captive she'd seen making a statement under duress. "We need to stop this rebellion before it gets out of hand. Let me repeat. Harley, if you're watching, please give yourself up. Call 911 and tell them who you are. Unless you turn yourself in by 10 a.m. this morning, they're going to kill me."

The image vanished, a broadcaster in a studio appeared. "That was David Diamond, brother of Harley Diamond, who is with a group of dangerous terrorists being hunted by forces of United Dominion. David Diamond was kidnapped yesterday by a group of radical Dominion supporters and, as you heard, they are threatening to kill him if his sister doesn't come out of hiding."

"That's Hector's work," Kahil said. "He's the one who kidnapped your brother."

"Harley, what're you going to do?" Lydia asked.

"I don't think I have a choice."

Kahil interjected, "I don't think they're going to kill him as long as they think David can use his abilities to find this hiding place."

Harley looked at Kahil, her face flushed, tears streaming down her cheeks. "I don't know what information you have, and I don't know what you're doing here, either. But I'm listening to what my brother is telling me. I'll give myself up, and everyone else can get away."

Harwood patted the air. "Now, just hang on, Harley. We've got a couple of hours. Obviously they don't know where we are or they would be here by now."

"That's right," Kahil said. "We're safe for now. I have a car here if we need to leave quickly."

Lydia stood up. "I'll scramble some eggs for everyone. I hope we have time to eat."

"I'll help," Alex said.

As she prepared the eggs and Alex made toast and sliced cheese, Lydia told him about her dream. "I made contact last night, Alex. I got out of body. I really did. And I found Risa. They're not on the ship. They're in Orlando. They're in the corrections center. I recognized it from stories I've done from there."

She glanced around to see Kahil standing in the kitchen doorway. "You're talking about your counterpart from the other world. Am I right?"

"Yes, but how did you know?" She slid the large iron egg-filled pan off the burner and turned it off. "I'm aware you and Alex didn't absorb your counterparts. I see energetic bodies. All *tulpas* do. You too became different than other humans after the merger."

"Really? You can see how we're different?" Alex asked.

"The energy around you is lighter, less dense. Also, you know about counterparts and the shift. That's not common knowledge. Not anymore."

When neither of them responded, he added: "You also both know that you're not going to survive much longer unless you find them. I can help you. Come with me now. I'll get them out of jail. You will all be together and something wonderful will happen. I am sure that it will."

Lydia remembered Harley's wariness about Kahil, that she'd sensed there was something hidden and deceptive about him. Lydia felt the same. Kahil was so different from other *tulpas* they'd encountered, and she couldn't tell whose side he was on or what his real agenda was.

Alex didn't trust him, either, and expressed his reservations. "You're right, we want to meet them, and soon. But if you're helping them escape from jail, I don't think Lydia or I should be anywhere nearby where we could get caught if your plan backfires."

"I agree with Alex," Lydia said. "If you can get them out of jail, bring them here."

He looked disappointed. "It would be easier if you came with me. I don't think you can stay here very long."

Alex glanced at her. "What do you think?"

Nothing good. She was feeling more apprehensive by the minute. "Kahil, why are you doing this? Why do you want to take such a chance to help two people escape from jail, who you don't even know?"

"I understand your feelings, but I do know about them. I know their importance. That's all I can say."

It wasn't enough, she thought. It felt like a trap. She shook her head, "I don't want to go."

"I'm staying with Lydia," Alex said. "Good luck."

Without saying anything else, Kahil turned and left, the porch door slamming after him. He crossed the yard and headed for the gate. She and Alex stood on the porch as he drove away.

"Where the hell is he going?" Jordan asked from behind them.

"He's on a mission, Reggie," Alex said. "Let's hope it's a good one."

Hector found David Diamond pacing around a small waiting room outside of Mackey's office, his shoulders twitching nervously. "Good, you're here. I found them." His map covered a coffee table and his rods rested on the center of the map, the tips pointed toward a small red circle on the corner of a lake.

"Where?" Hector stepped closer and the blur of lines came into focus.

Diamond stabbed a finger at the circle. His fingernail touched the corner of the narrow lake. "They're in Lake Helen. In a house by this lake and right at the intersection of two roads. One goes by the lake, the other passes the side of the house."

Hector pulled out his cell phone and hit a number for the Volusia County sheriff, whose deputies were involved in the ongoing search for the fugitives and Harley Diamond's Honda. He studied the map closely, and waited for Sheriff Stone to pick up. "General Hector Gomez here. We've got a lead." He described the location of the house.

"I know exactly where that house is," Stone said. "It used to be a bed and breakfast until some Yankees from Vermont bought it. They rent it out by the week or month."

"I want a perimeter set up around that house within fifteen minutes. I've got a chopper on the roof ready to go. I'll be out there shortly."

He ended the call and turned to Diamond. "You better be right."

"I want my sister cleared. She's not one of them."

"Yeah, you told me. But I don't see her turning herself in to save your ass."

"They're probably holding her captive."

Hector motioned toward the door. "Let's go. You're coming with me."

Diamond snatched up his dowsing rods, but left the maps. They moved down the hall at a quick pace and Hector created an image of Gogola in his mind's eye. He silently called out to her. Moments later, a flash of light followed by an internal clicking sound alerted him that their mind-link was open. He told her what he was doing. *I'll assess the situation and get back to you.*

Take them alive. What about my clients, the nameless ones?

Not nameless any more. I'll bring your clients to you after we catch the others.

"No, it's already being handled.

By who, he wondered as they reached the stairway at the end of the hall. But she'd already closed the connection. At the top of the stairs, they pushed open a door to the roof where the chopper and troops were assembled.

"We'll find out how accurate you are very soon, Mr. Diamond. And for your sake, I hope you are *very* accurate."

26

Escapees

ALEX

I stepped out onto the porch from the dining room where the others were still gathered, and glanced at my watch. Kahil had been gone forty minutes. He should be at the jail by now. Maybe even on the way back.

He'd left in a huff, not even telling the others what he was doing. Lydia and I had tried to explain, but we were both drained of energy. We were fading fast. I felt like I was talking underwater. It was a complicated scenario that didn't make any sense to them, except for Harley. But her mind was occupied and she didn't join in the explanation about the merger and counterparts.

She was ready to surrender in the hopes of saving her brother. But once she was in the hands of Dominion, we couldn't stay here. Meanwhile, CNN continued playing the video of David Diamond over and over again with a countdown to his execution now just an hour away.

An SUV with a sheriff's logo on the door pulled up to the gate. "Oh, shit." I darted across the porch, threw open the door. "There's a cop car at the gate. What are we going to do?"

"Get in here," Reggie snapped. "Fast."

"Hey you! Hold it there!"

I looked back. A uniform stood at the gate. I'd hesitated too long. If I ignored him, it would look suspicious. Maybe he was looking for the owner of a lost dog.

I met Reggie's alarmed gaze, then turned toward the cop and walked along the porch toward him. "Can I help you?"

"Doc Harwood, where is he?"

Now what, do I give him up? Is he fishing, or does he know Harwood is here? Before I made up my mind, the door opened and Harwood came out. "What's going on?" he called out.

The officer, a tall muscular man in his mid-thirties, wore a vest, as if he thought he might be fired on. But his weapon remained holstered. He motioned for Harwood to come closer. "Everyone out. Now! This place will be overrun with cops in less than five minutes."

"You know him?" I asked.

Harwood nodded. "That's Dawson. He's one of us. C'mon, let's go."

We piled into the back of the SUV, through the open lift-gate. The seats had been folded down so we crawled forward on hands and knees and laid on our bellies and forearms.

Harley hung back, watching. I craned my head. "C'mon, Harley, there's room. Hurry. We gotta go."

She shook her head. "I'm staying. I want my brother freed. I'm surrendering."

"Tell them you were held prisoner," Harwood said.

She nodded and closed the lift-gate. We pulled away and I took one more look back. I didn't feel good about leaving Harley, but there was no time to argue.

Chatter on the radio told us that several cars were about to descend on the place. The cop swung off the main road and followed side roads out to the highway entrance. Traffic was slowed to a crawl on I-4. "Damn, they got a roadblock up already," Reggie groaned, cradling his injured arm.

"We can still turn around," Lydia said.

Dawson shook his head. "It's too dangerous to go back. We're going through. Unfold that blue tarp back there and cover up,"

Just before I pulled the corner of the tarp over my head I heard the thumping rotors of an approaching helicopter and spotted a black military chopper as it passed overhead.

LANG

We were stuck in adjacent holding cells, waiting to be transferred to the court for our appearance before a judge. We had no idea how that would go, especially if our lawyer didn't show up. We couldn't see each other, but we could talk. I was feeling weaker by the minute, but tried not to focus on our dire situation. "I wonder what our counterparts are doing. I bet we're not too far from them."

"Far enough, if we're locked up," Risa responded.

"We're going to find them. I don't know how, but it's going to happen. I can feel it." I was surprised by the confidence in my tone. Ever since we'd realized that we were in another world, my driving urge had been to find Alex. If anything, the urge had intensified. Nothing else mattered. Except Jennifer. Somehow, I had to rescue her from this counterpart nightmare, but I had no idea how I would do that.

"I'm glad you're so positive, but I don't think we can last much longer," Risa said.

When I didn't reply, she said, "I wonder if our lawyer's going to show up."

"If she does, it won't be as our lawyer. You were right in your suspicions about her."

"Why do you say that?"

I knew they might be recording our conversation, but I didn't care anymore. "I figured it out after I saw him, Hector, the general. Our so-called lawyer used to be a waitress..."

"What, no! Oh, shit. I think you're right, Lang. It *is* her. The fucking god-mother of all *tulpas*."

"Exactly."

"But how did you know she was playing waitress?"

"From Alex, I guess. In fact, I think I saw him in the window up there in the stateroom. He was pointing at her and warning me not to trust her.

"What can you tell me about him right now?"

I thought a moment. "Fear. He's in trouble. They're coming for him. He's got to get out right now. He wants to find me as much as I want to find him."

"How are you getting that?"

"I don't know. It's just an impression. I feel it."

"I'm getting something similar from Lydia. She has hope now. She knows we're in this building."

A man's voice from outside the cell suddenly spoke: "Those are bleed-throughs."

"Who's there?" I heard a soft scuffling sound, then the voice again, louder this time. "You two better watch what you say."

A shadowed figure stood in the hall outside our cells. He stepped forward into the light and raised a palm, revealing the *tulpa* trident tattoo. When he lowered his hand, I saw pale blue eyes, white hair, an ageless face. I didn't know whether to be overjoyed or fearful.

"You're Kahil."

"Good guess, Lang."

He held up a set of keys, then unlocked our cells. We stepped out, not certain what was about to happen. "Are you the one taking us to court?"

"I'm the one getting you out of here. No time to talk. Stick out your hands." He held up a pair of white plastic handcuffs.

Cuffed again, we moved down the hallway, turned a corner, and hurried after Kahil. What was the rush? This felt more like an assisted escape than a transfer to a courtroom, and why would Kahil be taking us to court? I wanted to believe, hell, I needed to believe, that he was taking us to Alex and Lydia. I was feeling weaker by the hour, and I knew Alex was feeling the same.

We reached the first black steel gate and Kahil unlocked it. It slammed closed behind us with an ominous clang. We moved toward the electronic gate. Kahil pressed a button that triggered a loud buzz. A minute passed before the pot-bellied guard, the one who'd informed on me, stepped up to a counter across from the gate. "What's this about?"

Kahil, who wore a dark suit instead of a Dominion uniform, straightened his tie. "I'm transferring these two prisoners to military custody at the Disney base."

"Let's see your transfer orders. And your ID."

"There was no time for the orders."

"No paperwork. No release."

Kahil held up his palm, showing the Dominion tattoo. "This is the only information you need. I'm taking these two prisoners to the commander-in-chief of Dominion, who wants to personally question them. If you hold me up for more than another minute, I will see that you will be relieved of your duties. You'll be lucky to get a job checking parking meters. Do you understand?"

He hesitated and, for a moment, it looked as if he was about to let us out. But then he changed his mind. "I'll have to check with my chief." He tapped a series of numbers on his cell and quickly explained the situation. He listened and nodded. "Okay, I'll tell them."

He ended the call and pressed a button. The gates spread slowly apart. "Chief Mackey is releasing the prisoners to your custody as long as you're not taking them to Disney World for the rides."

Kahil considered the question. "You can tell her there's no time for Mickey Mouse, but the fun is just beginning."

We exited the corrections center under Kahil's guidance. In spite of his seemingly heroic effort to get us out of jail, I remained wary of his intentions. I was also annoyed and embarrassed. After so many years working as a cop and detective, I hated the idea that I was out in public in handcuffs like a criminal. My crime and Risa's, however, were unique in the category of b&e's. We remained under arrest essentially for breaking and entering into this world. But how much longer could we last here?

As we crossed the parking lot, I puzzled over Kahil's arrival. "How did you know we were here?"

"Lydia found Risa in jail."

Risa suddenly stopped. "I saw her briefly standing in front of me in the drunk tank. I thought I was hallucinating. I made an effort to find her, too, and ended up on a porch somewhere."

"I know that porch. You were in the right place."

None of this explained what Kahil was doing here. My suspicions were bubbling over and he sensed it. "I'm here because you two and your allies are key to defeating Dominion."

"How do you know anything about us?

"Let's keep moving," he said.

He led us to a black Suburban Lexus with government plates above the rear bumper. "Did you steal this vehicle?"

"It's on loan from renegade FBI agents." He opened the side door.

"Where are we going?" Risa asked.

"Get in and I'll tell you. We're in a hurry. Both of you, in the rear. Let's make this transfer look official."

Risa slid in and I followed. Kahil started the engine and we drove away. Out of jail, but I didn't feel free.

"I was going to take you to the safe house where your counterparts were waiting for you. But plans have changed. Now we're going to a gas station at the Sanford I-4 exit."

"Are you saying Lydia and Alex will actually be there?" Risa sounded overjoyed.

"That's the plan."

ALEX

The car slowed as we approached the roadblock. Beneath the tarp, I reached for Risa's hand.

"Okay, nobody move, nobody make a sound," Dawson said.

I felt warm air flowing in and the road sounds grew louder. Voices, cars peeling away from the roadblock, the smell of the pavement.

A voice from outside. "Hey, what're you doing out here, Dawson?"

"Checking on you, asshole. Do you know who you're looking for?"

"No, we're just stopping cars, looking for hot babes. Of course we do, bitch. We got pics of the five, the ones that have been on the news. Three men, two women. Not many vehicles with that combination."

"Keep the photos handy. They could be split up."

"Hey, are you going to help or just sit there and give orders? What the hell you got in the back there?"

"A delivery."

"Oh, yeah. What kind?" The voice sounded closer. I could imagine feeling the suspicious cop's breath against the back of my neck, through the tarp.

"Fully auto weaponry from Dominion. I'm supposed to take them to Orange County headquarters."

"Let me see this shit." I heard metallic clicks as the outside cop tried the side door, pushing the button on the handle. Locked. Thank God.

"No way. They're not for us."

"Are those bastards out here again?"

"Dominion? Hey, don't bad mouth our soldiers. The army is the army. Right?"

"Oh, look who's sounding self-righteous now. Are you okay, Dawson?"

"Hey, catch these terrorists and you won't see Dominion around here. I gotta go. See ya."

We gained speed and I slowly lifted my head. "Are we clear?"

"You can take off the tarp, but stay low."

"That was close," Lydia said.

"I'm taking you to Sanford. Then you're going to switch to a private vehicle."

"Where to from there?" Harwood asked.

"Don't know, and don't want to know. I'm doing my part for the cause, but I'm trying to keep my head down at the same time."

"That's fine," Harwood said. "We need you to remain safe on the inside."

"You saved our asses," Lydia said.

Hector was outraged. He stood in the dining room of the rebel house hovering over the Diamonds, who were seated at one of the tables and looking scared and extremely uncomfortable. Harley had surrendered when the first patrol car arrived, but she hadn't given up a thing about the rest of the rebels. If she knew where they were headed, she wasn't saying. She'd claimed she was in the house when they left and didn't see the vehicle that took them away. He didn't believe her.

"You say you weren't one of them, but you picked them up and drove them here."

She crossed her arms defensively over her ample bosom. "They blocked the road and said they had a gun. I was afraid, and after we got here they wouldn't let me go home."

"Why did they leave, Harley?"

"They thought it was too dangerous. They saw David's video."

"What did they do, call a cab?"

"No, like I said, someone came to pick them up. I don't know who it was."

"Were they waiting for the ride?"

She thought a moment. "No, they seemed surprised and didn't know who it was at first."

"So the rebels were tipped off."

"I don't know."

"What kind of vehicle was it?"

"A dark-colored SUV. I didn't get a good look at it."

It was too coincidental that their ride came just minutes in advance of the assault on the home. But who in the jail would know that David Diamond was dousing for rebels? Was it Jane Mackey, the chief of corrections? He didn't want to believe that the rebel cause was gaining that much traction. She had too much to lose. Who else could it be? Could a renegade sheriff's deputy have had time to get them out?

He straightened up in his chair, fingers curling into fists. There was one other person and he was seated right in front of him. These two were both psychics as well as siblings. The bastard had sent her a telepathic message. That had to be it.

"I've had enough of you two today and your fucking mind games." He pulled out his Glock and pointed it at David Diamond's forehead. "Where are they going, Harley? Last chance."

"I don't know." She choked back a sob. Let me...try to... to see." She shut her eyes, adjusted her breathing. After a few moments, she choked back another sob. "Okay. I...see they left in a police car... an SUV. They're...moving south. On I-4, I think. Going to a gas station. Lake Mary or Sanford."

"Too vague," Hector barked. "Give me an intersection."

She shook her head. "Shit…shit, I don't know. I'm not good at…at reading addresses."

"Try harder," Hector said.

"Okay… Sanford, I think it's Sanford, a gas station right off I-4. The first one."

"You're just guessing, Harley."

"Let me try," Diamond piped in.

"Oh, really, you think you can find them?" Hector lowered the gun. "No, I don't think so. You're too slow with your dowsing rods. They'll be gone before you figure it out."

He raised the Glock and shot Diamond in the forehead, turned and jammed the barrel right in Harley's open mouth and fired.

He left their slumped bodies, the mess of blood and bone, and walked outside. At least a dozen patrol cars with flashing lights lined the road. He found the burly sheriff standing by the gate, talking with a couple of detectives. "Sheriff Stone, the terrorists were aided by one of your deputies. They're headed in one of your SUVs to a gas station right off I-4, Sanford exit. Get them."

"I'll radio Seminole County. They can have officers there in two or three minutes."

"Good, and when you're done with that, call the fire department and tell them to burn down this house."

Stone frowned. His red cheeks brightened. "We haven't finished the investigation. Why destroy the house?"

"The investigation is over. There is no need to gather any more evidence. I don't want anyone to go inside. You burn it down from the outside. This is a military-ordered action against a terrorist threat."

He would wait to make sure the sheriff followed his orders. He turned away and softly whispered Gogola's name. He immediately glimpsed an image of her in his mind's eye and quickly related what had happened. He didn't tell her about killing the brother and sister or his plans to torch the house. But she knew, of course, and wasn't pleased about it.

Keep your focus on the rebels. We don't win minds and hearts with collateral damage.

He couldn't help thinking about Gogola's plan to dramatically reduce the population. How would that win mind and hearts?

That will happen in the appropriate fashion. The survivors will understand that it was a necessary cleansing. Not so with your fire. Get back here as soon as the rebels are captured.

LANG

As we sped along I-4, I was impressed by the lack of road noise. After the constant battering of waves against the ship and the racket aboard the helicopter, we were actually traveling in sequestered silence and could hold a conversation. But I was too exhausted to talk. Risa, who was slumped in her seat, looked pale and sick. I probably looked the same. Everything was riding on our rendezvous with Alex and Lydia.

After a few minutes, I finally spoke up. "Kahil, where are we going after the gas station?"

"The plan is another resistance safe house. But let's first see what happens when you meet your allies from another world. My guess is that there won't be any need for a safe house."

Risa sat up. "Really? Why's that?"

"You asked me before how I know anything about you. *Tulpas* can see energy. When I saw Alex and Lydia after the merger, they were energetically different from everyone else. I knew that they hadn't absorbed their counterparts from the other world. The question was what happened to them. When a couple turned up on the radar, who had no IDs and no backgrounds, Gogola took an interest. And I tuned into it."

Now I had questions. "You said we could defeat Dominion. Were you kidding? How is that even possible?"

"It's an energetic matter. This world is not as stable as it seems, and Gogola knows it. A single person who doesn't belong here, an independent entity, combined with that person's counterpart, could create a dynamic shift of energy and disrupt the stability of this world. Multiply that by two and who knows what might happen."

"But you don't want Dominion destroyed, do you?"

"Oh, but I do."

What possible benefit could he see in disrupting this world? The *tulpas* were in charge. "Why?"

"I have my reasons, Lang. One more mile." Kahil shifted into the right lane and raced up to the exit. "I hope they haven't been waiting long."

ALEX

I was feeling more hopeful when we finally left the interstate and pulled into the gas station where we would switch cars. I could just imagine Kahil pulling up in that black SUV he drove this morning and we'd find that he had two passengers—Lang and Risa—waiting for us. I didn't know what would happen, but I had to see Lang, face to face, not just as a voice in my head. I was even glad that I'd trimmed my beard this morning. Maybe I'd somehow known this was the day and I'd unconsciously made myself more presentable.

Dawson turned into a Shell station a quarter mile from the interstate and eased up to a pump. "Can we get out now?" Lydia asked. "It's kind of uncomfortable back here on our bellies."

"Hang on. When the car pulls up next to me, I'll hit the automatic lift-gate. You climb out, get right into your new ride, and I drive away."

Suddenly, I started to panic. "What if the other car doesn't show up?"

"I'll wait five minutes. If it's not here, you go inside like you're buying some stuff. Just watch for someone looking around for you."

"That doesn't sound very good," Jordan said.

"Sorry, but I'm already taking a big chance."

We were five minutes away from being abandoned. "Do you know who's coming?"

Seconds after the words were out of mouth, a car raced up to us, pointed at an angle, then another in front of us, and a third behind us. Two patrol cars arrived, filling the gaps. Headlights and top lights flashed in an array of colors. A voice on a mike ordered everyone out and down on the pavement.

"Oh, shit!" Dawson groaned and slammed his fist against the steering wheel. "That fucking Kahil. He turned on us."

Uniforms and plain clothes poured out of the cars. There was no escape. The lift-gate opened and we were dragged out feet first. Within seconds, I was on my belly, cheek to the pavement, my wrists cuffed behind my back. Jordan howled in pain as his arm was yanked from the sling and twisted behind him. I lifted my head and saw Dawson, his hands cuffed behind him, led to the backseat of one of the cars. Apparently, he would be dealt with separate from the rest of us.

Our chances of ever finding Lang and Risa were diminishing rapidly. I felt as if I were drowning and needed to get to the surface to breathe. I wouldn't last much longer. Our time was just about up.

27

Back to Disney

LANG

"We are late."

That was all Kahil said as he drove slowly past the gas station. From the road we could see several bodies face down on the pavement, surrounded by cops.

"Fuck! After all this?" I groaned.

Risa choked back tears.

Behind us a deep horn blared. A camouflage military vehicle that looked like a combination of an oversized SUV and a tank pulled into the gas station and several Dominion soldiers leaped out. Kahil continued on a quarter of a mile and swung into a McDonalds. He quickly made a U-turn and headed back toward the interstate. As we passed the gas station, we saw the cops retreating as the soldiers loaded the captives aboard their vehicle. I momentarily glimpsed the back of the head of a man as he was shoved forward and wondered if it was Alex.

"Now where to?" I asked.

"There's only one option. We're going to Disney World."

"What?" Risa cried out.

"I'm sorry. But that's your only chance now. That's where Alex and Lydia are headed."

"How're we going to find them?"

"I will take you in as captives, and hope for the best."

"Do you think Gogola will put us in the same cell as Lydia and Alex?" Risa asked.

"No, not a chance. But she will have some plan of her own for the four of you, I am sure."

ALEX

I had no idea it would come to this…this insanity. What was the point of these costumes, just to embarrass us? I was drenched in sweat, barely able to move, but I had to keep walking. Lydia was lagging behind and there was nothing I could do to help her.

After we were captured and cuffed, we were gagged, blind-folded and forced to lie in a fetus position. I'd gotten a glimpse of Dominion troops and their machine when one side of my blindfold slipped down. One of the soldiers immediately adjusted and tightened it.

Lydia was bundled next to me and I assumed Reggie and Harwood were also squeezed into the rear luggage compartment of the vehicle. Several minutes passed as we huddled together unable to talk, barely able to move. I could hear muffled voices outside, and the sound of cars pulling away. I knew Lydia was next to me by the smell of her hair. I nudged her with my foot and she responded with a knee to the back of my thigh.

Doors slammed as three or four of our captors climbed in. Finally we were moving. We quickly picked up speed and I knew we were back on I-4. I was disoriented and couldn't tell which direction we were headed. Maybe we would end up downtown in the correction center. Maybe Lang and Risa would still be there.

I realized how far my life had descended. I was actually hoping that I would end up in the drunk tank. And, if Alex was there, what would we do, stare at each other? Would I really feel any better in his presence? Even if we were both revitalized, we would still be captives.

Traffic slowed and I knew we were near downtown. But we didn't take the exit. After crawling along for several minutes, we gradually accelerated until we reached speed, and I realized the correction center wasn't at the end of this journey. We continued on for nearly half an hour before making a series of turns and came to a stop. Doors opened and slammed, and I heard a few sharp exchanges, as someone issued orders.

The hatch opened and we were dragged out. I heard a helicopter and more voices around me. It wasn't hard to figure out that we'd ended up in Dominion's Disney World. I was hustled about fifty feet and pushed against something metallic. A gravely voice said, "Take two steps up, turn to your right, and sit."

When I hesitated, I was shoved and stumbled my way onto a cushioned seat. "You want water?"

I nodded and the guard pulled off the gag. A plastic water bottle was pushed against my lips. I gulped a couple of times, then gagged, and water spilled over my chest. "Where are we?"

"You're in a golf cart, and you're about to get a ride."

"To where?"

"To hell no doubt."

I figured I'd be locked in another cell to await a kangaroo court, but the madness was just beginning. After a short ride, the guard guided me out of the golf cart and over pavement, either a walkway or a parking lot. A door opened and I was pushed inside. I stumbled and dropped to my knees. I heard the others stumble in after me.

"Okay, get them ready."

I instantly recognized Hector's distinct nasal tone, and remembered the first time I'd seen him a lifetime ago in Merida where this nightmare had begun for me. He stood directly behind me. After listening to him for weeks in the hotel, I would never forget that voice, high-pitched for a man, but low for a woman. When I first encountered him, he'd spoken English with a Spanish accent. But as we'd talked at the airport his image changed from an old beggar to a man in charge and his English gradually lost its accent.

The blindfold and gag were yanked away and I blinked and saw that I was in a large room with the others who were crouched on the floor. Hector had moved over to Lydia, removed her blindfold and gag. She stood up on her knees and our eyes met. Hers were wide, terrified. Plastic cuffs still bound our wrists behind our backs. A soldier stood behind her, his rifle poking into her back. The barrel of a rifle sank between my shoulder blades. Hector continued over to Harwood and Jordan.

I looked around. This place reminded me of a locker room with benches, a row of lockers, and on one wall an enormous closet. It was partially open and I could see hanging costumes and the heads of creatures resting on a shelf. It must be where the people who played the Disney character got dressed.

Hector directed the soldier to lift us onto our feet. I saw that Reggie's face was cut and bruised, his injured arm hanging useless at his side. Harwood had a cut on his brow, the blood now dried. Hector paraded in front of us as if inspecting his troops.

"You're not looking so well. You're going to clean yourselves up and get ready for some fun." He smiled at me and nodded. "You ready for that, Alex?"

"What kind of fun would that be?"

He pointed at me, then Lydia, Harwood and Jordan. "Mickey, Minnie, Donald Duck, Goofy. Get your costumes on. It's time to entertain the crowd.

Hector watched the rebel betrayers fumbling with the costumes. The guards stood by poking them in their backs with the muzzles of their rifles. Hector, finally took charge and ordered two of the soldiers to stand down and help them into the costumes. He couldn't imagine why Gogola thought this was such a wonderful idea. He was just carrying out her directives, and no longer felt that he was on the inside of her circle of power.

Don't worry, Hector. I haven't abandoned you. I have some good news for you about Kahil.

Once again Gogola was tuning into his private thoughts. That never was a problem in the dream world. But now with his new emotional awareness, he hated the intrusion. His thoughts should be his alone.

He is bringing in the outsiders, the ones who weren't absorbed. I want you to go out and meet them.

So Kahil had been working with Gogola all along. Again, she responded to his thoughts.

No, he's defective. He doesn't know if he is a tulpa or a human any longer. He must be eliminated. Now you will have a chance to learn how to disperse his essence.

That made him feel better. That skill would be very useful in the future.

Minnie Mouse stumbled and fell. A guard pulled Lydia back to her feet. Hector shook his head. "Let's get them outside. Disney security will take over." They were going to look like a bunch of drunk Disney characters, he thought, and hoped there was a reason for this craziness.

Oh there is, Hector. There really is.

LANG

As we approached Disney World, I had a difficult time grasping what I was seeing. But Kahil summarized it perfectly as we approached the first check post. "What we have here, Mr. Lang and Ms. Risa, is a post-apocalyptic theme park. Part military base, part entertainment complex."

Most of the vast acres of parking had been converted into a military encampment. Yet, visitors in limited numbers still came to the theme park after being selected through a lottery process. "There are no long lines anymore," Kahil continued as we drove down a roadway bordered by tents and makeshift buildings. We stopped at a second checkpoint and Kahil flashed his palm and said, "Executive parking." The guard told him to wait and disappeared into a nearby prefab building. A black chopper rested on a pad a hundred feet from the building.

I leaned toward Risa and we exchanged a quick kiss. "Not much foreplay with handcuffs on."

"That all depends," she answered with a smirk.

"Good one. How are you feeling?"

She shrugged. I knew what she meant. I was convinced we had only hours left. Our sparks of life were burning low, our batteries were running down into single digits. We needed to be re-charged and there was only one way that could happen. "When did you last see Alex and Lydia?" I asked Kahil.

"This morning. I left their safe house to find you."

"How did they seem?" Risa asked.

"Anxious, just like you two. They know their time is limited."

"Why the hell didn't you take them with you?" I asked.

"I invited them, but they refused. They're like you two. They don't trust me, because I don't act like other *tulpas*."

"Do you think Gogola will let us meet them?"

"That is yet to be seen. As I've said, she's unpredictable."

The guard emerged from the building followed by a familiar face. Kahil made a grunting sound when he saw him. "That man wants to kill me."

Before I could reply, Hector opened the back door and slid in next to me. He nodded at me and smiled at Risa. "We meet again."

"Hello, Hector. Or do you prefer I call you General Gomez?

"Call me whatever you want, Lang. Drive ahead, Kahil. I'll show you where to park. Then we'll go see Gogola. I'm sure she'll have some surprises for us," Hector said with a laugh.

ALEX

So now Lydia and I and the others were meandering around Fantasyland in the Magic Kingdom, trailed by non-uniformed guards with side arms hidden under sport coats. Apparently Hector didn't want to frighten the kids away with armed soldiers following the costumed characters. But I knew this insanity wasn't Hector's idea. Gogola was behind the charade. That was her M.O.

Hector had guided us out here and told us to interact nicely with the kids, that he would be getting reports every few minutes. Then he'd walked away. Gogola might be crazy, but she wasn't dumb. She had some plan for us in mind, but I had no idea what it was.

We were outside of Ariel's Grotto near a huge statue of Neptune holding a trident, a symbol linked to Dominion. I'd seen it too many times on the left palm of *tulpas*, and it made me angry to see it. One of the guards was shooting a video of three kids hugging Minnie Mouse. I was surprised Lydia was still on her feet. I was about to collapse. We'd been out here nearly an hour and the costume was cumbersome and hot. But that wasn't the only problem. I felt disconnected, as if I wasn't fully in my body. I could literally watch myself weakening. For a few moments, I would find myself floating above Mickey, looking down on the scene, then I would snap back into my body, into Mickey, as if waking up.

Now the kids were looking my way. They two boys and a girl, about eight or nine, maybe one of the boys was ten or eleven. I had an idea. I wasn't going down without a fight. They came over, yelling: "Mickey, Mickey!"

I lowered down to one knee and wrapped my arms around all three. In my best high, squeaky voice, I said: "Kid, I want you to turn and wave to the camera and shout, 'Give us our park back, Dominion!' Can you do that?"

They nodded and I pointed at the camera. They did exactly as I said, then the older one yelled: "Yeah, screw you, Dominion!"

Everyone froze for several seconds, then parents rushed in and pulled the kids away. Two guards grabbed my arms, pulled me up. "Help!" I called out in a high-pitched voice, attracting the attention of everyone in the area. As the men dragged me away, I shouted: "Dominion is kidnapping Mickey!"

I looked back to see uniforms surrounding Minnie, Donald and Goofy. I was pushed into a room with a wall of monitors and a uniform seated behind a desk. "What's going on?" the man asked.

Before the guards could respond, I said in the same cartoon voice: "Mickey's in timeout!"

I was pushed into a chair. I didn't care any longer what they did to me. I couldn't stay in my body much longer. I was ready to shed it like a snake molting its skin. What would happen to me, the bodiless me, was a mystery. Would I just fade into nothingness or move into a spirit world? I had no idea. But I did know, or at least believed, that whatever happened to me would also happen to my counterpart Lang. We'd go down together, fellow passengers on a crashing plane.

28

The Destroyer

Gogola studied herself in the full-length mirror. She wore a long blue frilly gown with ruffled sleeves and billowy shoulders. Her long curly blond locks flowed over the front of her dress, hiding the swell of her breasts. She spoke to the mirror.

"Cinderella, let's have a ball."

She crossed her bedroom and opened the door to the outer room where Hector awaited her. He wore his dress uniform, as she'd requested, and was pacing, hands clasped behind his back. He looked her up and down, smiled. "You look wonderful, Gogola."

She gave him an appraising look in return. "Thank you. You, on the other hand, look nervous."

"Excited, not nervous."

"About?"

He looked surprised. "About my new mission. To disperse Kahil."

"Oh, of course." Giving him the key to dispersing the essence of a *tulpa,* even a rebellious one, was potential suicide. There would be nothing to stop him from turning on her, and he would be much more direct than Kahil, who was still playing both sides.

"Are you certain that you want to learn this skill? We don't have many reasons to put it to use. We need more *tulpas,* not fewer."

"I will be very careful with the knowledge."

She met his gaze, remained silent. When a *tulpa* was in her presence, she couldn't open the network to read his thoughts. It was her weakness. It was why she often stayed distant from those closest to her. Hector knew that, too.

She nodded. "Here's what you do."

LANG

We sat at a banquet table in Cinderella's Castle with no food, no drinks. No nourishment. It didn't matter. Risa and I were not going to last long. Kahil sat to our right at the end of the table, hands clasped, staring. "Don't worry. She's coming down. We will have a reunion here."

"You mean with our so-called lawyer," I asked.

"Yes, and more. I believe she will bring your counterparts. She wants you together."

"You said that would be dangerous for her," Risa said.

"Maybe not. You won't be able to see them, even though they will be here."

I shook my head. "I don't understand."

"I don't either right now. That's the information she fed over the network. She's telling all of us that this is a momentous occasion, that she has found a way to destroy much of humankind. Tulpas will survive and build a new world from the remains."

"How is that going to happen?"

"Humans will lose their counterparts, which are essential to their awareness as physical beings. When that happens, most will fall into comas and die."

"We're not going to be used like that!" Risa's voice was weak, her face pale. She started to stand up, but collapsed back into her chair.

I reached out and touched Risa's arm to comfort her. "How does Gogola know that's true?"

Kahil beamed. "Ah, the skeptical journalist remains true to his profession. How do *tulpas* know anything? She has access to a field of energy that manifests as knowledge. Humans could enter that field as well if they knew the path."

"So you're saying that she's all-knowing?"

"The Maker, Gogola, is more about power than knowledge. You've seen what she has done. Destroyed your world and moved a dream world into the physical world. She is a god of destruction. She has syncretized her existence with the Hindu god Shiva, who holds a trident, which represents the threefold qualities of nature: creation, preservation and destruction. Gogola is not so concerned with preservation. Her goal has always been to create a *tulpa* world by destroying humanity."

I felt empty, and powerless. Suddenly, I was hovering above the scene, released from my body. *Am I dead?* At the thought, I dropped back into my weakened frame. Risa and I were near death and oddly I didn't care. In spite of my willingness to let go, I still felt an underlying urge to bond with my counterpart.

I heard voices and Risa clasped my hand. "Look!"

I turned and saw Cinderella in a frilly blue gown approaching gracefully on the arm of her general, who wore a spiffy black dress uniform with gold epaulets, ribbons and metals. Cinderella curtsied as Hector pulled out the chair at the end of the table, opposite from Kahil. Cinderella took her seat. Hector remained standing at her side, overlooking the scene.

"Nice of you to visit," Cinderella said in a little-girl voice. In spite of the voice, I recognized her as our 'lawyer,' as Gogola. Her makeup and blonde wig, neatly disguised the cool intellectual-looking counselor with her big glasses and short dark hair, but those green eyes were the same.

Risa made the same connection. "Hello, Heather. Nice make-over. Did you give up on law?"

"I don't know what you speak of, madam," she said in the same voice. Then her tone deepened and she sounded annoyed. "You're spoiling my fun."

"You look beautiful, Gogola," Kahil chimed in. Then added: "In a sort of cartoonish way. Personally, I like you best in your spaghetti strap top, torn jeans and high heels."

She frowned, her mouth pouted, giving her a comical look. Her voice dropped in pitch and sounded menacing. "Anything else you care to say, Kahil?"

"Yes, why don't we order pizza for everyone? I'm sure my

friends here are starving." He regarded us a moment. "Although they now might be too weak to eat."

Hector's eyes narrowed and settled on Kahil. He continued staring, but his eyes were now glazed so that he seemed to be looking past Kahil or through him. Hector stabbed a finger at him. His body was tense, his eyes looked as if they were about to pop from his skill. "Kahil, you're a goddamn traitor. You're with the rebel-terrorists and now you're hiding here in plain sight."

It looked like some kind of showdown between the two *tulpas,* another performance directed by Gogola, I thought. Whatever Hector was doing, it was having more of an effect on him than on Kahil, who stared at him, an amused look on his face.

Kahil's expression suddenly shifted to one of surprise. His mouth opened, his eyes widened. I looked back at Hector and saw that he was fading. I could see right through him. His head turned to face Gogola, an incredulous expression on his face, and then he vanished. I peered around the banquet hall, wondering if my eyes had deceived me and Hector was actually still here.

"He's gone," Gogola said in a soft voice. "His essence has dispersed. Even though we are here in the physical, *tulpas* remain inorganic beings. We are mind stuff and we can be snuffed. The general was very interested in learning the technique, so he could personally eliminate Kahil. Unfortunately for him, his gallant effort left his mind wide open and I saw he was intent on blowing up my essence, and taking total control."

"He thought you had lost your mind," Kahil said. "He told me once that we can't be ruled by someone who is insane."

"Partially true," Gogola said. "He tolerated my eccentric role-playing. But when he learned what I was planning to do here today, he became frightened. He didn't think it was time to destroy humanity. It was only my threat to disperse him that kept him from killing Alex and Lydia after they were captured."

"They may die anyhow. Same with their counterparts."

I felt as if I was about to fall off the chair. Risa's eyes were like glass. I guessed she wasn't in her body.

Gogola motioned to a young man stationed at the doorway. He glided over on light feet, leaned toward her and nodded as she whispered to him. He looked fresh-scrubbed, a recent creation no doubt. He hurried away, disappeared around a corner.

Within seconds, several soldiers appeared at the entrance of the banquet hall. There seemed some confusion, then in walked Mickey Mouse, Minnie Mouse, Donald Duck, and Goofy. I groaned softly. I couldn't handle another Gogola charade. What the hell was she doing?

The soldiers hustled the Disney characters forward and pushed them into chairs across the table from us. I didn't smile. I didn't welcome them. I became aware of myself looking down at the assembled group around the table from somewhere near the ceiling. Then I was back again.

Even though I couldn't see his face, I sensed Mickey Mouse staring at me. Minnie abruptly bolted to her feet. "Risa, Risa. It's me." She reached for her mouse head and tried to pull it off. But two soldiers moved in, pushed her down in her seat.

"Hey, Lang. We're here!" Alex called out from inside the Mickey costume.

"I see. Sort of." Alex could see me, but I couldn't see him through the dark lenses on the costume's eyeholes. Now I knew what Kahil had meant when he said they would be here, but invisible.

Simultaneously, Alex and I reached across the table, leaning as far as we could, and our fingertips grazed before guards pulled us apart. Risa and Lydia did the same, lunging across the table, fingertips momentarily touching. Guards jerked them back into their seats.

Nothing seemed to happen. As soon as that thought came to mind, I realized it wasn't quite true. I was feeling normal for the first time in days. No, far more than normal. I felt as if a hundred-pound weight had been lifted from my back. Energy had rushed back into me, as if I'd just gotten a shot of adrenaline or bathed in the Fountain of Youth.

Gogola watched us closely. I tried not to show how much better I felt. Even though I couldn't see Alex, his presence empowered me. I noticed he was no longer slumping over the table and sensed that he too was being restored.

After a couple of minutes, Gogola looked distracted, as if she were making silent connections to members of her network. I couldn't tell if she was pleased or disappointed. Then something clicked and she made a decision. She stood up and walked to the other end of the table. "Kahil, take Mr. Lang and Dr. Ferraro upstairs to my sitting room, where you will do just that, sit and wait."

She signaled to a couple of the soldiers who had brought Mickey, Minnie, Donald and Goofy here. They quickly strode over to her, apparently well aware that this Cinderella wasn't just another Disney character. She ordered them to guard us closely, and make sure no one leaves the sitting room. We were guided away from the table, down a hallway, and then up a winding staircase. At the top of the stairs, Kahil opened a door that led into a long rectangular room with a couch.

"Sit down, my friends. We might be here awhile." One of the guards was posted just inside the door, a pistol on his hip. The other remained outside. I'd glimpsed their hands and, for what it was worth, neither were *tulpas*.

I didn't like the feeling of this room. Something strange went on here. I didn't feel good about whatever Gogola was planning, either.

"What just happened down there?" I asked.

Kahil paced the length of the floor, as if measuring it, and eyed the guard as he moved past him. "You were brought together as she planned with one pair disguised."

"But nothing happened."

"Don't be so sure about that. Certainly, you two seem like you've been revived."

"I'm feeling much better," Risa said.

"I know, that's great, but that wasn't her intent," I said. "She wanted something more than that."

Kahil stopped in front of us. "That's true. We experienced no great eruption, no earthquakes, no tsunami, no great fire in the sky. The world didn't shudder when you encountered your hidden counterparts. But something more subtle is happening.

I'm sensing it now through the *tulpa* network. I think Cinderella is getting her wish."

"What do you mean?" Risa asked.

"The die-off is beginning."

"What's going to happen to us?" Risa asked.

Kahil squatted in front of us as if he were addressing a couple of children. "My guess is that she will deal with Alex and Lydia first, and the other two, Harwood and Jordan. Then she will join us for more fun."

I folded my arms tightly over my chest. "What kind of fun would that be?"

"She can't let you live. You don't belong here. She will no doubt disperse my essence, since I betrayed her, then send you two to your deaths in a more traditional manner—bullet to the head possibly from this fellow and his partner outside. A human killing humans. I'm sure she finds that appropriate."

The soldier drew his pistol from its holster, and pointed it at Kahil. "No more talking!"

Kahil looked amused, but didn't reply. He sat down on the couch next to Risa and clasped his hands behind his head. When the guard wasn't paying attention he leaned toward me and whispered. "I think Gogola made a mistake."

ALEX

As soon as Lang and Risa were gone, Gogola told us to get out of our costumes. Gladly, I thought. My stint as Mickey was over. I wanted to quickly get the head off and scratch my itchy beard.

Even before I was out of the costume, I was feeling like a new person, more energized than I'd felt for a long time. I'd barely been able to walk from Ariel's Grotto to Cinderella's Castle. But now I didn't feel any aches or pains, no sense of lethargy.

As soon as the four of us had shed our costumes, we were pushed back down into the chairs by a couple of beefy guys in polo shorts and khakis with badges that said castle security. It occurred to me that the soldiers, guards, and various security forces in Disney World probably outnumbered visitors by three to one. And that didn't count the battalion of troops stationed in the parking lot.

One of Gogola's *tulpa* assistants appeared with a computer. He sat down across from us, and without looking our way, tapped away on the keyboard. *What the hell was he doing?* I noticed the trident tattoo on his left palm when he waved to get Gogola's attention. She'd been standing several feet behind him, conferring with a high-ranking Dominion officer in hushed tones.

She walked over and the techie moved away after showing her where to point the mouse. She clicked something on the screen, then turned the computer to face us. I glanced at Lydia, who looked terrified; her own image appeared on the screen.

One rebel diatribe after another was played. Some featured Lydia, others were my own anti-Dominion commentary. Gogola had all of our favorite hits. Even though they were removed from You Tube within minutes of appearing, they'd all been captured and saved—for this moment, no doubt.

After several minutes, the clips ended. I looked up to see the techie *tulpa* now filming us, a professional video camera perched on his shoulder.

"There you have it. The evidence against you. You two are betrayers and you joined the rebel-terrorists with the help of these two, who were already part of the resistance. What do you have to say for yourself, Alex?"

"First of all, we were never betrayers. We were captives forced to do your propaganda. When we escaped, we went with the only ones who could protect us." I nodded toward Harwood and Jordan, who looked resigned to their fates.

"And a fine job they did." She smirked at them. "Do you have anything else to say before I pronounce your sentence?"

"Yeah, I don't know where you're from, but where I'm from I know that Cinderella would be on our side."

"I second that." Lydia turned her gaze from Gogola to the camera. "Before you sentence us in your kangaroo court, I want to thank these two brave men, Dr. Bruce Harwood and Reggie Jordan for risking their lives and helping us escape. They are heroes."

"That's enough, Lydia. You can be assured your comments

will be appropriately edited."

"This is a total farce," Lydia scoffed. "You're acting as prosecutor, judge and jury."

"You should know from your own history that in time of war civil rights are the first casualty." Gogola studied the purple polish on her fingernails. "Sorry about that."

Harwood stood up from his chair. He looked weary and beaten. "Let them go, Gogola. They're journalists. They were captives. Reggie and I are the rebels."

Soldiers moved in closer as Jordan stood, clasping onto his injured arm. His wound was bleeding and the right side of his shirt was soaked red. "Yeah, go ahead," Reggie said. "Make us heroes to the cause. You have no idea of the strength of the opposition. It's growing daily."

"He's right," Harwood said. "The opposition is spreading throughout every part of society. That includes Dominion. The troops will soon turn on you."

Gogola laughed. "No, we are the ones who are growing. There are more *tulpas* every day. There are *tulpa* farms around the world. Many sub-makers. We'll fill the vacuum when your kind is gone."

Harwood's back arched awkwardly, his head fell back as if he were staring at the ceiling. Then he collapsed, knocking his chair over as he fell. He didn't move. Jordan bent over, reaching for Harwood. Lydia screamed in distress. Jordan's body began to twitch, then he stumbled away and dropped to the floor a few feet from Harwood.

I shot to my feet. "What the hell did you do to them?"

Gogola smiled. "Actually, nothing. You did it!"

LANG

Risa and I both stood up from the couch. We'd heard shouts and a scream. "What's happening down there?" I turned to Kahil, who looked stunned. I guessed he was listening to something other than the sounds from downstairs.

He focused on me, as if seeing me for the first time. "Like I said, the die-off has begun."

"What?" Risa asked.

"There will be fires soon, enormous fires in every part of the world. The sky will be smoldering for months to come with the smell of burning bodies."

I spun around as the soldier at the door collapsed. His body shook for a few seconds, then went still. A clattering sound erupted on the other side of the door. Kahil dragged the body away from the door. I opened it and saw that the other guard had tumbled down several stairs. He lay still in the curve of the tower's stairway.

Kahil led the way and bent over the guard on the stairs and felt for a pulse. "That's odd," he murmured. I didn't wait to find out what he meant. I took Risa's hand and we stepped over the prone guard, past Kahil, then hurried down the stairs.

I nearly tripped, but grabbed the railing in time. We pushed through the door, ran down the hallway and into the banquet room. Several people lay on the floor. Everyone seemed stunned by the chaos of falling bodies. Someone was filming and the camera was jumping about.

I spotted a bearded man a decade younger than me, and a dark-haired woman. Alex and Lydia. Their costumes gone. Our eyes met eyes from across the room.

"Shoot them! Shoot them!" Gogola shouted.

They both moved toward us as we rushed toward them. Risa, just ahead of me, loped toward Lydia. I couldn't stop. My momentum carried me forward. It was as if my feet weren't even touching the floor. I was about to collide with Alex. I raised my arms, but the impact never happened. I flowed right into him, right through him and into nothingness.

PART FOUR

New Worlds

If we are continually shaping our future physical reality by today's collective thoughts and actions, then the time to wake up to the alternative we have created is now.

- Helen Wambaugh and Chet Snow, *Mass Dreams of the Future*

PART FOUR

New Worlds

29

Back in Time

LANG

My shoulders jerked as I came awake. I caught my breath. I must've dozed off. Sex knocks me out. The best sleeping aid ever. *How long was I out anyhow?* I turned and saw that Risa had also fallen asleep. That kind of surprised me. I thought only men passed out after sex.

An image of Cinderella in her castle swam through my mind. And then I was flooded with memories. I bolted upright, instantly alert. *Whoa. Wait a minute. What the fuck? How did I get here? What happened?*

I swung my legs over the side of the bed, grabbed my jeans, and pulled them on. I quickly moved through the house and realized it was Risa's house again, not the altered version owned by someone else. I opened the front door and ran outside confused, disoriented. Someone shouted: "What the hell happened?"

Several people were out in the street. They all look dazed. A woman stumbled and fell. She began weeping and a man nearby helped her get up. A bald man wearing only bikini underwear that were nearly lost under his bulging belly walked out into the street and pointed at the sky. "Born again! Born again!" he shouted over and over.

I spotted someone sitting on the sidewalk, looking around, then two more people on the ground near the corner. One was rolling around on his back, the other on his hands and knees, struggling to stand up. They weren't homeless people who'd slept on the side of the street. They were tourists or locals who had fallen into a coma just before the shift. Now they were back and severely disoriented.

I turned to go back inside and was relieved to see Risa's car and my pickup in the driveway where I'd left it. I walked over to it, put my hand on the hood, and it felt warm. I heard a ticking sound the engine made as it cooled. That didn't make any sense. I'd been gone for days, maybe weeks. I wasn't sure. I remembered hiding in the house, the Prius, the hitchhiker, captive on a ship, in jail in Orlando, Disney World…people dying…then rushing toward Alex and into oblivion.

Risa, I have to wake Risa.

I scrambled back inside, slamming the door behind me. Risa stood in the living room, her arms crossed over her silky violet robe. She stared at me with a look of disbelief.

"We're back," I said.

"Are we, Lang? Look at that television."

"What about it?"

"You don't remember because you were only here once. But that's not my TV. I had a 48-inch Sony on the wall. That one's a Samsung, and it's huge, maybe sixty inches."

"That *is* strange. You got upgraded. Maybe a spin-off from that other world. But everything else looks normal, right?" I tried to make light of it, even though it put me on edge. I wanted to believe that we were back, that it was all a shared nightmare. Then I remember the comas. And where was Jen? I felt a terrible urgency to find her.

Risa pointed and clicked. A pastoral scene appeared, then another, and a few seconds later another. It was like a nature slide show. "That always comes up when I've got a connection problem."

Were we back or not? "I'm going to the hospital to look for Jennifer. You want to come with me?"

"Sure. Let me get dressed. If I've got any clothes!" She hurried to her walk-in closet, flipped on the light switch and looked around for several seconds. She weaved her hands through the hanging clothes, then turned to me, a perplexed expression on her face. "Most of my clothes are here, but there's some new stuff. It's nice and it's my size. But where did it come from?"

I couldn't help wondering what had changed at my place. "Let's get Jennifer, then head to Sugarloaf."

I heard a familiar chime, my cell phone, a call from Jen. I looked around, and found it on the floor in the bedroom. The phone hadn't worked after the shift and I'd left it here. "Jen, where are you? I was just going to look for you at the hospital."

My voice sounded like a croak and I could barely hear Jen. What was she saying? Then everything just faded away.

I sat up in Risa's bed and looked around. I was naked and wasn't holding my phone. "Oh, shit. What a mind-fuck."

Risa raised up on her elbows, rubbed her eyes. "What's going on? Oh my god, I just dreamed that we woke up here in my house, and your daughter called."

"Yeah, I dreamed the same thing. It seemed so real."

"Lang, I don't want to wake up in Cinderella's Castle or in jail. I want this to be real."

I rubbed my arms. "Let's go take a cold shower. Then we'll know for sure that we're awake."

"We're awake. But are we awake in a dream?"

"If we are, then it's a nightmare because we already did this."

My cell chimed. I leaned over the bed and found it. "Here we go again." I pressed *accept.* "Hey, Jen, where are you?"

"Dad, I'm in the hospital." She sounded scared. "It's crazy here. Could you come get me? People are acting really weird. The nurse said we were all in comas and woke up about the same time."

It was wonderful hearing her voice and I wanted more than anything for this to be real. "You bet. I'm just relieved to know where you are. I love you, Jen."

"I love you, too. Please hurry."

I remembered that Sharon had called from the hospital. "Where's your mother? She was there with you."

"She was? I haven't seen her."

"Hang on. I'll be there as soon as I can. Are you okay?"

"I think so. I was with this girl. A younger girl. It's strange, like a dream. Her mother was also an FBI agent and divorced. I was with her, but I didn't seem to have a body. I was like a part of her."

"Okay. We can talk about it later. See you in a little while."

"How is she?" Risa asked.

"Good, but confused, like us."

I picked up my jeans and polo shirt, the same clothes I'd been wearing before I was garbed in the orange jumpsuits on the floating jail. But now they smelled freshly laundered. I quickly pulled them on. I kept telling myself over and over again that this was real, not a dream.

"You want to come with me?" I asked Risa.

"Of course I do. Let's hope the medical center is there this time."

"Oh, shit. I forgot about that. But we're not in that world any more."

"Let's hope not."

While Risa got ready, I walked out into the living room, picked up the remote for the TV, but simply stared at the blank screen.

"Hey, are you okay?" she asked.

I set the remote down. "I was going to turn on the TV, but then I remembered when we stood here and saw Dominion soldiers guarding the White House. If they're here, I don't want to see it."

She nodded. "The good news is that's my TV, and my clothes are my clothes. Let's go."

ALEX

I lay on my back staring at a spinning ceiling fan. My memory banks suddenly kicked in. It was like hitting a jackpot on a slot machine. I rolled over onto my hands and knees. I was in bed, but where? Lydia lay next to me and was starting to rouse from sleep. The room seemed familiar, but it took a few moments to place myself. I realized I was back in that little town with all the mediums. Cassadaga.

But what happened to the banquet hall and Gogola?

Lydia groaned, then sat up, the sheet falling away from her small pointed breast. "*Ah, caramba!* Alex, what's going on?"

"I think we're back where we were when the merger happened, when the worlds merged."

"How did we get here?

"No idea. But it's better, much better here than where we were."

"How do you know?"

I laughed. "Well, for one thing, that Cinderella bitch Gogola isn't shouting for somebody to shoot us."

"That's right. Oh my God, Alex." She hugged me. "I was so frightened that my mind blanked out."

"Wait a minute. This already happened. I dreamed this same thing."

"You're right. I did, too!"

A pounding erupted at the door to the hallway.

"Shit, get dressed!" I hissed.

I rolled out of bed and scrambled for my clothes. I could hear a man's voice, but couldn't make out what he was saying. The room had two doors, one to the hallway, another to the porch. I looked out the porch window, but didn't see anyone. I remembered doing the same thing in the dream and suddenly knew who was at the door.

"Lydia, Alex. Open up. It's me, Kahil."

We looked at each other, confused, astonished. Suppose I was wrong? I slowly approached the door, then opened it. Kahil grinned. "Can you believe this? We are back here."

"Yeah. How did you get here?"

"Same as you. It seems everyone has gone back to the time of the merger. My guess is that you triggered a new world."

"How did I do that?"

"You two and your two counterparts blew apart the world, as we knew it. It just took bringing the four of you together."

"What about Lang and Risa? Where are they?"

"Probably where they were just before the worlds merged."

"A lot of people died. Gogola called it a major die-off, that billions of people would die."

"You saved many of them," Kahil said. "If they weren't dead, their counterparts separated and went back."

"You said the same thing to me in a dream."

Kahil smiled. "Maybe you had to hear it twice. So you would not forget."

I never knew how to take what Kahil said. Sometimes he seemed trustworthy, but always he seemed to be hiding something. "I want to look around."

"You'll see that the hotel is busy. The streets are full of people, the same ones who were here at the time of the merger. They're a little confused, but happy. After all, they're no longer carrying around ghost-like beings inside them. Their counterparts were released back to where they were when the shift occurred."

I thought about that as we walked down the hallway and entered the crowded hotel lobby. I wanted to feel good about what happened, but something about Kahil's explanation didn't ring true. Then it struck me. If Kahil was in this world, then so were Gogola and all the *tulpas*. Maybe we had created a new world, but it was one with the *tulpas*.

LANG

Driving in Key West was always a challenge. Even though Risa lived several blocks from Duval Street, the tourist hub of Key West, groups of visitors tended to parade down the middle of the streets throughout Old Town, as if they were in a theme park. Today was no exception. Actually, it was much worse than usual.

Locals and tourists alike meandered around, crisscrossing streets with no regard for traffic. Some people actually lunged at us, shouting as if we were responsible for their confusion. Others seemed directionless and lost. From the expressions on faces, comments and weird behavior, people were not adjusting well.

"I'm not sure we came back to the same world," Risa said. "It just doesn't feel right to me. I saw a couple of houses that I pass all the time on my way to the office that were painted different colors than I remember."

"That's no big deal. You probably just hadn't noticed until now."

"Maybe." She sounded doubtful. "But everything feels less real to me."

I tapped my horn and veered to the left side of the street. A young couple, naked and holding hands had started into the roadway. They wore biking helmets, that was all. "Well, you don't see that everyday."

"It *is* Key West, but that's beyond normal."

I was glad to get to U.S. 1, and out to Stock Island. I turned onto College Road and passed the Tropical Forest and Botanical Garden. Then I spotted the Lower Keys Medical Center exactly where it was supposed to be and relief poured through me. Since the lot was full, I parked on the grass. Supposedly, the hospital had been crammed beyond capacity with people in comas, including the staff and doctors. Now they were waking up, but I didn't see any sign of people leaving.

We hurried over to the main entrance and tugged on the door. Locked. A sign read: *Due to severe overcrowding, hospital closed until further notice. No visitors allowed.*

"*What?* Since when do hospital close when they're filled with patients?" I texted Kari. *I'm here, but can't get in.* A few seconds later, I wrote again: *What's going on in there?*

Dad, they won't let me go! They think we're infected with something.

My concern escalated to near-panic. *Tell the doctors in charge I know what happened to everyone.*

I didn't notice we had company until I heard a man's voice. "Do you think anyone will believe you?"

Behind me stood a short man with a shaved head, wearing the saffron robe of a monk. His features were Euro-Asian, his skin was nut brown. "Believe me about what?"

He smiled. "About what you want to tell the doctors. How you and your companions destroyed a world, brought everyone back, and revived those in comas." The monk shook his head. "All the doctor will remember is a dream that is now fading."

"Who're you? How do you know so much about us?"

When he didn't reply, Risa spoke up. "I bet you're from the monastery where the first *tulpa,* Gogola, was created."

"Impressive," the monk remarked. "You absorb knowledge well from your free counterpart. And yes, my name is Norbu. I had waited a long time to find a pair of awakened dreamers who could make up for my error. You two had no idea how to manifest your abilities until I began guiding you. You quickly learned to involve your body and all of your senses in the dream."

His perfect English held a slight British accent. But I was confused. Was he even speaking aloud? I couldn't tell. "How did you find us?"

"Risa was the key. She is the reincarnate of an English woman who boldly came to Tibet and learned about *tulpas.* She led me to you even before you two met in person."

"But I've never seen you before now."

"In dreams, all things are possible, Bruce Lang. Even now you are in a lucid dream, awake but dreaming."

"No way this is a dream," I snapped.

"You must recognize it as one. When you do so, you become more lucid, more aware, more present in the illusion of life. You are *not* moving back into the world you remember, but into a new world. You will move into it seamlessly, because you have already been there. Your unconscious minds, the deeper part of you—your true selves—have jointly created it."

I considered what Norbu said, but before I could reply, he began fading. Then he was gone. I heard my cell phone ringing and wondered if I was about to wake up in bed again.

"Are you going to answer that?" Risa asked.

I looked at the phone in my hand and saw that it was Jen. "Dad! I didn't think you were ever going to answer."

"I'm here at the hospital."

"I know. I can see you. Why are you just standing there? Look up to your left, to the second floor."

I did and saw a figure waving in a window. I waved back. "Are you okay?"

"I'm fine. Can you get me out of here? They won't release me unless someone comes for me. I've got to tell you where I went in my coma."

"I know. The girl, Kari."

"Yeah, I'm confused. Were you there?"

Someone shook me. "Lang, wake up. You're talking in your sleep."

"Christ. How many times am I going to wake up?" I turned to Risa. "What do you remember?"

"The monk. He said we were dreaming."

"Yeah. I thought we already woke up from that dream."

ALEX

Lydia and I walked over to the coffee bar in the lobby of the Cassadaga Hotel and settled onto a couple of stools. An impressive array of commercial coffee machines were aligned behind the bar. I ordered an Americano—a triple shot of espresso topped off with hot water. Lydia ordered a cup of chai tea.

As we waited for our drinks, I noticed the people browsing through the New Age shop with its stones and crystal, candles and herbs, metaphysical books and fanciful apparel. Others wandered around the lobby and wide porch or headed to the restaurant. Maybe they were all dreaming. *Dismiss that thought*, I told myself.

"What happened to Kahil?"

Lydia shrugged. "I didn't see where he went."

Then I saw three men in Dominion uniforms enter the lobby, pause and look around. I instantly turned away and told Lydia what I'd seen.

"Shit, should we get up and walk away?" she whispered.

"Too late. They're coming this way." I watched them in the mirror behind the bar. They moved behind us, peered into the shop. One of them made a comment and the other two laughed. They turned and strolled back in the other direction. I glanced over my shoulder. They stopped at the check-in counter. I didn't think they were here to get a room. "So much for going back to our room."

"Maybe they're not looking for us," Lydia said.

"So they're here for readings? I doubt it. I bet there are more of them outside."

Our beverages arrived. The server wore a gold-colored vest, had long hair and a handlebar mustache. "You folks staying at the hotel?" he asked.

I touched my back pocket, making sure I still had my billfold. "I'll pay cash." I handed him a ten-dollar bill.

I was about to suggest that we take our drinks out to the porch so we could look around and assess the situation when someone took the seat next to me. His head was shaved and he wore the saffron robe of a Buddhist monk.

He nodded and smiled as I collected the change. "Hard cash." He chuckled softly as if he'd said something humorous, and made a sweeping gesture with one hand. "It all looks very real and solid, doesn't it?"

I wrapped my knuckles on the wooden bar. "Yeah, pretty solid."

I knew enough about Buddhism to know that one of their prime tenets was that the everyday world was an illusion. If you were a monk and lived in a monastery in the Himalayas, it might be easy to see it that way. But for someone like me who worked as an international journalist when I wasn't being held captive or on the run, it was a bit difficult to dismiss every day reality so easily.

"But what is this thing you call reality?" the monk asked.

I laughed. We were in danger of being arrested and now we had a guy going Zen on us. "Good question."

"Alex, Lydia. What is it you want to know?"

"How do you know our names? Who are you?"

"My name is Norbu. I think you know who I am."

Lydia nodded. "Yes, we do. You have something to do with the *tulpas*, don't you?"

"Dominion is a passing phenomenon, like everything else."

"*Tulpas* can't be killed," I countered. "So they're not exactly a passing phenomena."

"They can't be killed in the normal sense. But their essence can be dispersed. It's quite simple once you understand the technique. You two could do it."

"Why don't you do it? They want to destroy humanity. They want the world to themselves."

"Unfortunately, my own creation stabbed me between the shoulder blades before I had the chance. I can pass on the secret, but that is all."

With a quick movement, his hand slid out of the loose sleeve of his robe and slapped my forehead with his palm. The blow momentarily stunned me. A second later, he did the same to Lydia.

Norbu smiled again. "The transmission is already complete. When you wake up, you'll possess the knowledge. But you won't have access to it until the time is right."

30

Not About Time

ALEX

Lydia and I simultaneously sat upright in bed. "What happened?" she exclaimed. "What do you remember?"

"We talked to the monk who created Gogola. She killed him and created her *tulpa* army."

"Exactly. We dreamed the same dream again."

"Oh, aren't we good. Welcome to Cassadaga again." I hugged her and we both fell back onto the bed, laughing at the bizarre absurdity of the unfolding events. The soft curves of her body aroused me and I wanted to linger, but I knew it could be a fatal mistake to make love here and now. The longer we remained in this room the greater the risk.

"But if it was a dream, how much was real?"

"Let's get dressed and go see. We need to get out of this room in case Dominion troops really are here looking for us."

"Alex, if we're back in time to when the shift happened, we were hiding here and there were no Dominion troops here."

I pulled on my jeans. "You're right. So I don't think we time-traveled. It's more like moving into an alternate universe."

"Kahil said we went back to where we were at the merger."

"That was a dream. This is real. I can feel it. But there's something about the dream that I'm missing, something important."

Lydia crawled out of bed, found her clothes, and headed for the bathroom. "I know. I feel it, too. But I remember something else. Norbu said that it—whatever it is—wouldn't be available until we needed it."

She closed the door and suddenly wished I'd gotten into the bathroom first. We were definitely awake. In the dream, I didn't recall either of us bothering with a pit stop.

"Lydia, I'm going to the lobby to use the bathroom. I'll meet you at the coffee bar. If I see any trouble brewing, I'll be right back."

"Don't get lost," she called through the door.

I picked up my laptop and hurried down the hallway. After a stop at the closet-sized men's room in the lobby, I walked over to the check-in counter.

A man in his thirties with a thin mustache and narrow-set eyes appeared from a back room. His hair was mussed, his clothes rumpled. I guessed he was the night guy and slept on a cot. He looked past me when the front door opened, probably hoping the day clerk had arrived.

"How can I help you?" His eyelids were hooded as if he'd been woken up too many times during the night. I was tempted to ask if the ghosts kept him up.

I held up my laptop. "What's the wi-fi code?"

He reached under the desk and handed me a card for the Cassadaga Hotel. I turned it over and found the hand-written code. "Thanks. Oh I'm looking for Harley, a medium who works in the hotel. Do you know her?"

"Never heard of her. She doesn't work here, not in the hotel. I know them all."

"How long you worked here?"

"Three years."

I wanted to ask him what year it was, but thought better of it.

I walked over to the coffee bar and ordered a cappuccino. If Harley didn't work here, then we weren't back at the time of the shift. Besides Harley's absence, there were far fewer people here than I remembered. The lobby and restaurant were nearly deserted. Different from the dream. So where were we in time?

I opened the laptop and tapped in the code. The last time we were here, I never went on-line because it was too dangerous.

Now I didn't care. Whatever happened in the banquet hall, when we were finally face to face with Alex and Risa, had launched us back to the merger, and into a dream. Or a series of dreams. Now we had awakened to another time...or another world.

I went to CNN to find out what was going on. Nothing. Maybe it was down for maintenance. I went to Huffington Post. Nothing. I tried a couple other news sites and got the same results. I stared at the Google box. At least there was that. I typed *Dominion*, but hesitated hitting the key. *Do I really want to do this? Yes.* I hit *enter* and the screen filled with choices. I hoped like hell that they were historical, that Dominion was something from the past.

The top one looked like an official site. I clicked it. Instantly, an image of a trident in a circle appeared—the Dominion logo. A headline followed: *A Smaller Population, A Better World.*

As I contemplated the headline, Lydia walked up to the coffee bar. "I don't know what the hell's going on, but the coffee's still good here."

"Have you seen Kahil?" she asked.

"No."

Lydia stared at the laptop screen on the bar. "That looks ominous. How old is it?"

I leaned toward the screen. "Posted three hours ago."

"I wonder if there's any resistance left?"

I went back to Google and typed: *Anti-Dominion rebellion.*

Another Dominion page came up. The headline read: *Resistance Quelled.* I clicked onto the article. It sounded like the kind of bullshit articles I used to write for Dominion. Essentially, it said the great die-off, which was attributed to a deadly virus, wiped out the resistance. And a couple billion others, I thought.

The article warned against using the term *tulpa* virus. No doubt people suspected the *tulpas* were behind the die-off in one way or another. An unidentified Dominion spokesperson had said that *tulpas* didn't carry any viruses. Anyone using that term could be fined and penalized in other ways. Like go missing, I thought.

Lydia read over my shoulder. "Do you think we've jumped into the future?"

"I think when the merger was destroyed, we were propelled into yet another world, one with a lot fewer people and with Dominion even stronger."

"Maybe the bastards have forgotten about us."

As I spoke, proof of my contention suddenly appeared. Harley crossed the lobby carrying a suitcase. She stopped a few feet away and stared at the list of drinks on the wall behind the bar.

"Harley?" Lydia uttered, standing up from her stool, an astonished look on her face.

Harley frowned. "Hello. Do I know you?"

"I'm Lydia, this is Alex. Now you do."

I realized she was just arriving to begin work here as a medium. She had no idea who we were.

"I get it. You work here and you knew I was arriving today. Good guess. Nice to meet you." She walked away.

We definitely had landed in a new world. Yet, I had the feeling that we wouldn't be staying here very long.

Gogola held up a pyramid-shaped crystal in her palm and examined it as if it were a diamond sparkling under the florescent light. She set it back on the shelf of the New Age shop inside the Cassadaga Hotel. She wore a long bohemian print skirt, sandals, a snuggly fitted white t-shirt and an open jean jacket, clothes she carefully had selected so she looked like a typical visitor to a spiritualist community. But she wasn't here to get a reading.

She was targeting the two familiar faces hovering over a laptop at the coffee bar. If they were *tulpas,* it would be so easy for her to disperse their essences. They would simply disintegrate and fade away. That's exactly what would happen to Kahil, too, if he showed his face here. Killing humans, however, was a messier matter.

She randomly picked a book off a shelf and gazed over the top of it through the doorway. She had a perfect view of the coffee bar. She needed to eliminate these two as quickly as possible. She could order troops to invade the hotel and kill them, or take them away, never to be seen again. But they might slip away before help arrived. Gogola had her own plan, and would handle this matter herself quickly and efficiently.

She'd made a mistake when she'd used human soldiers instead of *tulpas* to guard Risa and Lang. When the guards were infected and collapsed, the pair had fled and Kahil hadn't stopped them. They'd returned to the banquet hall where Alex and Lydia awaited them.

Those two—Lang and Risa—were out of her reach. But their counterparts were in her cross hairs. Even though she'd brought the two pairs together knowing they would create havoc worldwide, their actions in the end had spun out of her control. She was unable to stop them from charging toward each other—and literally through each other. In doing so, they'd pushed her into this new world, and she didn't like it. There was something wrong here, and it related to her connection with all the *tulpas.*

She felt vulnerable in this world. She couldn't hear any hidden thoughts when she communicated with her generals or lower level *tulpas*. Her network in this world was substantially weaker. That was a serious concern and she suspected there were traitors in her ranks. As a measure to protect herself, she'd dispersed her three top generals. No sense taking any chances.

While she couldn't hear thoughts, she could feel the tension among the *tulpas,* and that just made her feel more frantic. She'd never felt real emotions in the dream world, certainly nothing like what she was experiencing. Now she knew what humans meant when they talked about someone being paranoid.

She needed to stop these two before they reignited the resistance movement. She didn't want to deal with that possibility, not with her suspicion of traitors in her own ranks. She lowered the book and for the first time noticed the title. *The Tibetan Book of Dream and Sleep.*

She dropped the book. *Bad sign. Move. Now.*

Wait. Who was that? Another familiar face. Harley Diamond, the medium Hector had killed. She recognized her from the wanted photos. Back alive in this world. But not for long if she didn't move her fat ass. Harley drifted off and Gogola slipped a compact handgun, a Ruger snub nose, from her purse. She walked purposefully toward the coffee bar. Just another visitor looking for a cappuccino. Two bullets, one to each of their foreheads. Bing, bing. Then walk right out the door.

She was ten feet away when Kahil stepped out in front of her. *Where did he come from?*

"Hello, Gogola!" The others now turned. She fired two shots at Kahil. She knew he would recover, but to her surprise the bullets didn't even knock him down. Panic erupted around them, people stampeded toward the door.

Finish the job.

But something unexpected happened. Alex and Lydia made no effort to flee and she felt an explosive burning sensation in her solar plexus.

LANG

I walked out into the living room, keys in hand, ready to head for the hospital. I'd just talked to Jen and she was anxious to get out of there. Risa had turned on the television, but all that appeared was the same slide show of pastoral scenes we'd seen in a dream version of this wake-up call. She turned it off and we left.

Once again, I was certain we weren't dreaming. But I was going to watch for signs that told me otherwise. "I feel like I'm Bill Murray in *Groundhog Day* repeating the same scenario."

"We're not dreaming," Risa said firmly.

As we approached my Ford Ranger, I put my hand on the hood of the pickup. "The engine's cold. I guess we took a dream truck on our last trip."

"It seemed real at the time. Do you remember seeing that naked couple in the street wearing helmets?"

"Yeah, I guess that should've been a clue."

I cautiously backed out of the driveway and followed the same route to U.S. 1. The streets were nearly deserted. No one acted manic. No one charged us or screamed at us. When we arrived at the medical center, there was no sign on the door telling us the place was closed. We walked in and headed to the second floor where Jen said she was waiting.

I'd expected the halls to be jammed with people. Not the case. There were plenty of people, staff and patients, but no beds in the halls, no crowded hallways filled with former comatose patients. Sharon no doubt had told me the truth when she told me to stay away. So apparently some people had not made it back from the *tulpa* world. Sharon among them, I suspected.

"Daddy!" Jen shouted, and hurried over to me, her blond hair flying off her shoulders. She hugged me tightly. "Am I ever glad to see you!"

I didn't want to let go of her. "I thought I'd lost you." Some day I would tell her about when I went looking for her and the hospital wasn't there. That was definitely a low point.

"Are you okay?" I asked, running my fingers through her hair.

"I'm fine. But just before I woke up, I had a dream that you were already here and left me."

I laughed nervously. "Don't worry. I'm not going to do that. Any word from your mother?"

"I called her. Her phone is turned off, I guess."

Before I could say anymore, Risa caught up to us and I introduced her to Jen. "Great to meet you, Jen. Are you checked out?"

"Yeah, the doctor said I could leave. He seemed as confused as the patients. He said there were more than three hundred patients here in comas with some weird virus, but he couldn't account for more than sixty-seven of us, and we all seem fine."

"What else did he say?" I asked.

"That some of us didn't come back, whatever that meant."

The world of Dominion was turning hazy. But I remembered that when Risa and I encountered the costumed Alex and Lydia, people were collapsing all around us. And all around the world, according to Gogola. If they'd died, their counterparts probably never returned.

"Let's get out of here and go to Sugarloaf."

"What's Sugarloaf?"

"What do you mean by that?"

"What is it?"

I exchanged a glance with Risa. Something was wrong. Maybe an after-effect of the coma.

"It's where I live, Jen."

"Ha ha, funny, Dad."

Now I was getting worried. Not only for Jen, but for humanity. If the survivors, possibly billions of people, came back and couldn't remember their past, the world would be total chaos.

As we passed through the lobby, I stopped and stared at a huge screen imbedded in a wall. Pastoral scenes appeared, similar to the ones we'd seen on Risa's TV. But across the front of the scenes was a bulletin that read: *April 15 is the last day to register for the Dome Cultural Exchange program. Don't miss the opportunity to spend up to three months in one of the 1,253 domes worldwide or one of the 846 specialty domes. Enjoy a new cultural, environmental and historical setting. Dome exchanges are limited and the earlier you apply the better your chance of being accepted.*

I pointed to the sign. "What does that mean? What are these domes?"

"Dad, are you okay? That's the exchange program I did last year in Morocco. It was great. You were jealous."

I didn't know what she was talking about, but decided to wait until we were in the car. When we stepped outside the building, my head felt like it exploded. Nothing I saw made any sense. Instead of a parking lot filled with cars, a lush garden spread out in front of us, with two narrow openings more like trails than roads. Several transparent egg-shaped vehicles hovered a foot above the trail. Each one had four seats and a longer version had eight seats.

"Christ," I whispered. "You seeing this, Risa?"

She nodded, but didn't reply. The blood had drained from her face.

"Are you two okay? What's wrong, anyhow?" Jen asked.

"What're those?" Risa said, pointing at the hovering eggs.

"Where have you guys been? That's the new style PMTs. Personalized Mass Transit."

Jen moved out in front of us. "C'mon. I'll drive."

We must be dreaming again, I thought. Then dropped my head back. No blue sky, no clouds, but an enormous dome swelled over the landscape.

ALEX

The moment Kahil's voice rang out, something snapped inside me. I knew how to eliminate Gogola. So did Lydia. The packets of information that Norbu had planted in us exploded, releasing all that we needed. I focused on her solar plexus, her weak point, directing energy from my solar plexus with the intention to disperse her essence. It was that easy, only it wasn't because she was firing her gun and Kahil momentarily blocked my view of her. But Lydia had kept her focus, and now we combined energies, intentions, and blasted away at Gogola.

She looked surprised. The gun fell from her hand. Her body shuddered, then seemed to disintegrate, as if it were made of sand. She faded and disappeared. She'd uttered a single word or maybe I'd heard it in my mind. She'd said: *Norbu!*

I looked at my hands. They were covered in blood. Then it was gone, just as Gogola was gone. Kahil stood in front of us. For a moment, I thought he might've picked up Gogola's gun and was about to finish the job for her. I had no power left in me to stop him. I was drained.

"You two did good. You not only eliminated Gogola, but all the *tulpas*. She had lost control of her network and when she tried rewiring it, she had tied the existence of every *tulpa* to her. When she vanished, so did they."

Lydia said what I was thinking. "But you're a *tulpa*, Kahil."

He shook his head. "No, I'm not." Like a mirage, his image shifted. A robed monk stood in front of us. Norbu smiled, then vanished.

ALEX

Not again, I thought as Lydia and I got dressed. Would this nightmare ever end? I'd been certain we were awake. But then

Kahil shifted into Norbu, who disappeared…and we woke up again.

"What could this mean, Alex? How could this be happening to us over and over?"

"I don't know, but I want it to end now."

"Do you think we actually destroyed Gogola and all the *tulpas* like Kahil said?"

"Sure hope so. I don't want to face her again."

I picked up a card on the bedside table. I hadn't seen it before. "What the hell is this?" I muttered.

The card read: *Cassadaga is a historical site that existed long before the first domes were built and has been preserved both because of its uniqueness as a spiritualist community and because its hilly environment allowed Cassadaga and nearby Lake Helen to remain above the sea level when much of Florida was lost. Today, it remains a specialty dome where up to 1,000 people live, and its spiritualist tradition has continued and thrived.*

"Is this a new dream?" Lydia whispered, reading over my shoulder.

I opened the door leading to the wide porch that spanned the side of the hotel. At first, everything looked the same. Then I noticed the houses and buildings had a newer look to them, as if they'd been refurbished or rebuilt. Whatever material was used, it wasn't wood.

"Look at the sky," Lydia burst out.

I glanced upward. We were enclosed in a sky-blue transparent dome.

I took Lydia's hand, grasping it tightly. We exchanged a glance. "Lets go take a look," I said. "I'm feeling this is where we belong."

She squeezed my hand and we started down the porch steps of the Cassadaga Hotel and into a new world.

About the Author

Rob MacGregor is the author of numerous novels and works of non-fiction. He's best known for his six-part Indiana Jones series, and adapting the script of *Indiana Jones and the Last Crusade,* a *New York Times* bestseller. He also won the Edgar Allan Poe Award for mystery writing for his novel, *Prophecy Rock,* and was a finalist for the same award for *Hawk Moon,* the second novel in the four-book series. His latest non-fiction book is *Secrets of Spirit Communication: Techniques for Tuning in & Making Contact,* co-authored with his wife, Trish MacGregor.

About the Author

[illegible]

www.ingramcontent.com/pod-product-compliance
Lightning Source LLC
Chambersburg PA
CBHW071127200626
46817CB00018B/2399
* 9 7 8 1 9 4 8 9 2 9 3 1 8 *